WI...
BRENDA NOVAK

When Lightning Strikes

HARLEQUIN®

entertain, enrich, inspire™

Recycling programs
for this product may
not exist in your area.

ISBN-13: 978-0-7783-1351-9

WHEN LIGHTNING STRIKES

For questions and comments about the quality of this book, please contact us at
CustomerService@Harlequin.com.

www.Harlequin.com

Printed in U.S.A.

To Pierce Rohrmann.

Your many talents and drive never cease to amaze me.
Thanks for your hard work on my behalf, your brilliant
ideas, your endless support, your wit and generosity—
and last but not least, thanks for picking me up, dusting
me off and shoving me back into the fight whenever
I try to escape. LOL You make one heck of a BFF!

Dear Reader,

I have had so much fun creating this new series—maybe because I live fairly close to Gold Country and have always been enchanted by it. My husband and I enjoy visiting Jackson, where we have dinner or stay over in a B and B. We've gone rappelling and spelunking at Moaning Caverns and driven the kids over to Coloma to pan for gold. But we've probably spent the most time mountain biking in the foothills. Even if we're not doing something special, we like just investigating the area. The history here in Northern California is as rich as the soil.

I love writing stories set in small towns, because of the depth of the relationships that so often exists there. A lack of anonymity affects behavior in interesting ways. A close-knit community can be a blessing; it can also be a curse. I think you'll find examples of both in Whiskey Creek—but for a movie star like Simon O'Neal, who needs a quiet place to get away and pull himself together, Whiskey Creek is just what the doctor ordered.

I love hearing from my readers. Please feel free to visit me on Facebook (search for Author Brenda Novak to "like" my page) or stop by my website at brendanovak.com, where you can sign up for my mailing list, enter my various giveaways or learn about other books in this series. There, you can also sign up for my annual online auction for diabetes research, which occurs every May. So far, we've raised more than $1.5 million for research!

I hope you enjoy *When Lightning Strikes!*

Brenda Novak

1

She was ruined. She'd become anathema—the Jerry Maguire of the Los Angeles public-relations biz. And it'd happened almost overnight.

"You don't look so good."

Gail DeMarco turned away from the phone she'd just hung up to focus on Joshua Blaylock. Dressed in a pair of skinny black jeans with long-toed shoes, a designer jacket and rectangular-shaped glasses, her personal assistant hovered at the corner of her desk, a hopeful yet worried expression on his face. Like her, he'd been hoping they could pull out of the nosedive she'd caused by making one impetuous call, and then a number of thoughtless statements, three weeks earlier. But she could tell Joshua had overheard enough to understand what her other employees didn't grasp quite yet. They hadn't just lost a few important clients, like Maddox Gill and Emery Villere; they'd lost them all. Big Hit Public Relations had fallen from its lofty perch at the top of the PR food chain to crash and burn at the bottom. And it was all thanks to one man. Simon O'Neal, the hottest male lead in the movie business, had flexed his superstar muscles and brought down her company so quickly and easily Gail could hardly believe it. She kept thinking she'd wake up to find that their feud was all a bad dream—or that others would see Simon as the train wreck she knew him to be and side with her instead. But America loved him. He was their new James Dean. He was screwing up right and left, but he had the most loyal fans in the world, fans who were as fascinated by his self-destruction as his talent.

She should never have told him she'd no longer work for him. One client after another had deserted her ever since.

But any self-respecting public-relations professional would've grown tired of Simon's antics. He'd done everything she'd specifically asked him *not* to, created so many media nightmares, and that made her, as his personal publicist, look as bad as he did. How was she supposed to represent someone like that?

"Hello?" His smile gone, Joshua snapped his fingers in front of her eyes.

Gail forced back her tears. For more than a decade, ever since she'd graduated with a degree in advertising and public relations, then interned for Rodger Brown and Associates, she'd devoted herself to building her company. She had no husband, no kids and very few friends, at least in the L.A. area. Her ambition hadn't allowed time for that. There was only the group of childhood friends in Whiskey Creek six hours north. She saw them every couple of months. But by and large she'd left both family and friends to make her mark in the big city. Here, her employees were closer to her than anyone else. And now she'd have to let them all go. Even Joshua.

"That was Clint Pierleoni." She groomed her voice into a careful monotone to keep it from cracking.

He blinked rapidly, as if he was tempted to cry himself. It wouldn't be the first time he'd broken down in her office. He was always getting upset over one man or another. She usually consoled him, actually enjoyed living vicariously through him since it'd been so long since *she'd* had a love life. But today she had no words of comfort because his pain was her pain, too.

"Don't tell me—" he started.

She broke in before he could get the words out. "He said it's time for him to find another PR company."

"But…Clint's been with us from the beginning. I've *slept* with Clint—after signing that form agreeing not to reveal he's gay, of course."

Gail ignored the last part of what Joshua had said. She didn't condone her employees having sex with the firm's clients. But she'd already written Josh up for his inappropriate relationship with Clint. It seemed pointless to go over her objections again, especially at this late date. What Joshua said about Clint was true. He'd been the first up-and-coming actor to take a risk on her. And she'd done a hell of a job for him at a steal of a price.

She'd expected more loyalty. They'd come so far together. He was bigger now than he'd ever been, and she'd helped make that happen. "He tried to explain—"

Joshua broke in. "Explain what? That he was caving in to the pressure of the Hollywood heavyweights who've joined Simon O'Neal and turned against us?"

"He's afraid staying with us will adversely affect his career. Simon promised him a part in his next movie, and he's positive it will disappear if he doesn't kowtow."

"Simon's a bastard! An *alcoholic* bastard!"

She narrowed her eyes. "You haven't slept with *him,* have you?" For just a moment, she allowed herself to imagine what it would do to the almighty Simon's career to leak *that* information. He'd never be able to play a romantic male lead again. But she knew what Joshua was going to say before he said it.

"He's yummy enough that I'd sleep with him if I had the chance. I don't know many people who wouldn't, except you," he added as an afterthought. "But…he's not gay."

"Right." She attempted a shrug, even though she'd had her fantasies about Simon, too. Who hadn't? "Too bad."

He leaned on his knuckles as if he was planning to reveal a big secret. "He *is* a womanizer, though. I bet we could come up with all kinds of dirt—"

She waved him to silence. "Not the kind that'll surprise anyone. His wife left him because he couldn't keep his pants zipped. His exploits in *that* area are second only to Tiger Woods's." Even if she had the goods, she doubted she could bring herself to destroy him. She was hurt and angry, but she didn't believe in creating bad karma.

"So what do we do?" Josh asked.

"What *can* we do?" Drawing a deep breath, she tried to sit tall in her chair, like she was used to doing when barking out orders and handling calls in rapid succession. She thrived on the adrenaline that sustained her on any given day. But her groove was gone, along with her clients.

Sagging against her expensive leather chair, she thought about calling the actors who'd fired her. If only she could talk them into coming back…

But it was no use. She'd already tried that. No one would cross Simon, except a few inconsequential clients who didn't care enough about him to follow his lead, and three of them were charities she repped *pro bono.*

"He's going with Chelsea Seagate at Pierce Mattie," she added dully.

"No!" Joshua punched the air. "That bitch has everyone!"

Also thanks to Simon. He'd been with Big Hit for three years, knew they were rivals, so he'd gone to Chelsea and taken almost fifty of Gail's sixty-four other clients there, too. "Pierce will regret letting Chelsea sign him. Simon will ruin them. There isn't a PR firm in America, or anywhere else, that can protect the image of a client so bent on self-destruction. Since his wife left, he's worse than Charlie Sheen ever was."

"At least PM will die a slow death," Joshua said,

dropping into the chair across from her. "How long before we have to close our doors?"

She pursed her lips as she glanced around her swanky office. There'd been days when she'd been unable to believe her own success. Now it all seemed to have been an illusion. "Two months?" Could she even hold out that long?

He rocked forward. "That's it?"

"Our overhead is huge, Josh. Rent alone is fifteen thousand. Together with salaries for twenty people… the money will dry up fast."

His next words were muffled; he'd buried his face in the stylish scarf he wore under the collar of his too-cool jacket. "When do we tell the others?"

She couldn't bear to see him slumped over like that. He'd told her not to cast Simon aside but she'd done it, anyway. Simon had deserved to be cut from her client roster—he'd been asking for it—but he wasn't anyone to mess with, and he'd proven that.

Struggling under the weight of her responsibility, she got up and walked to the interior window overlooking the expansive lobby designed to impress visitors. The staff cubicles and three other offices branched off to the right. They couldn't be seen from where she stood, but she could make out the back of Savannah Barton's dark head as she lounged in the doorway of Serge Trusso's office. Savannah was a single mom with two kids. Where would she go? Serge would land on his feet. He saved money, never took anything for granted. But what about Vince Shroeder, one cubicle over? He had a disabled wife. Then there was Constance Moreno, barely twenty years old. She'd come from New York two months ago and signed a year's lease on her apartment. How would she pay the rent?

These people depended on her. Why had she been so determined to punish Simon, to see that he received some type of backlash?

Gail tapped her forehead on the cool glass. "You'd better call a meeting. I'm sure they already know trouble's brewing. It's been dead around here. They're out there throwing spitballs at one another."

"You want me to get them now?"

She thought of Simon's movie premiere tonight and the fact that he'd be at the after-party, probably roaring drunk but enjoying the fame and fortune that followed him everywhere. He shouldn't get away with what he'd done. She'd been in the right, damn it. But... if she wanted to save her employees, she was going to have to humble herself and apologize, maybe even *beg*.

She'd rather throw herself in front of a bus, but there was more at stake here than pride. She had a good team; they didn't deserve to lose their jobs. "No, wait."

"You think something's going to change?" he said with a telltale sniff.

She didn't dare hope. But she had to make one last-ditch effort to save the firm, just in case it was still possible. "Give me until tomorrow."

He toyed with the expensive pen set he and the rest of her staff had bought her for Christmas. "For what?"

She turned to face him. "A Hail Mary."

2

Simon spotted Gail immediately. In a sea of silicone, Botox and spray tans, she stood out. Maybe it was her chest, flat by L.A. standards, the severe cut of her business suit with its starched white shirt or the stubborn set to her jaw. Or maybe it was her general disdain for Hollywood parties and the licentious behavior that went on, and her unwillingness to dress up and join the fun.

Regardless, Simon had always liked the fact that she wasn't an adoring fan—almost as much as he hated it. One would think she'd at least *try* to blend in if she was going to crash the party. He was fairly certain she hadn't received an invitation.

"What's wrong?"

He jerked his gaze back to the stunning blonde sitting in the booth next to him. A "hot yoga" instructor he'd met about twenty minutes earlier, her name was Sunny Something, and she was smarter than the stereotype her short skirt and low-cut blouse brought to mind. She was a nice person, too. But he was bored.

These days the women he socialized with seemed virtually interchangeable.

"Nothing." He tossed back the rest of his drink. "Why?"

She angled her head to see where he'd been looking but skimmed right over Gail. She probably couldn't imagine such a nondescript woman being of any consequence to him. If not for the guilt that plagued him, he might not have given Gail a second thought. When he'd told Ian Callister, his business manager, that he wished she'd go broke and return to the small town she called home, he hadn't meant it literally. He'd been drunk when he made that statement. But Ian had decided to take revenge for her defection, and Simon had been preoccupied and angry enough to turn a blind eye. He hadn't even asked what Ian was up to. Part of him figured Gail DeMarco deserved whatever she got. The other part didn't see why Ian would go to *too* much trouble.

But just yesterday he'd learned that Ian had called all her clients and "suggested" they might like it better with Chelsea Seagate at Pierce Mattie. Almost every one of them had promptly switched.

"You were frowning," Sunny said. "Is there someone here you're not happy to see?"

"No," he lied.

"What did you say?"

She couldn't hear him for the music. He raised his voice. "Just getting tired, that's all."

"Tired? Already?" She offered him a pout. "It's barely ten."

His lack of interest was an insult to such an attractive woman. He understood that. If he were a better man he'd pretend to be entertained, but he simply couldn't fake it. Not tonight. He did enough acting when the cameras were rolling. Besides, he didn't care if she moved on to someone more attentive. He'd been telling the truth when he said he was tired. He'd been tired since before he came, hadn't slept in days. Every time his mind grew quiet, the regrets that tortured him returned.

"Would you like another drink?" he asked.

She didn't get a chance to answer. When Gail started making her way over, he couldn't help shifting his attention again. She'd located him, as he knew she would. She was nothing if not focused. And it wasn't as if he could disappear into the crowd. He was always the center of attention whether he wanted to be or not.

What would happen from here on, however, was anyone's guess. He'd never dreamed his ex-PR agent would have the moxie to show up at an event like this, where he'd be surrounded by friends and supporters, not to mention the regular contingent of hangers-on—people who were willing to kiss his ass regardless of what he did.

The girl had guts. He had to give her that.

"Simon?"

He looked up at her from beneath his eyelashes, as if he was too lazy or intoxicated to move. Maybe his temper, and what he'd said to Ian, had sparked the conflagration that had consumed her business, but he hadn't intended for Ian to be quite so vindictive and didn't want to take responsibility for it. Barring a few minor faults, Ian was a good manager. He'd certainly never done anything like this before. She could call Ian if she wanted to discuss the problem. It wasn't as if she was entirely innocent; she'd vented her fury by making a series of unflattering statements that had wound up in the press.

Maybe when Simon O'Neal grows up, he'll realize that women are good for more than just one thing.

Simon O'Neal is his own worst enemy. He hates himself in direct proportion to everyone else's admiration. Why is anyone's guess. The guy's had it all. As far as I'm concerned, there's no excuse for his behavior....

Maybe some people find him attractive. But I wouldn't sleep with him if he were the last man on earth. There's no telling what kind of disease he's carrying....

There were other comments he couldn't remember verbatim. Something about how he needed more therapy than even a fortune like his could support. And another about his being a waste of God-given talent, a man without decency, a charming Dr. Jekyll on-screen and an evil Mr. Hyde off...

"What can I do for you?" he replied, using the same overly polite tone with which she'd addressed him.

She lifted her chin. "Could I have a word with you, please?"

Was she crazy? He had no interest in walking off with her. "'Fraid not. Maybe you don't remember, but we don't have anything to discuss these days. And in case you haven't noticed, I'm with someone." He could feel Sunny's interest in their exchange; she watched them but didn't say anything.

Gail ignored her completely. "It'll just take a minute."

He flicked his hand, hoping she'd interpret the gesture for what it was—an indication that she should take herself off. "I'm busy."

Unfortunately, she didn't go anywhere. With a decisive tug on her tailored jacket, she cleared her throat. "Fine. We'll talk here. I—I'd like to offer you an apology."

He didn't want an apology. People were beginning to stare, to realize she was the PR woman who'd dissed him. Everyone would want to hear what she had to say. He should get rid of her as soon as possible. But she'd just given him an opportunity to challenge the integrity she clung to like a battle shield, and he couldn't resist.

"Are you saying you didn't mean all the terrible things you said about me?" he drawled.

She hesitated while searching for words, eventually coming up with a response designed to placate him without being overtly untruthful. "I shouldn't have said them."

Damn right she shouldn't have said them! She'd drawn first blood. She'd been so sanctimonious while sitting on the throne of her PR empire that Ian had shown her just how vulnerable she was. It'd been tit for tat, no big deal. And as far as Simon was concerned, their little...*disagreement* was over.

"No problem. I'm willing to let bygones be bygones if you are," he said. "Have a nice night."

"That's it?" Her blue eyes widened.

He slung an arm around Sunny, slouching into her so he'd look comfortable and cozy and unlikely to go anywhere. "Were you hoping for more?"

Her bottom lip quivered as tears filled her eyes.

Ah, shit.

"I was hoping that you might—"

Jerry Russell, the director of his latest project, interrupted by walking up and bending to look in her face. "What's going on here? You making the ladies cry already, Simon?"

"You got trouble, Simon?" someone else piped up, and that was all it took to send a murmur through the crowd that made everyone turn toward him.

Tears rolled down Gail's cheeks. He could tell she was trying to hold them back but that only seemed to make matters worse. She was emotionally strung out and under scrutiny.

He had to get her out of here before he wound up on the front page of the tabloids again. One picture of her sorrowful face and some stupid paparazzi would report that he'd purposely and vengefully acted to destroy her: Box Office Hit Simon O'Neal Sends Small-Town PR Girl Packing. Which, thanks to Ian, was close enough to the truth that he wouldn't even be able to fight it.

He couldn't afford to give his ex-wife any more ammunition for the bitter war she was waging. If he didn't clean up his act he'd never gain even partial custody of his son. The judge had been very firm about that.

People were starting to converge on them. He had to act now to avoid a spectacle.

"No trouble," he said with a reassuring smile and, telling Sunny he'd be right back, slid out of the booth. "It's damn hot in here. I think we'll get some air."

Taking Gail's hand, to throw any curious onlookers off the scent of another disagreement, he led her at a measured pace, nodding and exchanging greetings as they passed through the other guests to an expensively appointed back room, one that'd been designated for his use. No one ever specified what such a room was for because it was for anything he wanted. He could do drugs in here, have sex, throw a private party…whatever.

He'd never been more grateful for it than now.

"What were you thinking coming here?" he growled as soon as he closed the door securely behind them. "And for the love of God would you stop crying?"

She dashed a hand across her face. "I'm sorry. I…I'm embarrassed, but…I can't seem to help it."

Tears made him feel inadequate. Especially coming from her. In the three years they'd worked together, throughout all the bookings and events and movie releases and good and bad publicity, she'd always been so composed. "Try harder."

"Thanks for the empathy," she muttered.

Partially so he wouldn't have to look at her, he crossed the room and poured a glass of champagne from the bottle that had been put on ice, then pressed it into her hands. "Here, maybe this will help."

"I don't drink."

He grimaced. "One of the many reasons I don't like you. Drink it, anyway."

She downed it as though it was water and the subsequent coughing fit distracted her enough that she was able to shut off the waterworks.

"So what is it you want from me?" he asked. "How do I make this...go away?"

The shrewdness in her eyes returned. "You mean me? How do you make *me* go away?"

After taking a second to think about it, he shrugged. "Basically, yeah."

"You can say that so nonchalantly after destroying my business?"

He considered explaining that he hadn't been as actively involved as she might imagine, but didn't bother. He doubted she'd believe him, anyway. "You need money, is that it?"

"No! I want my former clients back. And not for my sake—well, not entirely. The way things sit right now, I'll have to let my employees go, and...they need their jobs."

Her situation was that dire? *Already?* He was going to kill Ian. Why'd he have to take it so damn far? "Fine. I'll contact a few people, see what I can do to reverse the damage. Call me next week. Good enough? Will you go home now and…watch TV or reorganize your cupboards or whatever exciting thing you do in your spare time? Maybe you can go online and look for a dress that would be appropriate for a party like this."

He could tell she was tempted to land a good jab of her own. He knew she was capable of it. But she held her tongue. With a sniff and a nod, she handed him the champagne flute and started to leave.

"And, Gail?"

She glanced over her shoulder.

"I don't have a disease, sexually transmitted or otherwise. I can provide the test results if you're interested."

At least she had the decency to blush. "No. Sorry," she said, and slipped out.

3

Joshua jumped to his feet the moment Gail breezed into her office. "Did you see it?"

She wasn't surprised to find him waiting for her. Not after what they'd discussed yesterday. Looking forward to being able to put his fears to rest, to reassure all of her employees, she smiled. It hadn't been easy eating crow at the party last night—breaking into tears had been downright humiliating—but as agonizing as those few minutes had been, they'd also been worth it. Simon had promised to right what he'd done and she trusted he'd follow through. He wouldn't want her bothering him again, especially in public; he'd made that clear.

She'd slept soundly for the first time since dropping Simon O'Neal from her client roster. After spending an hour at the gym, she'd stopped off at a different coffeehouse than her usual one, just for a change, and was really enjoying the new blend. It was a good morning.

"See what?" She handed Josh her coffee while she removed her jacket and hung it on the rack.

His own smile a bit smug, he held up the folded tabloid he carried in his other hand. *"Hollywood Secrets Revealed."*

"No." She hadn't even signed on to her computer yet. She'd skipped that part of her morning ritual because she hadn't been worried she might find some damaging anecdote or tell-all about one of her clients in the gossip blogs or Hollywood e-zines. She wouldn't have to worry about *that* until she'd recovered some of her list. "Did Simon do something stupid after I left last night?"

This seemed to take Josh aback. "What do you mean?"

"At the premiere party."

"You went there? You saw him?"

She sent him a conspirator's smile. "I sure did."

His mouth hung open in surprise as she took her coffee. "What for?"

"To apologize. Why else would I go? He's agreed to do what he can to help us get back on our feet. We're going to be fine." *Hallelujah!* What a weight had been lifted from her shoulders. She felt so light, as if she could walk on air—until she noticed that Joshua wasn't reacting to this news as favorably as she'd expected. "What's wrong? Aren't you relieved?"

Stumbling back, he reached behind him to locate a seat and sank into it, clasping *Hollywood Secrets Revealed* to his chest. "Heaven help me…"

She felt her eyebrows go up. "Heaven help you *what?* I said we *wouldn't* be filing for bankruptcy. I fixed things. We'll be okay." She gave his arm a reassuring squeeze and sipped her coffee while waiting for him to absorb the good news. "So...what's in *HSR* this morning? A mess for Chelsea Seagate to clean up?"

With a chuckle for poor Chelsea, she started to round her desk, then stopped. "Why do you look like you just swallowed a marble?" she asked as her assistant's horrified expression finally dispelled the euphoria that had carried her to work this morning.

"I—I didn't know you planned to make up with Simon. You didn't say that. Not exactly. You said you were going to throw a Hail Mary. I thought that meant you'd try and beg Clint to come back, or...or apply for a loan...or go after Chelsea's old clients...or consider branching into fashion and beauty PR. I never dreamed he'd accept your apology even if you offered him one."

She remembered the argument she and Simon had had when he'd been charged with public drunkenness. "Neither did I. He's been a bear lately, angry all the time. I must've caught him in a benevolent mood." She gestured for Josh to give her the paper. "Let me have a look at what's got you so worked up."

Closing his eyes, he dropped his head back as if his neck could no longer hold it up.

"What's wrong with you?" She laughed because she couldn't take him seriously. He tended to be overly dramatic. And whatever was upsetting him couldn't be worse than the problem she'd just solved. Absolute disaster had a way of putting lesser setbacks in proportion. "Josh? The paper?" she prompted when he made no move to hand it over.

At last, he held it out. But he didn't look at her. He acted as though he couldn't bear to see her reaction.

Frowning, Gail opened the paper, read the headline—and felt her coffee cup slip out of her fingers. "Oh…my…God!"

He covered his face and groaned.

Clutching the paper, she jabbed it with a finger. "How did this happen?"

"It's all my fault," he mumbled from beneath his hands. "I…I met a friend at the paper for drinks. I thought Big Hit should go out with a bang instead of scuttling off like a dog with its tail between its legs. I told her she had to be careful how she wrote the story—to protect the magazine and to protect us. And she was. There's nothing directly attributed to you. It's all hearsay."

Gail wasn't even listening anymore. The ringing in her ears drowned out all other sound as she read and reread the opening paragraph. This had to be a joke. It couldn't be happening, not now. But she could tell from Josh's body language that it was most definitely for real.

Simon O'Neal Accused of Sexual Assault
An unnamed source from Big Hit PR, the firm that recently slammed its doors on Hollywood's biggest bad boy when he started a fight on the set of his latest movie, has revealed that the trouble between Simon and the owner of the firm, PR princess Gail DeMarco, stems from an evening the two spent together almost a month ago.

Although details remain murky, and both sides are rushing to cover it up, there has been talk about a sexual assault....

Ignoring the coffee fanning out on the expensive carpet, Gail leaned on her desk so she wouldn't fall. "I've never accused Simon of assaulting me," she gasped.

"The article doesn't claim to have proof," Josh said.

"But the media will be calling day and night, hounding me for details. If this was true, it'd be the biggest story of the year. And—" She reached into her purse for her cell phone. No doubt she already had dozens of messages. She'd turned it off when she went to the gym to save battery power and hadn't yet turned it back on. "I'm going to be sick."

"I know the feeling," Josh said.

"What made you think I'd ever condone such a lie?" She pressed the button on her phone that would start the power-up sequence. "Simon is trying to get custody of his five-year-old son." She held the paper in front of her. "Even though none of this is true it'll give his ex-wife one more stone to throw at him in court."

Wearing a sheepish expression, Josh lowered his hands and sat up. "I wasn't thinking straight. I was so...angry. And she says *talk*."

He'd already pointed that out. It didn't help. "She says I was Simon's victim! And now I *will* be his victim. He's going to strangle me! He'll destroy the company, and then he'll come after me. And I can't blame him. Don't you understand? All he cares about is regaining contact with Ty. It's the divorce and what he did to cause it that's eating him up inside. This will… Oh, God. I'll refute it. Of course I'll refute it, but that won't help."

"He deserved to have his wife leave him. He was cheating on her with half a dozen other women—"

"I know. It doesn't make much sense. But he loved her. A lot. Even I could tell that much."

Josh got up and began to pace. "I admit, now that I'm sober, what I did seems…reckless. And impetuous. And foolhardy. But…he gets away with whatever he does, and I didn't want to let him get away with what he did to us. I wanted him to pay a price."

The phone rang, the sound jangling Gail's nerves. It was eight o'clock, the time the answering service transferred all calls back to the office.

She glanced across her desk but didn't reach for the handset. She remained rooted to the spot until Ashley poked her head into the room. "A reporter from *The Star* is on the phone. They're offering loads of money for the exclusive. But…I'm not sure you're going to be interested in that."

"I'm definitely *not* interested. Tell him so." She needed to get her bearings, make a plan to stop the spread of this story. She could do that, couldn't she? Avoiding this type of disaster, or minimizing it, was what she did for a living. She'd just never had to do it for herself.

"Got it." Ashley lowered her voice. "I know this can't be easy for you. I have to admit I didn't agree with refusing Simon's business. But now I don't blame you one bit. I'm sorry I've been complaining behind your back about what a stupid decision it was."

"You might try thinking before you open your mouth next time," Gail muttered.

Ashley winced. "Not exactly behind your back. Yeah, I guess I'll shut up. But…I am sorry. Are you okay?"

No. She wasn't okay. She was in the middle of the worst nightmare of her life and couldn't figure out how she'd gotten there. She was always the one in the right, the problem-solver, the first with good advice. She'd made a living out of these strengths, only to have Josh shove her firmly into the wrong.

Ashley stepped closer. "What can I do to help?"

She curled her nails into her palms. "Get Josh out of here before I start yelling."

"Excuse me?"

"I'm sorry." Josh was distraught, but Gail wasn't ready to hear his apology. Not yet. Maybe he'd done what he'd done in some misguided attempt to defend her, to defend them all, or at least get in a good swing at the Goliath in their lives. Considering the situation, that was understandable, especially if he'd been drinking. But there was no escaping the fact that he'd crossed the line, and she was going to pay dearly for it. They all were.

"Josh?" Ashley said uncertainly. "You coming?"

"I'm sorry," he said again, and burst into a full-blown wail.

Gail breathed deeply as he ran out. "Let him cry."

"So…what should I do when other reporters begin to call?" Ashley was still waiting for direction, and not about how to handle Josh.

"Tell everyone that I'm unavailable. Whatever you do, don't even hint that I'm here or put anyone through. Not until I give the word."

"Does that go for the police? Because they left a message with the answering service."

Oh, no…

Ashley wrung her hands. "You're so white. You're not going to faint, are you?"

"Maybe." Was it just last night she'd gone home and congratulated herself on having a second chance?

"Should I get you something? A glass of water or— Oh, you've dropped your coffee. Look at the mess."

A stain couldn't compare to everything else that was going on. Gail pointed to the door. "The other line's ringing. Someone has to answer."

"Right. Of course. No one will get through. You can count on me," she said, and snatched up Gail's cup before scurrying out.

Bracing herself for what she might find, Gail checked the call log on her cell phone. Sure enough, she had thirty missed calls. All of which had been left in the past two hours.

Almost every one of them came from Simon or Ian.

What was she going to do?

She had no chance to decide. A second later, the outside door banged open and everyone started screaming while trying to stop the man who'd stalked inside. It was Simon. And he had his eye on her office as he shoved one person after another out of his way.

4

Gail jumped to her feet and put her desk between them. She had no idea what else to do. She'd never seen Simon this angry, not even when he'd punched out his costar for calling him "Tiger Woods" after news of his divorce, and the reason behind it, broke.

"What the hell kind of game are you playing?" he yelled. "I told you I'd reverse whatever Ian did to your business. We agreed last night. Didn't you believe me?"

The veins that stood out in his neck made Gail as uncomfortable as his bloodshot eyes. If she had her guess, he hadn't been to bed since she'd seen him. Unshaven, with his thick black hair mussed and his clothes wrinkled, he had lines of fatigue bracketing his eyes and mouth. But he still looked gorgeous.

Gail considered that more than a little unfair. At six feet tall, he wasn't even short like so many other male actors.

"I'm not playing games," she said. "I believed you, and I can…explain. If you'll just give me a chance."

He pulled *Hollywood Secrets Revealed* out of his

back pocket and slapped it down. "This is bullshit! All of it. And you know it."

Her knuckles ached with tension as she clasped her hands in front of her. "I do. And I'll admit it. I promise. We just need to brainstorm how…how to proceed from here, figure out the best way to neutralize the damage."

He tilted his head as if a new thought had occurred to him. "Is that why you did it? To get me back in here? So we could work together again?"

"What?" Losing some of her fear, she stood taller. "Absolutely not. I'm the one who kicked you out to begin with."

His lips, so sensuous-looking in the movies, thinned. "But now you regret losing the income."

"I regret that it cost me my other clients. I don't regret that it cost me *you*. You're a mess and it's time someone had the guts to tell you."

"*I'm* a mess?" he repeated. "At least I'm not falsely accusing anyone of a felony!"

She cringed. "Right. That's bad."

"If you agree, then *why?* I've never laid a hand on you—and I've had plenty of opportunities. How many times have we been alone in the back of a limousine, coming or leaving an event, or meeting after hours right here in this office?"

Not many. And certainly never for very long. Ian, his business manager, was usually with them, or Serge, who worked for her and helped with the bigger accounts. Sometimes one of Simon's bodyguards came along. But she wasn't going to quibble over such a small detail.

Especially when he added, "Not that I wouldn't like to wring your neck this very second."

"You wouldn't want to make matters any worse." She edged away when he took a few steps to the left, always keeping the same distance between them. She doubted he'd really hurt her. He'd never been known to strike a woman. But he'd been unraveling pretty fast since the breakdown of his marriage. She wasn't taking any chances.

"Matters *can't* get any worse," he ranted. "I've been accused of a lot of things, but never *rape!* Don't you realize what this is going to do to me? My ex-wife's lawyers have already called. They're going to use this to delay my next custody hearing. It could slow the process for months, make it impossible for me to get my little boy back...." When his voice broke, his muscles bunched as if he'd rather slug the wall than show her his softer side, the side that actually cared about something. "If that happens, if I lose him, I'll make you sorry you were ever born."

Gail couldn't help cringing again. He meant it. "I apologize. Sincerely. Please, calm down and—"

The door swung open and Ian Callister charged in. Face mottled with emotion, blond hair standing on end as if he'd just rolled out of bed, he was obviously in a hurry. But he didn't seem to be looking for her. At least, not yet. He had eyes only for his frazzled client. "Simon, let me handle this. You don't need to be here, okay? This is dangerous. You touch one hair on her head and it'll just exacerbate the problem. Why don't you go home and try to get some sleep? I'll call as soon as I have this resolved. We'll work it out. I swear."

"Like you worked out taking away her clients?" Simon asked. "Why do you think she did this?"

"*I* wasn't trying to get revenge," Gail said. But the men weren't listening.

"She was too full of herself," Ian replied. "I was just giving little miss prim and proper a much-deserved wake-up call."

Full of herself? Was that how she came off? Gail opened her mouth to offer some sort of defense; she wasn't the one who'd acted badly when she'd represented him. But Simon was already responding.

"What the hell am I even doing here?" He threw up his hands. "What's done is done. There's nothing we can do to take it back. As far as I'm concerned, you can both go to hell. Good luck saving your business," he said to her. "Because I won't lift a finger to help you, and you'd better be prepared to defend yourself against a slander suit. And you." He pointed at Ian. "You're fired."

With that, he left, but not before slamming every door he encountered.

In the wake of his noisy departure, Gail could see her employees creeping toward her interior window. They gazed in at her with wide eyes and mouths hanging open.

She ignored them. Ian was still in her office, breathing heavily and eyeing her as if *he'd* like to wring her neck on Simon's behalf.

"Thanks for that," he snapped.

She swallowed hard. "You deserved it. If you really went after my business the way he said, you don't deserve to work for him. Or anyone else in Hollywood."

"Like *you* deserve to work here after the little stunt you pulled? Accusing an innocent man of rape?"

"I didn't leak that bogus story!"

"Then where'd it come from?"

She felt too much loyalty to Josh to reveal his complicity. Since he worked for her, she was responsible for what he'd done, anyway. Caught between her disapproval of his actions and her understanding of the frustration that had fueled them, she shook her head to avoid answering. "Regardless, it's become public. Now we have to decide what to do about it."

He paced to her credenza and back. "What, exactly, do you suggest?"

The sarcasm that dripped from those words implied that there was no way out. But there had to be.

She pressed her fingers to her temples. "First of all, we have to calm down so we can think." Her employees, all except Ashley, who was busy with the phones, were still gaping at them, trying to figure out what was going on. Irritated by the lack of privacy, she waved them away.

"Easier said than done when we're all facing the end of our careers," Ian grumbled, frowning as their audience reluctantly dispersed.

"This article is just the latest in a series of bad developments," she said. "The real problem started long before now. Simon's been rolling downhill for months, drinking too much, fighting, acting belligerent, walking out on jobs and getting sued for breach of contract. He was already in trouble."

"That's no excuse for what you've done. Chelsea Seagate and I have been trying to get things turned around, but you've just made his situation exponentially worse."

She wondered what Chelsea was going to say about this, how she'd try to contain the damage, and was actually grateful that she might have some help. "I agree. I'm saying this isn't a *new* problem. It's more of the old problem. Simon needs a fresh image. We've got to pull him out of circulation until he can decompress and get hold of himself."

Ian shoved a hand through his thick, unruly hair. "How do we pull him out of circulation? He has a new movie coming out. He's contractually obligated to promote it. That puts him on every major talk show in America."

He'd probably show up drunk at those appearances because he couldn't bear to do them sober anymore. She'd never seen anyone so burned out. "What if he had a good reason to change things up? What if we gave the movie's producer such a great PR angle he'd be thrilled *without* the usual dog-and-pony show?"

"I'm not following you," he said, but he seemed somewhat mollified and encouraged by her tone.

"It's been six months since Simon's divorce."

"And he's still not over it."

She threw him a dirty look. "We're talking about *solutions*. He's available again. That's the bright spot."

He stood by the window and peered out through the blinds. "What are you saying?"

"That what we should do is—" her mind scrambled to focus the idea that was coming to her "—find a nice girl for him to marry."

The blinds snapped as he let go of them and swung around to face her. "*Marry?* After what Bella the Bitch has done, I don't think he'll ever marry again."

"But consider what a new relationship would do to distract from, and counteract, all the bad press. *If* we could find the right person."

He prowled around, examining the awards she'd won, tossing her paperweight from hand to hand. "And who would the right person be?"

"Someone sweet enough to soften his rough edges. Someone whose character is sterling, above question, so there won't be any shocking revelations down the road."

He sighed. "Too dangerous. Anyone could end up being unpredictable."

"Not necessarily. This will be a business deal. The woman will sign a prenup as well as a contract outlining exactly what she can and can't do. If she fulfills her obligations, she'll be generously compensated. But she'll get paid only if she abides by the terms. We'll make sure she says nothing that isn't nice about him and acts with proper adoration in public. He'll have total control."

Ian still seemed skeptical. "There's no such thing as total control. How do you know that whoever we get won't turn out to be a psycho? Or cause bigger problems? It's not like you're going to find someone who doesn't know who he is. Any woman would smell money."

"You have so much confidence in the female gender," she said with a grimace.

He shrugged at her sarcasm. "I'm just sayin'. What if she gets tired of putting in the time and sells her story to the tabloids to make a quick buck instead? Reveals that she's a plant? Tries to blackmail him or take him to the cleaners?"

"That would be breach of contract."

"So?" he said, exasperated. "People break contracts all the time. And once the truth is out there—"

"The wife would have to be someone we trust," she conceded, "someone who has no appetite for fame and no interest in pursuing the Hollywood crowd."

"Someone who appears dutiful and devoted," he added.

He was starting to see the potential, which ignited a flame of excitement in Gail. What she was picturing could work, even for someone as far gone as Simon. "The public will eat it up. Who doesn't enjoy a good love story—especially one in which beauty tames the beast?"

He hesitated as if tempted, but ultimately shook his head. "No. What're we thinking? That's crazy. Even if we could find the ideal lady, Simon would never agree to this. He's had enough of women—er, marriage. That ex-wife of his ran his heart through a meat grinder."

Gail propped her hands on her hips. "And he didn't do the same to her?"

"Maybe he did. But he never used their son as a weapon against her, like she's doing to him. He hasn't been able to see Ty for weeks. And there's a lot more you don't know, because Simon refuses to make her look bad. He's taking full responsibility for the breakup of the marriage, even though she's no gem."

"I'm glad to hear you think *her* actions are reprehensible, since destroying someone's business doesn't seem to bother your conscience. At least you have your limits."

He made a face at her. "You asked for what I did. You left Simon in the lurch, then compounded the problem by opening your big mouth."

"He showed up at his ex-wife's drunk and tried to bust into her house!"

"Because he wanted to see his son!"

"And accomplished just the opposite. Now she has a restraining order against him."

"What she's doing hurts Ty as much as Simon. Ty has to be wondering where the hell his daddy is, and that tears Simon up. Anyway, Simon's ex isn't the one who's paying my bill, so I'll let someone else worry about what's best for her."

"Right now *no one* is paying your bill," Gail reminded him. "If you want Simon back, you're going to have to make him an offer, show him a way out of the mess he's in."

"And you think a fake marriage is the ticket?" Suspicion entered his eyes. "Or are you setting me up for failure?"

Gail spread her hands wide. At this point, she wanted them all to regain their footing, even Ian, so they could move on. "I'm not setting you up. To prove it, I'll handle all the PR for this myself, free of charge."

"Which includes…"

"I'll get the information into the hands of key people, position it as one of the best-kept secrets in town that Simon has a new love interest. Everyone will be salivating to learn who the lucky girl is. Meanwhile, you can find the best candidate. Once that happens, I'll sell the exclusive to *People,* and he can use those funds to pay her if he wants." Satisfied that she'd come up with the perfect fix, she raised her hands palms up. "Or Chelsea could take my idea and run with it."

"No way," he said, shaking his head. "Why would Pierce Mattie be willing to get involved in this, to put their reputation on the line?"

"The money? Or the challenge—"

"No way. They'd never go along with it." He cracked his knuckles.

"Then I'll do it, like I said."

"That's better. But how am I supposed to find an innocent woman in the circles Simon's been hanging out with lately? He's so afraid he'll actually be tempted to trust someone he's sworn off all women except the most jaded and easy. You're the only one he knows who—" His head jerked up. "That's it!"

Gail wasn't sure why, but she took a step back. "What's it?"

"*You'll* be his wife. That way even Chelsea won't have to know. It'll stay between us. The three of us."

"You're not serious...."

"Of course I am. It's got to be someone he knows or people will see this as the ruse it is. Besides, you owe us, and you need the money a lot more than Chelsea Seagate. She has all your old clients, remember?" he added with a devilish grin.

"How could I forget? But I'm not cut out for the part of Simon's wife!"

"Sure you are. You're perfect. No one will pay attention to the rape claim because they'll know that if you're marrying him, it couldn't possibly be true. Everything will be tied up with a neat bow."

Was she really the one who'd come up with this idea? She was beginning to feel faint again. "But Simon and I aren't the least bit compatible. Seeing us together, the way we interact, will be a dead giveaway."

"He's an actor, and a damn good one. He can pretend to love even you. And you're a PR agent, which requires no small amount of stretching the truth."

She considered what his suggestion would entail and gulped. "Wait a minute..."

"For what?"

For the room to stop spinning. "What about my business? I'm needed here."

"You said you don't have any business left."

"I don't, but I was...hoping that—"

"We'll send your staff on vacation until we have everything set up and ready for you to return."

"That won't work. My employees can't survive without a paycheck, even for two weeks."

"Then they can stay and work. Simon will cover your payroll."

He was overcoming every argument. "And the rent until we can make a comeback?"

"Simon will cover that, too."

Her knees buckled, and she sank into a chair. She had to admit she'd had her fantasies about Simon. What woman in America hadn't imagined his mouth on hers? She'd imagined a little more than that. But those were silly daydreams about characters who didn't exist, not the flesh and blood and very fallible man who played those larger-than-life parts. At least, that was what she'd always told herself....

"I'm not sure I can do this."

Shoving his hands in his pockets, Ian came closer. "Why not? Who better than a PR pro to stay at Simon's side night and day? If that won't keep him out of trouble, what will? Besides, you'll know exactly what to say when someone shoves a microphone in your face."

Gail grabbed for the one remaining argument she could think of. "How can you promise that Simon will pay my employees and my rent or anything else on his behalf? Last I heard you were fired."

He winked at her. "Simon needs us. He'll understand that once I've had a chance to talk to him."

Maybe he'd refuse. He wouldn't like this idea. No question about that.

But if he thought it would give him Ty he'd do it in a heartbeat.

5

"Seriously? This is what my life has come to? A fake marriage?"

Suddenly finding it too much of a distraction, Simon put the football game he'd recorded on his DVR on pause. Ian was hoping to retain his job, so it was understandable that he'd come here with some crazy idea that was supposed to save the day. But even if it had been a *good* idea, Simon doubted he'd take him back. In his opinion, Ian had revealed some disturbing character flaws.

Then again, Simon knew he probably wasn't anyone who should be pointing a finger.

Ian sat on the edge of his chair. Showered and ready for the rest of the day, his sunglasses dangling from one hand, he looked refreshed and energetic, which counted for more than anything he'd had to say so far. His manner made him convincing. Simon needed *someone* who felt ready to tackle the world. *He* felt as if he'd just been hit by a truck.

"It wouldn't be fake," Ian said. "It would be real."

"That makes it worse. I'd be acting my own life."
Simon brought his recliner upright. He spent a lot of
time in this room. It had no windows, so it was completely dark if he wanted it to be, and that helped whenever he had a headache. It was comfortable, too. After
barging into Gail's office and ranting like a madman
early this morning, he'd come here to calm down and
recover from a raging hangover. But he wasn't succeed-
ing, at calming down *or* feeling better. Every time he
thought of Gail and that rape charge, he wanted to put
his fist through a wall. And although beer sometimes
helped with a hangover, it didn't seem to be doing much
today. His head pounded as though it might explode.

What he needed was sleep. He hadn't slept well in
weeks. But nothing he did, short of pills, made sleep
possible.

"This is what you come to me with?" he asked Ian.
"*This* is how you plan to prove your worth?"

Surprisingly, his manager—possibly ex-manager;
Simon was still trying to decide—didn't back down.
He was completely convinced he had the answer to all
of Simon's problems. "Yes. It's brilliant."

"It's crazy!" He winced. Raising his voice had been a
mistake. "There's got to be another way out of the mess
I'm in," he added more calmly. "I've got more money
than I know what to do with. Let's put it to good use."

Ian shook his head. "Money's not enough this time,
Simon. You need a more drastic solution."

"This is drastic, all right," he responded with a hu-
morless chuckle. "Are you listening to yourself? You're

suggesting I pay Gail DeMarco, a woman I don't even like, to be my wife."

"She's a PR professional, the best in the business. We can't expect her to give up two years of her life for free."

"Two *years?*" The sour taste of the beer was making his stomach queasy. He should've eaten something.

"You've got to create a track record of stability, give her time to build the illusion of peace and happiness, a life in control."

Simon said nothing. He was too busy trying to subdue his nausea. Maybe he didn't want to admit it to Ian, but he knew one thing—he couldn't go on like this. He'd known that for a while.

"Think about it," Ian said. "You won't have much to do with her. It's mainly for appearances. You get married, you lie low, you get Ty back and then you part amicably. This is a PR campaign, not a marriage in the normal sense. You're taking it way too seriously."

"Then *you* marry her."

"I would if it'd help."

Simon tried to picture Gail as his wife and couldn't. They'd worked together too long in carefully defined roles that rarely crossed into their personal lives. And what he'd seen of her on a personal basis hadn't impressed him. Talk about a straight arrow. Could he tolerate having this person in his life on a day-to-day basis? "Who picked the length of time?"

"She did. But it's a worst-case scenario. If our plan works sooner than expected, we can make adjustments."

He sure as hell hoped it wouldn't take two years. At

the moment, Bella had full custody of their son and, thanks to a hard-ass judge who'd ranted on about his "moral corruption," she'd managed to deny him visitation rights. Yet she was leaving Ty with one nanny after another while she had surgery to fix cosmetic flaws that didn't exist, took expensive trips with men she'd barely met and tried too hard to be seen, to be part of the Hollywood "in" crowd, as if she wanted to be famous herself. After his mother died, Simon had been raised by nannies. He didn't want that for his son.

"It beats rehab," Ian murmured when Simon didn't respond. "Something has to be done."

Surely marriage would do more for public perception than a rehab program. But it would only work if he could get his drinking under control.

He turned his beer around and around in its holder. "How much is she charging?"

"The price of the wedding photos. Whatever we sell them for, that's what she'll get. She'll even negotiate the sale and handpick the placement so we get maximum publicity."

"*People* magazine will want them. And they'll pay a couple mil, at least."

"That's a lot, but it's money you wouldn't have without her, so she's essentially paying for herself, right?"

He didn't care about the money. He just wanted to understand the setup. "Apparently you two have thought of everything."

Ian smiled. "This will work, Simon. If you'll let her take charge for a while, do everything she tells you,

you'll get Ty back. I fully believe that. Will you meet with her?"

"Not today." He wasn't sure he could trust himself not to lay into her again. Every time he remembered that whole assault thing, he wanted to go ape shit.

"Tomorrow, then?"

Why not? It was worth a shot. Gail DeMarco wasn't the most appealing woman in the world, but she was better than the alternative. "Fine."

Ian slapped his knees and stood. "Fantastic. So…are we good? Are we back in business?"

Simon hated to give in so easily, but in his current condition he didn't have the wherewithal to do much else. "Yeah, I guess so. For now," he added grudgingly.

"You'll be glad you hired me back. I promise. But…"

"What?" Simon said when he hesitated.

"No drinking tonight, okay? I don't want Gail to see you like this."

Simon gave him a wry smile. "You think she'll walk out on two million dollars?"

"I know she will. Her reputation will be on the line. She'll only do it if she believes we can succeed."

He was probably right. That was partly why Gail had always made him a little defensive and uneasy. His money didn't matter to her. Neither did his fame. And he wasn't too strong in any of the categories that did.

It was a beautiful Saturday afternoon. Pale October sunlight drifted into the living room of Simon's Beverly Hills mansion through a series of large front windows, but Gail barely noticed. They'd just come in from outside, where Ian had taken pictures of her and Simon wrapped in each other's arms, their mouths only millimeters apart as if they'd just kissed or were about to. They planned to kick off the campaign by leaking those suggestive photographs to the press. It was all calculated and arranged. It meant nothing. And yet…standing so close to Simon had left Gail a bit breathless.

She tried to pretend otherwise, but Simon immediately threw her off balance again.

"What about sex?" he asked, taking a seat on the sofa, while she stood closer to Ian, who had his laptop on a table and was downloading the pictures.

Gail had been planning to cover this herself. She just hadn't found the nerve. "What do you mean?" she asked, stalling while she formulated her response.

He held the club soda he'd poured himself. "You've told me that from this minute on I can't drink a drop of alcohol. You've negotiated your price. And you've covered how we'll make the marriage look real by leaking information and photographs to the press. You've even had Ian take the pictures you plan to start with." He motioned to his manager. "He'll be emailing them to you any minute. Don't you think it's time to address how we're going to handle our marriage on the *inside?* I'm assuming I can't cheat—"

"Of course not. That would endanger the whole campaign!" she broke in.

"So what am I supposed to do?" He slid one hand down his thigh as he shifted, adjusting the fit of the faded jeans he wore with a simple T-shirt and expensive-looking house shoes. "If we were talking about two months it might be different. But we're talking about *two years*."

Dressed in a standard business suit, since she considered this a business meeting, she fiddled with one of her buttons. "I realize that sounds like a long time."

"Damn right," he said. "An eternity. You're not suggesting I go without, are you?"

Hoping he'd explain why her answer had to be what it was, Gail looked at Ian. But he merely glanced up from his computer and arched his eyebrows, implying that this one was all hers.

"Thanks for jumping in to break the bad news," she grumbled.

He grinned for the first time. "It's kind of funny to watch you flounder. I've never seen a grown woman turn so red."

She grimaced. "With my coloring, it doesn't take much." Which hardly seemed fair, since the two of them were tanned to a perfect café au lait despite the fact that summer had ended two months ago.

Ian's grin stretched wider. "I'm starting to like you, you know that? For someone who's so uptight and controlling, you're not bad."

God, he made her sound like her father. She cringed at the militant image that presented. But she was her father's daughter. She'd heard that before. She'd even inherited his freckles and strawberry-blond hair, both of which she hated as much as his intensity.

"I don't care if you like me or not," she said. But it wasn't true. She was the worst kind of type A, worse than her father, because she was also a pleaser, which meant she'd work herself to death to meet everyone's expectations, no matter how unreasonable they might be.

"Is there an answer in my near future?" Simon shook his drink, causing the ice to clink against the glass.

Lifting her chin, she addressed him herself. "Yes."

"Yes, what?"

"Yes, I expect you to go two years without sex. That's what the job requires."

He took another drink of his club soda as if this didn't bother him, but a subtle tightening around the mouth and eyes said otherwise. "So you'll be my wife in name and pocketbook only."

"Basically. Although I'll be signing a prenup, so I'll have enough to make you look generous and in love, but no access to your millions. You'll pay for our wedding rings and the kind of wardrobe your wife should have. The sale of the pictures will cover my contract."

She got the impression he was circling, searching for vulnerability, like a buzzard.

"A rock on your finger and a few clothes. That's all you'll need from me to get you through the next two years?"

"That and some privacy. Once I'm Mrs. O'Neal, my business should recover on its own. I say we go our separate ways behind closed doors, don't you?" How else would they survive suddenly being shackled to each other, two people who were so opposite and ill-suited?

"For the most part…yes."

She'd expected him to be more adamant that she keep her distance whenever possible. He'd had no interest in her on a personal level before. In the past year, neither had he listened to anything she'd told him professionally, despite paying a hefty monthly retainer for her guidance and advice. He was only listening now because he'd bottomed out.

"We'll need personal space and time alone," she went on. "Considering the number of mansions you own, having our own space shouldn't be a problem." There was definitely room enough for two at his twenty-five-thousand-square-foot home in Belize, for instance. Room enough for her to handle her business remotely, with Serge's and Josh's help; it would grow by leaps and bounds as soon as word of their union got out. Simon could…read scripts or whatever he did when he wasn't shooting a movie. "We should live a few weeks here and a few weeks there—preferably out of the country as much as possible. That'll help us keep ahead of the paparazzi, control which details get out."

He pursed his lips. "You won't miss sex? It won't be hard for you to sleep alone for two years?"

She gestured carelessly. "I'll *miss* it, but…my world doesn't *revolve* around getting lucky. I'm a mature adult. I can delay gratification until our marriage is over."

If he got her hint that he should be able to do the same, he didn't let it deter him, didn't act the least bit chastised or embarrassed. "And if I feel more strongly about not having to go so long?"

She curled her fingernails into her palms. "I'm afraid you—you don't have any choice. It's the only way this will work."

"You could change your mind."

That was what he'd been getting at all along. Gail's anxiety rose until the muscles in her back felt like rubber bands twisted to maximum torque. "I'm sorry. That's not going to happen."

He jiggled one knee, an obvious sign of agitation. She'd seen him do it before when he was on edge or growing impatient—or anytime he had to sit still for too long. "What if I let you keep the ring? A big diamond. One of your choosing."

Of course he'd think he could buy anything he wanted. He was richer than God. And every decision they'd arrived at so far had been reached through negotiation. But he had to understand that this was different. She had her limits. "I won't trade sex for money."

"Oh, quit being such a prude," he said with a roll of his eyes. "We'll be married. It's not like you'd be standing on a street corner. And if you won't let me get it anywhere else, I need to know we have some sort of… arrangement, in case I get desperate."

"Desperate?"

He didn't bother to apologize. He'd been cross all morning, supremely unhappy with the problem as well as the solution. But Simon was always cross these days. The only thing that mattered right now was procuring a commitment to the no-sex rule, just as she had with the no-alcohol rule, so they'd both be going into this with the same expectations.

"I understand that you're trying to be practical," she said. "And I realize two years is a long time for…a man of your age and, uh, limitations." She smiled, knowing she'd just jabbed him back. "But our relationship isn't real, so we won't be sleeping together no matter how desperate you become."

"Why the hell not?" he demanded, finally losing the battle with his temper.

"Because I'm not an object! And we don't even respect each other!"

There was more to it. For one thing, after the sex goddesses he'd been with, he was certain to find her lacking. And what could she possibly gain? Nothing. Sleeping with Simon would only set her up for future disappointment. It wasn't as if she could expect the relationship to last, even if she wanted it to.

Fortunately, she could stand on principle and wouldn't have to explain the more embarrassing reasons behind her refusal. "Look, don't make a big deal out of this, okay? This is acting. You don't *really* get to sleep with the female leads you pretend to make love to in the movies, do you?"

Too late, she realized that might not be true offset and couldn't believe she'd let her tongue get so far ahead of her brain.

"Only eighty or ninety percent of them," he responded, and Ian began to laugh.

When she shot Simon's manager a dirty look, he

laughed even harder but tried to speak through it. "Come on, we all know the number of women who fall at his feet. Why pretend otherwise? In any case, you can't expect him to give up the good life—"

"You were with me on this!" she complained. "We talked about it last night."

Obviously sensing how easily their deal could fall apart, Ian sobered. "I agreed that he couldn't have any extramarital affairs. I *didn't* agree that he couldn't screw his own wife."

She'd said no sex, right after no alcohol, and he hadn't corrected her. "But I won't really be his wife!"

"You'll be legally married."

"That doesn't mean anything."

Finished emailing her the photos, he closed his computer. "It means he should be able to sleep with you if he wants."

"No, it doesn't."

"Then what else is he supposed to do?"

"He could try exercising a little self-restraint!"

"Like you?" Ian asked. "Someone who wouldn't know how to have fun if it came up and bit her on the ass?"

Fun had never been her top priority. Her mother had walked out when Gail was eight. Since then, she'd had too much to prove to her father and brother. "That won't change my answer."

Ian expelled a loud sigh. "He *will* be exercising some restraint. If he gives up booze and refuses the women who hit on him, he'll be exercising a lot of it. But you have to be realistic. If you take other women away, you have to provide *something* else instead."

Gail dropped her purse to the floor. "No matter how undesirable."

She'd imbued her voice with enough sarcasm to wither them both on the spot, but it didn't seem to make an impact. If anything, her words had the opposite effect. It was almost as if she could see them mentally offering each other a high five for scoring a direct hit. They respected her professional ability—she knew that much—but they'd never been particularly fond of her. She and Simon had too often been at cross-purposes, with him trying to do what he wanted regardless of the consequences and her trying to protect his image.

"It's a fair question," Ian insisted.

"A sabbatical might be good for him," she argued, "give him a chance to pull his life together."

Simon came to his feet. "This is bullshit! You'll have my name, my ring and two years of my life, and I can't even climb into bed with you?"

Suddenly Gail realized that this conversation had nothing to do with the topic. He wasn't attracted to her; he'd made that clear. He was responding to being nudged out of the power position and wanted to get back on top in some way. So he was demanding she make a difficult concession, one that couldn't be over-ruled simply by pointing to the fact that it would compromise the campaign.

"Sleeping together is *not* part of the deal," she re-iterated.

Jaw set, he slammed his glass down on the coffee table. "Fine. I'll make some sort of discreet arrangement with a third party."

"No, you won't! We've been over that."

"It won't matter if no one knows."

"Isn't that the kind of thinking that got you into this mess? Word *would* get out, eventually. Your bed partners are too anxious to brag about their good fortune." Besides, she wouldn't want to lie awake night after night imagining what he might be doing in another part of the house. "Can't you look at this as a job? Pretend you're preparing to play a monk and celibacy is key to getting into character? If you can stay focused and put in the time, we'll all get what we need in the end. Then you can have a whole harem if you want."

Pivoting, he spoke to Ian as if she was no longer in the room. "This won't work. I'm already going without alcohol. I'll be cut off from my friends, in case they see through this…sham of a marriage or—" he made quotation marks with his fingers "—lead me astray. And I'll be connected at the hip to someone who'll be monitoring my every move and, no doubt, criticizing it."

"Stop it," she told Simon before Ian could respond.

Simon whirled on her. "Stop *what?*"

"Stop looking for a way out. If you don't want to do this, fine. But don't justify blowing up the deal by acting like you would've jumped in with both feet if only I'd been reasonable."

"You're *not* being reasonable! It'll be hard enough giving up alcohol."

"You said you could do it. I said maybe you should go into rehab instead. We'll just make matters worse if we attempt this and fail. And *you* said you weren't addicted."

"I'm *not* addicted, but…God, I could use a little help. A shoulder to cry on, if nothing else."

She folded her arms. "I'll lend you my shoulder, if you've got to have one, but nothing else. And I won't be criticizing everything you do," she added. "If it has no impact on the campaign, I won't say a word."

"You won't *have* to," he said. "I'll be able to see it in your face, which happens to reveal every thought you have. In any event, I have *no* intention of going without sex for two years on top of everything else. The way I see it, getting lucky every once in a while might be the only enjoyment I'll experience in two hellish years. Why would I give that up?"

Gail held her ground even though her high heels were beginning to pinch her toes and she was dying to sit. "Because you've let your son down and this is the only way to make it up to him, that's why!"

His hands curled into fists as if he wanted to strike her, or strike something. Maybe it was only verbal, but she'd slugged him where it hurt. She'd had to. If they didn't stay focused, keep their goals in sight, they'd fail before they ever got started. And she had a lot riding on this, too.

"How hard can it be?" She went on more calmly, hoping to placate him. "You've already made it abundantly clear that I don't appeal to you."

His eyes, now glittery, roamed over her, making her want to cover herself even though she was fully dressed. "I assumed you'd be better than nothing. But maybe I was wrong."

"Oh, stop acting like a—" She caught herself before she could call him any names. He was looking for a fight. Why accommodate him? "Never mind. Forget it. No sex. Do I have your agreement?"

"I wouldn't touch you if you stood in front of me naked and begged," he grumbled.

Fabulous. She had what she wanted. But somehow it didn't make her feel any better. His capitulation, and the sentiment behind it, stung enough that she couldn't resist a final salvo. "Fine, because I have some standards myself, you know, and dissolute movie stars aren't high on my list of must-have men."

"That's the best you've got? *Dissolute?*" Wearing a pained expression, he turned to Ian. "Does anyone in the real world even use that word these days?"

"I've seen it in books," Ian said, his voice speculative.

She rolled her eyes. "I doubt you've ever picked up a book. It means—"

"You're not the only one here with a brain," Simon interrupted. "I know what it means. And as far as comebacks go, it sucks. Do you think I haven't heard it all before? That you're the only person with an opinion on how I live my life?"

All the things she'd wanted to tell him in the past but hadn't seemed to rise in her throat and propel her forward, until she stood almost nose to nose with him. At six feet, he still had her by a few inches, but the heels helped. "You probably haven't heard the half of it," she said, "because I'm the only one who'll state it plainly, the only one who's not out to get something from you. Who else will tell you that you need to pull your head out of your ass? The people who depend on you for a paycheck?" She motioned at Ian. "Him? Mr. Suck-up?"

Ian pressed a hand to his chest as if she'd just shot him. "Ouch! I take back what I said. I don't like you at all."

Simon ignored him. "Seriously? I hear how rotten I am all the time. My ex has said much worse than you could ever come up with—and she's said it to the papers so I have the print version in case I forget."

She'd made some comments that'd been printed, too, but she didn't want to remind him. "Yeah, well, you can't trust Bella, either. She's hurt and she's angry, and she's determined to have her revenge. I'm honest, not vindictive. If *I* tell you something, it's true. And I'm telling you this—you need to pull your head out!"

"Maybe she's not so bad at comebacks." Ian was obviously trying to break the tension, but it didn't work.

Sending his manager a dirty look, Simon returned to the couch. "You're not some sort of oracle, Ms. De-Marco, so quit pretending. I won't take advice from a repressed PR failure with her jacket buttoned up to her neck. And you *are* hoping for something from me. You want me to save your business and cut you a hefty check when this is all over."

She put her hands on her hips. "If you'd like to marry someone else, I'll do the PR for free. But two years of *my* life doesn't come cheap. And you're the one who destroyed my business in the first place. You *owe* me."

She thought he'd come right back at her, tell her it was Ian who'd gone after her and not him. But without his name Ian wouldn't have had the power to pull off what he'd done.

Simon didn't attempt to argue, however. A sigh hinted at how tired he was. Had he even been to bed last night? He looked like he'd been up for days. "Maybe I do," he relented, "but you don't have to make this so hard."

She got the feeling that they weren't talking strictly about sex anymore, but it was more comfortable to respond as if they were. "I'll be going without, too."

"You don't seem to have a problem with it, which doesn't say much for your love life."

He'd hit a little too close to the truth. She wasn't sure whom she'd sleep with even if she wanted a bed partner. Her last relationship ended three years ago; she hadn't been with anyone since. But she wasn't about to admit that to him. "Let's leave my love life out of it."

In an effort to turn the conversation around, Ian abandoned his seat by the computer and came forward. "Look—" he touched her elbow to get her to face him "—this'll be a piece of cake for you. What's so terrible about a couple of years spent eating at the best restaurants, shopping at the most expensive stores and flying around the world?"

Besides the fact that it meant she'd have to endure two years of knowing Simon found her completely unattractive and, worse, unlikable? Could her self-esteem survive such a constant beating?

Simon jumped to his feet, suddenly decisive. "I'm calling it off. She's not up to the task."

Gail felt her jaw drop. "That's it? We just wasted the past two hours?"

"I guess so."

"Fine. I'm out of here." Grabbing her purse, she headed for the door.

6

"Wait!" Ian caught her arm. "Don't leave. He's upset, not thinking clearly."

"He can't control his emotions and appetites long enough to implement a simple plan, let alone one that'll be as tricky as this," she said. "That's all we need to know."

"I can do whatever I have to," Simon said.

"Then why do you need me?" she asked.

With a grimace, he dropped onto the couch, leaned back and draped an arm over his face. "I don't know. You haven't helped matters so far."

Gail told herself to leave, as she'd intended to a moment earlier, but she couldn't seem to convince her feet. She wouldn't let him purposely destroy this opportunity to get his life back on track the way he'd destroyed all the others since he started acting out a year ago. He had *so* much potential. It drove her crazy to watch him self-destruct, especially in the public eye. Regardless of her opinion of him these days, he'd once been her favorite actor. His performances still captivated her.

"You don't get it, do you?" she said. "No one can do this for you. If you want to see your life improve, you need to stand up and fight."

"What do you think I've been doing?" he mumbled into the crook of his arm.

Fighting the wrong kind of battles. And if he didn't change that soon, he'd learn how much worse his life could become. "Lashing out randomly in anger isn't what I'm talking about."

When he didn't respond, Ian's alarm seemed to grow. "Simon, we talked about this. When you hired me back, you said you could do it. You said you *would* do it."

"I know." Deadpan. Resigned.

"So…are you backing out or not?" Ian asked.

Simon muttered something Gail couldn't decipher; it sounded like a curse. But then he said, "I'm in if she is. I'd walk through fire for Ty. Do anything."

That didn't mean he had to be happy about it, and he wasn't, which would make her job that much harder. "Give me one reason I should trust you to pull this off," she said.

He lifted his arm so could look at her. "I can pull it off. I'll pour it on so thick there'll be times when even *you'll* think I'm in love with you."

More than a little fatigued herself, Gail slumped into a chair. "There's no danger of that."

The fact that she'd cracked, shown some exhaustion and weakness, seemed to surprise him. The tension in his body eased. "What about you? You don't particularly admire me, and you've had no experience with acting. Can *you* be convincing?"

Self-conscious about her clothing ever since he'd made the repressed PR failure comment, she unbuttoned the top of her jacket. "I won't have to be. No one will bother to question how I feel. They'll take it for granted. Average-looking no-name lands big movie star. Why wouldn't a girl be happy about that?"

He sat up so he could study her with that intense expression she'd seen him wear so often in the movies. She'd said something that made him think or caused him to reevaluate. After all the bickering and chafing at their new roles, she couldn't imagine what it was. But acute interest transformed his face from dark and brooding to arresting, and she found it impossible to look away.

"Even if we do everything we can, it'll take some luck for this to work," he said at length.

"Yes," she agreed.

A frown tugged at his lips. "These days I'm not sure I can depend on luck."

She tucked the fine hairs that'd fallen around her face behind her ears. "Feel free to hire a real actress, if you think it'll help." She hoped he would. Then she could have him return as merely a client, which would be enough to protect her business, and life would go on as usual.

Ian jumped back into the conversation. "Simon, no. We don't want anything to do with a woman who might be interested in using you to get famous. You never know what someone like that will do. I say we stick with what we've got. Gail's a known entity."

"She's inflexible." He spoke in the third person even though his gaze never wavered from her face.

"She's trustworthy." Ian shifted his gaze to her, too. "That's more important than flexible. Two years will go by quicker than you think."

Gail held her tongue. She got the impression Simon was testing her to see how she'd respond. But despite what he said about her, criticizing him further wouldn't help. She had a feeling he already thought the worst of himself. At least *she* gave him credit for his talent.

"There's just one more thing," she said.

Stretching out his legs, Simon crossed one ankle over the other—another deceptively casual pose. "What's that?"

"My father."

Lines formed on his forehead. "What about him?"

When she'd agreed to be Simon's "wife," she'd been thinking of it primarily in the context of PR advantages. She'd been so focused on how to pull it off, she hadn't considered the impact it would have on her other relationships—probably because, until now, L.A. and what she did here had always felt so removed from Whiskey Creek. Despite being a small town of barely two thousand, it was a world unto itself. But news of her marriage would travel everywhere. There'd be no way to keep it from getting back to her family and friends. She had to allow for that, prepare for it. Which meant she had to include them in the process.

"Before the wedding, we'll need to take a trip to my hometown so I can introduce you to everyone."

He didn't consider that for even a second. "Absolutely not. I'm not going to some Podunk town to be judged by your family."

Her friends would be just as hard on him, maybe harder. She'd hung out with the same crew since grade school. But she wasn't about to mention that. "If we don't enlist their support, my father or brother will drive to L.A. to convince me that I'm making a mistake marrying someone with…shall we say…such a tarnished reputation."

Ian spoke up. "So go to your mother. Tell her you're in love, get her to intercede."

Gail straightened in her seat. "I don't have a mother."

Simon was still watching her. "Why not? Is she dead?"

"No, but she might as well be." Gail hadn't seen her in twenty years. "We don't have a relationship."

Ian raked his fingers through his hair. "We've got everything else worked out. This can't be *that* hard. Tell your father he has nothing to worry about. You'll get a big settlement even if your marriage turns out to be the worst thing you ever did."

"News of the prenup will be in the press," she said. "We have to make sure it is. It has to look like love and only love is the reason we're getting together."

"So?" he argued. "You'll be receiving other money."

"But I can't tell anyone about that, not without letting them in on our little secret." To Martin, having her marry someone he'd consider morally bankrupt would be bad enough. Getting paid for it would be worse. "Anyway, he doesn't care about money. That's not what matters to him."

"What does?" It was Simon who asked. She could tell he was leery of the answer. Knowing her father, he had reason to be.

"Me." Martin DeMarco also cared about character. But a list of Simon's faults had come from her own lips as recently as a few days ago, when she'd last spoken to her dad. In retrospect, what she'd said during that phone call was unfortunate; telling Martin she was marrying Simon O'Neal would be no better than announcing she was marrying Charlie Sheen or Tiger Woods. "That means we'll *have* to visit, show him you're a changed man."

"Forget it," Simon said. "I'm a good actor but even I'm not *that* good, or I wouldn't need to be doing this in the first place. If your dad is such a stickler, he won't accept me even if I grovel."

"So what do you suggest?" she asked.

"You'll just have to cut ties with him for a while," he replied.

"What?" She tightened her grip on her purse. "I can't disappear from my network of family and friends for *two years*."

Finished with his drink, Simon set it aside. "That's what you're asking from me, isn't it?"

"It's *your* image that needs improving! Your associates are the ones who threaten that, not mine."

"I don't care. Considering everything I'm giving up, you can make a sacrifice, too. I have enough to deal with. Why should I put up with people who are convinced I'm the devil out to drag you off to hell?"

"Because you're the one who has to face down what you've done." Why did her sacrifice have to be equivalent to his? She hadn't screwed up her life the way he had.

"Not with your father looking on I don't. I just have to survive the next two years without doing anything stupid. The rest is up to you."

"Why are you making this so difficult?" she demanded.

"You started it."

"Going without sex isn't the same as giving up my family and friends!"

"I think it's pretty equal," Ian inserted, but both she and Simon ignored him. They were locked in battle.

"I make some concessions. You make some concessions," he said. "How's what I'm doing so unfair?"

He was attempting to punish her, but she wouldn't let him. "You'd know if you had a family to bother with!"

When a muscle jumped in his cheek, she realized what she'd just said and had no idea how she'd allowed herself to be so callous, even to someone who provoked her as much as he did. His father, a dissolute movie star himself, had conceived Simon with his wife's sister. For obvious reasons, the relationship between father and son had always been strained. His father's wife refused to have Simon anywhere near her. And his mother, who'd been disowned by the rest of the family for sleeping with her sister's husband, had died of breast cancer when Simon was ten. After she was gone, he'd been moved from the small house he'd lived in until that time to his father's estate, where he'd been raised by the hired help that slipped in and out of Tex O'Neal's life, not all of whom were particularly reliable. Rumor had it that the one nanny Simon had loved most had gone to prison for embezzlement.

"I'm sorry." Her cheeks burned as she gaped at him.

He glared back. "I'm not going anywhere close to your family," he said, and got up and walked out.

"Simon, you okay?" Ian's expression filled with so much concern that Gail was tempted to believe he really cared about his employer, beyond just the paycheck, but Simon didn't respond.

"Did you have to go that far?" He turned to face her once it was clear that Simon wasn't coming back.

She was so busy kicking herself she didn't need him to pile on, too, but she couldn't blame him. "I didn't mean it. I—I'm overwrought. Couldn't sleep a wink last night. Other than that, I have no excuse."

"You're in the public-relations business, damn it!"

"I wish I could take it back." She honestly hadn't meant to hurt Simon, hadn't realized she could. He seemed so...impervious. Still, she prided herself on using restraint and diplomacy especially in difficult situations. What had gotten into her?

Sinking onto the sofa, she tilted some of the ice left in Simon's glass into her mouth. She'd turned him down when he'd offered her a drink, but she shouldn't have. She needed something to relieve her dry throat, and she was rattled enough not to care where she got it.

"For what it's worth, he's going through hell," Ian said.

She set the glass, now empty, back on the table. "You've mentioned that. But he's not the only one, okay? I don't like this any more than he does."

"Of course you don't." He made a noticeable effort to calm down. "You're out of your comfort zone, and that's understandable. But…can't you…I don't know… put out for him once in a while? Just to help him stay on the straight and narrow? I bet he'd agree to meet your dad if you do."

She smacked her forehead with the palm of her hand. "Tell me you're kidding."

"No! Come on, what would it hurt? You'll be married so it won't be illegal *or* immoral. Even Mother Teresa couldn't object."

When she didn't respond, he seemed encouraged.

"It might be something you'd enjoy," he added. "He could loosen you up. Teach you a few things. If this marriage is going to work, he'll need an outlet."

"I am *not* going to become his blow-up doll." Something to be used and tossed away when he was done, something that would never mean anything to him. She had to live with herself when this was over.

"Forget it. I shouldn't have brought the subject up again." He shrugged. "Time will take care of it."

"What are you talking about?"

"You'll see. You're going to want it as bad as he does. I mean, you've got to have *some* physical desires of your own. You're what, thirtyish? And not bad-looking. A bit pale, maybe, but if you were to forget the business suits, let your hair down and laugh once in a while, you could get laid."

She held up a hand in the classic stop position. "Please, don't try to cheer me up."

"Just my two cents," he said with an attitude that indicated he was as obtuse on this as he sounded.

"Could you shut up for a second, please? I need to think."

He shoved his hands in his pockets while she tried to sort out her thoughts and feelings, but silence didn't offer the clarity she'd hoped for. She kept coming back to two things. She couldn't bear to cast her employees aside. And she couldn't return home in defeat. Whether she liked it or not, that left her with only one option— to ignore her frustration and unhappiness and marry Simon.

But the second she said, "I do," she'd step into the spotlight that followed him mercilessly and attract far more attention than she'd ever feel comfortable with. And if Simon refused to make an appearance in Whiskey Creek, her father would be positive that she'd turned out as disloyal as her mother, and her friends would feel snubbed and betrayed that she hadn't included them in the "courtship."

"Don't." Ian broke into her thoughts.

She lifted her head. "Don't what?"

"Back out. You're Simon's only hope for getting even partial custody of his kid. He's counting on you."

But what about her family? "What if something goes wrong—we can't get along or…whatever? I don't want to make matters worse."

"This marriage won't be easy, but if anyone can do it, you can. I've never met a more talented publicist."

"Really?" His confidence in her actually made her feel a bit better. She eyed him, wondering what he was about to add that would twist the compliment into something less flattering, but he seemed to be in earnest.

He lowered his voice as if he thought their host might be standing outside the door. "This will give Simon a second chance. I think he deserves one, if that makes any difference."

Someone as shallow as Ian probably wasn't the best judge of character. But it would give Big Hit PR a second chance, too. Considering the money she stood to make, she'd have her payroll covered for a long time, even if things turned bad again. But could she really do this? Could she placate her family and friends with calls and emails for a few months by pleading Simon's busy schedule?

If so, maybe she could convince her "husband" to visit Whiskey Creek for Christmas. Or at least let *her* return for a visit. "This is going to require such a commitment," she said, feeling the weight of it. "And for so long."

"Not *that* long, not as far as marriages go. Think of

it as a job, like you told Simon to do." He bent at the waist to catch her eye. "Okay?"

The years she'd toiled to get on top came to mind. So did the fact that she had nowhere to go if this didn't work out. She couldn't bear the thought of moving back home; she'd done everything she could to escape Whiskey Creek the first time. "Okay."

"You're making the commitment?"

She stood. "I'm making the commitment."

He crossed to the minibar and brought the prenup they'd painstakingly devised on the phone last night. "So when should we have the wedding?"

She glanced over the legalese Simon's attorneys had thrown together on short notice, made sure everything was in order and signed before panic could overtake her. "A month from now is the earliest we could have the ceremony and make the relationship seem credible. Check Simon's schedule. See if he's free the first Saturday in November."

"I'll clear off whatever else he has going."

"What are you going to tell Chelsea Seagate?"

"Nothing. I've already called her to say we're canceling our contract with Pierce Mattie and returning to you."

She wished she could take some small pleasure in that. "Fine."

When she handed him the contract, he smiled in apparent relief. "Thanks. First Saturday, private ceremony in Vegas. The two of you will take his jet, of course. But that doesn't give us much time to prepare."

"Then we'd better get to work." She left the house but stopped in the drive, her finger hovering over the send button on the pictures he'd emailed her. Once she forwarded them to Josh and he leaked them to his friend at *Hollywood Secrets Revealed,* there'd be no turning back.

A creeping sensation gave her the feeling that she was being watched. Twisting around, she spotted movement in a second-story window. It was Simon, looking out at her. They stared at each other for a few seconds. Then she held up her phone to let him know they were at the point of no return.

After a slight hesitation, he nodded, and she pressed Send.

7

Gail hadn't expected her other life, the life she'd known in Whiskey Creek, to intrude quite so quickly. But as she walked into the office, which was closed up and dark on a Saturday afternoon, Callie Vanetta, a member of the clique she'd grown up with, tried to reach her on her cell phone. Gail let it go to voice mail because she wasn't sure she wanted to talk to anyone from Whiskey Creek at the moment. She'd just left Simon's and hardly felt prepared.

"You okay?"

She was standing in the middle of her office, staring at her phone and feeling guilty about avoiding Callie when she heard Josh's voice. She glanced over her shoulder, surprised to see him in the doorway. Her employees typically took weekends off, unless they were working on a big project. When she'd sent Josh the pictures, she'd assumed he was home and would forward them from there. But he knew she spent most weekends in her office, catching up on what she hadn't been able to finish during the week. Considering what was going on, he'd probably made a special trip to see her.

"I'm fine, why?"

"You need me to explain?"

She turned to face him. "No." She knew perfectly well why he'd asked.

"So?" Eyes wide with curiosity, he closed the door. She wasn't sure why, since they were alone. Just more of his sense of drama, she supposed. "Give me the low-down. How'd it go?"

Could she classify the meeting she'd had with Simon and Ian as *good?* They'd worked out a lot of details, launched "The Plan." But whether or not they'd regret what they'd started remained to be seen. "Simon's in." That was about all she could say, all that was certain.

"I figured, when you sent me those pictures. It's the dirty details I'm after." His voice took on a husky undertone. "Were you two really kissing in that photo? Or did it just look that way?"

They hadn't kissed. But they'd stood awfully close. Close enough so she could smell the toothpaste on Simon's breath. Close enough to feel the warmth radiating from his body. When her breasts accidentally grazed Simon's arm as Ian pressed them into ever more compromising positions, she'd jumped back as if he'd burned her, and Simon had scowled.

Maybe she *had* overreacted. But that brief contact had sent a jolt through her.

"It was all staged," she assured Joshua. "We weren't kissing."

He flopped into a seat. "How disappointing."

It *had* been a little anticlimactic to continue their discussion while her heart was pounding like a jackhammer. Thanks to her line of work, she associated with the rich and famous quite often, but she'd never gotten so worked up over anyone else. In an effort to fight the effect Simon was having on her, she'd searched his face, only inches above her own, for one significant flaw, something to convince her that he wasn't as attractive as she'd originally thought—and found nothing.

His eyes were especially distinctive. An unusual sea-green color contrasted with thick black lashes and even thicker eyebrows, they reflected too much cynicism. That wasn't attractive, but there was a hint of the lost little boy in there, too. His fine build, combined with those eyes and that sense of hidden vulnerability, packed a punch that had left her reeling.

She'd been pleased to find his bottom teeth slightly crowded.

Not that such a small imperfection really mattered. Thanks to *Shiver,* his last suspense thriller, she'd seen what he could do to a woman with his lips and tongue.

"You should've made out with him," Joshua said.

She pulled a skeptical face. "Right. In front of Ian?"

"Why not? He was *hoping* to get a steamy pic. You could've blamed it on the PR campaign. I can't believe you missed the opportunity to indulge. *I* would've made out with him to my heart's content."

Instead, she'd been clinging to her control, trying not

to get swept up in the lust surging through her veins. "Simon's too feminine for my taste."

"Are you *kidding?*"

Kidding herself, maybe. High cheekbones and a prominent jaw, not to mention the perennial shadow of beard growth, added more than enough of the masculine to compensate for his pretty eyes and pouty lips. But she had to create some kind of defense. There were moments when she was afraid the hero worship she'd once felt would reassert itself and undermine what she knew of the real Simon. "I'm just saying he looks like his mother more than he does his father."

"Doesn't make him *feminine*."

"Did you get those pictures off?" she asked instead of responding.

"As soon as they hit my in-box."

Rounding her desk, she straightened her blotter. "And…did you get confirmation that they've been received?"

"Immediately. Sarah's ecstatic about breaking the story—and avoiding any heat from that other mess we created."

"Good."

"So." He crossed his legs. "You're sure you'll be able to make yourself go through with it? You'll marry him?"

"I don't see that I have any choice. I've already signed the contract."

Hanging his head, Joshua peered at her through the

hair, dyed a stark black instead of his usual brown, falling into his eyes. "I feel so bad about what I did."

"I know."

"I endangered Sarah's job, too."

"Yes." Gail drummed her fingers on the desk. "What'd her boss say?"

"He's every bit as excited as you'd expect. Anything Simon does is big news."

That picture they'd taken in the backyard would soon be online. Other magazines and bloggers would jump on the publicity bandwagon before she could blink.

Sick at the thought of all the calls that would pour in, how *she'd* become the focus of the paparazzi who'd harried her biggest clients, Gail propped her chin on one fist. "Do you think this is a disaster waiting to happen?"

"Could go either way, but you're saving my ass by doing it, so I can't tell you how grateful I am." He gave her a childlike smile. "Makes me love you all the more, if that helps."

"It doesn't," she said, but smiled back.

He sobered. "I deserve to be fired."

"Except that you've been great at your job and I can't judge your entire performance by one stupid, drunken mistake."

"I appreciate that. I really do." His mood brightened. "Tell you what—*I'll* marry Simon."

She pictured the fury in Simon's face when she'd said what she had about his family, or lack thereof. At this point, he'd probably prefer *anyone* to her—maybe even Josh. "I wish you could."

She prided herself on being able to handle anything, but she was out of her element here. Maybe she was better at running other people's lives than her own. "What if he won't stop drinking?" she asked. "Or he secretly bites his toenails? Or sleeps in a coffin? Or burns incense and offers up prayers to his own picture?"

"All movie stars are eccentric—or get that way if they go unchecked for too long. Just roll with it. The marriage is only temporary."

Two years didn't feel as short as he made it sound. "But he might be more insufferable than I'm expecting. Maybe he's...abusive."

Josh grimaced. "He's not abusive, not physically, anyway. With his ex running her mouth to anyone who'll listen, we would've heard about it if he'd ever even threatened to hit her or the kid."

"He's hit a few guys," she mused. "He got in that fight on-set, remember?"

"I'm not likely to forget. That's the reason you refused to work for him anymore."

Ignoring the censure in his voice, she proceeded to prove it wasn't the *only* reason. "What about that time a few months ago when he tried to force his way into his ex-wife's house and got in a shoving match with her brother?"

"Maybe he had a good reason for what he did."

"On *both* counts?"

"That's how we tried to spin it," he said with a shrug.

"He could've walked away."

"We both know he's not the type. Too short a fuse."

"That's no excuse." She searched for other examples to support her "Simon's unstable" theory. "And those bikers?"

Joshua adjusted the scarf he wore with his pink button-down shirt. "I think he *wanted* to get his ass kicked that night. Why else would he drive to the shitty side of town and confront so many dangerous gang-bangers? He was all alone, had no chance from the beginning."

That was what she thought, too. Nothing else made sense. After the judge signed the restraining order that would keep Simon from his wife and son, he found a seedy bar he later admitted he'd never been to before, one with a row of motorcycles out front, and picked a fight with three Hells Angels. They would've destroyed his face, maybe a lot more, if not for one of their own. Fortunately, a member of the club happened to be a big fan. He saved Simon an extended hospital stay by pulling the others off and pushing him out of the joint while he could still walk—but the biker later confessed he was disappointed that Simon didn't really know kung fu. He'd expected more from him after watching *Take It or Leave It,* Simon's most violent movie.

"Honestly? I think the worst he's done is cheat," Joshua said.

"You say that like it's nothing."

"It's nothing to you."

She cocked her head in challenge. "I'm only his future wife!"

He cocked his head right back at her, exaggerating

the movement. "But you don't love him. Cheating on you would be more of a...breach of contract."

"It'll be adultery to the rest of the world! And he might have other problems, ones we haven't discovered yet. Maybe he's a sex addict." He'd certainly made a big enough deal about her refusal to service him....

"You should ask."

"I did. Ian and I talked about the possibility last night. He says no. Claims there were extenuating circumstances to Simon's extramarital affairs."

"Like...he got bored and horny?" Josh said with a laugh.

"Ian doesn't know for sure. He thinks she may have cheated first, but he can't substantiate that and it doesn't really make sense. Wouldn't Simon have said so if it meant keeping custody of Ty?"

"No doubt." Josh swung his foot. "You didn't confront Simon himself?"

"I'd already called him an alcoholic. I didn't think it would go over too well if I accused him of being a sex addict, too."

"So what do you want me to say, Gail? Don't do it?"

The anger drained out of her. "More or less."

"Then don't do it. We'll...go into promoting beauty products or something."

If that happened, she'd have to start over alone. "What about Sonya? And Serge? And you and everyone else? I *have* to do this."

"Then keep Simon in bed."

"*Excuse* me?"

Eager to convey his point, he leaned forward. "If you're so worried he might stray, keep him in bed, darling. Don't give him time for anyone else."

Sometimes Gail wished she could be as sexually unfettered as her assistant. She was beginning to feel a lot older than she was.

What are you doing this weekend?

Working.

Any plans for Friday night?

Catching up on some paperwork.

Tell me you have a hot date for Valentine's Day.

With my television.

She'd fallen to a new low when she went to a movie alone on her birthday. She was still mad at herself for not heading back to Whiskey Creek, but she'd been so slammed with new clients she hadn't wanted to take the time off.

"Thanks for that piece of advice, but I don't want to talk about what I should do to keep Simon interested on a sexual level." He wasn't interested to begin with.

"Why not? You can do it. So what if you're a late starter?"

"I'm not a late starter. I'm *selective.*"

Josh formed a steeple with his fingers. "You didn't lose your virginity until you were twenty-six. That definitely qualifies as a late start."

She should never have admitted that. Josh had a way of getting personal information out of anyone.

"I was twenty-*five,*" she corrected. "But who's keeping track?"

"Just me."

"Thanks for that."

"Maybe it's good you're tying the knot. Maybe this is the only way you'll ever say 'I do,' seeing as you cross every guy off your list before you even give him a chance."

"Before I sleep with him, you mean."

"Same thing."

She arched an eyebrow. "Not quite."

A soft knock interrupted them, which surprised her. She'd figured they were alone.

Bracing herself in case it was the beginning of the media onslaught—some reporter who'd somehow gotten in—Gail called out, "Yes?"

It wasn't a reporter. It was Ashley, her receptionist, who poked her head into the room. "Thought I might catch you here."

"What brings you to the office on your day off?" Gail asked.

"The answering service contacted me. They're being inundated with calls from a guy with *The Star,* who claims he has to talk to someone in the office right away." Barely five feet, Ashley looked more like a child than a twenty-one-year-old woman. Her large-framed glasses added to the effect; they always gave Gail the impression she was playing dress-up. "I thought maybe it was important, that someone should get back to him."

Joshua's eyes latched on to Gail's. "You know what this means."

"I do. Word is getting out." It was time to quit fighting what she'd agreed to do and throw herself into her role. If they had any hope of pulling off this campaign, there could be no halfway measures. She had to play the part even for her own employees.

But when it came right down to it, she couldn't lie, bald-faced, to Ashley. She knew she'd feel ridiculous saying that one of the most famous men in America had fallen in love with her, especially when he'd never so much as given her an appreciative glance.

She couldn't bear lying to the rest of the people who worked for her, either. Which meant Josh had to do it. "Josh will explain the situation to you and everyone else."

Josh blinked at her. "I will?"

"Yes." Maybe it'd be more believable if everyone heard it secondhand while she went underground, anyway. She'd take the phone off the hook and hole up in her house for two or three days. That would go far toward convincing everyone that her "relationship" with Simon was real. If she suddenly went quiet instead of going on the record with an admission *or* a denial, the press would chase after the story that much harder and break it that much bigger.

The paparazzi would be waiting for her when she emerged, of course. She wouldn't be able to avoid them altogether. But hiding out until Wednesday would save her a lot of acting, which she feared wasn't her strong suit despite the misplaced confidence she'd exhibited at Simon's.

Josh cleared his throat. "Right, I will. And you…"

"Will be at home for a couple of days," she finished while packing up her briefcase.

"Right again. Not coming in is probably a good idea. We'll do what we can without you."

"Thanks." In a moment of clarity, Gail realized she'd set a match to a trail of gunpowder by making that agreement with Simon. But it was too late to put out the fire.

All she could do was try to survive the explosion.

8

Relieved to be safe in her little beach house, Gail lowered the blinds in her bedroom, curled up on her bed and stared at Callie's picture and contact information on her cell phone. She'd never purposely ducked a friend's call before. At least not one of her friends from Whiskey Creek.

"Oh, what the heck," she mumbled. "Get it over with." Once the news that she was seeing Simon O'Neal broke, she'd have to worry about her phones being tapped or her house being bugged—laughable considering she was no head of state or criminal informant. Her only claim to fame would be that she was "dating" a box office hit.

But tabloids were big business, hence the worry that someone could stoop to such means to get inside information. She might as well use this time to prepare her friends and family, before sightings of her and Simon began to appear in the media.

Her father should've been her first call, but Gail preferred to break into this easily. It was the weekend. She had that going for her. With so many people out doing other things, word wouldn't spread quite as fast as it would on a weekday.

Callie picked up on the second ring. "Jeez, there you are. I've been trying to reach you all day."

"Sorry. Been working."

"On a Saturday?"

Gail pictured her curvaceous bombshell of a friend. She used to wish she looked like Callie, who resembled Marilyn Monroe. "Always."

"You should really take a day off here and there."

"You've mentioned that before. What's up?"

"I've been *dying* to tell you something."

"What?"

"You're not going to believe it."

Callie wouldn't believe what Gail had to say, either. "Try me."

"Matt's moving back to town!" she announced with a "ta da" flourish.

Sure she must've heard wrong, Gail gripped her chest.

"Hello?" Callie said. "Did I lose you?"

She'd forgotten to breathe. Air. She needed air. Taking a big gulp, she sat up and forced words out as she exhaled. "No…I'm… I haven't gone anywhere."

"Did you hear what I said?"

This had to be a mistake. Matt wouldn't leave Wisconsin in the middle of football season. "What happened? He didn't get injured again, did he?"

"Not a new injury, no. Just more of the same old stuff. Knee's acting up."

Gail wasn't sure how to react. She'd been in love with Matt since she was in middle school. They'd finally gone out in July and nearly wound up in bed together. But, to her severe disappointment, he hadn't called since. "So…is he out of the NFL for good?"

"I don't think so. They had to do a second surgery, and he's in therapy, but he's planning to return to Green Bay next season."

Too agitated to remain on her bed, Gail got up and began to pace. "How did you find out? You talked to him?"

"No. My mother heard the news while she was having her hair done. You know what this town is like."

Gail had been hoping Matt would come home eventually, had dreamed of it. Given the opportunity, she thought he might ask her out again. But she found herself cringing at the possibility that he wouldn't be able to continue playing football. He loved the sport like nothing else. "Do you know how long he'll be staying?"

"Months. Until he's recovered."

"Wow." She pivoted near the French doors that opened onto her postage stamp of a backyard. "I hope… I hope it heals well."

"You mean you hope it heals *slowly*," Callie said with a laugh. "I thought of you as soon as I heard. He'll be here when you come home for Thanksgiving in a few weeks." She put some innuendo into her voice. "With you two in the same town for a few days, you never know what might happen."

Nothing would happen now because Gail wasn't going home. And even if she did, she'd be married. She'd been waiting years for this news—and it had to come on the day she'd made a business arrangement to marry someone else. "He's probably got a girlfriend," she said. Maybe that was why he hadn't called her after their date last summer. Maybe there'd been someone else all along....

"Nope. Word has it he's as single as he's ever been."

So they would've had a chance?

Suddenly claustrophobic, Gail went out onto the patio where she liked to read or answer email. Normally, she loved it out here, but her piece of heaven didn't hold the same magic for her today. Her heart had been yanked back to the Sierra Nevada foothills, to the historic gold-mining town where she'd grown up and so many of her friends still lived.

The sound of laughter and voices from the beach, only ten feet or so from her fence, engulfed her. So did the cool, moist air of autumn and the briny scent of the ocean. She closed her eyes as she considered backing out of the deal with Simon. But the practical side of her wouldn't allow it. What did she think—that she and Matt would bump into each other and he'd suddenly regret not pursuing the relationship? Why would that happen now when he'd gone back to Wisconsin and basically forgotten about her after they'd all but had sex?

It wouldn't. For the sake of her future and her employees, she needed to live up to the commitment she'd made to Simon. "There's just one problem," she heard herself say.

"What's that?"

She felt she sounded wooden, mechanical, but soldiered on. "I can't come home next month."

"Why not?"

"I'm…sort of involved with someone else, someone who lives here." She figured she'd be better off not mentioning the "M" word. She could always justify her marriage by saying it was an impulsive act, something they'd done while visiting Vegas. Otherwise, she'd send the whole town of Whiskey Creek into an uproar.

There was a slight pause. "Since when?"

"It's been a few months."

"You've never mentioned anyone."

Gail slipped past two trellises to gaze over the fence at the inline skaters rocketing down the walkway, the athletes playing sand volleyball beyond that and the waders at the water's edge. "I didn't think it would go anywhere."

"If you're willing to miss seeing Matt, it must be serious."

The scent of damp wood and seaweed filled her nostrils. It didn't matter that L.A. and Whiskey Creek were in the same state. They were as different as two places could be. No wonder she hadn't thought of all the complications she'd bring to her personal relationships when she'd decided to save Simon's image—and her business—with a temporary marriage. "More serious than it was before."

"Are you in love, G.?"

"I...might be." She was waffling, but her response shocked her friend enough that Callie didn't seem to notice.

"Oh, my gosh! Who's the lucky guy?"

Wincing at the reaction she'd receive when she uttered the name, Gail made her way back toward the bedroom. "Simon O'Neal."

Callie's pause extended into awkward silence. No doubt she'd expected Gail to add, "Not the Simon you're thinking of." When she didn't, Callie said it for her.

"You're not talking about *the* Simon O'Neal, are you? The actor? I know he was your client before you fired him. But you said he was an asshole."

Gail was going to get this a lot. She'd complained far too much to her friends. "I was frustrated when I said that."

"So it *is* Simon."

The wind chimes on her porch tinkled softly. "Yes."

"You're dating him even though you told him you wouldn't work for him anymore?"

Her bedroom seemed far cooler and darker than before her excursion into the afternoon sunshine. But she went inside and closed the door. "The stress of trying to have a professional relationship while seeing each other caused everything to blow up. You can imagine how difficult it would be to date someone so famous. We were sneaking around, and he was...acting out because of…you know, the divorce, and I was wondering how I could continue to represent him if I was emotionally involved with him. I swore I'd never date one of my clients. You've heard me say that. It's just not wise." She was talking too fast and too much and throwing in too many justifications. She needed to be careful but couldn't seem to catch herself until Callie interrupted.

"Speaking of the divorce, it's only been a few months since he and his wife split."

Gail kicked off her flip-flops and smoothed her bare feet against the plush rug near her bed. "Actually, she took Ty and moved out over a year ago. The divorce has been final for six months."

"Okay. About a year, then. He could still be on the rebound, Gail. If he ever loved Bella to begin with. You can't tell me his behavior doesn't spook you. It would have to. What about all the things he's done?"

He spooked her, all right. But she'd never be able to do business in L.A. again if she didn't come through. "The divorce was an acrimonious one. I'll be the first to admit that. But you have to understand it's been really, really hard on him."

"I don't think it's been any easier on his ex-wife. Last I heard, he showed up at her house drunk and got into a fight with her brother. You shouldn't be dating someone who…who's spinning out of control, G."

Gail laughed uncomfortably. "Come on, Callie. He'll get turned around. It's not easy living under a microscope."

"I understand. But…you're the most stable, level-headed girl I know. Why would you get involved with someone who needs so much therapy? He cheated on his wife with *six* different women."

At last count. Gail was pretty sure he'd been shooting for Tiger's record. "He screwed up, ah, literally." She managed a weak chuckle at her bad pun. "But it's killing him to be kept from his little boy."

"I'd like to believe you, but most people who feel bad about losing their kids resist jumping from one bed to the next because they know it won't help their case."

Gail squeezed her forehead. "He was depressed, fatalistic, going through a rough time. That's not who he really is."

"The pictures in the tabloids, showing him with one woman after another, sure don't make him look depressed and fatalistic. He's living the high life."

Gail suspected that appearing so happy in public was a purposeful cover, a way to save face, but she couldn't use that in her argument. And if this was how it was going with Callie, she cringed to think of the conversation she'd have with her father.

Suddenly Gail was glad Simon had refused to go to Whiskey Creek. She needed to keep him away at all costs. "The tabloids make up a lot of that stuff."

"You once told me there's a kernel of truth behind most of those stories."

She'd been so transparent about everything that she had no wiggle room left. "It's more complicated than it seems. He had a horrible childhood."

"So…you feel sorry for him? For a rich, spoiled, self-indulgent movie star?"

"You don't even know him. How can you judge?"

"His mistakes are public knowledge!"

"I see a different side, okay? He's a good man." She cringed because she had no confidence in that statement. She'd fantasized about him as much as anyone, but she'd known in her heart that the real Simon couldn't live up to the man in her dreams. "Can you give him a break? Please? For me?"

"I'm just saying…before you get too committed to Simon, maybe you should come home and see if there's anything between you and Matt. Matt's a great guy."

Callie would know. He'd been her neighbor growing up. But Gail had too much on the line to risk it all on the hope that Matt Stinson would finally return her interest. Dropping onto the bed, she watched the fan rotate overhead. "My relationship with Matt has been completely one-sided."

"You kissed last summer."

"He hasn't called since."

"Because he's too focused on his career. He doesn't want to risk getting involved with someone like you, someone who's marriage material. He's not ready for that kind of commitment. He's said as much."

"He has?"

"Not in so many words," she hedged. "But I know he thinks you're amazing."

Torn, Gail rubbed her face. "He could've followed up, come to see me."

"At the moment football is his whole life. But at least he's not some hotheaded philanderer who's using his power and money to destroy everyone around him. Where can you expect your relationship with Simon to go? If even one-tenth of what I've read about him is true—"

"Have some faith in me, Callie. I don't fall in love easily. There's…something inside him that's worth fighting for." She believed that much. Occasionally she caught a glimpse of Simon's good side, saw how warm and generous he could be. If she could figure out a way to avoid his rougher edges, they might be able to establish an equilibrium of sorts—build a friendship over the course of their marriage. "Besides, people can change."

That was the classic line used by every woman who'd ever dated the wrong guy, but it couldn't be refuted so she had to go with it. People *could* change. But they seldom did, and Callie latched on to that immediately.

"And if he doesn't? Why take the risk? His last wife was heartbroken and publicly humiliated—"

"You don't know what caused the breakup of his marriage."

"I think six affairs would do it, don't you?" Obviously Callie thought being with Simon was a huge mistake. The other people who cared about Gail would, too. But they didn't know she already understood how the whole thing would play out, that she wasn't in love with Simon and never would be, because she knew too much about him.

"You're being really hard on him. You'd like him if

you gave him half a chance." Simon had to be the most charismatic person on the planet—but only if he cared enough to bother pouring on the charm.

"When will we get to meet him?" Callie asked.

"Maybe I'll bring him home for Christmas," she said, but just talking to Callie had convinced her that she'd never contest his decision not to visit her hometown.

"Okay, but…I wish you were coming next month. Everyone was looking forward to it." Callie's voice reflected her disappointment. No doubt she thought a few days with the old gang would set Gail straight.

"I'll reschedule soon." The buzzer that indicated someone was at her front gate sounded, so Gail got back on her feet. She wasn't expecting anyone. Would the paparazzi be bold enough to come to her house and ring the doorbell?

Some would. Her gate faced the narrow street leading down to the beach, which meant it was accessible to anyone passing by. And the value of taking the right photographs made the paparazzi unbelievably intrusive.

"I've got company," she said. "I have to go. Don't tell anyone about Simon, okay? Not yet. First, I need to break the news to my dad."

"I won't say a word, but…good luck with Martin." Callie knew he wouldn't take the news well.

"Thanks. I'll call you in a few days." Gail disconnected as the buzzer went off again.

Setting the phone aside, she hurried out of her small cottage and down the flagstone path dividing the abundance of plants in her front yard. There was a man at her gate. Despite the foliage that provided her with a modicum of privacy, she could see part of his dark head above the tall stone fence and arch of the gate. He appeared to be wearing a uniform, one typical of a courier service, but that could be a trick.

"Who is it?" she called.

He tried to look over at her, so she flattened herself against the gate and peered through the crack.

Unfortunately, he was standing too close for her to see more than a four-inch square of his chest.

"Courier," he said. "I have a package for you."

"Go ahead and leave it."

"Can't. Requires a signature."

Really? She opened the gate by a wary inch, just enough to see a little more of the guy.

He seemed legit. He wasn't holding a camera, he seemed to be alone and an ID badge hung from the collar of his shirt.

"Are you going to sign for this or not?" he asked impatiently. "I've got other deliveries to make."

When she spotted a small truck with his company logo double-parked on the street, she finally released her death grip on the gate and swung it wide. "Yes. Sorry."

He handed her his clipboard. "Right here."

She scribbled her name, and he gave her the small box he'd been holding.

"Thank you," she murmured.

He walked off without responding; a moment later, she heard the rumble of his delivery truck. No doubt he thought she was some kind of paranoid hermit. But she didn't care. She had reason to be skittish.

After shutting and locking the gate, she examined what the courier had given her. The return address indicated it had come from O'Neal Productions—Simon's company.

Ian had said he'd mail her a copy of the contract once Simon had signed it, but this wasn't flat. The size and shape resembled a jeweler's box.

Most likely the wedding ring, she supposed. But that wasn't it at all. Once she opened the package, she saw that Ian—she assumed it was Ian—had sent her a pendant, one with a giant ruby and two diamond baguettes. Classy, solid and probably expensive, it was exactly what she might've chosen herself if she'd had a cool ten or twenty grand to drop on a necklace.

"Nice," she breathed. But...why the unexpected gift?

She guessed it was Ian's way of keeping her moving in the right direction—a sample of the finer things she'd enjoy while married to someone so rich. But when she read the accompanying handwritten note, she realized the pendant hadn't come from Ian at all. It was more personal than that.

"I'll make it up to you where I can. Simon."

9

It was late evening by the time Gail summoned the nerve to call her father. She would've called him a little earlier, but she'd been on the phone with the police. They wanted to get a statement from her, make sure that no crime—no assault, sexual or otherwise—had been committed.

Taking responsibility for a lie she hadn't uttered was embarrassing, but she'd managed to assure them that it was just a lovers' quarrel and they took the news pretty well. They'd probably heard crazier stories. The officer on the phone was very professional, and because there was no evidence to support any charges, none were going to be filed.

She was relieved to have that out of the way, but now she had another hurdle to clear. The photographs of her and Simon were already posted online. She'd checked. That meant the fervor was starting and she risked having her father find out before she could tell him. Fortunately, Martin DeMarco wasn't fond of the internet. He didn't watch a lot of TV, either.

Still, sooner or later—and probably sooner—someone in Whiskey Creek would see the pictures of her "kissing" Simon. Then her father would hear about it from everyone in town. Back home, in "the heart of the Gold Country" as the town slogan went, it only took one person to start a social epidemic.

As she sat in the dark of her living room, blinds drawn and clock ticking closer and closer to ten, she imagined how it would go when the news did get out. *Have you heard? Gail is dating that no-good bastard, Simon O'Neal. Yes,* that *Gail—and* that *Simon!*

She almost felt sorry for her soon-to-be husband. If he thought his name had been maligned before, he hadn't seen what they could do in her conservative hometown. The people who lived there had deep roots and strong values. They prided themselves on living circumspect lives. In Whiskey Creek, his celebrity could not outweigh his notoriety. Not anymore. He'd passed that point six months ago.

As Gail pictured the Old West boardwalk and historic architecture of Sutter's Antiquities, Black Gold Coffee and Whiskey Creek Five and Dime, she realized that she would, for once, supplant Matt Stinson in the gossip arena—even with all the speculation about his knee injury and the possibility of early retirement. She was Whiskey Creek's hometown girl made good: valedictorian of her high school, a Stanford grad and, to all appearances, a successful entrepreneur. They'd see Simon as using her, and them by extension, and it wouldn't go over well.

Too bad she'd helped shape their hard feelings when she visited last month. Their prejudice would only make things more difficult. But back then, she and Simon had been in the heat of battle. She'd had no clue she'd wind up *marrying* him.

Steeling herself against her family's reaction, she picked up the phone. All things considered, the evening had been a quiet one. But it felt rather ominous, like the calm before a storm.

She had a feeling that storm was about to break.

"'Lo?" Her brother, Joe, had answered. Not only did he and her father own the gas station and towing service at the edge of town, they shared the same house, at least since Joe's divorce four years ago.

Gail attempted to put a smile in her voice. "Hey, big brother. How are you?"

"Hangin' in. You?" Although he was more connected to the world outside Whiskey Creek than her father was, he didn't seem to have heard anything that upset him. He was treating her like he always did.

She breathed a sigh of relief. She'd called in time. "Fine. Busy, as usual."

"How's the biz?"

"Getting better all the time." Or it would soon....

"So it didn't hurt you to cut Simon O'Neal from your list? I know you were worried about that."

She'd been far too vocal about *everything.* "Um, not so much. It's going to work out in the end. Dad around?"

"Right here."

"Who's at the station tonight?"

"Sandra Morton."

"I thought she only worked days during the week-end."

"She's asked for some extra hours. Robbie's getting married. You might've heard about that."

"No." When she'd spoken with Callie earlier, that detail must've gotten lost in the news of Matt's return. "Robbie's just…what, seventeen?"

"Yep. A senior in high school. Knocked up his girl-friend."

Maybe she wasn't the *only* one Whiskey Creek would be gossiping about. Matt's return and Robbie's shot-gun wedding would also be hot topics. She would've been relieved to have competition for the best scandal in town, except this wasn't good news for Robbie or his mother, whom she liked. "I'm sorry to hear that, for everyone concerned."

"They claim they're in love, want to get married and keep the baby."

"What does Sandra say?"

"She's determined to let them." He didn't sound like he thought the marriage had a snowball's chance in hell, but that was probably because he blamed the failure of his own marriage on settling down too early.

"They'll be living with her?"

"Until they finish high school, anyway."

Sandra was a widow, mostly dependent on social se-curity. "How will she afford to feed them?"

"He's working at the station now, too. He does nights. She's training him."

For all his exacting ways, her father had a soft heart. He just didn't want anyone to know it—and could be darn good at hiding his secret. "Do you and Dad really need that much help?"

"Can't hurt, I guess. Dad's grabbing the phone," he said, and passed it off.

"'Bout time you checked in." Her father's voice was as commanding as ever.

She stayed in close touch, but he was never satisfied. He wanted her back in Whiskey Creek, like Joe. "Sorry, Dad, my life's been crazy."

"What's going on?"

Hesitant to launch into what she had to say about Simon, she searched for other things they could talk about. "Just…work. You know how it is."

She asked about the station and Sandra and Robbie. He confirmed what Joe had told her. Then he mentioned that Matt Stinson was coming back to town and assured her Matt's knee would heal. How he knew anything about it wasn't clear. Matt and her father spoke only if they bumped into each other on the street. But her father was the last word on everything, regardless of his lack of firsthand knowledge. Ironic though it was, he was usually right, too.

"That boy's not done playing football," he said.

"I hope not. He loves it."

"And we love watching him. You know what it's like around here when the Packers have a game." She did. Forget the San Francisco 49ers. As long as Matt played for the Packers, Whiskey Creek would be wearing green and gold.

Eventually her father said it was getting late and he had to be up early. At that point, Gail knew she'd waited too long to broach the subject of Simon. With Martin about to hang up, it would be even more awkward to give him her news. But she had no choice.

She cleared her throat. "Before you go I, uh, there's something I want to tell you."

This met with silence. No doubt he'd heard the nervousness in her voice.

"Everything okay, Gabby?"

Where he'd gotten that nickname, she had no idea, but he'd used it like an endearment ever since she was a child. "Yeah, of course. I'm fine. It's just—"

"What the hell?" Joe spoke so loudly in the background that he interrupted their conversation. "Give me the phone."

"What's the matter with you?" her father responded, but the phone changed hands, and Joe's voice came back on the line.

"Tell me it's not true, Gail! Tell me Simon O'Neal didn't rape you."

She bit back a groan. "No, he didn't. That was… Well, it doesn't matter. The important thing is that it didn't happen and I never said it did."

"You're sure? You'd tell us if you'd been hurt…."

And have them attempt to punish Simon? Probably not. She'd let the police handle something like that so her father and brother wouldn't end up in jail. But she didn't say so. "Of course. I'd speak up if I had anything to tell. That claim is one hundred percent false."

He wasn't completely mollified. "That's what it says on AOL. But you wouldn't lie about something like that. If you said it, it's true."

"I *didn't* say it. One of my employees got drunk and started that rumor."

There was a slight pause while Joe considered what she'd told him. "You've got to be kidding me."

"No."

"Which employee?"

"It's been taken care of."

"Whoever it is should be fired."

"It's been handled, like I said."

"Is the same person responsible for the rest of it, too? Because Dad's reading the article right now, and it says you and Simon have been secretly seeing each other for several weeks."

Saying a silent prayer that this would go better than she feared, Gail changed her phone to the other ear. "My employee has nothing to do with that part of it."

"Which means…what? It can't be true! I can't believe you'd go out with a man like Simon O'Neal. Any woman who got involved with him after all his bad press would be asking for trouble."

"I… He… We're not… I mean, I've been out with him a few times, but it's not serious." She told herself to calm down so she could at least speak coherently. "The media is making more of our relationship than it is."

"There's a picture with the caption Simon O'Neal's

Love Life Heats Up Again—with PR Maven Who Cried Rape."

"Like I said, we went on a few dates, that's all."

Her father took over again. "Gail? What's this all about?"

"I mentioned to Joe that Simon and I have gone out a couple of times, Dad. But it's no big deal."

"There's no truth to the rape stuff?"

"None. I didn't say it, and it didn't happen. The rumors about Simon are crazy. He can't do anything without the press making an issue of it."

He didn't let her comment about media exposure distract him. "Your brother's right. Getting involved with someone like Simon is asking for trouble. You don't want to screw up your life, do you?"

Imagining what he'd have to say when he learned about the marriage, she wrung her hands. "No, of course not. But…he—he's not as bad as I thought."

"Don't you believe it, Gabby," he warned. "If you have any doubts, all you have to do is ask his ex-wife."

"It's not like Bella and I are friends, Dad. Besides, I don't get the impression that the divorce was entirely his fault." In reality, she had no idea, but she had to use what she could.

"She's got a restraining order against him, doesn't she? That tells you all you need to know right there."

It looked pretty cut-and-dried from the outside. Simon had been convicted in the court of public opinion. At one time—not long ago—she'd convicted him in her own mind, too. But Ian had suggested there was more to the story, and that made her a bit defensive. America only knew so much—Bella's side. Not only that but Gail was *Simon's* publicist. She was wearing his ruby necklace. And she'd agreed to become his wife. If she didn't stand up for him, who would? "Does that mean he's not worth helping through a rough time? That he should never get another chance to straighten out his life?"

"He's had plenty of chances. You've told me that yourself. You don't want to risk your heart on someone who's sure to break it."

She'd expected that response, and yet it bothered her. "I'm thirty-one, Dad. I'm quite capable of deciding who I want to date."

"Not if you're talking about a guy who can't keep his pants zipped, Gail."

The endearments were gone; she was Gail now. "He's trying to change his life. Have I not communicated that part?"

Her father snorted. "If he wants to change, more power to him, but keep your distance or you'll be sorry."

"He's fighting to gain custody of his son. That means he cares."

"If he cared he never would've lost custody to begin with. A court doesn't take your children away unless you deserve it." The way her mother had deserved it. But Simon wasn't her mother.

"You're coming on really strong, Dad. Could you just…back off a little?"

The sudden chill told her she'd offended him. And

he didn't forgive easily, even small slights. He'd probably withhold his love and approval for weeks over this call. But she didn't have the opportunity to apologize or try to make amends.

"You're making a mistake, Gail," he said, and hung up.

Gail stared at the phone in her hand. Part of her was inclined to call her father back. She'd always fallen in with his wishes before, and she certainly couldn't deny the wisdom of his words. But firemen couldn't avoid a burning building just because it was dangerous. *Someone* had to rush in and look for survivors.

Simon was standing in a burning building and, as belligerent, sarcastic and aloof as he could be, he didn't know how to get himself out. He had too much anger and self-loathing working against him. Did she try to help? Risk getting burned herself? Or did she turn a blind eye, walk on and leave the job to someone else?

Who would do it if she didn't? He had everyone he trusted cowed. And he wouldn't cooperate with anyone he didn't trust.

Why was it always someone else's responsibility, anyway?

It wasn't. This time she was holding the fire hose and she was going to use it whether her father approved or not. She might live to regret her actions—whenever she crossed her father she usually did—but if she were Simon, she'd want someone to brave the flames.

Taking a deep breath, she redialed.

Her father didn't answer. He had to teach her a lesson for disrespecting him. But she wasn't going to succumb to his emotional blackmail. Not today. She had a date with a burning building.

Joe answered. "Hey, Gail. I don't know if Dad wants to talk—"

"I'm not asking him to speak to me. I just called to tell you both that I'm going to marry Simon," she said, and disconnected.

10

Simon had had every drop of alcohol removed from his house, including the cooking sherry. He'd canceled all outings and appearances, lest he be tempted. And he'd agreed to have his chef administer random Breathalyzer tests every day for the first week, as a fail-safe to keep him honest. If he screwed up, Ian and Gail would be notified and it would all be over.

Those were extreme measures, and yet he was beginning to wonder if they'd be enough. It was only day three of Operation Desperation, as he secretly referred to it, and already he was having fantasies about gulping down the rubbing alcohol under his bathroom sink—anything to give him a few moments' peace from the constant craving. He'd let drinking become such a big part of his life, had used it to create a buffer from all the things he'd rather avoid. When he was too bored, he drank. When he was too angry, he drank. When he was too frustrated or disillusioned, he drank. Alcohol even helped him sleep, if he consumed enough of it. Now he had to deal with all the emotions he'd purposely dulled, and he'd never felt more exposed to his enemies, more...*raw.*

As he glanced around his son's old bedroom, he suffered a tremendous sense of loss. That was what he'd really been hiding from—his own inadequacies and what they'd cost him.

"Simon? Where the hell are you?"

Hearing his manager in the hallway, Simon stepped up to the window as if he was interested in what was going on outside. He didn't want Ian to know he'd been sitting here for an hour or more, just missing his kid. "In here."

The thump of footsteps stopped as Ian came to the open doorway and leaned against the frame. If he thought it was strange to find Simon in Ty's old room, he didn't say. His eyes swept over the stuffed animals in the hammock, the portrait of father and son taken a few days after Ty was born, the alligator-shaped rug on the floor and the extensive bug collection hanging on the wall, but he said only, "Holy shit, man. You scared me. Why haven't you been answering your phone?"

Simon turned back to the spectacle of a woman with a camera attempting to scale his back fence. "Don't know where it is."

"Might be wise to keep track of it for the next couple of weeks, make yourself accessible to Gail and me, don't you think?"

No, he didn't. Keeping his phone close by would also make him accessible to his other friends, and he wasn't supposed to see them, didn't even want to hear their voices. Although he'd promised himself he'd get control of his life many times in the past few months, now he had no choice. He had to hold the line without a single mistake. Gail had been right when she'd said he was on his last chance. His attorney had called this morning to tell him that Bella's side had been successful in convincing the judge to postpone the next hearing. He no longer saw that as a bad thing, since it gave him a chance to prove he'd changed. But it was absolutely imperative that the next several months go by "without incident."

There won't be anything I can do, his lawyer had emphasized, *unless you make this reprieve work to your benefit....*

He got that. He was trying.

"Figured you'd find me if you needed me," he said.

"You could make it easier. Takes twenty minutes just to go through this damn house."

Simon preferred not to talk about why he'd been so hard to find. He didn't want Ian to realize he was hanging on by such a slim thread. Somehow, despite the fact that he'd broken every promise he'd ever made to himself or anyone else since the real problems with Bella began, he'd managed to convince Ian and Gail that he could play the part of a sober, doting husband. Why erode their confidence? Their expectations, their willingness to trust him, were all that kept him going right now. That was why he'd sent Gail the necklace. In his better moments, he could acknowledge that his publicist's life had been doing just fine until he'd come crashing into it.

He had a habit of bringing people down, whether he intended to or not. The least he could do was compensate her with a nice gift. "How's the campaign coming along?"

Ian rubbed his hands. "Now that the weekend is over, the news is spreading fast."

Simon was glad *someone* was excited about this. He was filled with trepidation and a sense of dread that he'd screw up again. "Good."

"You haven't heard anything?"

"No." He'd avoided the computer and the TV, had spent his time in the woodshop, building a playhouse and jungle gym. He liked working with wood, enjoyed the physicality of sanding, sawing and hammering. And constructing something so elaborate for Ty helped him have faith that one day his son would be back to use it.

"Hollywood's in an uproar," Ian said. "*Hollywood Secrets Revealed* put the pics online right away. I guess they didn't want to get scooped. Then everyone ran with the story. Facebook, Twitter, celebrity blogs. They're all buzzing about it."

Simon had witnessed some added activity outside. He knew that his security personnel were having more of a fight than usual keeping people off the premises. "What are they saying about the rape accusation?"

"That it's bogus, just like we wanted. Have you heard from your attorney on that yet?"

Yes. Harold J. Coolridge, attorney at law, had used

the false accusation as his excuse for supporting a post-ponement of the hearing. He'd told the judge that there were too many issues that needed to be resolved before the court could make a fair decision, so he agreed with Bella's motion. But Simon didn't want to go into that with his manager. The more intricate details of his personal life weren't any of Ian's business. "No."

"Then you will, and I'm sure he'll be relieved." He gestured at the window. "What's so interesting out there?"

"Some chick's sitting on the fence. She just flashed my security guys."

"No kidding?" Ian hurried over to see for himself. "Hey, look at that." He whistled long and low. "Nice tits. God, it must be great to be you."

Simon rubbed his neck. "This place is crawling with crazy people and paparazzi."

Ian didn't take his eyes off the spectacle unfolding outside. "It hasn't been this bad since Bella called the cops on you. How's security holding up?"

"They're managing, I guess. Godzilla—" also known as Lance Pratt, Simon's best bodyguard "—had to knock some fat guy on his ass when he slipped through the front gate along with the delivery truck that brings my groceries, but…that's been the worst of it."

Ian shook his head. "I wouldn't want to tangle with Godzilla. He's a bruiser."

He was also a loyal friend. Simon knew Lance would get him a fifth of vodka if he asked for it and not tell a soul, but that wasn't the kind of friend he needed at the moment. He needed more people like his hard-hitting publicist. Maybe she wasn't a barrel of laughs, or even particularly good for his ego, but she demanded he follow the rules—more so than anyone else.

"How's Gail handling the onslaught?" he asked. The paparazzi had to be all over her; she'd never had to protect her privacy so was therefore much easier to reach.

"Haven't talked to her. She's shut herself in her house like you have and won't come out." Pointing outside, he clicked his tongue. "Aw, they got her."

Simon didn't care about the girl with the camera. He had too many other things to worry about. Besides, women acted in zany ways to get his attention all the time. "Will Gail be able to handle the pressure when she does come out?"

Now that there was nothing exciting going on, Ian turned from the window. "Of course. She's tough. You know that."

Truer words were never spoken. Gail had such control of herself, her life. Simon envied that. When he'd married Bella, he'd been so sure he was doing the right thing, so sure he'd do a better job of being a husband than his father had.

"When does she plan on surfacing?"

Ian clipped his sunglasses to his shirt. "Don't know. I checked in with Joshua this morning. He said Gail won't pick up, even for him. I guess the news that she was seeing you got her in some kind of fight with her family."

Simon felt his muscles tense. "They don't think I'm good enough for her?"

"You know how judgmental people can be. Give her father a Ferrari and everything will be fine."

Simon didn't get the impression Gail's father was that easy to placate. "She's old enough to make her own decisions. It's none of their business."

"Doesn't matter. They don't want her with someone who has a reputation for sleeping around."

Ian's words cut, but Simon had gotten damn good at pretending nothing could hurt him. He was actually surprised that something this small *could* bother him. It was the lack of alcohol, the new vulnerability. He had to figure out how to shield himself some other way.

"On top of that she's afraid her phones are bugged," Ian went on. "She won't trust her cell, either. Even Josh insisted on calling me from somewhere other than the office." He chuckled. "She's militant, man. That's what makes her so great at her job. I'm being straight up with you. I wouldn't want to go into this with anyone else."

Simon agreed and—suddenly—wanted to see her. His manager meant well but often did more harm than good. Maybe he could draw some strength from Gail's no-nonsense, do-or-die approach to life's tougher choices. Maybe spending a few minutes with her would give him a fresh shot of determination. "When are we supposed to get together for that romantic dinner?"

"The one where we leak your location to the press but pretend we're shocked when they show up? We talked about next week sometime, right?"

"Let's do it tonight."

Ian straightened. "It's already after noon. How will I get a message to her if she won't answer her phone? I guess I could text, but who knows if—"

"Go over there."

"And if the paparazzi follow me?"

"That's what they're supposed to do, isn't it? That's what this whole thing is about."

Simon wasn't looking his best, but the restaurant was so dimly lit Gail couldn't discern any one reason. He was well-groomed, well-dressed—more so than when she'd sat with him in the living room and plotted out their marriage. So...maybe it wasn't his looks that were off; it was something else. The bravado that was normally such a part of him was gone. The way he kept shifting, he seemed tired, stressed, restless. She would've assumed he was bored, except that he'd drawn out the meal as long as possible, even though he had no apparent interest in eating. He'd downed five Cokes while barely touching the oysters on the half shell he'd ordered or the salmon and Italian sausage pasta he professed to love. When she asked him why he wasn't eating, he said he wasn't hungry.

"You okay?" This was the second time she'd asked, but she didn't dare say more. Not in public. Although a gaggle of people holding cameras had thronged them at the entrance, the restaurant had done a good job of keeping out the paparazzi. That didn't mean she and Simon could forget the roles they were playing until they had to emerge onto the street, however. The other patrons and the restaurant staff were watching them carefully and could report what they saw, especially if there was any money to be made.

To keep up the illusion of intimacy they'd come here to create, she reached across the table for his hand, and he threaded his fingers through hers. She'd expected him to be receptive. They were here to canoodle in public. But she hadn't expected the little hitch in her chest at his touch, or the relief that came over his face when they joined hands.

There was more of the lost little boy in him tonight than ever before. Usually, he hid it quite well; at times, she wasn't even sure it existed.

She cleared her throat. "Are you going to answer me?"

His chest rose as if he'd just taken a deep breath, but then a smile broke across his face. It looked so natural she was tempted to believe it was—but he was acting. She could already read him more deeply than even a few days ago. "I'm fine."

In case someone was using a device that amplified their voices in an attempt to pick up on their conversation, she didn't push for more. "My dinner was delicious. Too bad you weren't very hungry."

"How do you like the pendant?"

Although she could tell he hadn't been too invested in any of their other chitchat, he seemed genuinely curious about this. The look on his face gave her the impression that he'd truly meant to please her, which was something new.

"It's lovely." She was wearing it; the solid weight of it rested just above her cleavage. "But...I'm not sure why you sent such an expensive gift. That really wasn't necessary."

"You're worth it."

More acting. Lies, false compliments and fake smiles were easy to combat on an emotional level. But his touch seemed so honest it confused her. It also set her on edge because she liked it. The movement of his thumb, rubbing lightly back and forth on hers, put butterflies in her stomach.

"I knew it would look good on you," he said.

For the sake of anyone who might be watching, she gave him a smile to match the one he'd bestowed on her and resisted the urge to withdraw her hand. "It was very sweet of you."

"Finished with your meal?"

"I am." She used the fact that they were about to leave as an excuse to let go of him. But after he tossed a couple of large bills on the table, he put an arm around her shoulders, which kept them in close contact. At first, she thought it was part of the show but his sense of purpose soon told her he was preparing for the crowd that awaited them outside.

"Are you ready for this?" he murmured as he guided her through the restaurant.

"This?"

"The paparazzi."

They wanted her picture as badly as his, and that was an experience she'd never had before. "As ready as I can be. I don't know how you put up with the loss of privacy."

"Part of the territory," he said. But she knew it bothered him more than he was letting on. She'd heard him make statements about "being hunted." He might have elaborated, but the restaurant manager darted into their path to thank Simon for his patronage.

"I hope you found each dish to your liking," he said, all but bowing in deference.

Simon gave him a stiff nod. "Everything was delicious."

Knowing the man must have noticed that Simon had eaten very little, Gail jumped in. "It was wonderful," she gushed. "The best!"

Relieved, he thanked her profusely and begged them to come again.

"What I said wasn't enough?" Simon muttered as they moved on.

Had she irritated him? "He was so…hopeful."

"That's how they all are."

The constant attention would get tiresome. She could see that. She could also see that being a celebrity was exhausting. Tonight that was more obvious than ever. Simon could never give enough to the people he encountered because there was only one of him and so many of them. He never got to feel he'd met others' expectations.

"There's no break," she said as they stepped out of the restaurant and into a sea of flashing lights.

Gail had told herself she'd smile and hold her head high whenever she encountered the paparazzi, just as she advised her clients to do. *Make them think you enjoy it, that you have nothing to hide.* After all, what were a few pictures? It was better to pose and get good ones. That was her classic line.

But because of the crush, there was a much greater sense of urgency than she'd ever seen or experienced before. And acting as if this was an unwelcome surprise was part of the campaign. She turned her face into Simon's chest to avoid being blinded by the strobelike effect and felt his arm tighten as he sheltered her from the most aggressive of the cameramen.

"Car's right here," he said.

One of Simon's bodyguards, who'd been waiting with their driver, had created a path. Relieved to have a safe resort, Gail slipped inside the same limousine that had picked her up at her house. Simon rarely traveled in vehicles like this, unless it was Oscar night, a premiere or some other special event where it was expected, but there hadn't been any point in holding back on the accoutrements for this date. Tonight he'd *planned* to dive into the shark-infested pool of celebrity obsession—and he'd taken her with him.

The silence that met them as soon as the door was shut felt odd, oppressive. But it didn't last long. The stereo went on, playing classical music, as the driver inched through the crowd, most of whom were still vying for photographs—from the curb, the street, anywhere they might gain advantage.

"Wow," Gail breathed. This was what she had to look forward to. Could she keep up the charade?

She thought Simon might be as talkative on the drive as he'd been in the restaurant, but he didn't say a word. Back to his laconic self, he stared out the window.

"So? How do you think it went?" she asked as they glided around the corner like a slow-moving parade float.

"Good." His response was clipped, perfunctory. Apparently he'd been acting a lot more than she'd realized. Maybe that vulnerability that appealed to her was part of the character he'd decided to play. She hoped so. It made her too eager to defend him, whether he deserved it or not. She'd always been an "underdog" kind of girl.

But a movie star of Simon's caliber and success could hardly be considered an underdog; she had to remember that.

They merged into traffic, finally leaving the scrambling photographers behind. "I played my part well enough?" she pressed. "It was convincing even though I'm not an actress?"

He didn't turn to look at her. "You did fine."

"Did it come across as natural when I reached for your hand?"

This seemed to pull him out of his brooding. "That was smart. It made you appear confident of my feelings for you and suggested that we're comfortable touching each other."

"Great." Especially since nothing could be further from the truth. Although it was easier to touch Simon in public than anywhere else, even that simple gesture had given her pause.

"But surprised the hell out of me," he added.

"Why?" He'd taken her hand earlier.

"Because you think I'm the big bad wolf."

"I don't know what you're talking about."

"Yes, you do. You're afraid to make even accidental contact."

Knowing him the way she did, she should've expected his candor. He always said what he thought, regardless of whether it put her on the spot. "I'm not *afraid.*" She searched for a better way to explain her reaction to him. "I'm just not groveling at your feet, dying to get a piece of you, like most people." Because she knew how superficial his attention would be, how quickly it would pass. "You should find that... refreshing."

The panel between the front and back opened before he could answer. "Boss?"

Simon's gaze cut to the rearview mirror and the reflection of his chauffeur's eyes. "What is it?"

"Where to?"

"My place."

"*Your* place?" Gail echoed. "You mean, after you drop me off, right?"

"We're being followed," he said. "Might as well let them think you're staying the night. We've already put this much into it."

She twisted around to look behind them. It made sense that the paparazzi who'd staked out the restaurant would want to know where they were going next and follow in hopes of another photo op. She couldn't pinpoint any specific driver as one of the people she'd seen outside the restaurant, but she hadn't looked at them as individuals—only as a pack. "Okay, but...won't they hang around for a while?"

Simon's gaze returned to the buildings whipping past them now that they'd picked up speed. "Some of them will probably camp out."

"How will I get home without them noticing?"

"You won't." His lips curved into a challenging smile. "I guess you'll just have to share my bed."

11

Once they got inside the house, away from the photographers' prying eyes, Gail suggested she sleep in the room next to Simon's, where they'd each have some privacy. She didn't want to worry about brushing up against him during the night, and she didn't see how having her own room in such a big house would hurt. With her hair mussed and her clothes wrinkled, she'd still be able to put on a good show for any media that had the tenacity to wait until morning.

But he said he had too many domestic workers who might notice and would, no doubt, find the arrangement odd enough to mention to others. So Gail relented. They had to look like lovers, which meant she'd probably be the first woman to spend the night in Simon's bed without taking off her clothes.

Actually, she did undress—but in his expansive closet, with the door closed. She borrowed a T-shirt and a pair of boxers so she could at least be comfortable. Then she climbed into bed beside him, propped some pillows behind her back as he'd done and watched an indie film he'd been meaning to vet on his big screen.

"You've got a nice setup here," she said when the credits began to roll. She was wondering what they'd do next. Even if he could go to sleep, she couldn't. Ever since they'd closed the door to his bedroom, she'd been trying to pretend that spending time with him was no different from hanging out with any other platonic friend. She and Joshua had shared a hotel room at various PR conventions, hadn't they?

But this didn't feel the same. Besides the obvious difference in Josh's and Simon's sexual orientation, Simon was sitting only a couple feet away from her wearing nothing but his boxers. She'd asked him to put on some pajamas, but he'd given her that look of his, the one that said he'd do as he damn well pleased.

His stubbornness on that point should've bothered her more than it did. She had a long list of complaints about his character, but she couldn't fault his looks or his sex appeal.

"It's not hard to have a nice setup when you've got money," he said, and used the remote to start flipping through channels. "It's the things you can't buy that are difficult."

Even in the dark, with only the glow of the TV screen to light the room, his bare chest drew her gaze. She knew most women in America would give anything to trade places with her, but all she wanted was to go home. Being here, feeling what she was feeling—it wasn't good. She was the one who'd insisted on the "no sex" mandate, and yet having sex with Simon was suddenly all she could think about. No doubt he'd been hoping that would be the case when he brought her home.

"Are you talking about peace of mind? Or personal relationships?" Using all the self-restraint she could muster, she shifted her attention back to the TV.

"Both."

She nodded. "You do need some help in those areas."

With a withering glance that said he didn't appreciate her comment, he switched to the Golf Channel.

"Golf? Really?"

"Wow, this *is* like being married." He kept surfing, but what he chose next didn't make her any happier.

"Oh, this is perfect," she said. "I'm equally interested in basketball."

One dark eyebrow slid up. "It's *SportsCenter*. And they're talking about the Colts. They're a football team."

She hadn't really been paying attention or she would've known that from following Matt's career. "Whatever. You sure know how to entertain a woman."

He gave her a crooked smile. "You're the one who tied my hands."

"Sort of makes you appreciate all those women who'll put out, doesn't it?" She manufactured a yawn.

"Sort of makes me mad you won't," he grumbled.

She couldn't help laughing at his surliness. Their date tonight hadn't been bad. As a matter of fact, she'd enjoyed it. Despite some of his comments since, she was beginning to believe they might actually get along. "We could always watch the shopping network."

"I'd rather stick a fork in my eye."

"But it's time I started spending your money."

"Who says?"

"Isn't that what wives of movie stars do?"

"You've made it abundantly clear that you won't *really* be my wife."

"And you've made it clear that I could still have some decent pocket change."

He got up. "Fine. I don't care. Just shop on your own time."

She pulled the blankets higher. "Whose time is this?"

"Mine," he said without looking back.

"According to who—you?"

"It's part of your contract." He went into the bathroom and shut the door.

"I didn't sign anything that said I had to watch TV with you," she called after him.

He poked his head out. "You don't. You only have to share my bed and pretend to like it. So feel free to roll over and go to sleep."

She tried. But she was too aware of every move he made.

A few minutes later, he was back in bed, surfing stations again. "How long are you going to be up?" she asked.

"It's still early."

"In which country? Because here it's after one o'clock."

"One more program."

"Fine," she said with a sigh. "But I'm going to sleep."

His hair stood up as he raked a hand through it. "Does that mean I can finally watch what I want?"

"Of course," she said, and flopped over, but she'd expected him to choose something sports-related, like before. She had no idea he'd settle on a skin flick.

Male and female moans immediately drew her attention back to the screen, where a woman with obscenely large breasts was having sex with a man whose body parts were equally exaggerated. It was low-budget, down and dirty, but it was effective. Gail hadn't been with a man in so long, a sight like this couldn't fail to trigger a deluge of hormones. "What are you doing?" she gasped.

He blinked innocently at her. "Watching TV."

"That's *pornography!*"

"You just said you were going to sleep. I said, 'Does that mean I can finally watch what I want?' and you said, 'Of course.'"

"But that's cheating! You're trying to get me interested."

He raised his hands as he shook his head. "Not my plan at all."

Then he was after revenge. No doubt he thought it was funny to arouse her, since she was the one who'd taken physical satisfaction off the menu.

When the woman threw her head back and cried out in ecstasy, Gail felt her face flush. "I don't want to watch this!"

"Fine. Then choose something else." Tossing her the remote, he scooted down and closed his eyes.

Gail selected a news channel for a few minutes, then a cop show for a brief time, then an old rerun of *CHiPs*. She'd won that skirmish, she told herself, satisfied that she'd gained control of the remote. But as the minutes lengthened and Simon's breathing grew regular, she couldn't help going back to see if the show he'd chosen was still on. And then she couldn't seem to pull away from it until it was over. By the time she turned off the TV and put the remote on the nightstand, she was far from sleep. As a matter of fact, she was so hot and bothered she wanted to slug Simon.

"Something wrong?" he asked when she couldn't get comfortable.

He hadn't moved in some time. She'd assumed he was asleep. "No, why?"

"I thought you didn't want to watch *Here Comes Pussy*."

She could hear the laughter in his voice and felt a certain amount of embarrassment. "I didn't really watch it. I was just…surfing around."

"Sure you were."

He'd caught her and he knew it. "It was your fault!" She threw a pillow at him, which he batted away.

"You were in charge of the remote."

"I told myself not to go back to it, but…"

"But?" he challenged.

She stopped searching for an excuse he wouldn't believe, anyway. "It was sort of fascinating," she admitted. "I've never seen anything like it."

This seemed to startle him. "Seriously?"

"Seriously."

"Damn, you really are straitlaced." He didn't sound pleased.

"And you're already corrupting me," she muttered.

"Just living up to my reputation." He covered a yawn. "Anyway, if I'd known it was that great, I would've watched it with you. What was so fascinating about it?"

She couldn't find the words to explain, but having those images on TV while he was lying next to her, all but naked, had been erotic. Which went to show how poor her sex life had been so far. He hadn't even touched her and it was still the best sexual experience of her life. "It just...was." Since he'd played the male lead in her fantasy, she decided she'd be much better off to let it go at that.

"Good to know you have a libido," he said.

She shot into a sitting position. "Was that some sort of *test?*"

"It was a joke." He reached out and took hold of her chin so that she had to look him in the eye. "But since it was a little more effective than I expected, I'll do right by you if you want."

She might've gone for it. There was a small part of her that was urging her to take what she could get. But he was laughing at her again. She could feel the bed shake with his mirth.

"You are *so* bad!" she said.

Dropping his hand, he sobered instantly. "I know."

These days, Simon slept only in snatches and giving up alcohol wasn't making getting through the night any easier. His mouth was dry, his hands felt shaky and he was nauseous. It was nothing for which he needed a doctor; just his body's way of trying to demand he return to his earlier habits. Maybe it was more of a psychological craving than a physical one. Regardless, he woke up only forty minutes later and couldn't go back to sleep.

Shit... He'd hoped by giving himself a bed partner, even one who slept on her own side and wouldn't let him cross that imaginary line, he'd have better luck, some reason to stay put instead of rambling around the house. But nothing seemed to help. He figured he could take a sleeping pill, but considering his state of mind, he was afraid of where that might lead. He didn't want to toss away one crutch only to grab another. Ty deserved a better effort than that.

Rolling over, he scooted toward Gail. He was afraid to get too close for fear she'd think he was making a move. But maybe the steady sound of her breathing and the solidity of her presence would anchor him, somehow ease his insomnia. If he kept his eyes closed, he could pretend she was Bella and this was before they'd torn each other apart—that Ty was still a baby sleeping in the next room.

It might've worked, but Gail wasn't asleep.

"What's wrong?" he asked, slightly embarrassed when he realized she was watching him.

"Don't you ever sleep?"

"Not much. Not these days. What are you doing up?"

"Thinking."

He punched his pillow. "Be careful. Don't do too much of that or it'll drive you crazy."

"Is that what it does to you?"

"Unless I stop the whole process by dousing my brain with alcohol."

"Which you can't do at the moment."

"Or any moment in the next two years."

"I'm glad you're taking that seriously."

He blew out a sigh. "It's been a whole seventy-two hours." He could've given her the minutes, too. He was pretty sure she understood that.

"So…now you're looking for other distractions."

"Except there's nothing on the list of approved activities."

She adjusted the bedding. "Is that why you didn't watch the porn flick you showed me?"

"Part of the reason."

"I suppose you could start gambling, if you must have a bad habit."

"I'm willing to consider anything."

"I believe it." When she laughed, he realized she was more attractive than he'd ever given her credit for. She wasn't a beauty in the classic sense, but…there was *something* about her.

"You're a lot prettier when you laugh," he said.

She didn't respond, just stared at him with those serious gray eyes, and he could tell she'd discounted his words as soon as he'd uttered them.

"I meant that as a compliment."

"You don't have to pay me compliments." Her shrug

suggested she didn't believe him, anyway. "I don't expect you to pretend to see something that's not there."

The silence stretched with only the swoop of the ceiling fan to interrupt it. "Is that why you won't let me touch you?" he asked at length. "You think, for me, it's all about the perfect body?"

She seemed to consider her answer carefully. "No, I don't think you care what I look like or that you'd even notice. For you, sex is like alcohol. You're just trying to deaden the pain."

She was right. Since the breakdown of his marriage he'd gone from one woman to the next. Some of them he'd never seen before or after, never even learned their names.

"You're going to be hard person to live with, Ms. DeMarco," he said.

Her lips curved into a wry smile. "Why's that? Because you can't bullshit me?"

"Because you see enough truth to think you know it all."

"I haven't been wrong yet."

"Yes, you have. I *do* think you're pretty," he said, and got up.

She leaned on her elbows. "Where are you going?"

"I have a project I'm working on."

"It's the middle of the night."

"I need something to do," he said, and pulled on his jeans.

Gail woke up alone in Simon's bed. After dressing in last night's clothes, she wandered out of the room and down to the kitchen, where his chef, a stout man who reminded her of Emil Villa, insisted on making her an omelet for breakfast. Once she was finished eating, Simon's driver, a handsome younger man of maybe twenty-five, came in through the French doors and announced that he'd be happy to take her home whenever she wanted to leave.

"Where's Simon?" She gazed out a wall of glass toward the pool—the direction from which the driver had come.

He set about gathering his keys. "I'm sure he's on the property. All the cars are here. But, honestly, I can't say where. He texted me earlier and asked me to drive you home whenever you're ready. That's all I know."

Arching a disbelieving eyebrow, she waited for him to look up. When he did, he acted a little embarrassed, as if he understood that she knew he was covering for his boss. From the driver's perspective, Simon had had his fun with her; now his job was to drop her off, like he'd probably done with so many women before her.

But why would Simon treat her the same as all the others when they needed to convince everyone he felt more for her?

"Or…I could text him and tell him you want to see him—if you like," the young man added reluctantly.

Mere platitudes. He didn't expect her to take him up on that offer. He was obviously skeptical it would do any good, even if she did.

Gail didn't dare risk having Simon brush her off in front of his staff. Not saying goodbye was bad enough.

"No, that's fine," she said, but to compensate she fondled the ruby pendant at her throat. "I'm ready whenever you are. I just wanted to thank him for the necklace."

On learning that Simon had given her such an expensive gift, the cook and the driver exchanged a meaningful glance, but they said nothing more. The chauffeur, dressed in a polo shirt and chinos, grabbed a pair of sunglasses off the counter and led her through the house to a tunnel that ran to the garage—a garage that appeared to be detached when viewed from ground level.

"This reminds me of the Bat Cave," she said.

He opened the back door of the limousine. "Comes in handy."

"I bet." Raking her fingers through her tangled hair, she settled against the leather upholstery. She had none of her toiletries, hadn't even been able to brush her teeth. Maybe Simon had done her a favor by letting her duck out with no farewell.

I do think you're pretty....

She'd mulled over those words long after he'd left last night. They rose in her mind now, but she quickly shoved them away. She could never compete with the kind of women he usually enjoyed. There was no reason to get excited about a "you're not so bad." What he'd said didn't matter, anyway. This was a job.

The driver began to back out, but she stopped him. "Wait! Do we have to take this car?" It attracted so much attention.

Eyes hidden by his silvery lenses, he looked in the

rearview mirror. "It has tinted windows. Simon said to get you home without letting anyone bother you."

So he'd done *something* to convince his staff that he might care about her well-being. She supposed she should be grateful for that small courtesy, but she was still a little put out that he hadn't bothered to see her. Had he ever come to bed?

She couldn't remember. Once she'd fallen asleep, she hadn't stirred until morning. "This is fine."

Her cell phone buzzed as they made a three-point turn and started down the drive. She'd gotten a text. From Callie. How'd it go with your father?

Not good, she responded.

I'm sorry. But...you might want to listen to him.

Gail didn't text back. She'd crossed her father and was ignoring her friend's advice because she'd already committed herself to this course of action. But...what made her think her plan would work? Simon had just sloughed her off on his hired help like he did all the women he didn't care about, even though he understood the need to treat her as if she was special. What was going through his mind?

She had no idea, but part of her feared he might be drinking. And if he was drinking she needed to know about it. She had so much riding on this campaign. There was more at risk than her business; she had her relationship with her father to consider, too. She wouldn't let Simon prove Martin right. Simon *could* change, pull himself together and stop his downward spiral. And she was going to do everything in her power to see that he did.

"Take me back," she said.

The driver slowed in surprise. They'd just passed through the gate. "Excuse me?"

"You heard me. I want to go back to the house right now."

12

Security didn't want to let her on the premises. But Gail wasn't taking no for an answer. She called Ian, told him the deal was off unless she could get onto the estate immediately, and somehow he arranged it. After fifteen minutes of haggling between him and a gigantic muscle-bound man named Lance, during which she was pretty sure Ian told Lance she was to be accommodated no matter what she wanted, the limousine rolled through the gate, down the long winding drive and into the garage.

By the time Gail got out, she'd called Simon's cell phone twice. She'd texted him, too. There'd been no response. Was he passed out somewhere? Dabbling with a maid? Or did he have enough of his wits about him to know he'd better hide?

Damn him. She'd gone out on a limb for him. If he was drinking...

"Ma'am? Ma'am, is there something I can help you with?" The driver hurried after her. He didn't like letting her have free run of the place any more than Lance, the security guard, did. But she didn't care. Avoiding the tunnel, she headed to the house by circling around to the front entrance.

The driver stuck with her, a few feet behind. "How can I help you?" he called again.

"You can find Simon," she called back, "because I'm not leaving until I talk to him." No way would she sit passively by and let her former client—her "fiancé"—ruin everything. They were all in this together now.

"Simon? Where are you?" she shouted as she entered the house. Sweeping staircases, to the right and left, a marble floor with nothing but a grand piano and a high ceiling made for perfect acoustics.

Simon didn't answer.

A maid came to the top of the stairs. Obviously surprised by the interruption, and the angry edge to Gail's voice, she stood at the railing and gaped down at her.

"Where is he?" Gail demanded when their eyes met.

The maid shook her head. "I don't know. I swear."

"Somebody here does." She marched into the living room where she'd met with Simon yesterday. Empty. She found a study, a library, a movie theater, a game room…too many rooms to count. But they were all perfectly clean and perfectly empty. When she finally reached the kitchen, she'd decided he was drinking for sure. She was going to bust him, then cut ties completely, no matter what happened afterward.

At the sound of her heels clacking on the tile floor, Simon's chef twisted around to look over his shoulder.

"Have you seen him?" she asked.

Unlike the maid, he'd been expecting her. He was sitting on a bar stool, having a cup of coffee with the driver, who'd given up following her once she started through the house. The stubborn tilt to the chef's round head indicated he wouldn't tell her anything and his words confirmed it. "No. But I rarely see him in the mornings."

"Because he's usually hungover," she muttered, afraid no one had seen him this morning for that same reason. "You're not doing him any favors, you know. I'm trying to help him."

"Looks like it," the chef said.

Suddenly she remembered the project Simon had mentioned in the middle of the night. "Where does he go when he's here but not in the house?"

They knew, of course, but were too loyal to tell her. The driver blinked at her. "I have no idea, Ms. De-Marco."

The chef spread his hands. "He could be anywhere."

She hadn't introduced herself. Either Simon had given them her name or they'd seen the pictures of her and Simon kissing and read about her online. But if that was the case, they didn't seem to be putting much store in the tales that were circulating. The press called her Simon's latest "love interest." They probably thought she was just another conquest, that she'd already passed out of favor or Simon wouldn't have foisted her on them.

"I'm talking about when he works on his project," she prompted. "Where does he go then?"

They glanced at each other but remained mute.

"Fine, I'll just have to keep looking," she said, and stalked out the French doors.

Before she could cross the patio, however, the driver came to the door and called after her. "Ms. DeMarco?"

She turned to see that he was frowning. Speaking up went against his training. But he had obviously gauged her determination and decided it was better to get what was coming over with than have her searching the property for hours, haranguing everyone she saw. "I've texted him several times, but he's not answering. At this point, I don't know what to do, so…I guess he can tell you himself if he wants you to leave. I'll take you to his wood shop."

Wood shop? Simon didn't seem like the carpenter type, but maybe the project he'd mentioned involved wood.

"Thank you."

Hurrying to keep up, she followed as he crossed the grass and went behind the tennis courts, past the pool house, the guesthouse, a second barbecue area, this one with a koi pond, and what looked like an outdoor dancing pavilion.

At last they came upon a giant cabinlike structure at the far corner of the property. "This is it?" she asked.

He waved her ahead of him. "This is it."

Heart pounding for fear of what she'd find, and the disappointment that might go with it, she knocked on the door.

There was no response but she could hear a saw going inside. She tried the handle.

It wasn't locked. She poked her head in. "Simon?"

At first she thought the shop was empty. She spotted the saw, but there was no one near it. The motor grated as the blade whirled freely. "I don't think he's here, either—" she started to say, but then she saw the blood. "Oh, my God!"

Simon's driver stood behind her. He noticed the drops the same second she did, but he found his employer faster. Pushing past her, he dashed across the concrete floor to where Simon sat, slumped against the wall, blood covering his hands and phone and staining his clothes.

She hurried over and crouched on the other side. "Simon? What happened?"

"I don't think he can hear you," the driver said, and he was right. Simon's eyes were glassy, his skin cold and clammy.

Standing, Gail pulled her phone out of her purse. Her hands were shaking so badly she could hardly dial, but she hit 9-1-1.

"How long do you think he was bleeding?" Gail stood in a corner of the hospital waiting room, conversing quietly with Simon's doctor.

"Considering the size of the cut?" the doctor replied. "At least an hour."

She attempted to swallow, but her mouth was too dry. "So…was it a suicide attempt?"

A tall, spare man with gray hair, the doctor pursed his lips. "I don't believe he was trying to kill himself, no."

"Then why didn't he seek help?"

"Who can say? Maybe he thought he could get the bleeding under control, that he only needed to sit down and put some pressure on it. But it was much worse than he realized and he eventually went into shock. To be honest, thanks to significant sleep deprivation and the lifestyle he's been leading, I'm not sure he was in a clear frame of mind to begin with."

She could certainly confirm that. "What about alcohol? Was he drunk when this happened?"

"No. There was no alcohol in his system at all."

For some reason this helped her relax and made her tear up at the same time. It meant he was trying. "He told me it's been three days since he's had a drink."

"How much was he drinking before?"

"A lot."

"Maybe he's going through withdrawal and that figures into this somehow. It can cause depression, anxiety, myriad other things. I'm guessing this accident is a culmination of a number of factors. Including exhaustion."

"But not suicide." For some reason, she needed to hear him say that again.

"I doubt it. A saw would be an emotionally daunting way to take your own life. Besides, only one of his hands is cut and not near the wrist. This was an accident, but...the fact that he didn't immediately call for help might say something about his state of mind. Then again, it might not. It could've happened like I said."

"Gail? What's going on?"

Ian had arrived; he was hurrying toward her. Thanking the doctor for taking the time to speak with her, she turned and greeted Simon's manager. "He's going to be okay."

His eyes darted between her and the departing doctor. "What the hell happened?"

She blew out a long breath. "I'm not sure. The doctor thinks it was an accident."

"You don't?"

The image of Simon sitting on the floor of his woodshop, cradling his hand and staring off into space as if he'd just as soon slip away came to mind. Why didn't he call someone? He had all kinds of domestic help on the property. The doctor didn't feel it was an *active* attempt to take his own life, but he'd intimated that it could have been a passive one, which still gave them plenty to worry about. "I don't know what to think," she admitted. "Except…Simon needs a break, Ian."

He scowled. "What do you mean?"

"I mean he needs a break, a real break. Some time to take care of himself, to get back on his feet emotionally and physically, to rest from all the demands on him."

"But he's under contract for promotion! I already told you that. And he's supposed to start another movie in two weeks."

She was so upset it didn't take much to set her off. "You said you could clear his schedule in early November for our wedding."

"I was talking about a weekend or maybe even a week. But he's slammed with work before *and* after."

"I don't care! Get him out of whatever obligations he's got. He shouldn't be working in this condition."

"I can't just—"

"Yes, you can." She grabbed his arm to make her point. "It's only money."

"Easy for you to say. It's not *your* money that'll be lost, not *your* career that will suffer. This film he has coming up—it's supposed to be the kind that makes or breaks a career. The producers are pressuring me to make sure he'll be at the studio and in good shape."

A couple on the couch glanced up, so she pulled Ian farther into the corner and lowered her voice. "He nearly cut off his hand. Whether that was an accident or not, he didn't seek help. He sat on the floor as if he didn't care whether he lived or died and nearly bled to death. If that isn't a cry for help, I don't know what is. Now get on the phone and call whoever you have to, but tell everyone that Simon will be unavailable for the next three months."

Agitated, Ian began to pace. "They'll think he's cracking up, that he's finally lost it. I've spent so much time trying to make them believe he'll be fine, snap back, get into it again."

She threw up her hands. "Then tell them it's because he's fallen in love and is getting married. We'll provide plenty of pictures to prove it. Making a commitment to someone stable should be a good sign, not a bad one."

"They don't know you're stable. Anyway, you could be perfectly stable until you hook up with him."

"Well, that's how we need to sell it, because I now

believe this is Simon's last chance in more ways than one."

Ian's mouth hung open for several seconds before he could find the words to respond, but at least he'd quit pacing. "So...I get him out of all his obligations, and then what?"

"We leave L.A."

"And go where?"

Gail's mind whirled. She was on to something. She could feel it. Her certainty grew as she considered the problem from all angles. Simon couldn't stay in Los Angeles. Here, he was surrounded by the same temptations, reminders, people and worries. How could he effect the changes he needed to make when he was mired in the past? When nothing else was changing?

Getting away made sense. But where should she take him? To one of his houses abroad?

No. What if the accident hadn't been an accident? She didn't want to be out of the country if something like this happened again. Or he went back to drinking. She preferred someplace she felt comfortable and safe and could get the help he would need. Someplace where he could dry out and recover without the intrusion of the paparazzi. Someplace where there were no painful memories of Bella or Ty, no friends who might encourage him to keep partying, no enticements from film-industry types to make another movie before he was ready.

She was sure he had other houses in America they could go to, but she didn't want an army of domestic workers taking note of everything that transpired, either.

They needed privacy, support, protection and a change of scenery. Given all that, the answer became obvious. "I've got it," she said.

Ian narrowed his gaze. "You've got what?"

Her father wouldn't like it. Neither would her brother and her friends. They were already convinced she was making the biggest mistake of her life. Even Simon would object. They'd all reject one another—at first. But the people who loved her were good people. They'd made her whole and happy despite her mother's defection. They'd been there when she needed them most. And they were still there for her.

Simon needed rock-solid commitment from the right sorts of friends and associates and for the right reasons. He needed to figure out what really mattered in life and what he wanted out of his own.

She couldn't think of a better place to do that than Whiskey Creek. "I'm taking him home."

13

When Simon woke up, he found Ian and Gail sitting on either side of his bed, glaring at each other.

"Why all the hostility?" he muttered.

Gail came to her feet. "What hostility?"

Whatever they'd given him made him groggy, but even then he could tell she was covering up. "You two act like you want to choke each other."

"So what's new?" She laughed, and Ian did, too, but their eyes were cold when they met and their smiles seemed brittle.

"Something. I can feel it." He glanced between them. "I thought we'd called a truce, that we were all playing on the same team again."

"We are," Gail told him. "Ask anyone—you and I are madly in love and having wild sex at your Beverly Hills mansion. Everything is fine. Right on track."

Except that she was treating him like he'd lost his mind—was probably wondering what kind of crazy man she'd gotten involved with.

Damn... Somehow, despite all his good intentions

and effort, he'd screwed up again. "Wild sex, huh? That's what they think?"

"How do you feel?" Ian stood up, too.

Simon had never seen his business manager so serious. "Drugged. What happened?"

"You don't know?"

He lifted his right hand to examine the bandage that made his arm look liked it ended in a club. "Nurses told me I cut my hand. They said it wasn't too bad, but they were somber as shit and it has to be more than a scratch or I wouldn't be here, right?"

Gail bumped up against the steel rail of his bed. "You don't recall the accident?"

He honestly didn't. The last thing he remembered was getting a text from Bella—a short video of her having sex with some guy and a note that said, Ty's new daddy. "No, I was exhausted, completely out of it." He realized how that sounded and hurried to amend his words. "But I wasn't drinking. At least…I'm pretty sure I wasn't drinking." He'd considered it. Had he given in?

"No, you weren't drinking," she said.

"There's a bright spot." He grinned, but when she didn't lighten up he stopped trying to charm her. "So… what? Are you backing out? Cutting me loose?" Why wouldn't she? He knew how this looked. He could tell by some of the questions the doctor had asked that he hadn't called for help when he should have.

They wondered if he'd purposely hurt himself. And maybe he had. He wouldn't be stupid enough to attempt suicide by power saw, but subconsciously he might've been sabotaging his own efforts to reform, or trying to save himself from failing through lack of willpower. He'd always been his own worst enemy. His father told him that all the time, even though it felt more like his father was his worst enemy. Their relationship had never been a strong one, but recently they'd become completely estranged.

He let his eyes slide closed. "You're off the hook, if you want."

He expected her to jump at the chance, provided he agreed to a stipulation that saved her business, but she surprised him.

"That's not what I want."

Opening his eyes, he found her and Ian watching him a little too closely. He nearly assured them he was stable, that he could cope with whatever he had to, but he'd been saying that for too long. His actions hadn't backed it up, so why bother? "Then, what is?"

She nibbled at her bottom lip. "I want to take you to Whiskey Creek."

Had he heard her correctly? "Isn't that where your family lives?" He didn't bother hiding the skepticism in his voice.

"That's right."

"We already discussed it."

"We did, but…" She folded her arms, which told him she was anticipating a fight. "A few things have changed since then and…now I think it's imperative to the success of our marriage."

He raised his eyebrows. "Why? What difference does

it make whether or not I meet your family? Are you *trying* to drive me to drink?"

He thought she could at least smile at his joke, give him credit for the effort he was putting into pretending he was okay, but Ian piped up before she could react.

"It'll mean canceling everything you've got going for the next three months."

So Ian wasn't excited about this change of plan.... Simon rubbed the beard growth on his chin. "I'll miss starting my next movie."

"Yes."

"That's a long time to be in Whiskey Creek."

Gail stood taller. "Given your injury and our wedding, you have a good excuse, a believable excuse, to clear your schedule without losing face. Take the out. It'll only make our marriage look more genuine."

He scowled at her. "How is Whiskey Creek going to do that?"

"It'll suggest you care enough to spend time with me and my family. And dropping out of public view will ultimately make it easier for you to regain custody of Ty."

The sex video Bella had sent and those taunting words—*Ty's new daddy*—floated to the forefront of Simon's brain. The images turned his stomach. But it was the idea of the man who was screwing his ex-wife replacing him as his son's father that hurt, as Bella knew it would. "You really believe it would make enough of a difference?"

"You couldn't go wrong in Whiskey Creek even if you wanted to."

He could go wrong anywhere. He'd proven it. But… she seemed so convinced and, whether he wanted to admit it or not, he was starting to trust her, certainly more than Ian. Ian had his strengths, but she was smarter, more disciplined. Just what he needed at the moment. "What would I do there?"

"Anything you want. I saw the playhouse you've been building. It's amazing! You like working with wood. Why don't we rent a house while you build us a bigger one?"

Building a house with his own two hands had always appealed to him. He felt a flutter of excitement, the first in a long, long while—but Simon refused to succumb to it. He didn't want to be disappointed. "Are you setting me up?"

"Excuse me?"

"Your dad's going to hate me."

"He already does," she said. "So does my brother. But you can win them over. You can win anyone over."

She was offering him a chance to be a regular person for a while, a chance to step out of the limelight and catch his breath.

"This'll cause damage to certain key relationships," Ian warned. "You're booked solid. And if I have to buy your way out of your next movie, it'll be pricey."

True, but his sanity was worth any amount. Simon had learned firsthand that even piles and piles of money couldn't buy happiness. That cliché was a cliché for a reason.

"The producers of *Hellion* will freak out if you postpone too long," Ian went on. "It'll put them in trouble with the rest of the cast, studio time, everything."

"If they can't wait, they'll have to find someone else," Simon said.

"Seriously?" Ian looked stupefied.

Simon couldn't imagine trying to make a movie in his current state of mind. "Seriously." He turned to Gail. "Okay, we'll go to Whiskey Creek."

"You'll do it?" She sounded skeptical, and he couldn't blame her.

He thought of all the hours he'd spent aching for his son while standing or sitting in Ty's room. Maybe it was time for a radical change. "Why not? Let your dad take his best shot."

They needed to get married before doing anything else. Only if Simon was legally bound to her and couldn't be easily relegated to the "temporary" category would Whiskey Creek even begin to accept him. Gail understood that, which meant they had to change the proposed timeline of their "courtship."

Because she'd never been engaged and had no idea of the process required to make a marriage legal, she used her smartphone while sitting at Simon's bedside to go online and figure out what they'd need to do to get a license.

Fortunately, it was going to be easy. As long as they had proper ID and proof of the dissolution of Simon's marriage, they could pay a fee, get a license on the spot and be married shortly after. No need for a blood test; no need to go to Vegas.

But they had to appear at the county clerk's office together, and Simon hadn't yet been released from the hospital so it wouldn't happen today.

Ian had stayed, too, although Simon was too drugged to do much talking. Mostly, he slept. There were moments when Gail was tempted to leave so she could prepare for their big move. But the number of hospital personnel who popped into the room bothered her. They all came in and fiddled with this or that, pretending to be on official business. However, Gail was convinced they were merely gawking at the big movie star, which felt wrong since he wasn't even aware of them.

How many times did a guy with stitches need to be checked? she wondered. It wasn't as if Simon had had a heart attack or any other problem that required such close monitoring. He just needed to catch up on his sleep, and medicating him made sure he was able to do that.

"Word is spreading," she told Ian as the door closed on yet another visitor.

Simon's business manager sat with his elbows on his knees and his head in his hands. "What are you talking about?" he asked, looking up.

"That's the fifth nurse to come in here in under an hour."

"I know. He'd probably be getting a blow job by now if you weren't here."

She could tell by the sulk in Ian's voice that he was

no longer happy to be involved with her. He'd expected her to keep Simon productive so that the next two years would run smoothly. Instead, she was pulling his client out of circulation. "Simon doesn't need a blow job. He needs a break from all the celebrity worship and scrutiny."

"You're sure about that, are you? Why don't we ask him if he'd like one of these cute little nurses to—"

"Stop it." She rolled her eyes. Ian was being crude on purpose, trying to shock her. "I've got a novel concept—how about if we give Simon what he needs instead of what he wants?"

"He doesn't need you to tell him what to do. He's a grown man."

She lowered her voice just in case Simon was nearing consciousness. "Who's on the brink of total collapse! You asked me to help for a reason, remember? The fact that you're fighting what's best for him tells me you're as bad as his other so-called friends. You're all vultures, hoping to pick his bones."

Ian shot to his feet. "That's bullshit! I care more about him than you do."

She stood, too. "Then prove it."

"I don't have to prove anything to you."

"At least quit pouting. You're driving me crazy."

"Feel free to go home if you don't like it."

No way. That was exactly what he'd been hoping she'd do. Then he could try to talk Simon out of going to Whiskey Creek. "Sorry to disappoint you but I'm not leaving you alone with him."

Ian leaned toward her. "What you're doing is crap, you know that? You're changing everything."

"I'm making necessary adjustments."

He combed his fingers through his hair, hesitated, then continued in a calmer voice, one meant to sway her. "Come on, I'll go with one month, okay? One month is plenty of time for Simon to be gone. We can put the producers of his next movie off until his hand heals but that's it."

"Sorry. Simon has to be out of circulation long enough to feel it, to unwind and focus on other—"

Yet another nurse popped in, but she got only halfway through the door before the look on Gail's face stopped her dead in her tracks. Mumbling a quick "Excuse me," she ducked out as if she'd entered the room by mistake.

Ian whistled. "You're a freakin' pit bull."

"You knew what I was like before you agreed to our deal."

"I had no idea you'd talk him into quitting work!"

"He's not quitting work, he's taking a break so he'll be able to salvage his relationship with his son and his career. And call me what you will, but now that I'm committed I'm going to do whatever it takes, so get used to it."

Simon shifted in the bed but didn't open his eyes. "Hey," he said. "Could you guys argue somewhere else?"

How much had he overheard? Gail exchanged a glance with Ian that essentially asked that question.

But she got the impression that Simon hadn't been paying attention to much more than the harshness of their whispering.

"Sorry," Ian muttered. "I think I'll take off."

Simon's eyes opened. "I'm surprised you lasted this long. You must be bored stiff."

"I thought you might need me, but…you're in good hands with Attila the Hun over there."

"Attila was a man," Gail snapped.

"I know that," he snapped back.

"Sure you did."

Ian lunged forward and gnashed his teeth. "He was ruthless, right?"

Simon put up his good hand. "Whoa, what'd she do to you?"

"How can I get some of the nurses to give me their number if she's chasing them off?" He smoothed his wrinkled shirt.

"You that desperate?"

"Desperate enough."

Simon didn't press him further. "Okay. Talk to you later."

"I'll get your schedule cleared," Ian said, his tone letting them know that he still thought it was a mistake.

As the door swung shut behind Ian, Simon raised his bed and turned his attention to her. "What's up between you two?"

Stiff from sitting all day, Gail rolled her shoulders. "I made it obvious that I wouldn't let him get in my way, that's all."

"And he backed down?"

"I prefer to believe he realized I was right."

"I don't know...." He studied her with a frown. "A blow job is never a *completely* bad idea."

So he'd overheard more than she'd assumed. "If you already knew what we were arguing about, why'd you ask?"

"Honestly? That's the only part I can remember."

She could tell he thought she'd snap at him, tell him to keep his priorities straight, but why would she? He wasn't serious. She was beginning to believe he purposely painted himself as shallow and hedonistic so the people around him wouldn't realize he was so sensitive. Somehow it was easier for him to outrage everyone than to allow them to see how deeply he was hurting.

"Enjoy your painkiller," she said. "Because that's all the feel-good you'll be getting here." She offered him a facetious smile. "And after that things will really go downhill because you'll be married to me."

"Wait, *I'm* the one who's supposed to put *you* down."

"We're getting to know each other so well, I can actually predict what you're going to say."

He didn't react to her sarcasm. "So...when's the big day? I'm guessing it's changed. You'll want to be married before introducing me to Daddy, am I right?"

Of course he was right. Then Martin couldn't talk her out of it or disapprove of their living together. "How'd you know?"

"You've got to have some way to make them accept such—what'd you call me? A dissolute movie star?"

He was slurring some of his words but she could still understand them. "*You're* going to make them accept you, not me. But to answer your question, I say we marry as soon as you're up and around."

"I'll be fine tomorrow. That's when we'll get our rings." His eyes drifted shut. He seemed to be having trouble remaining lucid, but he managed to say something else. "You don't have to stay here if you don't want."

Given his strained relationship with his family, who else would come? One of his bodyguards? His driver or a maid? That seemed so impersonal. "Sorry, but I've dedicated my entire day to beating back these nurses, and I won't quit now."

As if on cue, the door opened. When a male hospital worker walked in, Simon offered her a wry look. "I'm safe with this one."

Gail was too preoccupied to respond to his joke. "Do you have some reason for being here?" she asked the young man.

A sheepish expression appeared on his face. "Actually, I'm a huge fan." He held up paper and pen as his gaze darted in Simon's direction. "I was wondering if…if maybe I could get an autograph. I've seen *Shiver* so many times."

"If you don't mind—don't mind an *X*," Simon said, but Gail knew he was too groggy to hold a pen. And it was his right hand that had been injured. This guy was probably a nurse or an X-ray tech or someone who should know better than to barge into a patient's room without a legitimate reason.

"Get out and let him rest," Gail said. "And if you don't post a sign on the door saying that only authorized personnel are allowed in, I'll file a complaint and then maybe a lawsuit."

The man's eyes rounded. "But...I didn't mean to... What kind of lawsuit?"

"I'm sure a good attorney could think of something. If you like your job, you wouldn't want to be the cause of all the trouble."

"No, ma'am," he said, and hurried out.

Simon chuckled. "Jeez, with you around who needs security?"

She sank into her chair, which felt no softer than it had before. "I'm glad you feel that way because you won't have any security in Whiskey Creek."

The humor fled his face. "I won't?"

"No. No maids or chefs or drivers, either."

He scowled. "Why the hell not?"

"It's too insular, too alienating, especially in a place as small as Whiskey Creek."

"*Somebody's* got to cook."

"I'll do it if you'll do the driving."

"Are you any good?" he asked skeptically.

"I'm not bad."

"Fine. Because I'm a hell of a driver. We'll bring the Ferrari."

She crossed her legs. "Do you want everyone to hate you even more?"

"Money's the one thing I've got left. I might as well enjoy it."

"Later. Otherwise, it'll look like a shield—or an enticement. This is about creating a humble image of reform."

He tried to adjust his pillow despite his bandaged hand. "You're making your hometown sound like a real bitch."

She'd been trying to make it sound like a second chance. That was what she believed it could be. And, unlike Ian, Simon understood, or he never would've agreed to go there. He even seemed a little excited by the opportunity, although she guessed that once the drugs wore off, he'd also be frightened by the challenge. It'd been a long time since he'd gone into any relationship on an even footing. In her estimation, that was why he had no true friends.

In Whiskey Creek, it would be different. Simon would be normal, just like everyone else, or as "normal" as someone so famous could be. She hoped that he'd engage others and develop some mutual trust and respect, self-sacrifice, deep feelings. Those were the things he needed right now.

"Most of them won't kiss your ass, but you'll survive," she said.

"I can hardly wait."

Chuckling, she called up the ESPN website on her phone. "Did you hear that the Lakers are taking on the Heat tonight?"

He rested his injured hand on his chest. "What are you talking about?"

"Basketball."

"I know *that*. I'm wondering *why*. You hate sports."

"I'm beginning to rethink my position. Anyway, you used to be a big fan of the Lakers."

"I haven't been following them in pre-season."

He hadn't been keeping up with a lot of the things he normally enjoyed. She thought that should be remedied, too. "I know. So?"

"So what?"

"They'll be starting out strong if they win."

"How many have they won?"

"Eight of their first ten games." She filled him in on the details before going on to the rest of the sports news. Then she moved to other sites and shared snippets of information about Egypt, China, Sudan, anything that involved people outside the U.S. She hoped doing so would remind him that L.A. wasn't the only city in the world, that there was much more out there than fame and the movie industry and his current problems.

Hearing about people being killed and driven out of their homes seemed to put it all in perspective.

"You think you're smart, don't you," he said.

He'd caught on. She smiled innocently. "Excuse me?"

"How am I going to put up with you?"

"Pretending to love me will be the biggest challenge of your acting career."

He didn't respond for a few seconds. Then he said, "How many people live in Whiskey Creek?"

"Population 2,000, give or take a hundred."

Sleepiness no longer seemed to be an issue. "And they're *all* going to hate me?"

She dropped her phone in her purse. "Give or take a hundred," she repeated.

His eyes narrowed. "I'll have them eating out of my hand in a matter of weeks."

"Glad to hear it." She had no doubt he could do it; she just hoped she wasn't one of them.

14

Every diamond was huge, much bigger than any Gail had seen before. And the prices… The average American house didn't cost this much.

Mr. Nunes, who sat in Simon's living room with the nondescript briefcase he'd carried in, had spread his entire cache of loose diamonds out on a piece of black velvet. "This one is the finest quality you'll ever find," he boasted as he held up yet another five-carat rock. "Just look at the clarity."

It was beautiful. But so were the others. "How much?" she asked, and braced herself for another shocking figure. The last one had been four hundred and thirty-five thousand.

Nunes was starting to show some irritation at her continued insistence on knowing the price. "If it's the one you like, I'm sure Simon and I can work something out." He leaned forward to gaze deep into her eyes. "This is your engagement ring. Price is no object."

Easy for him to say. But, surprisingly, Simon didn't argue with him about that. He didn't ask for smaller or cheaper diamonds, either. He simply looked on, wiggling the fingers that dangled out of the sling on his arm.

"It's an ideal cut," Nunes added. "And it has absolutely no color. Diamonds of this size, with a D grade *and* an IF clarity, are very rare."

"Is it more money than the last one?" she asked.

He made a dismissive motion. "Not by much."

What did that mean? Five thousand? Ten? It irritated her that he wouldn't be specific. Just because Simon was rich didn't mean he shouldn't be concerned with getting a fair deal. "How long will it take you to set it?"

"I can have it ready in three days. You will be my top priority."

At that price, she should be. But… "I don't know." Overwhelmed by the prices and the selection, she frowned at the twinkling display. "Maybe…maybe Simon and I should talk about this."

Simon stared at her as if he couldn't figure out what the problem was. "Talk about what?" he asked. "There must be a hundred diamonds here. Surely you can find *one* you like."

She gave Nunes an apologetic smile. "Excuse us for a moment."

"Just pick one so we can decide on the setting," Simon insisted, but she grabbed him by the sleeve of his good arm and led him out of the room.

"What are you doing?" he asked when they were alone in the foyer.

"I think we should forget about the diamond."

His eyebrows shot up. "You need a wedding ring."

"We both do. But gold bands will be fine."

"Why would you settle for a gold band?"

She wasn't sure. There was something...hollow about choosing a big diamond when there was no meaning behind it. She felt as if they were mocking all the traditional wedding symbols. She could see someone with his wealth buying a stone like that to express his devotion to the love of his life, but she wasn't the love of his life. So it was just...wrong. Especially when she knew that canceling his next project would cost him a fortune already. "I don't want to be responsible for such an expensive piece of jewelry," she said. "What if I lose it?"

"It'll be insured."

But a diamond, particularly of this caliber, wasn't part of her contract price. At least, that wasn't what she'd meant when she said he'd have to buy the rings. Her conscience would demand she return it when they divorced, so why get attached to it? What was the point? "There's no need to invite comparisons between me and Bella. Let's keep it simple, modest, understated."

"You're serious."

"I am. I think we should sell the public on the fact that this marriage is different from the typical Hollywood marriage. That we're about the things that really matter. No pomp or ceremony. No obvious publicity stunts. No lavish lifestyle. Just the two of us in love, living in a small house in my hometown—until we grow apart and divorce amicably, of course."

He studied her. "Does this have anything to do with

the offer I made you before? Are you afraid you'll owe me sex in return?"

"No."

"Then what? You don't want to have *any* positive feelings for me?"

"That's not it, either," she said, but she couldn't quite meet his eyes and he jumped to his own conclusion.

"Wow, even my money isn't good enough," he said. "Fine. No problem."

When he headed back without her, she knew she'd offended him. He thought she wouldn't let him redeem himself even where he could, that she found him unworthy of *any* approval.

But that wasn't the problem. She found him appealing whether she approved of him or not.

And she couldn't see how adding a half-million-dollar diamond ring to his side of the equation would make him any easier to resist.

It took nearly a week to get ready for the ceremony and still the time seemed to come up fast. They'd given Simon a chance to recover a bit, gotten the marriage license, purchased the wedding bands. Ian had found some guy on the internet who could legally officiate. For an additional fee, he was willing to come to Simon's house. They'd have a small, private affair with only Josh and Ian as witnesses.

The ceremony would make their marriage legal and binding, and in less than an hour it would all be over.

This wasn't exactly the type of wedding Gail had

dreamed about when she was a little girl, but she'd never imagined that her mother would abandon the family, either. She had to deal with what life handed her, just like everyone else.

She sat in Simon's bedroom, where she'd been staying most nights for the sake of appearances, and painted her fingernails. She'd just finished one hand when someone knocked on the door.

"Who is it?"

"Me. You okay?"

Josh. He'd come to find her. Thank God. Just hearing his voice steadied her nerves. "I'm alive," she said, and jumped up to let him in.

"Wow, you look beautiful," he told her as soon as she opened the door.

He seemed honestly impressed. She liked her outfit, too. Yesterday, Simon had sent her to Rodeo Drive with his credit card but, given the recent press, she'd felt too conspicuous among all those exclusive shops. Pulling on a pair of sunglasses for camouflage, she'd driven to the closest mall, where she felt more comfortable and was able to blend in with the crowd. There, she purchased yet another suit to add to her already extensive collection. She knew that probably wouldn't be a popular decision with Ian or Simon. But this one was teal in color and reminded her of the tailored fashions of the 1940s. She almost felt she should be wearing a fancy hat.

"Really?" She turned in a circle. "This is okay?"

"It's stunning on you. Simple but classy."

She released a nervous sigh. Josh was a fashionista if

ever there was one. If she didn't look good he would've told her. "You prepared to be a witness?"

He whipped a small camera out of his pocket. "As well as the official photographer."

She knew he'd also help with the sale of those pictures to *People*. They'd agreed on that beforehand. "Great. Is Simon downstairs?"

"Waiting in the library. That's where they've decided to hold the ceremony."

"What's he wearing?"

"A suit and, man, does he look delicious—even with his hand all bandaged up."

"You think he looks delicious in anything."

"He does."

She couldn't argue with that. "What about the officiant? Is he here, too?"

"Officiant?"

"That's what they're called. At least, that's what I read on the internet."

"Oh, you mean the *minister*. He's not here yet, but he's on his way." He lifted the hand with the fingernails she hadn't painted. "Shouldn't you get on with this?"

"I was about to." She brushed on the pink lacquer while he talked, but when she finished, he looked at her closely.

"Oh, boy, you're not going to pass out, are you?"

"No, why?"

"You look pale."

"Pale is my usual color," she said, but her shaky laugh confirmed that she was more than a little out of her element. What they were doing invited bad karma. She and Simon would be making promises to love, honor and cherish each other for as long as they lived, with no intention of fulfilling those promises. She wasn't superstitious, but she couldn't help wondering if she was jinxing her future.

"I saw the rings," he said. His tone indicated he wasn't impressed.

"What do they look like?"

"You don't know? They're gold bands. What a cheap asshole. Why didn't he get you something expensive and gorgeous?"

"I didn't want that." She fanned herself to dry the polish. "I'm trying to keep what's happening *somewhat* real. Otherwise, it'll all feel too...outlandish."

"I have news for you, Ms. DeMarco. You're marrying one of the most famous movie stars in America. There's no way to avoid outlandish. I would've asked for the biggest diamond I could find."

"Why make him go to the expense? It wouldn't mean anything. And I'd just have to give it back."

He looked at her as if she was crazy. "Who said?"

Another knock interrupted. "Ms. DeMarco?"

"Yes?"

"They're ready for you in the library."

Simon had sent a maid up to get her. Squaring her shoulders, she offered Josh another tentative smile. "Shall we?"

"Allow me," he said and, with a gentlemanly flourish, escorted her downstairs.

As promised, Simon was in a suit. Freshly shaved, with his hair combed back, he looked every bit as good as Josh had said. Ian stood next to him, also in a suit but clearly no longer as enthusiastic about the idea of their marriage as he once was. The only other person in the room was a distinguished-looking man with silver hair who introduced himself as Reverend Bob Grady, a minister with the United Disciples of Christ Church.

Gail wasn't remotely familiar with the beliefs of that church, was pretty sure she'd never even heard of it, but she figured that didn't matter.

"It's nice to meet you," she said.

"I was just discussing with Simon the type of ceremony the two of you would like," he told her. "Some people write their own vows, but he said you'd both prefer a simple recitation of the traditional promises. Is that right?"

"Yes, that's fine." Her heart was beating so hard, she dared not look at Simon, but she could feel his gaze on her. Was he feeling hopeful? Relieved that the time had come and they'd be able to get this part over with? Hesitant to go through with what they'd planned? She didn't know and she didn't *want* to know for fear it would undermine her own resolve.

The minister bent his head. "Then that's what we'll do. If you two will join hands—as best you can," he said in deference to Simon's injury, "and face each other in front of me, we'll get started."

Simon stepped up and did as he was asked. At that point, Gail *had* to look at him. He seemed pensive.

Maybe he was as nervous as she was. And she could guess why. He'd sworn never to marry again. Even if this wasn't a regular marriage, wasn't real in the same sense, it sure *felt* real.

She almost pulled away to verify that they all believed they were doing the right thing, but Simon tightened his grip to hold her in place and she decided it was his commitment that mattered.

Sweat ran down her back as Reverend Grady began—and her fear of bad karma grew worse, especially when he reached "in sickness and in health" and then "till death do us part."

Still, she managed to repeat her vows. Simon did the same without sounding too panicked. As a matter of fact, he seemed…resolute.

They exchanged rings and the minister said, "I now pronounce you husband and wife. Simon, you may kiss the bride."

Gail knew Simon was in acting mode. He was used to such intimate contact, didn't think anything of it. But the warmth of his lips against hers made her knees weak. Hoping to play her part as well as he was playing his, she slipped her arms around his neck—until Simon's tongue entered her mouth. Then she drew back.

If she'd shocked the minister by stopping the kiss, he didn't show it. Smiling his approval, he gave her elbow a squeeze and, when Simon turned away to speak to Ian, lowered his voice. "I hope you can bring him peace."

"I do, too," she murmured.

They posed for several pictures. Then Josh swept

her into a hug. "Congratulations. You'll be fine, you know that?"

"Of course I do. We both understand—" she dropped her voice to a whisper so the reverend wouldn't overhear "—what's riding on this." She forced a bright smile as she stepped away from him but felt dangerously close to tears.

"Thank God for every new day you have together," the minister said. "May you have a long and fruitful union."

When Gail heard Simon thank him, she was once again embarrassed and uncomfortable with the lies they were telling. But it wasn't until Simon went to show Josh, Ian and Reverend Grady out that she allowed herself to sink into one of the leather chairs along the wall and drop her head in her hands.

"They're gone," Simon said when he came back.

She looked up. "I can't believe we did it, that we went through with it."

He leaned against the door. "You were thinking of bailing on me?"

"No, not really. But…" She finished in a whisper so that no one else in the house could hear. "I felt like an idiot taking those vows. Didn't you?"

He stared at her for what seemed like an interminable time. "I don't know how I missed it."

She had no idea what he was talking about. "Missed what?"

"You're completely…*innocent*."

Her mind scrambled to put his comment into some sort of context. "Because I don't watch porn or—"

"No." He chuckled as if his meaning was obvious, but she couldn't imagine what he was trying to convey. She'd never had anyone call her innocent. It wasn't a word most people associated with a business professional, especially one over thirty.

"Then what?" she asked.

He shook his head. "You're so tough and inflexible that—"

She held up a hand. "You've mentioned my lack of better qualities before."

Ignoring the interruption, he moved closer to her. "That I keep expecting you to be jaded and self-serving. But you're not. You're not that person at all."

Shifting in the giant but soft leather chair, she studied the polish on her nails to avoid looking up—but ended up looking at him anyway. "I'll probably kick myself for asking, but…according to you, who am I?"

"Someone who's honest, sincere and too tender-hearted for her own good." He frowned as if these things were terrible, the latest blow in the long series of blows he'd recently been dealt. "As I said, innocent."

"And you don't like innocent any more than you like tough and inflexible, is that it?"

He did what he could to loosen his tie with one hand. "That's where you're wrong. I *crave* innocent. It's so rare in my world that I'm immediately drawn to it. Which is why I think we might have an unexpected problem."

"Admiring some of my positive traits is a problem?"

"It could be, for you. So I'll add my voice to all the others who've tried to warn you away. If you know what's good for you, you'll walk out of here right now and petition for an annulment."

He was serious. "I can see you're feeling confident in our success. That's encouraging."

"I'm feeling guilty," he clarified.

"For taking vows you don't mean?"

"For knowing I'll probably end up destroying your innocence."

"And how do you think you'll do that?"

"You haven't been through what I've been through, haven't lost the ability to fall in love." He jerked his head toward the door. "So get out while you can. I'll still be your client, do whatever you need to help get your business back on solid ground."

And what would *he* do? Continue to battle his demons with alcohol? He'd certainly made a mess of his life. She wasn't sure he deserved the second chance she'd constructed for him, but she wanted to see him take it.

"You're reading too much into one kiss. It was nothing. I was embarrassed to have an audience, that's why I reacted the way I did."

He said nothing. But his skeptical expression goaded her on.

"Come on, you're not *that* irresistible." She merely had to remind herself of the dangers involved in falling for him and she'd be fine. It wasn't as if she was going into this with her eyes closed. Even *he'd* been up front with her about his limitations.

His gaze lingered on her body. "I give it a week."

"A week for what?"

"That's how long I think you'll last with your no-sex rule."

The awareness that had slammed into her when she was in his arms returned with a vengeance. She wanted him and he knew it. She'd wanted him ever since she'd first seen him on the silver screen.

But most women did. She wasn't stupid enough to act on it.

"Quit trying to scare me off. We've already come this far. We're going to see it through." She got to her feet. "I'm heading home to pack. I suggest you pack, too. We leave for Whiskey Creek in the morning."

"You're staying somewhere else tonight?"

"Yes."

He laughed softly. "See?"

That proved nothing. "See what?"

"You felt it."

"I felt nothing. I just have a lot to do," she said, but she had to sleep sometime, and the fact that she'd decided to stay in her own bed said something, even to her.

He stiffened as she brushed past him but didn't stop her. Neither did he try to talk her into coming back.

"We'll be taking my Lexus to Whiskey Creek, so be ready when I come by in the morning," she said, and left.

15

Simon's introduction to Gail's hometown started with a sign posted on the meandering highway they'd been traveling since leaving Interstate 5: Welcome to Whiskey Creek, the Heart of the Gold Country. They'd passed through other places, similar in size and architecture. Jackson and Sutter Creek also dated from the Gold Rush—era of the 1800s and looked it. But there was something different about Whiskey Creek. Subtle though it was, Simon noticed it right off. There was a definable unity here, a certain pride evident in the way the buildings were maintained and cared for that made him believe it should've been named Happy Valley.

"What do you think?" Gail adjusted her seat belt so she could turn toward him.

"It's…interesting." He'd insisted on driving, even though he wasn't familiar with the route. He had to retain *some* semblance of control, and she hadn't fought him on that. She seemed happy enough to play the role of navigator.

"You don't like it?"

Resting his left hand over the steering wheel, he used his injured right to slide his sunglasses down and take a better look. "The surrounding countryside is gorgeous. I've just never lived in a small town. I'm not sure how I'll adapt."

She lowered the passenger window and stuck her head out as if she couldn't wait to smell the air. "There's nowhere like the foothills, especially in the fall."

That she loved the area so much surprised him. Although they'd never really socialized when he was her client, they had spent significant time together. Other than an occasional mention of where she came from she'd never talked about Whiskey Creek. But then... she'd always been straight-up business. This was the first glimpse he'd had into her past. He'd never had any reason to take an interest before.

"Why'd you leave here?" he asked.

She lowered the volume on the radio. "For the same reasons I keep coming back. My family lives here. And I know everyone."

"Those are bad things?"

"My father can be...a bit overbearing and opinionated."

He'd already gotten that impression.

"And when you know everyone, there's no chance to break out and be anything other than what people expect," she added. "It can be...confining." She rolled her eyes. "Then there's the inevitable gossip."

"I can't imagine *you've* ever been gossiped about.

You always play by the rules." He glanced over to see if she'd refute that statement.

"I've had my less-than-stellar moments."

"Name one."

"No, thanks. Those incidents were painful enough when they happened. No need to relive them." She rummaged through her purse and came up with a pack of gum. "Now that we're married, there will, of course, be more gossip."

"Unlike you, I'm used to being gossiped about." He shook his head when she offered him a piece. "I don't think I could feel at home anywhere I wasn't the center of attention," he teased.

"Then you'll feel right at home here." She tossed him a grin. "Anyway, I had to leave. There's not much opportunity in Whiskey Creek for a PR firm."

"What about in Sacramento? According to the signs I've seen, it isn't far."

"It's still an hour, which makes for a long commute. Unless you want to run one of the stores around here, or maybe a B and B, and we already have two, you're pretty much out of luck in the business world."

He nodded toward A Room with a View Bed and Breakfast, a quaint Victorian perched prominently on Main Street, where the road made a ninety-degree turn. "Tell me we can stay there," he said, but he knew it wasn't likely that she'd change her mind. She'd told him they'd be staying with her father until they could find a rental. He'd heard her confirm it on the phone earlier. He was going to be Martin DeMarco's guest even though he wasn't particularly welcome.

"We have to stay at my dad's, at least for a day or two, or he'll never forgive us," she explained.

"*Us?* He doesn't want me there."

"I can't let him reject you. We're married. We're a package."

"I'm being rescued by a girl." He sighed. "I can't believe my life has come down to this."

If he thought she'd give him a bit of sympathy, he was mistaken. "I hope it's as humbling as it should be," she said.

"Good thing my ego is all but indestructible." He let his gaze stray to the V of her tan dress, which had distracted him all day. As much as he didn't want to find his new "wife" too appealing—they both knew their relationship would best be handled as simply a business transaction—he was intrigued on a number of levels. Mostly, he liked her mind. He'd always admired her quick thinking and no-nonsense, honest approach to life, or he wouldn't have hired her as his PR agent. But there was something more, something about her that just felt…right. She inspired him.

If that was the extent of it, the next two years should progress uneventfully. But in the past few days he'd actually been wondering why he'd never noticed how flawless her skin was. Or how her lips quirked endearingly to one side when she was trying to tell him he was full of bullshit.

"Stop it," she said, nudging his shoulder.

"What?" he asked innocently.

"Just because you're wearing sunglasses, don't think I can't tell what you're looking at."

It was their wedding kiss, he decided. Ever since she'd drawn back almost as soon as their lips touched, he'd been preoccupied with kissing her again. But that wasn't a welcome realization. If he wasn't careful, he'd drag her down before she could pull him up.

"I'm happy to hang out on my own at the B and B, if I'm bothering you," he said.

"Nice try, but I'm not going to my father's without you."

The reminder of what they would soon face quashed his libido. "How difficult *is* Mr. DeMarco?" he asked, slowing for a traffic signal.

"What do you mean?"

The light turned green before he had to stop. "He's never been abusive with you...."

"No. I hope I didn't give you that impression. He's a good man, a *really* good man. It's just that he expects so much of me, and is so easily disappointed. The... force of his personality can be hard to take."

Simon considered that and grimaced. "I don't do well with authority figures."

She didn't attempt to convince him otherwise. That was another thing that made her different. If she said something he could believe it. "No kidding."

He adjusted his seat to give himself more legroom. "So...how do you think this is going to work?"

"We'll figure it out," she said. "At the very least it'll be interesting."

Besides the B and B, they passed an antiques store called Eureka Treasures, Black Gold Coffee, Whiskey Creek Five and Dime, 49er Sweets and a smattering of mom-and-pop-style restaurants, including a diner called Just Like Mom's that could've come right out of the 1960s. There wasn't one fast-food joint or chain grocery store that Simon could see, which made this town and others in the area different from most.

Farther down the street there was a post office, a bike store named Crank It Up and a barbershop, complete with the traditional pole.

"When do we get our own house?" He came to the second stoplight and glanced over to see some flyers taped in the window of Harvey's Hardware. One advertised a tour of a nearby gold mine. Another enticed visitors to go spelunking at a place called Moaning Caverns. The display behind these flyers featured Halloween decorations.

"As soon as Kathy Carmichael, down at KC's Gold Country Realty, is able to find us something suitable."

The hill to the right sported several century-old homes. Others—those along Sutter Street—had been turned into gift shops or art galleries. "Doesn't look like there's a big housing market around here. Will there be anything to choose from?"

"Not much but—" she gave him a pirate's smile "—thanks to you, money's no object, so we'll just take the best one we can get. Picking our lot and getting started on the house you'll build will take more time."

Not if he could help it. He needed to stay busy or he'd revert to his old ways before she could raise a disapproving eyebrow. She'd removed all his coping mechanisms. They hadn't been working particularly well, but they had always provided an escape. "You realize I can't build a house by myself. I've never taken on a project quite that big."

"I have a good friend who's a general contractor. I'm sure he'll be happy to provide any support and guidance you need—for a fee."

"And you think we can build a house in the time we plan to stay here?"

"Probably not, but you can always have Riley take over when we go back to L.A. Then we'll have somewhere to stay when we visit." She conjured up an expression of mock innocence. "Unless you'd like to stay with my father whenever we return."

"Point taken," he grumbled.

Her attention shifted back to her hometown as if she was making note of any subtle changes, but he broke the silence again. "So…you were serious about three months, right? I have to last here for three months and then our Whiskey Creek days are over, except for an occasional visit?"

She touched his arm. "Give it a chance, okay?" She gestured at a small side street jutting off to the right. "Turn here."

* * *

Somewhere in his late fifties, Martin DeMarco was a tall, grizzled redhead with erect posture, big shoulders and hands large enough to palm a basketball. He treated Simon with cool reserve, wouldn't address him directly, but said nothing overtly unwelcoming. He didn't say much at all. He greeted his daughter with a stiff nod and suffered through a brief introduction. Then he helped carry their luggage from the car to Gail's old bedroom in his home, which resembled a large cabin. After putting down her suitcase, he gave Simon one long, assessing look, frowned as though he wasn't happy with what he saw and turned back to his daughter.

"Dinner's in the fridge. Go ahead and heat it up if you're hungry." He didn't say it, but the intimation was there: *And feed him if you have to.* "I've got a problem at the station, but it shouldn't take long."

"Anything serious?" she asked.

"No, just Robbie. He can't figure out how to open the till to give change—the little idiot."

"Where's his mother? I thought she was training him."

"She's been trying, but she's not feeling well. This is his first night on his own."

"He'll learn," she said.

With a skeptical grunt, Mr. DeMarco left, but as far as Simon was concerned his absence did little to improve the situation. Joe, Gail's older brother, was still at home, and he was just as tall, just as imposing and just as unhappy with Gail's choice of husband. He'd spent the whole time they were coming in leaning against the counter, drinking a cup of coffee and sizing Simon up.

When they returned to the kitchen, the disapproval rolling off him was offensive, but Simon had expected to encounter disapproval. He did his best to ignore it—until the sound of the older DeMarco's engine disappeared and Joe addressed him. "So. You're the badass."

"Joe! You don't have to be rude," Gail cried, but Simon talked over her. He didn't want her sticking up for him. He'd face these people down on his own. Maybe he'd get his ass kicked by her Goliath of a brother, but he wasn't sure that would be entirely a bad thing. A bit of violence would provide an outlet for the emotions he could no longer dull with sex and alcohol. His temper had never been closer to the surface.

"That's right." He adopted the cocky air so effective in pissing people off. "How'd you know?"

"I read the papers."

Simon lowered his voice as if divulging a fact Joe should already know but was too stupid to figure out. "Do you mean the tabloids? Because in case you hadn't heard, they're quite often full of shit." He spoke at a normal volume again. "But don't let that change your mind. I'm as badass as they come."

"Funny, too. I like that." Lifting his coffee cup, Joe smiled, looking perfectly comfortable—except for the muscle flexing in his cheek, which said otherwise. "But the fact that you're a big movie star doesn't matter that much to me."

Simon felt his muscles tense. "Then why'd you bring it up?"

He set down his cup and straightened. "There's one thing you need to know."

"Joe—" Gail tried to break in. She'd been glancing between them, a worried expression on her face, but Simon pulled her behind him so she couldn't get in the way.

"What's that?"

"I don't care how rich or famous you are. All the shit you're used to getting away with? Won't fly around here. You step on someone's toes in Whiskey Creek, they're going to knock you down a peg. And if you cheat on my sister, I'll be handling that myself. Understood?"

He deserved the lack of faith, the censure, so Simon tried to take it like a man. But that wasn't easy when it came from someone who had no clue what his life had been like with Bella. "I won't embarrass you or your family. You have my word."

Joe turned to rinse his cup. "For what it's worth," he muttered under his breath.

Had he not added that, Simon would've been able to let it go. As it was, the angry words he'd been biting back rose to his tongue. "Now that we've covered what went wrong in *my* marriage, what happened to yours?"

The question took Joe off guard. No doubt thanks to his size, he'd expected to swagger around and do the big-brother routine without any backlash. "Come again?"

"You heard me."

"None of your damn business." He dried his hands and tossed the towel aside.

"Simon," Gail warned, but Simon ignored her.

"You can keep a scorecard on me but I can't keep one on you?"

Joe sneered at him. "I don't know what you're talking about."

"Sure you do. Few women walk away from a perfect husband."

When Joe's face flushed, Simon thought he'd start swinging. He had more than three inches and fifty pounds on Simon. With an injured right hand, Simon wouldn't even be able to land a decent punch. But he wasn't about to back down. Trying to change his life was hard enough without taking the crap this guy was dishing out.

Fortunately, Joe didn't start a fight. Chest rising and falling fast, he sent an accusing glare at his sister, as if she must've revealed his situation, and stormed out. A second later, his truck's engine roared to life and tires squealed as he peeled down the drive.

"Wow," Gail breathed, and crumpled into a chair at the kitchen table.

Prepared to defend himself further, Simon whirled to confront her. He thought she might be upset that he wasn't willing to tolerate her brother's abuse, but her next words surprised him.

"Good job."

"Good job?" he repeated. "I just pissed off your brother."

"He was pissed off to begin with. He's probably been waiting to do that to you ever since I told him we were getting married."

Simon gave himself a couple of seconds to process the fact that she wasn't going to turn on him. "But now he hates my guts."

"That's okay. At least he understands that he can't push you around. Respect is more important than anything else. Respect will create a foundation. But, just so you don't walk into something you aren't prepared for in the future, you need to be aware that he has his limits."

"So do I," he grumbled.

She regarded him quizzically "How did you know?"

He had no idea what she was talking about. "What?"

"That he's been married before. That Suzie left him."

"There's a picture of him with a woman and two little girls hanging in the hallway."

"Oh…right." She nodded. "Of course. But *he* could've left *her*."

"I figured he wouldn't be living here if that was the case."

"I see." She studied him. "It's going to be tough settling in."

"I can handle it," he said. "Don't worry about me." But he was suddenly craving alcohol so badly it was all he could do not to head for the closest bar or liquor store. "Let's get out of here, go to dinner."

She hesitated. "You're sure you're okay?"

"Fine."

"There's a good Italian place around the corner."

"Great. Maybe there's a casino nearby, too."

"As a matter of fact, there is. Some of the locals work there, but I'm not sure that's the best place for you to go." She picked up her purse. "Still on the hunt for an acceptable vice?"

He pulled her car keys from his pocket. "I need some kind of distraction. And I'm guessing you don't want to provide it."

"What happened to his hand?"

Gail sat at the kitchen table, only now it was her father who stood at the sink. She'd had Simon drop her off after dinner. Although she wasn't happy about the risks involved, he'd insisted on heading to the casino. He said he needed a break, some time alone. She'd finally agreed because she knew she'd ensure the failure she was trying to avoid if she smothered him or pressed him too hard. Besides, she'd wanted some private time with her family, felt that might take the edge off their reaction to her marriage, but Joe hadn't yet returned. "He had an accident with a power saw."

The smell of the coffee her father had just put on filled the room as he eyed her skeptically. "Are you sure he didn't get in another fight? Go after his ex-wife's brother again?"

She scowled. "I'm sure," she said, and left it at that. The details wouldn't help convince Martin she'd made a good match.

With a click of his tongue, he shook his head. "What were you thinking, marrying someone like him, Gail?"

"Someone like him?" she echoed.

"Someone so shallow…and reckless…and stupid…"

Since he seemed to be searching for more adjectives, she stopped him before he could continue. "Simon is anything but stupid." The other things made Gail defensive, too. Coming into their "deal," she'd felt the same irritation and repugnance for Simon's behavior as her father did. She'd sympathized completely with Bella. But Simon's lack of action when he cut his hand had made her realize that his behavior wasn't the result of elitism or arrogance, as most people believed. He'd been so emotionally distraught he couldn't cope.

She wanted her father and everyone else to put his past in the proper context, but Simon wouldn't allow anyone to get close enough to gain any sort of understanding. If not for his meltdown, and how she'd been drawn into it, she wouldn't have come close enough to understand him, either. "He's been through a lot."

"So you've said. But if you're talking about his divorce, I don't buy it. I went through a divorce, too. And I had kids to raise and not nearly as much money."

Her mother had walked out on her father for an old high school sweetheart. They were now married and living in Phoenix. Gail knew how painful losing Linda had been for Martin. She also knew it had changed the way he behaved every bit as much as Simon's divorce had changed him. He obviously felt his situation had been harder. But Gail wasn't convinced. At least there'd been no fame to complicate matters, no media coverage to broadcast every sordid detail, which would've made everything that much worse, especially for such a proud man. Even so, Martin had become strict and controlling, especially where she and Joe were concerned. There were times Gail suspected her mother would've remained a part of her life if not for her father, who could be autocratic and difficult to deal with.

Gail wanted to tell him those things, but she knew he wouldn't take kindly to the criticism. Besides, *he* could allude to her mother, but Linda was still a taboo subject for everyone else, even after all the years that had passed.

"He's worth trying to save," she said simply.

"That's what you're doing? *Saving* him?" He shook a finger at her. "You can't save people from themselves, Gail. You're foolish to think you can."

"So…I should quit without even trying?" she challenged.

He didn't seem to have an answer for that.

"We're already married, Dad. All I'm asking is that you treat him with some respect while we're here, give him a chance."

The door opened, and they both glanced up. Gail feared it was Simon. She wasn't quite ready for him. But it was Joe who walked in.

Her brother gazed around the kitchen, then speared her with an angry glare. "Where's pretty boy?"

Prepared to take on the two of them, if necessary, she squared her shoulders. "You started that fight, Joe."

Her father pulled out a chair and sat down across from her. "What fight?"

"After you left, he tried to belittle Simon," Gail explained.

"That couldn't have been hard," her father said wryly.

She folded her arms. "Maybe not, but he lived to regret it. Simon feels attacked on all sides. He'll snap at anything, even if he's the one who'd take the worst of any fight it might cause."

"Why'd you bring him here?" Joe demanded. "You know how we feel."

Scooting her chair away from the table, she stood. Her father and brother were so big, so…overpowering, they could be intimidating even when they weren't teaming up against her. "What are you saying, big brother? That I should've come without him? Or that *I* should've stayed away, too? Because Simon and I can head over to the B and B if you don't want us here—"

Her father raised his hand in a calming gesture. "Hold on. There's no need for that. Simon's here now. We'll make the best of it."

Joe wasn't willing to let it go quite so easily. "You don't expect this marriage to last, do you? Because I can tell you right now it won't."

For a second, Gail wished she'd be able to prove him wrong. But that was crazy. Under normal circumstances, Simon wouldn't have given her the time of day. No doubt, once he had Ty back, he'd return to Hollywood and all the women who'd throw themselves at him—and forget about her. He was with her for Ty's sake, and only for Ty's sake. He'd made that clear from the beginning.

"Maybe it won't," she admitted. "But that's okay."

"No, it's not," her father argued. "You don't want to go through a divorce, Gail."

"It's too late to worry about that! I took the risk when I married him. All I ask is that you don't make my life or my marriage any more difficult by rejecting my husband."

Her words met with silence. She'd made an impact, showed them no good could come out of how they were acting. She could tell by the sheepish expression on her brother's face and the stoic one on her father's that they suddenly understood it was too late to talk her out of being with Simon.

"He needs friendship," she went on. "I'm asking you to offer him that and see what you get in return. If you hate him, just be sure you hate him because he's earned it. Don't hate him on principle."

Joe sagged into the seat next to her father and propped his elbows on the table. "You want us to forget what we've heard about him and give him a clean slate."

Intent on her appeal, she sat down again, too. "Why not? You don't even know him! All you know is what you've read and heard in the media."

"And from you," he pointed out.

Her conscience pricked her. "I was wrong to say what I did. I was reacting to…false perceptions. Just like you're doing now. Anyway, can you imagine going to your wife's home and being treated the way he was treated tonight?"

Joe toyed with the sugar bowl sitting on the table. "I

know what that's like. My in-laws hated me because I wasn't interested in their religion."

"Exactly."

"You always did know how to make me feel like shit," he muttered.

She managed a halfhearted grin. "We're siblings. That's my job."

Her father got up to pour himself some coffee. "So tell me this, Gail. If the two of you are so in love, why are you here in Whiskey Creek and not on some extravagant honeymoon celebrating your marriage?"

She could no longer meet his eyes. "This is about something more important than that."

"Like what?"

The memory of finding Simon on the floor of his wood shop came into sharp focus. After that, a honeymoon hadn't even crossed her mind. She'd just wanted to help him recover. "This home has always been my safe harbor."

Her father's eyes widened. "But it can't be the only place someone who's *that* famous has to go."

"Anywhere else wouldn't have the support he needs. This is the best place *I* know. The one I trust. I want him to have the peace of mind you've both given me. *That's* why I brought him here."

After setting his cup on the table, her father came over to crouch in front of her. "He's not a stray dog, Gail," he said, taking her hands. "He's a wealthy movie star who'll probably break your heart—"

"If he does…he does. He's human, Dad. And he's

going through hell. Sure, he's asked for a lot of it but everyone screws up now and then. He needs a way to break his fall. I'm trying to give him that."

Another silence descended as he considered her words.

"Fine." Her brother relented first. "I'll be on my best behavior from here on out. You can get us to do anything. I think you know that."

Tears filled her eyes, which surprised her. She hadn't realized this meant so much to her. "Thanks, Joe. Just give him a chance. That's all I ask."

"Okay." Her father squeezed her hands and stood as if that made it official. "Far as I'm concerned, he has a clean slate. But if he hurts you—"

"He can't hurt me, Dad. I know what to expect."

He returned to his coffee. "You just want to help him. That's it."

"That's it." She wasn't sure when her motivation had changed, when she'd become more interested in seeing Simon get back on his feet than in saving her business, but there was no doubt she was far more emotionally committed than she'd been before.

"At least it makes sense to me now," her father said. "But pity is a hell of a reason to marry someone."

It was more than pity. It was sadness over his lost potential, even a little of the hero worship she'd felt for her favorite movie star. She knew that worship was what frightened her family. It frightened her, too. Maybe she'd become disenchanted with him in certain ways, but it was hard to get on an equal footing with an idol.

"Thanks, Dad."

"You're too good for him," her father added when she came around to kiss his cheek. "But I'm willing to give him the opportunity to prove me wrong."

She offered them both a watery smile. She'd known they'd come through for her. They always did. "Thanks."

for several reasons. A DUI would destroy what she was trying to accomplish with his image, not to mention all the worse things that could've happened if he'd been driving while intoxicated. "Gambling's an expensive vice."

"Maybe I should go back to drinking."

"That could cost you even more."

He motioned to the dark, shadowy porch behind her and the swinging chair she'd ignored. "What are you doing out here?"

"Just getting used to being home."

His eyes narrowed in disbelief. "Really?"

"And wondering when you were coming back." She figured she might as well admit it; he'd already guessed she'd been worried.

"You thought I might be breaking the terms of our agreement."

She felt bad for doubting him, but she knew the first few days and weeks were going to be the hardest. And the way her brother had treated him... That could've acted as a trigger. "Yes."

"I almost did," he said, and circumvented her to go inside.

At least he was honest.

Gail waited another fifteen or twenty minutes. She wasn't sure what to say to Simon. One part of her wanted to know which had been more of a temptation—alcohol or women. The other part was too afraid to hear his answer. As Josh had so aptly pointed out, she had no claim on him in an emotional sense. But it still wasn't easy to acknowledge that the man she'd married, for whatever reason, might've been tempted to go home with someone else.

The next two years were going to be even more of a challenge than she'd realized.

When she thought he'd had enough time to go to bed *and* to sleep, she carried her empty cup into the house, rinsed it in the sink and crept up the stairs. The house was quiet and all the lights were off. She didn't turn any on because she didn't want to wake her father or brother—or Simon, for that matter.

Simon was in bed. She could see the shape of his body in the moonlight streaming through the window. Her room faced the yard, which wasn't really a yard so much as raw land that backed up to the mountain. Without any neighbors around to worry about, she rarely bothered to lower the blinds.

Being as quiet as possible, she yanked off her sweatshirt and slipped under the covers.

But Simon wasn't asleep. When he shifted, she got the impression it was to avoid contact with her, which gave her some idea of how he was feeling. "Something wrong?" she asked.

"I'm not sure I'm going to stay," he said.

She'd been so afraid he'd give up, had felt the tension of that fear, the worry eating at her ever since she'd said, "I do." "Why? What happened tonight?"

"I almost took off, drove to L.A."

Was that what he'd been doing in the car? Thinking about leaving? "I'm sorry if it was my brother who—"

"It wasn't his fault," he broke in. "He has every right to be defensive of you. I'd be defensive, too, if you were my sister."

She fussed nervously with the blanket. "Then what caused the…flight response?"

"I don't see how my involvement in your life can be a good thing."

Releasing the blanket, she curled her arms around her pillow. "Why not?"

"Because it'll end. In two years, just like we planned."

She lifted her head, trying to see his face in the dark. "What makes you think I expect anything else?"

"I'm afraid at some point saving your business won't be enough to compensate for what you'll sacrifice."

"There's more in it for me than that. There's the money, of course. It might not seem like a large sum to you, but it's a fortune to me. Don't get me wrong. I'm earning every penny of it, so I won't feel bad taking it, but…there's that. And it'll be gratifying to see you on your feet again and in control of your life. I feel as if I'm doing America a great service by helping you salvage your career. They want to see more of you in the movies, and so do I."

"But I'm afraid you don't really understand what'll happen on a personal level."

"We spelled everything out in the contract. What else is there to understand?"

"This could get very complicated."

"It's already complicated."

"Not as bad as it will be with time." He rubbed a hand over his face. "This is just the beginning."

"What are you talking about?"

"I'm talking about met and unmet expectations and desires, our developing friendship, the obligations that'll go with it, becoming accustomed to having each other around. I'm talking about jealousy, familiarity, entitlement and all the other ways our lives will become entwined, including relationships we form along the way with the people around us. Our 'deal' sounded simple enough when we made it, even to me. But I didn't really like you then, didn't see myself as *ever* liking you. I certainly didn't anticipate coming to Whiskey Creek and getting to know the people who are closest to you."

"Sometimes you can be too blunt," she said.

"I'm trying to be fair!"

"That's the problem? That's what has you so freaked out? You *like* me?"

"Yes, and you seem to like me."

"I do, but that's good. It means our marriage won't be as miserable as we both thought."

There were a few seconds of silence. "The problem is, I will never *love* you, Gail," he said. "You understand that, right? I don't want to find myself in the same situation I was in with Bella—*ever.* I won't allow another woman to hold that kind of power over me."

She nibbled her lip. He had loved Bella. He was *still* in love with her, just as Gail had expected. "I'm not trying to keep you, Simon."

"I know that. Now. But…what if it changes? What if we make love and—"

"We're not going to make love. I've already told you that. We can keep it simple if we want to. You just worry about staying clean and sober and acting like the dutiful husband in public. I'll take care of myself."

He was staring at her; she could see the shine in his eyes. "I just hope you don't live to regret getting involved with me. I don't want to leave you worse off than when I found you. I have enough on my conscience," he said. Then he rolled over and went to sleep.

When Gail woke up, she had her face pressed to Simon's back. He was wearing a T-shirt and a pair of pajama bottoms, probably because her bed wasn't as big as his and that meant there wasn't much room to avoid each other. But she didn't care about staying on her side at this particular moment. She was too relieved he hadn't left. When she'd finally dropped off into an uneasy sleep she'd worried that he'd be gone by morning.

But he was still here, and it seemed he'd actually stayed in bed and been able to get some rest. She was so happy about those two things that she slid an arm around his waist, gave him a squeeze and kissed his back. "You made it."

"Hmm?" His arm covered hers, holding it in place, but he seemed reluctant to wake.

"Your first night in Whiskey Creek is behind you."

Letting her go, he stretched and turned to face her.

"Once I closed my eyes I didn't even stir. I can't tell you the last time that's happened to me."

She leaned over him, smiling. "It's a sign. Don't you think?"

Reaching up, he tucked her long hair behind one ear. "What kind of sign?"

"That last night you were worried for nothing. You're where you should be. I'm glad you didn't give up."

"I was too exhausted to drive, anyway."

He could never take any credit when he did something right. That would destroy his bad-boy image. But she was so proud of him she couldn't help bending her head to kiss his whisker-roughened cheek. "We can both get everything we want—as friends."

"You're becoming pretty comfortable with me," he said as she pulled away.

"We like each other now, remember?"

His gaze dipped to her braless chest. "I think I'm liking you a little too much."

"Meaning…"

"What do you have against friends with benefits?"

She made a face. "Quit pretending. Last night you acted as if sex between us would be a terrible thing."

"It would be. But that doesn't mean I don't want it."

"Sorry. We can be affectionate but not intimate. That's how we'll get through the next two years."

He covered his eyes with one arm. "Sounds safe— but boring."

Now that he wasn't watching her, she let her gaze range over him. He was so attractive—even with the imprint of the bedding on his cheek and his hair mussed. She loved the rough-hewn angles of his face, the smoothness of his golden skin, the thickness of his unruly hair.

"You like what you see?"

She felt herself blush. "So I was looking. Big deal. You're handsome. Everyone knows that."

"Don't worry. In case you haven't heard, it's only skin-deep."

She'd believed that once, but not anymore. He had plenty of good qualities. One of them was an active conscience. Who knew?

"Fine. Then I won't be tempted. *Safe* is our new buzzword," she said, and hopped out of bed.

His biceps bulged as he propped up his head with his arms. "Are you really getting up?"

"We both are."

"Why? It's early."

"We have a coffee date."

He watched as she searched through her suitcase. *"We?"*

"As in...both of us?"

"That's the 'we' I thought you meant. Who are we meeting?"

"The friends I grew up with."

"What time?" He didn't sound particularly enthusiastic.

She glanced at the clock. It was 7:10. "In twenty minutes."

Sprawling across the bed, he shoved his head under her pillow. "Can't we put it off for an hour or two?"

"I wish. There's no time to even shower. But...unlike us, they have to work."

"How many people are we talking about?" His voice was muffled, but she could understand him.

"Depends. It's a standing date for anyone who can come."

"Do your friends know you're back? Are they expecting you?"

She came up with some black jeans, a pair of gorgeous leather boots and a turquoise sweater she'd bought with Simon's credit card at the mall. It was an attractive outfit—one that made the most of a slender figure. Maybe she'd known these people for years and their opinion wasn't likely to change, but she wanted to look decent. She certainly didn't want her husband to outshine her, although that was pretty much a given.

"No. My dad's the only person I told," she said. "And he's the one person in this town you can trust to keep what you tell him quiet. Everyone except Joe is on a 'need to know' basis." Callie had tried to reach her several times, but except for a few texts saying she was happy and not to ruin it for her, she hadn't responded. She hadn't been ready to deal with Callie's reaction to the news of her marriage. But she'd be doing that this morning—with all her friends.

Checking over her shoulder to make sure Simon still had his head under the pillow, she faced the corner to change. But a second after her tank top hit the floor, the clarity of his voice indicated he was looking right at her.

"Okay, that's going too far."

She glanced at him again. He was watching her with predatory interest. The intensity of his expression lit a fire inside her, but she did her best to shrug it off. "Surely you've seen a woman's bare back before."

"I don't think I've ever seen one as tempting as yours."

"Getting desperate already?" She laughed to let him know she wasn't convinced he was remotely sincere, and he didn't argue with her. But when he spoke again, the gruff edge to his voice left no question as to how her near-nudity affected him.

"Turn around."

It was a challenge, a command. She told herself she'd be crazy to respond. They'd just gone over all the reasons they had to be careful not to let their situation get too complicated. But categorizing their relationship as affectionate friends somehow took the pressure off. It made her feel safe, as if she could relax a little now that they'd recommitted themselves to the rules.

"Just for a second," he coaxed.

He *did* sound desperate. And she *was* tempted. Especially when she considered that over the course of the next two years they'd probably see each other in various stages of undress all the time. It wouldn't be a catastrophe if he caught a glimpse of her now, would it?

Telling herself to lighten up and do something wild and exciting for a change, she hesitated. She'd always been too conservative, and she'd never felt more like a stereotypical librarian than since she'd started hanging out with Simon.

Innocent. Straitlaced. Inflexible. Those were the words Simon had used to describe her....

Determined to shake him up a bit, she turned while she had the nerve.

His expression was worth it. She'd shocked him—just as she'd intended.

"God," he whispered as his gaze latched onto her breasts.

She didn't stick around long enough to find out what he might say or do next. Suddenly willing to risk having her brother or father catch her sneaking into the bathroom to change, she put on her sweater, grabbed her bra and jeans and fled.

That was a mistake.

It took Simon all of ten minutes to get his heart rate to return to normal. He should never have baited Gail. He'd mostly been teasing when he'd thrown out that challenge, had done it to see how she might react. She was so prim and proper; it was fun just to make her blush.

Never had he expected her to turn and show him her breasts....

And now he couldn't get the vision out of his mind.

She'd certainly gotten the last laugh in that encounter.

She knocked softly, then opened the door and poked her head through. "You coming?"

"Gail…" he started.

She raised her eyebrows. "What?"

She was pretending it had never happened. Considering what they'd discussed last night, it was probably best if he did, too.

"Never mind," he said. "I'll be right there."

17

For all of Whiskey Creek's old-fashioned charm, the coffee shop felt current. It listed the menu on a chalkboard, boasted of selling only fair-trade coffee, used organic beans and offered chai and other options. Several people sat with laptops at small round tables, taking advantage of the free Wi-Fi.

"Now *this* feels like home." Simon breathed deep, enjoying the comforting scent of fresh-ground coffee as the door swept shut behind them.

Gail didn't respond. She was too busy searching the crowd.

She waved to a group sitting in one of two large booths. "There they are. Over in the corner. Looks like…" She angled her head to see them all. "Ted, Eve, Callie, Cheyenne, Riley and…oh, boy. Sophia."

"What's wrong with Sophia?" Simon asked.

She lowered her voice. "No one likes her."

"Maybe no one will like me, either."

"Don't worry." She patted his back. "This won't be as painful as you're expecting."

"Why would I expect it to be painful? Meeting your family was such fun."

She nudged him. "Stop with the sarcasm."

Her friends quickly spotted her.

"Oh, my gosh! Gail's home!"

"Where?"

"Look...and she's brought Simon!"

"Here we go," she murmured. "I hope your acting's up to par."

He wished he hadn't left his sunglasses behind. He didn't care if it was too dark inside the café to bother with them. The world he was living in since Gail had started this latest PR campaign felt so much more up-close and in his face. "Hey, I'm a pro, remember?"

By that point, everyone in the coffee shop had turned to stare. But Simon was used to attracting attention. Pretending not to notice, he waited for Gail to order, then asked for an espresso. She hurried over to her friends while he paid, leaving him to approach them on his own, but she'd been right. Joining the group wasn't nearly as awkward as he'd initially feared, once the suddenness of their marriage had been handled and they moved on to other topics.

Fortunately, these people weren't as obvious in their disapproval as Gail's brother and father had been. A few of them sent Simon sidelong glances, as if they weren't sure what to make of his presence, but they smiled politely if he caught their eye and shifted their attention—to whoever was speaking or their coffee or fruit and yogurt.

As they chatted about this or that, Simon was more than happy to kick back and enjoy his espresso. He liked watching Gail, he realized, liked how animated and expressive she was, especially now that she was in her element. Of course, he also liked recalling the image of her standing in the bedroom this morning, wearing nothing but her pajama bottoms as she turned to face him—

"Ted's an author," Gail explained, cutting into his thoughts.

Simon had lost the thread of the conversation. Sitting up, he cleared his throat and attempted to pretend otherwise. "What kind of books does he write?"

"Thrillers. Already has two out."

With that enthusiastic lead-in, Simon expected Ted to ask for the usual favor. Hundreds of authors sent their work to his production company, hoping to gain interest in a movie adaption. But to Simon's relief, the conversation moved on to another guy, someone by the name of Kyle Houseman, who wasn't there. Kyle was going through a nasty divorce. It soon became apparent that everyone blamed his wife.

Simon guessed he was the only one in the group who felt sorry for the maligned soon-to-be ex. He knew how being "the problem" felt. He also knew that a divorce was never as clear-cut as it appeared.

After the talk of Kyle's divorce, a woman with black hair and a widow's peak—Eve Something—spoke up. "What would you guys think if I started a new marketing campaign for the B and B focusing on those scary stories we used to pass around as kids?"

"The ones where we claimed the inn was haunted?" This was Sophia. Simon had noticed that every time she tried to contribute, everyone else immediately stiffened.

"Last I heard, you wanted to keep a lid on the history of the place for fear of scaring off patrons," she said.

Eve shrugged in response but wouldn't quite meet her gaze. "That's true, but…times have changed. I need to try a more aggressive approach."

All of these people were attractive, Simon thought. Sophia, with her wide blue eyes, brown hair and porcelain skin, was probably the prettiest, but he wasn't as taken with her looks as he would've expected to be. He returned his attention to Eve of the widow's peak. "You own A Room with a View?"

She blushed as if she was surprised he'd get involved in the conversation. "No. The other B and B—the Gold Nugget Inn. It's not quite as nice or as prominently situated."

"It *is* nice," Gail chimed in. "But Simon hasn't seen it." She turned to him. "Eve's parents bought it just after they were married and fixed it up, so it's been in her family for years. It's around the bend, heading out of town to the north. Cheyenne—" she motioned to her other friend "—helps run it. I'll show it to you later."

Riley entered the conversation. Gail had introduced him as her contractor friend, so Simon had made a special note of his name. "Do you think that story we used to tell is true? About the young daughter of the couple who built the Gold Nugget being murdered in the basement?"

"It is." Cheyenne contributed this remark. She'd been listening quietly, seemed to hang on every word, but she came across as the type who typically kept her thoughts to herself. "When we first moved to town my mother dragged me and my sister into the cemetery and said if we didn't take good care of her while she was sick, the same evil that got little Mary Hatfield would come after us."

"That's so out of line." This came from Callie, the only member of the group who seemed unwilling to accept Simon. She'd frowned when they were introduced and bristled whenever he looked at her. "But knowing her, it doesn't surprise me," she added.

"You were in high school when you moved here," Gail said to Cheyenne. "I hope you knew better than to believe her."

Cheyenne's somber gray eyes focused on Gail. "I absolutely believed her. There was no telling what she might do."

"That was so unnecessary," Ted put in.

"Exactly," Eve agreed. "They would've taken care of her. Look at them now that the cancer is back."

"She's my mother," Cheyenne said. "What else can I do? Anyway, I don't want to talk about Anita. We were talking about the inn."

"Tell them what you found at the library, Chey," Eve prompted.

"You tell them," she responded, but Gail joined Eve in prodding her.

"What'd you find?"

Cheyenne stirred the whipped cream into whatever drink she'd ordered—hot chocolate?—as she began to speak. "When Eve first mentioned the idea, I went down to the county library and researched the story. I found an old newspaper article dated August 1, 1898, that said the girl's father came upon her strangled in the basement."

Ted nodded. "That's the same story I heard. They never figured out who did it."

"I used to be so afraid of seeing Mary's ghost," Eve said.

"And you want to use that tragedy for marketing purposes?" Callie looked horrified. "Don't you think that's kind of…morbid?"

Eve shrugged. "It is but, like I said, I've got to do something."

"That'll be taking things in a new direction, all right," Riley said with a laugh.

It was obvious that Eve didn't appreciate his attitude.

"Will you change the name, too?" Sophia wanted to know. "All Hallows Inn would be chilling."

Slumping in her seat, Eve played with a sugar packet. "I'm willing to do anything. The place needs updating and repairs, and I don't have the money. I don't want to lose it to the bank. So I'll have to get creative. If I make the wear-and-tear part of the theme, I might be able to limp along for another year or two until I can get on my feet."

"Makes sense to me." Gail reached across the table to squeeze her hand. "When you're ready, I'll help you put together a press packet so we can get the word out."

Eve smiled her thanks.

"I don't know...." Riley wasn't convinced. "Might be too gimmicky, Eve."

"I disagree," Cheyenne piped up. "I think we should do it."

Everyone seemed surprised that she would argue with him.

"There's so much interest in the supernatural," she went on. "We should hire some good fortune tellers and offer free tarot readings on check-in, really go with the theme."

Eve turned her attention to Simon. "What do you think?"

Simon hadn't expected to be singled out when he was the least likely to have an opinion. He searched his mind for some useful idea. "Well, if you want to go in a darker direction...I could come up with some interesting props from various films that might add an Alfred Hitchcock air to the place."

She perked up. "That's a great suggestion! But... won't real movie props be expensive?"

"They don't have to be," he said. "I happen to know some people in the industry." He heard a few chuckles at the understatement. "I'll see what I can arrange."

"That's *so* nice." Eve looked at Gail as if to say she

liked him, and Gail smiled, but the atmosphere grew tense as soon as someone mentioned a guy named Matt.

"Have you seen him yet?" Ted asked Gail.

Everyone fell silent. Clearly, they'd all been dying to ask the same question.

Gail poured more cream into her coffee even though she didn't usually take very much. "No, not yet. We just got in last night."

"He's been here a couple days already," Sophia said. "I saw him at Just Like Mom's last night."

"How does he look?" someone else wondered.

Eve answered. "Better than ever."

"What about his knee?" Gail asked.

"He's wearing a brace, but he's walking on it," Ted told her.

Gail added even more cream to her coffee. "Will he ever get to play again?"

"Hard to say," Riley replied. "No one knows."

Simon's gaze circled the group. Normally he would've let this go, as he had the talk about Kyle Houseman. But there was a definite undercurrent here, and it seemed to be swirling around Gail. "Matt is…"

Gail seemed eager to answer before anyone else could. "Just another friend."

"He plays football for the Packers, when he's not injured," Eve said.

"He's part of the group?" Simon asked, trying to clarify.

"Not really." This came from Eve again. "I mean…

he's not one of the original members. We all graduated the same year. Matt's three years older."

"He's a *great* guy." When Callie said this as if he was the perfect contrast to Simon, Gail made a point of checking the time.

"Whoa, don't some of you need to be at work?"

"Yeah, Chey and I are already late," Eve agreed. "Jane's there cooking breakfast, but she'll need us to help serve."

Everyone stood. As they cleared the table of plates and cups, Callie pulled Gail aside, but Simon could hear what she said.

"What the hell are you doing?"

Gail met Simon's eyes over her friend's head. "Nothing, why?"

"I can't believe you married him. Already! Didn't you think we'd want to know you were that serious before seeing it on TV?"

"I told you we were dating."

"Dating's a little different, Gail."

"We didn't plan it, Callie. We just…decided to do it. It happened very quickly."

"I'm sure it did. Let's hope you don't end up brokenhearted and divorced just as quickly." Callie whirled around to glare at Simon. "Nice of you to come and meet the family, even if it is too late for us to talk her out of ruining her life."

"I didn't realize we needed to get your approval," he responded dryly.

Callie turned back to Gail and said something else

18

"You just met six of my friends. And you want to talk about one who wasn't even there?" she said as she put on her seat belt.

This was clearly a deflection. But Simon allowed it. For the moment. "Okay, let's talk about Sophia." He buckled his own belt. "Why did you refuse her invitation to dinner?"

"I didn't refuse it. I said I'd call."

He started the car. "Will you?"

"I don't know."

"Why?" he asked as he shifted into Reverse.

She blew out a sigh. "I'm having a hard time forgiving her."

"For?"

Facing the window as he backed out of the parking space, she waved at Ted, who was climbing into his SUV. "A lot of reasons."

"We're here for three months. I think you've got time to explain."

"It's old gossip," she said as if it didn't matter, but obviously it did, or she wouldn't be holding a grudge.

They reached the exit, where he waited for an opening in traffic. "Everyone else knows, right?"

"Of course. There are no secrets in Whiskey Creek."

"Then you might as well fill me in."

"Fine." She turned off the radio. "Back when we were in high school, her father was the mayor. She was an only child and very spoiled. She was also the most popular girl in school and dated Scott Harris, the best basketball player Eureka High has ever seen." Her voice softened. "Scott was Joe's best friend. And he was like another brother to me."

Simon merged onto Main Street: Speed Limit 25. Just as well he hadn't brought the Ferrari. "This story doesn't feel like it's going in a good direction."

"No. He lost his life in a drunk-driving accident, and most people here blame Sophia."

He winced. "Including you."

"Maybe. To a point," she said, obviously not wanting to commit herself. "It's hard *not* to blame her."

A bicyclist swerved around the corner. Simon swung wide to make room. "What happened?"

"He was expecting her to join him at a party one night, but she didn't come. When someone mentioned that she'd been seen with another guy earlier in the day, he took off to find her, even though he was far too drunk to get behind the wheel."

"No one tried to stop him?"

"Of course. He pretended to change his mind, then

slipped out when the rest of us relaxed and stopped paying attention."

Simon could guess what happened next. "He crashed?"

"Wound up in a ditch. It was too late by the time the paramedics arrived."

"I'm sorry."

She seemed lost in the memory. "He would've made a wonderful husband and father, had he been given the chance."

"*Was* she with someone else?" he asked as they came to a red light. He couldn't help wondering.

"She claims she wasn't and no one's stepped up to say, 'I'm the other guy.' There have been rumors, though."

"Of course. It's a small town. But blaming her for his drinking and driving is like blaming Bella for my bad behavior. Last I checked I don't get to do that."

She studied him. "You haven't even tried."

Because it felt too much like cheating. He had his faults but blaming others for his actions wasn't one of them.

"Come to think of it, you should be commended for that," she added.

Surprised by her concession, he glanced over to make sure she was serious. When he saw that she was, he shrugged. "So I have one redeeming feature."

Her lips curved into a smile. "You've got a few others."

A dose of sexual awareness warmed his blood. "Feel

free to elaborate," he said, tempting her to flirt a little more, but she backed off.

"I think you know what they are."

The light turned green. "If you're talking about my looks, I'm not particularly flattered. I had no control over the face I was given."

"You've worked hard for that body."

"All part of the job. But I'm glad you noticed."

She scowled. "I've also noticed how easy it is for you to light up a room, how fast you neutralized all the people who should've been defensive of me. They fell for your charm almost immediately."

He got stuck behind someone in an SUV who was waiting for a parking spot on the street. "Really? Because Callie seemed completely immune."

"She'll come around."

Maybe. Maybe not. She'd seemed pretty unhappy. "What was that bit about Cheyenne and her mother?"

"Anita's a piece of work. You wouldn't believe what Cheyenne has been through. When she and her sister were little, her mother dragged them from one town to the next. They lived out of cars or in cheap motels. She didn't even go to school until she moved here, and by then she was fourteen!"

The people who owned the Jetta in the parking space the SUV wanted began the process of loading up, but they had a baby and a toddler to strap in, and a stroller to contend with. "How did she fare?"

"Not as badly as you'd think. She'd taught herself a lot by then, is naturally very smart. But it took most of high school for her to catch up. And, of course, she didn't get the chance to go to college, like the rest of us."

"Her name's unusual."

"She thinks she was named after Cheyenne, Wyoming."

"One of the cities they passed through."

"You guessed it. Who knows where she'd be right now if Anita hadn't gotten sick? That's the only reason they settled down."

"A haunted B and B, someone who didn't start school until the age of fourteen, a woman blamed for the death of a local sports hero… You have an interesting group of friends."

"And everyone knows too much about everyone else, like I told you before."

"I guess that's the downside of living in such a small place," he said. "No one can forget. No one can forgive."

"Publicity has made the whole world that small for you."

That was one of his problems. The other was that he didn't seem to be the best judge of character. Had he been able to detect the deep reservoir of insecurity that lurked beneath Bella's beautiful face he would've had some inkling of what he was getting himself into. But he'd been oblivious. Or maybe Bella was right— and he'd somehow created her insecurity. To him, it seemed as if he'd tried *everything* to convince her he loved her. He *had* loved her, more than he'd ever loved anyone—other than Ty. She just couldn't believe it for any length of time, had to make him prove it over and over and over.

Finally, the Jetta pulled into the street and the SUV took its place. "Tell me this," he said.

"What?"

"If Sophia knows she's not wanted, why did she show up at the coffee shop?"

"The news that we got married has been flying around." She put a piece of gum in her mouth. "Maybe she was hoping we'd be there."

It hadn't felt as if she'd come to gawk at him. He'd gotten the impression that she was honestly trying to make friends, maybe even make amends, but who was he to say? He'd just met her. "Tell the truth. You were tempted to feel sorry for her because she looked so depressed when you waffled on dinner."

"No, I wasn't. She did a lot of other things I haven't told you about. As far as I'm concerned, if people don't want to have dinner with her it's because she deserves it," Gail said, but he could tell she was torn.

They had to stop at the next red light, too. Simon felt annoyed by the pace of life here—until he realized there was no point in hurrying. For once the world wasn't going to fall apart if he didn't make it to a certain place by a certain time. And he had nothing to fear about being out in the open. There were no paparazzi, no cameras, no Bella and no reporters with uncomfortable questions. He wasn't even afraid of being recognized, because being recognized here didn't turn into an embarrassing worship session. These people just sort of stared and murmured, then glanced at their toes if he caught them gawking.

The light turned green, so he gave the car some gas. "Okay, now tell me about Matt."

She let her head fall against the seat. "We're back to him?"

"Is there someone else you want to talk about first?"

"Not if it won't distract you."

The Jetta he'd been following turned, and he came up on a Prius that was barely creeping along, looking for a parking place—obviously more tourists out to visit the shops on Sutter Street. "He's *that* big a deal to you?" Simon said. If so, why hadn't she ever mentioned him? He would've expected that information to come out *before* they got married.

"He's a professional football player. That makes him a big deal to everyone, at least around here."

She'd taken the personal element out of his question, so he put it back in. "I want to know what he means to *you*."

"Nothing. We went out once last summer. That's it."

Although she tried to shrug it off, Simon didn't believe he'd misunderstood what he'd sensed at the coffee shop. "Then why does everyone seem so interested in your reaction to him?"

"I couldn't tell you."

The Prius found a car with some people who looked like they might be loading up, but they were only storing their packages. "You're a terrible liar," Simon said. "Has anyone ever told you that?"

"I'm not lying…exactly."

"Then what are you hiding? Did you sleep with him?"

Her hesitation told him he'd hit somewhere not far from the truth.

"You don't have to conceal any indiscretions from me," he reminded her. "I'm pretty much the poster boy for sin, remember?"

"I didn't sleep with him."

"But…"

"We went out once and came close."

"Aha! Here we go. So he's your local love interest and everyone knows it."

"No one knows anything, because nothing really happened. It was one date. So he's not a…*love* interest, per se."

At last the Prius found a spot. "You're not head over heels," Simon said.

"No."

They reached the turnoff to her father's. "Tell me where we're going."

"Home, to shower and get ready for the day. I want to check our media hits and see what Josh has arranged with *People* on our wedding pics. Then we'll contact Kathy and see when she has time to show us whatever rentals are available."

Still intrigued by her self-conscious reaction to his questions about Matt, he returned to the same subject. "Has he called you since the big night? Was he expecting to see you again?"

"What does it matter?"

"Maybe I want to be sure you'll keep your end of our marriage contract, now that *you're* the one facing temptation."

She folded her arms, which made her look even more prim than usual. "Give me a break. You have nothing to worry about. It's always been a very one-sided crush. I mean…not crush. Brief infatuation."

"*It's* is present tense," he pointed out. "And *always* isn't brief."

Her face turned red. "Can we drop it, please?"

She was getting flustered….

He pulled into the driveway, to the far left, just in case her father or brother returned. Their vehicles were gone—thank God—which meant he was going to get a reprieve from the we-hate-Simon vibes that had bombarded him yesterday. "I just want to be sure I'm not holding you back."

"You're not."

After putting the transmission in Park, he cut the engine. "You've got feelings for Matt. I can tell."

"No."

"What do you see in him?"

She opened her door. "Callie already told you—he's a nice guy."

He came around to meet her. "And I'm not. She made the distinction very clear. Which brings me back to Callie—what do you see in *her*?"

"Don't hold the way she acted at the coffee shop

against her. She'll warm up to you. She's just being protective."

"She's being judgmental. Hasn't she ever done anything wrong?"

"Most people haven't crashed and burned quite as publicly as you have. You have that going against you."

"Such is the price I pay for being rich and famous." It was a glib response, designed to cover how it felt to have his every mistake and shortcoming advertised to the public. If not for that added dimension, maybe he wouldn't have become so determined to prove he'd do exactly as he pleased, regardless of the world's shock and recrimination. To a certain extent, the worst of his behavior was simply his way of giving the world—and everyone who judged him—the finger.

"Are you sorry you didn't have sex with Matt while you had the chance?"

Clearly, she wanted to be done with this conversation, so it took him off guard when she suddenly stopped and whirled around. "Yes," she said in exasperation. "I am. Especially now that I'm getting paid *not* to have sex for the next two years."

He put a hand to his chest as if she'd just wounded him. "Who's paying you not to have sex?"

"Our marriage will fall apart the second we cross that line, and you know it."

The stubborn glint in her eyes offered an irresistible challenge. Gail was so…normal. That was one of the things he liked most about her. She kept problems in perspective and demanded he do the same. Since she'd taken charge, his life had begun to make sense again.

But she was also a bit starchy, and that made her fun to bait. "I'm willing to compromise in that area," he said. "I'll give you a night off from our deal if you'll give me one." He adopted a sultry tone. "Think about it…all that pent-up desire could be unleashed on your old crush."

Oddly enough, he didn't want her to accept, but he was curious whether or not she'd be tempted by the offer. That alone would tell him how important this Matt the Football Player was.

She didn't take the bait. Grabbing his shirtfront, she tried to yank him toward her. When she couldn't budge him, and he started chuckling at her efforts, she stood on her tiptoes so she could come nose to nose with him instead. "Don't mistake the tranquil setting here in Whiskey Creek for privacy or anonymity. *Everyone's* watching. You do one thing wrong in this town and you can say goodbye to making yourself remotely respectable." She let go and brushed the wrinkles out of his shirt. "And I'd rather you didn't make a fool of me in front of the home crowd, if you get my meaning."

He lowered his gaze to her lips. She was so close he could smell the mint of her chewing gum. If he kissed her, he'd probably taste it, too. "I guess that leaves us with only one alternative."

"And that is?"

Tilting her chin up, he brought his mouth within a hairbreadth of hers. "You can't guess?"

"Sure I can." Shoving his good hand up against his crotch, she said, "Have fun," and walked away.

Apparently she'd had enough of his teasing. But something about her reaction to her old flame triggered an unpleasant response in him.

It couldn't be jealousy, he told himself. It had to be wounded pride. He wasn't used to being upstaged.

Unwilling to let her have the last word, he called after her, "You're supposed to want *me*. *I'm* the movie star!" as if he was the egotistical ass so many of the tabloids described.

"Some women prefer professional athletes to self-absorbed movie stars," she retorted, and when she reached the stoop, she tossed a taunting smile over her shoulder. "You should see how *big* Matt is."

Simon felt his eyebrows jerk together. "You're talking about height, aren't you?"

No answer. She was trying to unlock the door.

He strode over to the porch. "You can't compare what you haven't seen. To be fair we should go into the bedroom and check it out. I'm not afraid of a little competition."

"I want a divorce," she grumbled as she finally got the door open.

Trying not to laugh, he swatted her bottom. "I seem to have that effect on women."

Bringing a movie star home to Whiskey Creek wasn't turning out like Gail had imagined. Her father and brother had reacted as defensively as she'd thought they would but, except for Callie, her friends had not. Probably because she and Simon were already married. Considering that, there wasn't much anyone could do to warn her away.

Still, she'd anticipated a bit more…concern.

At breakfast, her old school chums had looked as if they couldn't believe her situation had changed so drastically, but she'd talked about the people on her client roster enough in the past that they associated her with a lot of big names. They were more surprised to have Simon O'Neal sitting at coffee with *them*. She'd never brought anyone home before, let alone an actor of his stature, and they were understandably flustered.

But, interestingly enough, they didn't seem to blame her for marrying him. The guys took it for granted that Simon would be able to have anyone he wanted, even her, regardless of what he'd done. And her girlfriends harbored no illusions that they would've refused him had he shown interest in any of them. So there'd been no frowns, no head shaking, no "what the hell were you thinking?" when they got together this morning. Everyone had been too busy trying to acclimate to having Simon around. Gail had almost laughed out loud as all but Callie succumbed easily to his potent charm.

That grin of his was like a slow-acting poison, she decided. It wasn't lethal but it could certainly incapacitate a woman. It entered at the eyes and jammed up certain frequencies of the brain, making the victim susceptible to almost any suggestion Simon made. That had to be the reason she'd been stupid enough to flash him this morning, even though she didn't want to be compared to his many other women, didn't want to become his temporary antidote to grief, didn't want to be just another meaningless lay. She already knew her self-esteem couldn't take it.

He'd win Callie over eventually, too. Callie was only holding out because she'd cautioned Gail not to get involved with him, and had been ignored. Callie couldn't swoon at his feet the second he walked into town or she'd look ridiculous.

"Hey, what's taking so long?" Simon called up.

Apparently he was off the phone with Ian, who'd been expounding on the difficulties of getting Simon out of his next movie. She could hear the TV but Simon's conversation seemed to have ended several minutes ago, probably around the time she'd finished reading all the blogs and articles posted about them on the web.

"Just handling a few details," she called back.

"How are we looking? Am I coming off as innocent? Reformed?"

"America hasn't gotten that far yet. Everyone's in shock."

"I still have the ability to shock people?"

She couldn't help laughing, despite the fact that she was wounded by so many of the comments she'd read. Being realistic about her own limitations was one thing. Reading so many snarky reasons he should've chosen someone better was another.

"They're calling me Plain Jane," she said.

"They don't know you," he responded.

Nice try. "That comment doesn't refer to my personality."

When she heard his tread on the stairs, she was about to turn off her computer. It'd been hard enough to read these remarks when she was alone. But he'd only demand she turn it on and show him some of the press. He had a right to be interested.

"Who's been writing about us?" he asked as he entered the room.

"'Perez Hilton,' 'Hot Hollywood Gossip,' all the usual celeb sites."

"'Hollywood Hunk Marries Plain Jane,'" he read over her shoulder. "The *hunk* part is pretty accurate."

She knew he was trying to soften the blow by making it into a joke, but that didn't help. She said nothing, just clicked on the other sites she'd seen so he could continue to skim through the headings.

"'Box Office Hit Simon O'Neal Ties the Knot… What's Simon O Thinking?… Simon O'Neal's Latest Debacle… The Real Cinderella… Big Hit PR Scores and So Does Its Owner, but for How Long?'"

"Looks like they're buying it," he said.

"Of course they're buying it. I may be plain but I'm good at what I do." She could at least take pride in that.

"Come on." He rested his hands on her shoulders and kneaded the tense muscles there. "I'll bet you anything that was written by a woman."

"John McWhorter would be an odd name for a woman."

"So a gay guy. A jealous gay guy. It's possible. I've gotten love letters from guys before."

"It doesn't matter." She really felt that way. She'd known what she'd be up against coming in to this. Known that everything would be criticized, especially her.

And yet…it wasn't pleasant to know that the world found her lacking as Simon's wife. This morning, when she'd flashed Simon, the way he'd looked at her had made her feel drop-dead gorgeous. No other man had ever made her feel so intoxicated with desire.

But Simon was out to get laid, and she'd made herself his only quarry. He was probably using all his acting skill in the hopes of achieving sexual gratification. Considering how beautiful Bella was, he couldn't have been as impressed as he seemed.

"That's what you've been doing up here this whole time?" he asked. "Reading all this negative crap about yourself?"

"I have to know what's being said or I won't know what we need to do to enhance or combat it."

He didn't seem pleased. "Why do people have to have an opinion on everything I do? Can't they just enjoy my movies and leave it at that? Close up and let's go."

"I haven't been crying over it, if that's what you think." She stopped him when he tried to shut down her browser. "I've been answering email."

That was true. She'd had to check on Big Hit, see what was going on with the new pitches and assure herself that Josh and Serge were covering for her in her absence. Josh had written, telling her not to read any of the blogs, that he'd keep track of their buzz, which should've warned her, but she'd had to look.

"Any word from *People?*" Simon asked.

"We have a two-million-dollar offer."

"Hold out for three."

"That's what I told Josh."

He kept rubbing her shoulders, but she didn't like that he was doing it because he felt sorry for her. "What about Kathy Carmichael? Have you reached her?"

"Not yet. I left her a message."

"What's happening at your office?"

"We're being deluged with calls. A lot are from media interested in getting whatever scoop they can on us, but there are others who are potential clients. Josh thinks we should hire two more publicists."

"Do you agree?"

She was surprised he'd ask. What did he care about her PR business? "We have to be able to grow quickly enough to accommodate our sudden popularity. And I don't want the quality to suffer. That would ruin my brand. So, yeah, I told him to do it. Maybe it's the news of our marriage that's bringing business to Big Hit, but only hard work will keep that business, especially after you and I split up."

"Are you okay with missing all the fun?"

Gail hated feeling so removed from what she'd created. She was too used to standing at the helm. But she had enough challenges right here, she reminded herself. One of those challenges was not moaning at the pleasure his fingers were giving her with his massage. Another was making sure her soft spot for him didn't get any larger. "I'm on assignment."

"And you'll see it through."

"Of course."

The rubbing stopped for a moment as he saluted her. "That's your brand, too."

"That's my personality."

He stared at her for several seconds.

"What?" she asked, growing self-conscious.

"You're right. It is your personality. You're responsible, dependable."

Although that sounded like it was meant as a compliment, being responsible and dependable wasn't flattering enough to counteract the negative comments she'd just read. It wasn't like being told she was gorgeous or sexy or charismatic, like he was. But she figured the world could use a few more dependable people. Lord knew she dealt with enough who weren't. "Be careful. I might get a big head—like yours," she said with a laugh.

He started to rub again. "I *like* responsible and dependable."

She watched him in the mirror of her dresser. "Sure you do. Being responsible and dependable is almost as good as being conscientious and trustworthy."

"You're not flattered."

"No."

His hands stilled. "Okay. Would you believe me if I said you have the prettiest tits I've ever seen?"

He was getting a lot closer to the things a woman really wanted to hear—even someone as practical, responsible and conscientious as her. But he couldn't be serious. She was barely a C cup. "No."

"Now you know why I didn't bother."

She told herself to let it go at that, but couldn't. "Is it true?" she asked warily.

A sexy smile lifted one corner of his mouth as he bent to whisper in her ear, "I'd be happy to convince you of my sincerity if you'll give me the chance," he said and his hands came around to cup her breasts through her clothes.

The heat of his palms made her nipples tighten. She told herself to get up and step away, but she could only stare at the sight of his dark fingers against her turquoise sweater. "Something must be wrong with me...."

His thumbs moved back and forth, and darts of pleasure raced through her. "No, there's not," he said, his lips against her neck.

She could hardly breathe. She wanted to let those well-sculpted hands delve beneath her top and really touch her. But she was determined to be smart about Simon. "I mean, there must be something wrong with *you* if you think I'm going to fall for that," she said, and knocked his hands away.

She'd thought he'd straighten and laugh it off as if touching her hadn't meant anything to him, anyway. As if it had been some sort of test to see what she'd do. But he didn't. When their eyes met in the mirror, she could plainly read his disappointment.

God, no wonder he could get any female on the planet, she told herself. It wasn't just his celebrity and appearance. There was an emotional honesty about him she found oddly courageous. Maybe he didn't always feel the way she might like him to feel, but he didn't hide the truth.

"What would it hurt?" he murmured. "You're my wife."

He wanted the physical intimacy a regular wife would give him. But he wouldn't be happy if she wanted the emotional intimacy a regular wife would expect in return. "I know you're not used to going without, that it's been a few weeks—"

"Ah, shit. Don't patronize me," he said, and walked out.

Gail sat there for several more minutes. She was waiting for the tingling in her breasts to subside. But every time she thought of Simon touching her with that intense look in his eyes, the sensation came back.

Finally, she told herself to quit being an idiot and went downstairs.

"Should we drive around and see if we can find any for-rent signs?" she asked.

He was sitting on the couch, watching TV, and didn't even bother to look up. "I've decided a for-sale sign would work just as well."

"You want to buy a house?"

"I'm just saying I'll take what I can get."

Of course. He wouldn't want to stay with her father

and brother any longer than necessary, and she couldn't blame him.

"You're mad at me."

"Frustrated," he said.

"Simon—"

"But I don't want to talk about it."

"Fine. Let's just…" She swallowed hard, feeling at a loss because she was frustrated, too, even torn. "Pretend nothing happened," she finished. "Come on."

Picking up the remote, Simon snapped off the TV and followed her through the kitchen. They were just stepping outside when Kathy called.

"Is it true?" the Realtor squealed.

Distracted by Simon, who insisted on driving even though she thought she should probably do it this time, since she knew her way around, Gail didn't immediately understand what Kathy meant. "Is what true?"

"That you married *Simon O'Neal?*"

Sometimes Gail couldn't believe it herself. "Yes."

"Oh, my God!" Kathy shouted. "Oh, my God! Oh, my God!"

"Kathy—"

"What's it like to sleep with him?" she asked.

Gail froze. This was the last question she'd expected from middle-aged, happily married Kathy Carmichael. Simon was so famous, people thought they had some sort of claim on him, which gave them the impression they had the right to ask such personal questions.

Simon had obviously overheard. He glanced up to see what her response would be.

"He's not all he's cracked up to be." She wasn't sure why she said that; she just couldn't stop herself from needling him.

Whatever Kathy said was lost on Gail, who was too focused on Simon.

"You keep saying stuff like that and you're going to *have* to give me the chance to prove you wrong," he told her.

Which was exactly what she wanted him to do. She was just afraid of what might come after. "Kidding!" she told Kathy. "He's amazing, of course. Just looking at him makes me drool." She stuck her tongue out so he wouldn't take that seriously.

"The truth at last," he murmured sarcastically.

"Lord, you and me both, honey," Kathy was saying. "I've seen *Shiver* at least half a dozen times. The way he makes love to Tomica Kansas in that movie is beyond anything I've ever seen. All I have to do is hear the musical score and..." Her voice softened. "Oh, my."

Gail didn't want to think of that movie but the images danced through her brain, anyway. "Don't hold your husband accountable if he can't duplicate that scene," she said. "I'm sure the director had a lot to do with it. And the music. And the magic of make-believe. Sex is never messy on screen."

Simon settled behind the wheel of her car. "Keep talking. You might actually believe it one day."

She couldn't respond to him. Kathy was murmuring, "You're one lucky girl, darlin'. That's all I'm saying."

Eager to change the subject before she had to hear

any more, Gail cleared her throat. "Thanks. Do you know of any places we can rent for three months, Kathy?"

"Only one that's good enough for Simon."

Gail covered the phone. "Did you hear that?"

"Yeah," he said. "Sounds hopeful."

"I'd better not run into this very often," she told him.

He raised a questioning eyebrow.

"The way people gush over you is so ridiculous it makes me sick."

"Is that why you're looking at me as if you'd like to tear my clothes off?"

She gaped at him. How could he see through her so easily? "You're *so* conceited!"

"What did you say?" Kathy asked while he laughed.

She removed her hand from the phone. "Sorry, I was talking to Simon. I told him you have just the place."

"I do," she said. "It's the old Doman mansion. You know it, don't you?"

"Of course. But…that's up for rent?"

"For sale. Why would someone like Simon pay rent, especially in your hometown, where you'll be coming again and again? This is pocket change for him."

That diamond guy had felt he should be able to tell Simon how to spend his money, too. "How much pocket change?"

"Two-point-five million. It's an entire compound, with ten acres and stables and everything."

"We'll take it." Simon was still listening in, but Gail had no interest in buying the old Doman place.

"I'm afraid that won't work," she told Kathy. "It's far more than we're willing to take on. Simon wants to get a piece of land and build us a house, but for now we just need something small and cozy, something temporary and a lot less work."

"Oh." Kathy seemed disappointed.

"If she doesn't have anything small and cozy, we're taking the Doman place," Simon informed Gail.

Gail gestured for him to be quiet.

"Well, in that case—" Kathy hesitated. "Meet me at the office. I can show you a couple of possibilities, but... there's not much on the market right now."

"I understand. We're on our way." With a triumphant smile, Gail hit the end button.

"What's wrong with the Doman place?" Simon asked, scowling. "Kathy seemed to think it would be perfect for me."

Gail fastened her seat belt. "You trust her more than you do me?"

"Hell, yeah," he said. "At least she recognizes a good love scene when she sees one."

"That love scene was...generic," she responded, but it was a lie, and they both knew it. That love scene was one of the best to ever hit the screen. Every time Gail climbed into bed with Simon she had to face the memory of his perfect mouth moving down Tomica Kansas's flat stomach....

His gaze lowered to her breasts. "That's not what your body is telling me."

She resisted the urge to fold her arms over the evidence of her arousal. "I'm not Tomica Kansas." She had to keep the distinction between her, at Plain Jane status, and the femme fatales who starred in his movies clear in her mind.

"You could've been fifteen minutes ago," he said, but he was no longer looking at her. He was checking the road as he backed out of the drive.

19

"This is it?" Simon didn't seem impressed with the house Gail wanted.

"What's wrong with it?" she asked.

He waited until Kathy was out of earshot. She'd gotten a call and was heading to her car for an address. "It's a two-bedroom, one bath that was built in 1880."

"So?"

"It's functionally obsolete."

"No, it's not."

"The only bathroom is in the hall, Gail. And it has a claw-foot bathtub. There isn't even a shower."

She rolled her eyes. "There's a shower head above the tub and a curtain you can pull around."

Obviously he'd seen the makeshift shower. He just didn't think it was an acceptable arrangement. "I don't want to have to stand in one place and turn in a tight circle. The entire bathroom is half the size of a normal closet!"

"By L.A. standards, maybe. But we're not in L.A. anymore."

He gave her a pained look. "I think I'm clear on that."

"We're not going to be here long," she said, trying to convince him. "We can get by with this place, can't we?"

After glancing into both bedrooms and the bathroom again, he sighed. "There has to be something else. This is barely...what did she say? Eight hundred square feet?"

"Eight hundred and seventy-five." She shoved the flyer at him, but he didn't take it.

Crossing his arms, he leaned dejectedly against the wall. "It's the size of my bedroom back home."

"But you heard Kathy. This is our last option. There are no rentals, and we saw the only other houses on the market. Neither of them were as nice."

"That first one was bigger," he grumbled. "We could fix it up."

"It was right in town. We don't want neighbors, do we? Certainly not nosy neighbors, and there isn't any other kind in Whiskey Creek. Here, we'd have some privacy. Better yet, we'd each have our own bedroom."

He turned to face her. "Being told I'll be sleeping alone? That's supposed to convince me?"

She grinned. "Convinces me."

He lowered his voice. "Only because you're *scared*."

"Of what?" she scoffed, but immediately regretted it when he cocked his head as if he had no intention of backing down.

"Of me. Of how much you might enjoy my hands on your body. Of what it might feel like to lose control."

She swallowed hard. "I'm not scared," she lied. "I'm just…not stupid enough to…" To what? To get too comfortable in a marriage that wasn't going to last?

He shot her a sullen glance. "To get involved with me?"

"I'm already involved with you. That's not what I was about to say."

"There's another way of looking at it, you know."

"Which is…"

"My way."

"Let me guess. You think I should let you use me until you're ready to move on."

"I'm offering you two years of endless orgasms. Why reject that out of hand?" He poked her. "You need an orgasm more than any woman I've ever known."

She stepped out of reach. "Quit treating me like I'm frigid!"

He lifted his hands. "Whoa, no need to get defensive. I wasn't implying that."

"But you think it."

"I think you're too uptight. But you have nothing to worry about. I'll take care of you."

He thought she was denying them both for no good reason. But he didn't understand what was at stake. How could he? Maybe sex meant nothing more than a fun time to him, but she wasn't built that way. "I might be uptight but I'm not shortsighted."

"Typically not," he said. "So why are you renting a house with only one bathroom?"

Arguing about sex *and* the number of bathrooms in

their first rental made her feel more married than she'd felt before. "We'll have to share it but…otherwise, this house is perfect."

Hands on his lean hips, he turned in a circle.

"Okay, it's quaint, but quaint is good enough." She drew him back to the living room, with its high ceiling, crown molding and hardwood floors. "Look at this place. Look at the fireplace mantel. It has so much character."

"I like the porch," he admitted, gazing through the gigantic front windows with the diamond-shaped cut-glass inserts above them.

"I *love* the porch," she said. "It's almost as big as the living room. Imagine sitting out there with a glass of iced tea as the sun goes down. Summers in Whiskey Creek are so gorgeous. And the kitchen's got potential," she added.

He followed her around the corner. "If someone were to gut it and completely redo it, maybe." He eyed the lime-green cupboards. "These cabinets are hideous."

"It wouldn't be that hard to renovate," she said. "Maybe we should remodel instead of build."

The screen door slammed as Kathy came back in. "So? What do you think?" she asked when she found them, but she had eyes only for Simon. What Gail thought didn't matter.

Simon stared at Gail for several seconds, during which she silently pleaded with him. Then he shifted his attention to Kathy. "We'll take it."

"You want to make an offer?"

"Give them their asking price," he said. "It's not much."

Gail had begun to figure out that Simon was a push-over when it came to money and possessions. She was pretty sure she could get just about anything out of him. His willingness to buy her a half-million-dollar diamond was proof. So she wasn't surprised that he'd let her have the house even though he didn't want it and that he'd agreed to the original price. She was surprised, however, when he leaned over and brushed a kiss across her lips. It was a loving gesture manufactured for Kathy's benefit, of course. They'd been holding hands for most of the day; it was beginning to feel natural. But that kiss. It was nothing, a split second of contact, and yet it stole Gail's breath.

She glanced up to see if he was laughing at her, if he realized how much she'd liked it, but he turned away before she could ascertain what he might be thinking.

"When can we move in?" he asked.

That night Gail made a Caesar salad, pasta and garlic bread. The cream sauce for the pasta had onions and peas and bacon. Simon liked it. But sitting at the table with Martin and Joe DeMarco, who were home from work for the evening, was a silent and awkward affair.

Gail must've said something to them about how they'd treated him so far, because they were on their best behavior. Martin no longer shook his head in disgust whenever he glanced at Simon, and Joe didn't seem so hostile, either. Both men bent their heads over their plates and shoveled in their food as if they were sitting at the table alone.

"Would you like some more garlic bread?" Gail asked Simon.

He looked up from his own plate. "No, thanks."

This polite exchange aside, Simon thought they'd go the whole meal without any conversation. Which was fine with him. He didn't have a lot to say to her family, anyway.

But then Martin wiped his mouth, tossed his napkin on the table and spoke. To *him*.

"What do you think of Whiskey Creek?" he asked.

There was a bottle of Napa Valley wine sitting on the counter. Simon had been given a glass of soda. Gail had poured herself a soda, too. But he could smell the wine from where he sat. "I like it."

"Great place to raise a family."

Was he referring to *his* having raised a family here? Or was he fishing to see if Simon and Gail planned to have children?

Simon supposed it was natural that the old man might hope for another grandchild. But even if they hadn't already made provisions for their divorce, even if he could get Gail to sleep with him, Simon would insist on using some form of birth control. Never again would he hand a woman a weapon as powerful as a child. Love was far too fickle.

"I'd like to bring my son here sometime." He'd sidestepped what he suspected might be the real issue, but he couldn't be faulted for what he'd said.

Joe nodded. "I was wondering if we'd get to meet him. My daughters come every other weekend."

Simon twirled another forkful of pasta but didn't bring it to his mouth. "Where do they live the rest of the time?"

If Joe recalled Simon's earlier words about his divorce, he seemed willing to let bygones by bygones. "In Sacramento. Their mother's a nurse at UC Davis."

"How old are they?"

People with children loved to talk about them, and Joe was no different. He took a couple of pictures out of his wallet. "This is Summer. She's ten." His face split into the proudest of grins. "And this little devil's Josephine. She's only seven, but she's a spitfire."

"Like her mother," Martin added dryly.

Joe clicked his tongue. "Yeah, her mother's something else."

Simon got the impression that wasn't a compliment.

He looked at the pictures long enough to seem interested, even though he didn't want to become embroiled in the family dynamic. "They're pretty girls. You're going to have your hands full when they get older."

"Ain't that the truth," Joe said.

"You planning to do another movie soon?" This question came from Martin.

"I'm thinking of accepting another romantic thriller in March, one called *Last Train to Georgia*."

"A thriller, huh? Sort of like *Shiver*?" Joe asked.

Simon couldn't help glancing at Gail. She was definitely familiar with his work in that movie. She turned red every time someone mentioned it, which made him want to laugh. If only she knew how hard he'd worked to get that love scene right. Tomica, the actress he'd been paired with, had worn the same perfume as his mother, which made it revolting for him to kiss her. He was proud of his performance simply because no one seemed to be aware of his repugnance. He'd considered demanding they hold off and shoot another day, but it would've cost the production company a shitload of money. "More or less."

"Who else is in the new one?" Joe asked.

"An actress by the name of Viola Hilliard-Paul."

Joe washed his food down with a sip of his wine. "Never heard of her."

"She's new. But she's got talent." And she didn't remind him of his mother. He had slept with Vi a number of times—although he couldn't remember whether he'd enjoyed it. He'd been drunk more often than not and had broken it off the minute she began taking it seriously.

Joe looked at Gail. "How are you going to feel about your husband doing love scenes, baby sister?"

She got up to put some more bread on the table. "He's an actor. That comes with the territory."

"You won't be jealous?"

"Why would I? It's not real."

Martin lifted his glass. "Better not be," he muttered.

Gail promptly changed the subject. "We found a place to live today."

"Where at?" Joe signaled for more wine, and since

Gail had just filled Martin's glass, she came around to pour it.

"You know that little Victorian where the Widow Nelson used to live?"

"The white one? All by itself at the end of Autumn Lane?"

"That's it."

A nostalgic smile curved Joe's lips. "How could I forget? She used to give out caramel apples at Halloween."

"Yeah, her place was always our first stop," Gail said.

Apparently in this area they didn't have to worry about someone putting razor blades in the apples. That was definitely an upside to such a small community. *Another* upside. Simon was finding quite a few of them.

Martin pushed back his chair. "I thought you wanted to rent. That house is up for sale."

"We've decided to buy," Gail informed him as she put the wine back on the counter.

"How much are they asking?"

Simon tried not to let his eyes latch on to the bottle. "Two hundred and fifty thousand."

"That's not bad," Martin told him, "considering the land."

"The house needs some work," Gail said.

Joe carried his plate to the sink. "You could have Riley fix it up before you move in."

Gail motioned in Simon's direction. "Actually, Simon is planning to do the renovations once he gets his stitches out. He's very good with his hands." She cleared her throat when she realized how that had sounded. "With wood," she clarified.

Joe turned off the faucet and set his plate on the counter. "Holler if you need any help with that," he said to Simon. "I'm not so bad with my hands, either." He grinned at Gail but seemed serious about the offer of help.

"Will do." Simon relaxed despite the relentless pull of the alcohol. There was something about Whiskey Creek *and* its people. Even with a wife who wouldn't let him touch her and the doubt Gail's father and brother had to be feeling about their marriage, Simon was beginning to feel comfortable. As a matter of fact, he hadn't felt this good, this *whole,* in months.

Maybe he was through the worst of it, he thought.

But then he got another text from Bella.

Gail could tell this night wasn't going to go as well as the last one. Simon had been fine for most of the day. Better than she'd ever seen him. There'd been times when they'd talked and laughed as if he was just an average person and not a celebrity desperate to recover his son.

But now he was restless, fidgety. He couldn't seem to shut down and sleep. After tossing and turning for a while, he seemed to doze off. But when she woke sometime during the night, she found him standing at the window, gazing pensively out into the yard.

"Is anything wrong?" she mumbled.

He glanced over his shoulder. He was still wearing the pajama bottoms he'd had on earlier but not his T-shirt. Gail had no idea where that had gone.

"No. You can go back to sleep," he said.

Unwilling to leave him up alone, she slid over to his side of the bed. Getting closer to him meant she could keep her voice down. "We could talk, if you like."

He shrugged. "There's nothing to talk about."

The moon outlined his profile in silver. Gail stared at his bare back, his broad shoulders, hunched just enough to show he was brooding even if he pretended otherwise. His hair stood up as though he'd run his fingers through it several times. Obviously he wasn't okay.

Could she get him to tell her what was troubling him? Or…somehow…help him stop worrying? She didn't want him to backslide. He'd made so much progress in the two weeks since they'd reached their agreement.

"Come here," she said.

Suddenly wary, as if he didn't trust what she might be offering, he glanced at her again. "What for?"

"I'll give you a massage. It might help you sleep."

"That's not necessary."

Under normal circumstances, he would've had a flip answer for her, or some sort of sexual innuendo; the fact that he didn't told her he was hurting too badly to accept help. Maybe he thought accepting help would be revealing he needed it, and heaven forbid he *need* anyone, especially a woman.

"Come on," she coaxed. As much as she hated to admit it, she'd been looking for an excuse to touch him ever since he'd kissed her earlier. No, before that. From the beginning. He'd just never shown any interest in her—not when he was a client, so she'd never allowed herself to seriously entertain the thought.

"There's no reason for you to be up all night," she said with a little more authority.

Sighing, he sat on the edge of the bed, and she got up to fetch the lotion from the bathroom across the hall. But when she returned and put a hand on his shoulder to urge him to lie down, he resisted.

"What is it?" she asked.

He gave her such an intense look she knew he wanted something other than a massage. "Kiss me instead."

Gail swallowed hard. Today, every one of his smiles, every touch of their fingers or accidental brush of their arms, had sent her nerves into a jangling riot of desire that reminded her of those few minutes when he'd cupped her breasts. It didn't help that she was beginning to really care about him, that seeing him healthy and happy was becoming more important to her every day.

She was in a very precarious position, had no reason to even consider his request. But she wanted to ease his discomfort. And she *wanted* to kiss him.

"You'd just like to check out of reality for a while," she said, forcing them both to face the truth. "And I'm convenient. But...whatever you're feeling...it'll pass by morning."

"Damn it, don't say that like I'm trying to use you," he snapped. "I'm tired of being psychoanalyzed, tired of being found lacking. I know more about what's wrong with me than anyone else does. I don't need you to tell me what I want or what I'll do."

He was impatient, irritable, probably unsure how to end the pain. He wasn't even in familiar surroundings. Gail feared that might weaken his determination, cause him to turn back to alcohol.

But if she gave in and had sex with him tonight, where would she be in the morning?

She'd be no better off than the other women who'd come before her.

"Relax," she said gently. "And lie down."

"One kiss," he pressed. "Show me you trust me enough to give me one kiss."

"You kissed me at the house today."

"That doesn't count. I want you to kiss me back, here in private, where we're not putting on a show. I won't take advantage if you do. I'm not as big a bastard as you seem to think I am."

"I know you're not a bastard."

"Then prove it."

"Fine." Planning to allow him a quick peck, nothing more, she leaned forward, already braced to pull away. But he was as good as his word. He didn't attempt to draw her up against him. With his left hand lightly touching her cheek, he kissed her so tenderly she wasn't sure he was looking for a sexual escape so much as he wanted human contact, someone to hang on to.

"That wasn't so bad, was it?" he asked, surprising her by breaking off the kiss before she was even tempted to pull away.

His gentleness and honesty shattered her resistance. As she stared into his face, she nearly slid her arms around his neck to kiss him again. *More.* That was all she could think about. "Not at all."

"You liked it."

"Yes," she whispered.

He raised his hands. "See? And you're no worse for wear. You're not contaminated or anything."

"I never said you'd...*contaminate* me." She *had* accused him of carrying disease, but that was back when they'd been fighting. He'd told her he was clean and had the test results to prove it.

"You believe I'm morally beneath you, that I don't care about anything except myself."

Because she *needed* to think that. It was her only defense against the onslaught of desire she had to battle on a daily basis. She tried to conjure up an appropriate response, one that explained without giving too much away. But he didn't allow her the chance.

"Now I'm ready for my massage," he said, and flopped down on his stomach.

20

When Gail woke up Simon was wrapped around her. She could feel the warmth of his bare chest at her back, feel his breath graze her ear and remembered the excitement she'd felt while touching him last night. As he'd begun to relax and fall asleep, she'd remained completely awake and vitally aware of him as a man. There'd been moments when she'd been so aroused, she'd nearly nudged him so he'd turn over.

She was pretty sure there'd been one moment when he knew that, too. She'd leaned down, kissed his jaw, then the side of his mouth. But as soon as she'd felt him stir as if he might respond, she'd pulled back.

They hadn't done anything. So why was his hand sliding up her shirt now?

At first, she thought it was purposeful, but the cadence of his breathing didn't change. He wasn't awake.

She considered removing his hand as soon as it touched her breast, but there was no intention behind his caress. He burrowed closer as he touched her, and she liked that. Liked all of it—so much that her body seemed to melt into his.

She wasn't sure how long she lay there, telling herself to stop him. But she never did, and eventually she must've slept because when she woke up again, Simon had left.

There was a note on the nightstand. "Went to the coffee shop. Join me when you wake up."

So this was Matt.

Transferring his laptop to his other hand, Simon turned to get a better look. But it was difficult to be discreet when he had to tilt his head so far back. The guy standing in line three people behind him had to be six-foot-six. He towered over Simon, over everyone, easily weighing two hundred and sixty pounds.

Simon sort of wished the guy had a crooked nose, or a gut that hung over his belt like some linemen, but Matt was all muscle. Not only that, he was blond, tan, with chiseled features—what most women would consider handsome. To top it off, he had a quick smile and was obviously well-liked. Three different people had hailed him since he walked in, which was what had drawn Simon's attention to him in the first place.

Gail had gone out with this guy. She'd almost slept with him. And Lord knew Gail didn't take off her clothes for just anyone.

"How's the knee?" someone asked.

While Simon took note from behind his Ray-Bans,

Matt gestured at the brace on his right leg. "Hurts like hell, but...I'm in therapy. I'll get it back eventually."

"I can't believe you're gonna miss the rest of the season."

"Me, neither."

"Good to see you, man."

"Good to see you, too."

"You think the Packers can take the Raiders on Monday?"

A woman broke in. "Excuse me? Can I help you?"

Simon had been listening so intently to Matt's conversations it took him a moment to realize that this voice came from a different direction. The barista was asking for his order. Forced to shift his attention, he requested his usual—an espresso.

Several more people approached Matt while Simon waited for his coffee, all of them excited to see their favorite football player.

"Your coffee's ready," a girl called, dimpling as she handed Simon the cup. On one side she'd written her number. But she barely looked eighteen. That wasn't a call he would've made even at his worst.

"Thanks," he said, and headed to a table. He'd been planning to read some scripts. There hadn't been much time for that this past year. He hadn't had much interest, either. But even with the new picture Bella had texted him last night still fresh in his mind—of her completely naked and posing with her hands on her breasts—he was eager to find a gem among the files Ian had sent, a character he was dying to play, a film that would get him excited about his career again.

He hadn't had a drink in two weeks, was doing everything he possibly could to get Ty back. As long as he stayed the course, he'd look a lot better in the coming hearing. No need to worry about Bella's threats. She could pose and taunt him all she wanted. He wasn't going to let her rub salt in his wounds anymore.

For a second, he debated turning that sex video and this latest picture over to his attorney, who would then present them to the judge deciding Ty's future. The way Bella was acting meant she cared more about hurting him than protecting her parental rights. But she knew he'd never tell on her. He couldn't. Because that might make the court decide neither one of them was fit to care for Ty. Then they might put him in a foster home, and that was the last thing Simon wanted. At least Bella was a loving parent. Ty was better off with her than complete strangers.

He opened a script called "To The Bone," yet another thriller, but he couldn't concentrate. His eyes kept wandering to Matt, who had his own drink now and was sitting with an audience in the same booth where Simon had joined Gail and her friends yesterday.

"You going to the crab feed over at the school?" one of his admirers asked.

"Of course."

"You give 'em anything to auction off?"

"A signed jersey, but I do that every year. Hell, everyone in town has my jersey by now," he joked.

"You'll have to go for a jockstrap next year," some-one quipped.

Suddenly Matt glanced up and met Simon's eyes. Something passed between them. Simon wasn't sure what. An acknowledgment of their interest in the same woman, perhaps. Simon expected Matt to realize he was being rude if not confrontational by staring at him with that challenging expression, but he didn't seem to care. He didn't glance away until someone addressed him again.

"You heard about Gail, right?" A man at Matt's table had noticed the exchange. Seeing Simon had obviously reminded him of Gail.

Lowering his gaze to his computer as if he was no longer paying attention, Simon strained to hear Matt's response, but it was impossible. The football player mumbled his words while turning in the other direction.

Simon almost got up to leave. There was no point in staying if he was too distracted to comprehend what he was reading, but before he could sign off his computer, Gail walked in.

The memory of waking with his hand up her shirt brought a deluge of testosterone. He hadn't touched her on purpose, but once he came awake he'd known in-stantly what he was doing. He'd stayed where he was for a few minutes, savoring the feel of her. It'd been an effort not to roll her onto her back so he could put his mouth where his fingers were. But then he grew so hard he was afraid she'd be able to feel his erection. So he'd gotten up and left before she could accuse him of trying to seduce her.

"Over here," he called with a wave.

She smiled brightly—until she saw Matt. Then she almost missed a step.

Wanting to be sure she came to him first, Simon stood to regain her attention. But Matt had spotted her, too. Getting up, he limped quite handily past Simon, despite his knee, and swept her into his arms. His bigger body all but engulfed hers, reminding Simon of the comment she'd tossed at him yesterday: *He's so big.*

Even with the memory of that statement ringing in his ears, Simon might not have minded. It was just a hug. Except that Matt held on a little too long—and Gail closed her eyes during the embrace, making Simon feel he was witnessing a far more intimate exchange.

When Matt finally released her, they had a short conversation. Then, without even glancing at Simon, Gail headed to the counter to place her order and Matt started back to his seat. Simon thought he'd pass right by. He'd already put on a show that underscored his importance in her life, which, Simon suspected, was exactly what he'd hoped to achieve. But he stopped, and he seemed more upset than smug when he rapped his knuckles on Simon's table. "She's a good woman," he said.

He gave Simon no clue how he was supposed to interpret that remark, but Simon could guess. And he didn't like the implication: *She's too good for you.* "Is that why you backed off last summer?" he asked.

A flicker of surprise appeared on Matt's broad face.

"Damn right. It's the *only* reason. She's the type you take seriously."

"You don't call marriage serious?"

"Not when you don't have any idea what marriage means."

Leaning back, Simon crossed his arms. "You're saying you do?"

"Damn right."

"Then I guess your loss is my gain."

"We'll see about that," Matt retorted.

"Excuse me?" he said, abandoning his relaxed pose.

Matt lowered his voice. "I'll be waiting when you screw up. And if I know you, that won't be long."

Simon couldn't help clenching his jaw. "You *don't* know me. That's the point."

"Everybody knows you," he said, and moved on.

Gail joined Simon a second later. She must have seen their interaction, but didn't ask what her old flame had to say. Obviously she didn't want to talk about Matt. "How do you feel this morning?" she said instead.

Simon felt as if he'd just been slugged in the stomach, which was an odd reaction considering his fear that *she* might get too attached to *him*. "As if I'm standing in your way," he admitted.

"Why?" Lines of confusion appeared on her forehead, but then understanding dawned. "You mean…" She dropped her voice to a whisper. "You're not standing in my way. I told you, it was one date. And he never called me after."

Simon sipped his espresso. "I think he's regretting not making his intentions clearer."

"I doubt it."

He *definitely* was, but Simon didn't argue. He wasn't used to being with a woman who wanted someone else. His ex had cheated on him almost from the start, but only because she relished his jealous reaction. No matter how much he professed his love, making him prove it was the one thing that reassured her he still cared. She'd thrived on getting him so angry he was ready to kill whatever man she'd been with, and the second their relationship settled into a calm or even semiregular routine she'd pull something else. Especially after Ty was born, because threatening to split up and take him with her instantly threw Simon into the panic she was hoping for.

Gail wasn't like that. She was emotionally stable, didn't indulge in theatrics. But she'd married him even though she was in love with someone else, and he wasn't quite sure what he should do about it.

Maybe nothing. In two years she'd be free to marry Matt. Still, making her put her life on hold for so long felt pretty selfish, particularly now that Matt seemed ready to step up.

Somehow Simon had lost interest in reading scripts. "Have you heard from Kathy?" he asked.

"I have." She put her cup on the table. "She left a voice mail while I was in the shower. She has a purchase agreement for us to sign, said we can drop by her office anytime." She motioned to his computer. "What have you been working on?"

"Nothing." He closed his laptop. "Can we get the key today? Move in?"

"If we sign a rental agreement covering the period until escrow closes, I don't see why not."

If they were in their new place, he couldn't wake with his hand up her shirt again because they'd be sleeping in separate beds. Now, more than ever, they needed to give each other space. "What about furniture?"

"We could head over to Sacramento and do some shopping."

"Sounds good." After meeting Matt, he could use a break from Whiskey Creek.

He packed up his laptop and led Gail out of the coffee shop. To her credit, she didn't so much as turn toward Matt, but Simon could feel the other man's eyes following them all the way to the door.

Gail knew she was being too quiet. It was becoming obvious that encountering Matt at the coffee shop had left her reeling. If he hadn't seemed so upset that she'd gotten married, maybe she could've taken it in stride. In the past few months, she'd convinced herself that he wasn't interested in her. But when he hugged her he'd muttered, "I blew it," and sounded genuinely disappointed.

She hadn't responded to that. There wasn't time, and she wasn't about to undermine the believability of her marriage to Simon with a "Wait for me. This isn't real."

For one thing, she'd look too mercenary, as if she'd done it for the money. She'd kept the secret for other reasons, too. Simon seemed to be stabilizing. The last thing he needed was for his new wife to become regretful or act as if she wanted to break up with him on account of an old crush.

She felt she'd handled the situation well, but she didn't have it in her to make small talk. She kept wondering…if she'd left Simon to solve his own problems and tried to figure out another way to rebuild her business, as Callie had suggested, would she and Matt have had a chance? Would they finally have gotten together? She'd planned on marrying him since she was thirteen!

As they drove to Sacramento, she stared out at the passing landscape, remembering how she and Callie used to take turns peering through a knothole in Callie's back fence while Matt threw a football with his father or older brother.

Maybe his knee injury and the possibility that his football career might be coming to an end were making him consider settling down. Maybe he wouldn't go back to Wisconsin, after all. He could stay in Whiskey Creek. He could even marry someone else while she was tied to Simon.

Wouldn't *that* be ironic? It was probably what she deserved for telling the world such a lie about Simon and her….

"You okay?" Since they'd left Whiskey Creek, Simon hadn't spoken much, either.

She dug through her purse for her lip gloss so she wouldn't have to look at him. She was afraid of what he might see in her face. "Fine, why?"

"Are we going to pretend?"

"Yes," she said simply.

He had the sunroof open. The warm, midmorning air ruffled his hair, but she'd put hers in a ponytail to keep it out of her face. "Why didn't you tell me you were in a romantic relationship?" he asked.

They were both wearing sunglasses, which helped hide their feelings and reactions. Today, Gail liked the buffer those glasses provided. She didn't necessarily want to know what Simon was thinking, and she sure as heck didn't want him to discern *her* thoughts. "I told you—I wasn't. I don't know what's going on. I think...I think Matt's return home is just bad timing."

"When you're ready, he's not. When he's ready, you're not."

"Something like that."

"We could make some changes in our...arrangement," Simon pointed out.

This was a business deal. She didn't mean anything to Simon on an emotional level so she didn't have to worry about hurting him. She understood that. But she couldn't dissolve the marriage too soon. He'd lose all the ground they'd just regained. And if that happened, it could be the trigger that would send him back to the bottle. He needed more time.

She could give him that, couldn't she? "I'm okay. I'll take one for the team."

His lips thinned. "Choosing me over him is taking one for the team? Wow, you really know how to flatter a guy."

"You have enough women drooling over you. You don't need me for that." Actually, she drooled over him plenty. She just didn't want him to know it. Whenever she was sure he wasn't aware of it, she found herself watching him. It was a good thing she understood the difference between reality and fantasy. Matt was someone she'd known her whole life, someone she had a right to hope for. Except for this brief period of time, and their very practical reasons for being together, Simon was as out of reach as the moon. Once their two years were up, he'd shoot back into orbit.

She just hoped she'd still have some semblance of her old life to resort to—and that she'd be satisfied with it.

His phone buzzed on the console, but he didn't even glance at it.

"You have a new text message," she said in case he'd been too preoccupied to hear.

"I know."

"Want me to read it to you?"

"No."

"Want me to drive so you can read it?"

"Don't worry about it. I'm not interested right now."

"Why not?" She looked down and saw the message. "It's from Bella."

He didn't seem surprised, which concerned her.

"Why would she be texting you?"

Lifting his bottom from the seat, he shoved his phone

in his jeans pocket. "If you knew Bella you'd under-stand."

"What does she have to say?"

"Nothing new, I'm sure."

Another ripple of alarm went through Gail. "You haven't been contacting her, have you?"

"No. Not once—at least, not in several weeks." He sounded adamant. Whether she was right to take his word for it or not, she believed him. She hadn't caught him lying to her yet. He'd actually told her some pretty harsh truths—including the fact that he was incapable of falling in love again. She figured he deserved the benefit of the doubt.

"She's been reaching out to you?"

"I wouldn't call it reaching out."

"What would you call it?"

"Bella's own brand of torture."

"Which means…"

"Doesn't matter."

"Sure it matters. Why is she texting you?"

"She sends shit she thinks will make me mad."

"Such as…"

He grimaced. "'Meet Ty's new daddy.' 'Before long your little boy won't even remember your name.' Crap like that."

Outrage gnawed at Gail's soul. "That's not fair! She has a restraining order against you. How is it that you can't contact her, but she can contact you?"

"Welcome to Bella's world, where nothing ever

makes sense. You can't fight emotion with logic. I learned that years ago."

"So you haven't gone to the police."

He looked at her as if she'd lost her mind. "What do you want me to say? 'My ex-wife keeps sending me upsetting texts?' How do you think that'll make me look?"

Gail supposed it did sound a little whiny. "Well… can you block her, at least?"

"I don't know. I've never blocked anyone. But even if I could, I wouldn't."

"Why not?"

His gaze slid over to her again. "Because she has my son, and I need to know if anything happens to him."

Gail adjusted her seat belt so she could turn toward him. "Does she ever send you anything to do with him?"

He passed a slower-moving Honda. "I'll get a picture every now and then."

"So she tries to be nice sometimes."

"Definitely not," he said with a laugh. "She's twisting the knife, but that's better than nothing."

Having full custody of his son had empowered his ex-wife. It tied Simon's hands behind his back while *she* was free to slug away. That drove Gail crazy. But as long as Bella had Ty, Simon would remain defenseless. He wouldn't fight her if there was any chance Ty could get hurt.

"She's taking advantage of your love for your son."

"Is that news?" he asked.

She thought most people would be pretty surprised if they ever learned the rest of the story. Bella had done such a good job of smearing Simon as a heartless, irresponsible, selfish bastard. "We're going to get him back."

He slid his glasses down until he could see over the top of them. "And Matt?"

"Matt's going to Green Bay to play football."

"While you keep up appearances with me."

"Yes."

"I can depend on that?"

She slipped her hand inside his and felt far more gratified than she should have when his fingers curled through hers. "You can depend on it."

"*What* is it you want me to do?"

Simon checked to make sure Gail was still engaged with the furniture salesman across the display area. Ian sounded understandably shocked, but what good was money if Simon couldn't use it to assuage his conscience? "I want you to call Mark Nunes, the diamond guy."

"I heard that part. But then I thought you said to buy Gail a five-carat diamond."

"That *is* what I said. Have him design the setting himself. Tell him it better be good, too."

Just out of hearing range, the salesman was having Gail try out another leather couch, one with a recliner at both ends.

"Why are you doing this?" Ian asked. "You got away with a gold band, man. Why would you buy her anything else? You know she'll just want to keep it when this is over, don't you?"

He didn't care about that. She was sacrificing more than he'd expected so she deserved a nicer ring. Or maybe it was the sudden competition. He wanted to appear more favorable than some dysfunctional movie star destined to devastate the town sweetheart. He had his shortcomings but he wanted people like Matt to know that at least he was generous with his money. Professional athletes made a fair amount, but chances were good, *very* good, that Matt couldn't give Gail a diamond of quite the same value. There weren't a lot of men who could.

"Just do it."

"Okay, but…how am I supposed to get it to you?" Ian asked. "I can't imagine the insurance company would cover it if it got lost in transit. They have stipulations on stuff like that."

They'd learned a few of those stipulations when Bella had lost her wedding ring and demanded that he replace it with one twice as expensive. Turned out, the insurance company was right to be careful. She'd been lying about losing the ring, had merely wanted to get another rise out of Simon.

"Drive it to me if you have to," he said, and hung up because Gail was coming toward him.

"Who was that?" she asked when she was close enough. "Not Bella…"

"No. Ian."

"What did *he* want?"

He could tell by her tone that she didn't hold Ian in the highest esteem. "He was giving me an update on some business at home."

"Everything okay?"

She was searching his face so he manufactured a bland smile. "Fine."

"Do you like this?" Drawing him over to the brown leather couch he'd seen her sit on, she insisted he try it out.

"Feels comfortable to me," he said as he settled into the recliner at one end.

"I like it, too," she mused. "But…it's almost ten grand."

The salesman, an older guy with a toupee, stood at a respectful distance so they could discuss their buying decision. If he recognized Simon as a celebrity, he didn't show it. He probably hadn't seen a movie since *Casablanca*.

"Would you quit that?" Simon murmured.

"Quit what?"

"Worrying about price!" Bella hadn't thought anything was too much if she wanted it. Buying her the best of everything was just another way he was required to prove his love. Gail acted as if she didn't want to be a burden.

She leaned down to whisper in his ear. "I don't see any point in wasting money. Who buys a ten-thousand-dollar couch when there are starving children in Africa?"

"I'll make a donation to compensate. We need a couch, and we need one today."

"We don't *have* to have one today," she hedged. "We could shop for something we like that's a bit cheaper."

"No. Enough shopping already." He was done traipsing through one showroom after another. "Let's have them ring it up. Otherwise, they'll close before we get anything at all."

"Fine," she grumbled.

Bedroom furniture came next. By the time they'd picked out two beds, including mattresses and box springs, and a kitchenette set, which was all that would fit in their small house, plus a couple of coffee tables and side chairs, they'd been gone all day. They arranged to have it delivered on Monday, since the store didn't offer that service on the weekend, and headed out, tired but happy.

"We still need a TV, a washer and dryer and some patio furniture." Gail ticked these items off on her fingers as they walked.

"It's after nine o'clock," he said.

"I know. At least we made a dent in it."

"Furnishing a house by yourself is a lot of work," he complained as he held the door for her.

"You probably haven't done it in a while."

"Not in a long while."

"But it feels good, doesn't it?"

He studied her tired smile. Being with her felt good. He was beginning to think it didn't matter what they were doing.

21

"Should we stay in our house tonight?" Gail had fallen asleep against the door of the car, so this was spoken through a yawn while Simon was still driving. But she seemed excited by the idea. Simon was sort of excited by it himself. He didn't know why such a simple thing—camping out at their new home—would sound remotely enjoyable to someone who'd traveled the whole world and had the finest of everything. But the idea made him feel light and free, unshackled for the first time in years. When was the last time he hadn't had to watch over his shoulder for determined paparazzi, an overly zealous fan or his ex-wife, who felt she could show up at his house whenever she wanted, despite the restraining order? Maybe his past was still following him around. He had to remain vigilant for more than a couple of weeks before he could outdistance his previous behavior. But he was feeling more like his old self. He wasn't even craving alcohol as much as he had in the past several days, which proved he wasn't an alcoholic. With enough determination he could let it go.

"Stay there without furniture?" he said.

"We could borrow my dad's blow-up mattress and a couple of sleeping bags."

"And get out from under his roof? I don't know—" he pretended to be giving it a great deal of thought "—you'd really have to twist my arm to do that."

This bit of sarcasm elicited a playful slug from Gail. "Stop. He was better to you last night."

"Considering how things began, there was only one way he could go."

"It was my brother who was rude," she argued. "My dad didn't say anything."

"Your dad was stoic. But he kept shaking his head as if he just couldn't believe his wonderful daughter would be stupid enough to hook up with me. I wouldn't call that polite."

When she laughed, he did, too. He'd once thought she was so much more appealing when she let down her guard and relaxed. Now she was appealing all the time.

How had he worked with her for so long and been unable to detect her charm?

He'd been blinded by his own troubles. Or by the glitz and glamour of Hollywood. Maybe he was as subject to following the crowd as anyone else, despite how jaded he'd become.

"How's your hand?" she asked.

"Starting to itch."

"That's a good sign." She tightened her seat belt. "You're leaving the stitches alone, though, aren't you?"

He shot her an are-you-kidding-me look. "What am I—five?"

"Sometimes you don't know what's good for you."

"I can't argue with that."

She cleared her throat. "So...about Matt."

Surprised that she'd return to this subject, he adjusted the volume on the radio so it wouldn't be distracting. "What about him?"

"I'm fine with our arrangement. You don't have to worry that I'll regret our deal or anything. My commitment hasn't changed."

He wasn't sure how to respond. He didn't want her to stay with him because she felt obligated—and yet that would make it easiest to split up when the time came. "How did you know I was worried?"

She pursed her lips in a smug fashion. "I'm starting to figure you out."

"Which means..."

"You're not as tough as you act."

"Oh, God. Now I'm losing all my mystery? How much worse can things get?"

He'd been joking, but she answered seriously. "Things are only going to get better. There hasn't been one negative article printed about you in two weeks."

"What about the windows?" Simon asked as they were packing up.

"What about them?" Gail responded.

He pictured how easy it would be to peer in at them in their new place. "They aren't covered."

"So? There aren't any neighbors." She said this while struggling to get her suitcase zipped. Simon chuckled at the sight of her sitting on it before waving her off so he could finish.

"What about the paparazzi?" he said. "They'll find us eventually."

She'd already moved on to closing down her laptop. "How would they trace us to Autumn Lane? No paperwork's been recorded—not yet."

Once he'd succeeded in closing her suitcase, he gathered up their bags. "We aren't making it a secret where we live. Pretty soon everyone in town will know."

"But not tonight," she said. "So far only a handful of people even know we bought a house."

Something else occurred to him. "What about water?"

She glanced up. "Don't you want to go over there?"

He did. Definitely. But he didn't want to be miserable. "If the utilities are on."

"Even if there's no water we can make it for one night, can't we?" She slipped her power cord in her briefcase. "We'll use the bathroom here before we go. At least we'll have a few hours of privacy without constantly worrying about how we're coming off to my father and brother." She grinned. "I'd hate to get you all excited about skipping out on my family and then renege on the deal."

He lowered his voice. Her brother wasn't home, but her father was asleep in his bedroom. "Too bad you'll never meet my family so you can see what meeting the in-laws is *really* like."

"You plan on avoiding them for two years?"

He thought of his father and how their relationship had flip-flopped through the years. When he'd married Bella, they'd actually been close for the first time in his life. He could hardly believe that now. "I don't have to avoid my family. They know to stay away."

"You're willing to give them up for good?"

"They gave me up first," he said. *Especially my father.* He started down with the suitcases, leaving her to get her computer and makeup bag from the bathroom.

Her brother walked in as Simon was going out to load the car. "You guys moving already?"

Simon stepped aside to avoid a collision. "Got our own place now."

Joe shook his head. "For the life of me I can't believe you're staying in Whiskey Creek."

"Why not? The people here are so friendly."

It was a joke, but Joe's ears turned red. "I meant since you're famous. Matt Stinson, who plays ball for the Packers, has been our only claim to fame. He probably hates it that you're in town."

"In more ways than one," Simon muttered, crouching to fix a wheel on Gail's suitcase.

"What'd you say?"

He lifted his head. "I said I'm going to get your sister a new suitcase."

"Oh." Joe lowered his voice. "You love her, don't you?"

For a moment, Simon felt tongue-tied. How could he respond to this? It was a question that begged an honest answer.

Fortunately, when he hesitated, Joe added, "You'd never do anything to hurt her...."

Grateful for the slightly different slant, Simon stood. "No. I would never do anything to hurt her," he said, and he meant it.

Her brother seemed relieved. "Good."

Gail hurried down the stairs with the last of her belongings and gave her brother a hug. "How'd it go at the station today?"

"Fine. I think Robbie's getting the hang of it. I stayed with him tonight so I could keep an eye on things while he did his homework."

"That was nice of you." She gestured toward the stairs. "Dad was asleep when we got home. Will you tell him we'll see him tomorrow?"

"Sure. By the way..." He caught them before they could leave. "There were some people asking about you at the station earlier."

Leaving the suitcases at the door, Simon turned. "People?"

"Reporters, I think. They didn't identify themselves. They wanted to know if Simon O'Neal had been in town."

"What did you tell them?" Gail asked.

"That I hadn't seen him. They didn't seem to realize I was your brother. But...I get the impression word is out that you're in Whiskey Creek, so…keep your eyes open for an ambush."

"So much for our short reprieve," she said to Simon. "Do we dare sally forth? We could always roast marshmallows here and watch a movie on Netflix or Hulu."

"Wouldn't be the same," he said. "I'm willing to risk it."

Someone knocked on the door of their new house even sooner than Simon had expected. They'd just hauled in their bags. Gail was in the bathroom brushing her teeth. He'd been wrong about the utilities; they had both water and electricity. But because of the late hour—it was nearly eleven—and what Joe had said, there was a greater chance of their visitor being someone Simon didn't want to see than someone he did. He couldn't imagine many people staying out so late on a weeknight here in the town that time forgot.

It had to be a reporter from one of the tabloids. Or some obsessed fan who'd managed to track him down. Simon had experienced both and didn't want to deal with either, especially considering his injured hand, which limited his ability to protect Gail, if it ever came down to that.

He peered out the window. He could see the dark shape of someone standing on the porch, but he couldn't tell who it was or anything about why he or she had come. The outdoor light wouldn't go on. He figured it was burned out, since the rest of their lights worked.

"Gail? It's me!" their visitor called. "I—I know it's

late, but Joe said you'd be here. And I wanted you to have this while it's still warm."

Suddenly more curious than defensive, Simon opened the door to find Sophia—the woman he'd met at the coffee shop, the one who'd alienated everyone years ago with her behavior.

"Sorry to bother you." She was carrying what looked like an apple pie and seemed flustered that he'd answered instead of Gail.

"It's fine." He held the screen door. "Would you like to come in?"

She ducked her head as she stepped past him, which brought her hair forward, concealing much of her expression. "I made you both a housewarming gift." Her gaze briefly met his. She was even prettier up close, but he felt no attraction to her. He wasn't sure if that was because she was married, or because he was.

"Thank you," he said as he took the pie. She had oven mitts on her hands, but the ceramic dish was no longer hot enough to need them. "Apple?"

"Yes."

"Smells delicious. I'll put it in the kitchen."

"Where's Gail?" she called after him.

"In the bathroom. She'll be out in a sec."

Gail came into the room as he was returning. "I thought I heard a woman's voice."

Sophia smiled in relief. She obviously didn't feel comfortable around Simon. But he didn't resent that. He was relieved to know she hadn't come because of him. "I brought you another pie. You really liked it the last time you were home."

Gail's eyebrows shot up. "Oh, right. I did. Thank you."

"I've been baking a lot lately."

"The last time we talked, you mentioned that you were thinking about getting a job. How did that go?"

She shrugged. "I decided against it."

"Why?"

"Skip doesn't think it's a good idea, not while Lexi's so young. He's worried about me not being around enough as she goes through puberty."

Simon couldn't help noting the double standard. Hadn't she told him at the coffee shop that her husband was frequently gone himself?

"But…you were talking about a few hours a week at the B and B with Chey and Eve—nothing too time-consuming."

"Turned out they didn't need the help."

Simon guessed that was a lie, but Gail quickly covered for her friends. "I think they're having a tough time staying in the black."

Sophia let it slide. "You're probably right."

"Anyway, I'm sorry you have to put off the job search."

"It's not a big deal. Really."

Gail motioned to the empty room. "And I'm sorry we can't offer you a seat…."

"That's okay. I can't stay. Skip will be wondering where I went—if he ever gets off the phone."

After shooting Simon a glance, Gail said, "He's home this week?"

"Got home late last night. He does that sometimes. Just shows up out of the blue." She laughed, although there was no real mirth in it, and when she tucked her hair behind her ear she immediately untucked it—but not before Simon saw the bruise on her cheek.

"What happened?" he asked.

She acted confused. "What do you mean?"

"To your cheek."

"Oh, that." She rolled her eyes. "I ran into the door. Can you believe it? Clumsy, huh?"

Gail stepped up to inspect her injury. "Looks painful."

"It's not. Not really. It'll heal."

"When did this happen?" Simon asked.

"Last night."

Before or after her husband came home? Simon had no reason to assume that Skip might be abusing his wife. Except that her excuse seemed flimsy. And the way she talked about her husband, as if he had the last say in everything, sounded suspect.

"I know this weekend isn't good for you with everything you've got going, but let me know if you can come to dinner sometime next week," she said, and headed for the door.

When Gail asked, "What day were you thinking?" Simon almost laughed out loud. He'd been right about how hard it was for her to withhold her friendship.

"Tuesday? Wednesday?"

"Tuesday should work. What time?"

"Six?"

Gail's smile grew more certain. "Perfect. Can we bring dessert? Or the wine?"

"There's no need. I've got everything. Thanks. Thanks a lot." Seemingly excited to have obtained a commitment, she left.

"Way to hold your ground," Simon teased after Gail had closed the door. "You showed her."

She groaned. "I know. I'm such a sucker."

"That's okay." He tweaked her nose. "I like suckers. Especially when they're as cute as you are."

"Because I'm a sucker for you, too," she said with a disgruntled look.

"Since when?" he asked with a grin. "If I'd known that, I'd have been taking advantage of it."

She was too busy berating herself for caving with Sophia to respond. "Why did I say yes?"

"Because you had to. She was trying so hard. And it'll be okay. I just hope she can cook." He took the mattress out of the box and began to assemble the pump.

"She can bake. I don't know about anything else. We've never been friends. I just agreed to have dinner with the girl who stole my date for junior prom simply because she could."

"You didn't tell me about that."

"Because it's not what matters. Not compared to Scott."

"Something like that is pretty traumatic to a teenager…."

"I couldn't blame the guy who ditched me. My

dad was so strict I had to be home by eleven o'clock, which counted out the after-party. And my prom dress would've looked like a gunnysack compared to everyone else's. He wouldn't let me show an inch of skin."

Simon smiled at the image she painted of herself as an embarrassed girl with a domineering father. "Ah, now I see where you developed your penchant for the boxy business suit."

Her eyebrows came together. "Why don't you like my suits? They're stylish."

He had to speak over the whine of the air pump. "It'd be nice to see you in something sexy for a change."

"That won't fix the red hair and freckles. I'm sure you can see how I might get passed over."

She had a lot more to offer than most women. But he didn't say so. *He'd* passed over her, hadn't he? It took a second look to really see her beauty. "There's nothing wrong with your appearance. Anyway, I'm glad you gave in on dinner."

"Why?"

"Beats kicking Sophia while she's down."

"Like people have kicked you?"

"Deserving it only makes it worse," he said with a wry grin. He squeezed the mattress to see how firm it had become. Almost done. "What about her husband? Is he any more popular than she is?"

Gail sat near him and pulled her knees to her chest like a child. She was so unaware of the assets she did possess. It was refreshing. Beyond refreshing—endearing.

"He keeps everyone at arm's length," she said. "But he has a good reputation. Most of Whiskey Creek has invested with him at one time or another. Even my father. And Martin's about as conservative as a person gets."

"I can only imagine," he said wryly. "What does Skip do?"

"Puts together venture capital partnerships, so he meets with investors all over the world."

Simon turned off the air pump. "Did you see that bruise on her face?"

"I did." She frowned. "The way she kept trying to hide it makes me think it didn't come from a door."

"Have there been rumors about abuse?" Simon rolled out the sleeping bags while she got up and plugged in her laptop.

"A few. She's been seen with other injuries. But it's hard to believe Skip would strike her. He acts like the perfect husband and father—makes sure his family always has the best of everything."

"Maybe they only look perfect in public."

"Or maybe we're jumping to conclusions," she said as she queued up the movie they'd selected, which was another indie film. Unless they were particularly well done, Simon had a hard time watching big, commercial movies like the ones he worked on. After being in the industry for so long, and being exposed to its inner workings even as a child, they seemed too predictable and formulaic to him. He preferred the off-beat humor or unusual situations and settings he could find in indies or foreign films.

"Could be." Lighting the instant log they'd bought on the way over, Simon started a fire. "Has anyone ever come out and asked her if he gets violent?"

Finished prepping the movie, Gail left her computer to warm her hands above the flames. "She'd never admit it, even if they did."

The smell of smoke and accelerant filtered into the room, chasing away some of the mustiness of the old home.

"Maybe she's afraid to leave him for fear he'll *really* hurt her," Simon said. "Or that she'll wind up with nothing. Does she have any education or job skills?"

"Not that I know of. Just her looks, but that's always been enough in the past."

As far as Simon was concerned, she was too Barbielike, which reminded him of so many of the women he'd met in Hollywood. "I guess she could always become a Playboy Bunny."

Gail arranged her laptop next to the bed he'd made and slipped into her sleeping bag. "I bet you could put her in contact with the right folks."

"I've been invited to the mansion."

"How was it?"

"I didn't go."

"Why not?"

He found that whole scene to be a little too misogynistic. Anyway, it was his father's crowd. But he didn't see any point in denying involvement, however minimal. Having avoided *one* mistake was hardly enough to improve his reputation. "I must've been busy that night."

"How unfortunate for you."

"Should I make the offer?" he asked, just to see what she'd say.

She glared at him. "Stay away from her."

Leaning over, he peered into her face. "Do I detect a note of jealousy?"

"Of course not. I'm just trying to keep you out of trouble."

"Then you won't be interested in this, but—" he caught a lock of her hair between his fingers "—I'd rather make love to you than her any day."

He probably shouldn't have said it. The admission made him that much more aware of her sexually. He wanted to touch her to see if she'd welcome it, to see if she'd respond with the same earthy realness she brought to everything else. She was so different from any of the other women he'd known, most of whom stripped before he could even suggest it. They wanted the bragging rights of having slept with someone famous, wanted to gain entrance to his world or to feel they had the right to ask him to recommend them for an acting role. His partners had used him as much as he'd ever used them. Even his ex had used physical access to her body like a weapon. Or an incentive.

But maybe he was merely justifying what he'd done....

Gail wanted something more from that aspect of a relationship, and that made him eager to see what "more" might feel like. He'd been so empty when she assumed her new role in his life, so disillusioned. But she'd made the little things important again.

He was trying to tell her that he felt differently about her, that making love with her would be different, too, but she wasn't listening.

"You just feel that way because I'm the only woman who's ever refused you," she said with a dismissive laugh, and reached for the hangers they'd brought for their marshmallows. "The second I give in, you won't be interested anymore."

When he didn't say anything, she glanced over to see his response and he forced a smile. "You've got me all figured out."

She studied him for a second. "I didn't offend you, did I?"

"Of course not." What she'd said shouldn't have bothered him. It wouldn't have, except he was beginning to care what she thought of him. Which was crazy. She'd seen him at his absolute worst. The past year he'd been her client, he'd done everything possible to let her know just how little he cared what she or anyone thought. So how could he expect her to see even a glimmer of something worthy in him now?

"Everyone knows what a shitty person I am," he added with a shrug. Then he straightened her hanger, stuck a marshmallow on the end and handed it back to her. "But I can roast a mean marshmallow."

22

Simon didn't talk much the rest of the evening. He was polite but the casual camaraderie they'd established since coming to Whiskey Creek was gone. Gail hadn't realized how much she'd enjoyed his companionship until that warmth was replaced with the old indifference.

Accusing him of wanting her only because he couldn't have her hadn't seemed like a big deal at the time, but it'd hurt him somehow. She was afraid it kept him from changing, becoming a better person. Every time he tried, every time he started to believe he could, she held up the mirror of his past and reminded him that there was no way to outdistance his deeds, that she'd never forget and therefore he couldn't, either.

He was probably confused and disappointed. So was she. She didn't want to send mixed signals. But no one had ever frightened her in quite the same way as Simon O'Neal. Charisma rolled off him in waves. If she let it carry her away, there was no telling where she'd end up.

"You okay?" she said at one point.

"Fine." He offered her another perfectly roasted marshmallow. But his emotional withdrawal made her feel as if the sun had suddenly disappeared behind a cloud.

Simon dozed off before the movie ended, but Gail lay next to him long after, wide-awake and feeling... she didn't know what. Remorseful. Conflicted. And attracted. Always attracted.

In the light of the log's dying embers, she admired the contours of his face while trying to decide how to keep this "marriage" on track. She was supposed to care about Matt. She'd yearned for him for years. The flutter she'd felt in her stomach when she'd seen him earlier had made her wonder what she'd done. Yet she'd scarcely thought of him since their encounter in the coffee shop. As long as Simon was around, nothing else seemed to matter.

But Simon wouldn't be around forever....

Suddenly he opened his eyes as if her intense regard had dragged him from sleep. She told herself to roll over and pretend she hadn't been watching him, but she refused to be that much of a coward. Even after his eyes met hers, she continued to stare just as intently and allowed him to do the same.

Finally he broke the silence. "What are you thinking about?"

"You," she admitted with a sigh.

"Don't waste your time on that." He turned over, but she refused to let him exclude her so easily. She put her palm on his back, and when he didn't move, she slid it up and into his hair. The thick, silky locks felt so good....

"What do you want from me?" he murmured without moving. "Sometimes the way you look at me...it's as if you want to be with me. And yet...the second I act on that, you shut me down."

"I'm sorry," she said.

After another strained pause, during which she went on touching his hair, he turned to face her again and unzipped his sleeping bag. "Come here."

Gail's heart pumped hard and fast. She'd done it now; she'd started down the path of no return. But she couldn't blame Simon. He was right about the way she looked at him. And what else could he assume when she kept touching him?

"Maybe...maybe we should lay down some ground rules first," she said.

"What kind of ground rules?"

"How about this can only happen once. And it doesn't mean anything. Those kinds of rules."

"There isn't any need."

But the next few minutes would change everything. At least for her. She wet her lips. "Are you sure?"

"Positive. You coming or not? Because it's cold, and I'm going to zip this thing up if you're not."

Supremely conscious of the fact that she'd chosen to wear a T-shirt and pajama bottoms—nightclothes that weren't the slightest bit sexy just so she wouldn't be tempted to do exactly what she was about to do— she took a deep breath and wiggled out of her own bag.

Fleetingly she wondered if her underwear was attractive enough. She thought so. She'd recently bought new ones. Just marrying Simon was enough to make her worry about her underclothes.

Thinking of her panties made her question whether she should undress before climbing inside his bag. They already had *his* T-shirt and pajama bottoms to remove, which wouldn't be easy in such a confined space.

The practical side of Gail suggested she strip now. But maybe that was unromantic. He didn't tell her to....

In the end, she didn't have the nerve. She figured he could get creative; after all, he had a lot more experience than she did.

"I'm a little self-conscious," she admitted.

"Everything will be fine," he said.

"But...talk about pressure." She worried her lip. "You've been with supermodels and actresses and Olympic athletes."

He surprised her with a laugh. "Where did you get Olympic athletes?"

"Just guessing. Some of them are pretty hot, right? And you can take your pick."

Sobering, he lowered his voice. "It's not a contest, Gail. You don't have to compete with anyone."

"I wouldn't want to be your worst. I'd at least like to hit somewhere in the middle."

"God, no wonder you don't want to sleep with me."

"What do you mean?"

"Never mind. Come on."

The nerves in her stomach were making her jittery.

"I'm just trying to tell you it's been a long time for me. I'm out of practice."

"How long has it been?"

"Three years."

He shoved a hand through his hair. "Wow, you really are selective. How many men have you been with?"

"At one time?"

He raised his eyebrows.

"That was a joke."

"You had me for a second. How many?"

She considered lying. Too few might make her seem like she wasn't playful or sexy enough—or someone guys sought out. But she figured he should know what he was getting into. "Two."

"That makes it easy to see why you're self-conscious. But it's just me, right? You don't have anything to worry about."

"Just you…" she repeated, and somehow managed to suppress a nervous giggle. She was going to sleep with one of the biggest movie stars on the planet. She figured she had a right to be anxious about it. But after he'd helped her inside his bag and managed to zip it up, he simply enfolded her in his arms. He didn't even kiss her.

"Simon?" she said when minute after minute ticked away and he didn't move. He seemed to be going to sleep….

"What?" he mumbled.

Sure enough, he sounded as if he was just on this side of sleep. "Aren't you going to take off your clothes?"

"No."

Shocked, she blinked at the darkness. She couldn't look into his face. The way he was holding her kept her cheek against his chest. "Why not?" she whispered.

"Because you'll only regret it in the morning."

This was not the answer she'd been expecting. He'd tried to make sex part of her contract, for crying out loud. "How do you know?"

"You don't trust me."

She considered that before breaking the silence again. "So…what are we going to do?"

His hand swept her hair back as his lips brushed her forehead. "Isn't it obvious? We're going to sleep."

"Have you ever just…slept with someone like this before?"

"Only my wife."

So she hadn't gone *too* far. He was offering her the comfort of his body in an asexual way and she sort of liked that. It certainly eased her fear and anxiety, even her self-consciousness.

As she closed her eyes and breathed in the scent of warm male, she experienced a strange sense of satisfaction. Maybe this wasn't as exciting as a sexual encounter, but it was oddly gratifying. "You smell good," she whispered.

His hand slipped up the back of her shirt. But he didn't bring it around to her breasts. He merely flattened his palm against her bare skin. Then, slowly but surely, his breathing evened out and hers must have, too, because the next thing she knew it was morning.

* * *

Gail had slept deeply. But when she came to full awareness, she realized that the contentment she'd felt the night before was gone. She liked being in Simon's arms just as much as before—didn't want to be anywhere else. But after spending the night pressed to his body, the awkwardness of climbing into his sleeping bag had vanished. So had her reluctance to touch him and be touched by him. As a matter of fact, all she could think about was getting naked so she could feel more of him.

The love scene in *Shiver* played in her mind as Simon's chest rose and fell with each breath. She imagined him making love to her as he and his costar had depicted, imagined his mouth moving down her stomach—

"What's wrong?"

Her breath caught in her throat. He was awake. But his thoughts didn't seem to be going in the same direction as hers. He didn't sound happy to be disturbed. "Nothing, why?"

"You keep moving."

"Oh. Sorry," she said, but shifted again—to bring their hips into full contact.

She noted his surprise as she glanced up at him, felt his irritation fall away as he came almost instantly to full attention. She'd attracted his interest; she could tell by his growing erection. He opened his mouth to say something. Then the doorbell rang.

"No way," she grumbled.

He rolled onto his back and covered his face with one arm. "Already?"

She pulled her cell phone closer to check the time. It was barely eight.

"Who do you think it is?" he asked without looking over.

"Probably Kathy," Gail guessed. "She said she'd bring us copies of the fully executed real estate contract, but I don't know why she has to do it this early. I'm sure she couldn't wait to see *you* again. I'll get it."

As soon as she left the sleeping bag, Simon got up, too, and went into the bathroom. She heard the door close just as she peered out the window. But the person on her porch wasn't Kathy. It was a man.

Did she know him? There was something familiar about him, but he was turned away from her....

"Who is it?" she called through the door.

"Tex O'Neal." At the sound of her voice he'd turned back to face her. It was Simon's father.

"Oh, God," she muttered. "Simon?"

She'd had to whisper his name. Simon probably couldn't hear her over the running water. In any case, he didn't answer.

"I need to talk to Simon," Tex called.

Gail pivoted to head down the hall. She wanted to check with her husband before letting Tex in. She knew he and his father weren't on good terms. Their relationship had always been rocky, more so in recent years. But what was the point of asking Simon whether or not to let him in? They couldn't sit inside their house and refuse to open the door when she'd already given away the fact that someone was home.

Self-conscious about her appearance, since she'd come straight from bed, she smoothed her T-shirt and cautiously opened the door.

Simon's father wasn't nearly as attractive as Simon. He didn't have the same bone structure—the kind that made Simon almost as beautiful as he was handsome. Simon had inherited those features from his mother. But his father's face was interesting the way Clint Eastwood's was. Shrewd. Tough. Unflinching. Despite their visual differences, father and son had the same powerful personalities, however—the same magnetism and keen intellect. At least that was Gail's impression.

"I want to see my son," he said without preamble.

His gaze swept over her, then shifted away as if he found her wanting, which made Gail regret her courtesy in answering his knock. "He's in the bathroom. If you'd like to come in, he'll be out shortly."

She stepped back, half expecting to hear the jingle of spurs as Tex walked in. He'd taken a lot of acting parts over the years, but none fit him better than that of a hardened gunslinger; that, of course, was where he'd gotten his nickname. He'd been called Tex for so long she couldn't remember his real name. Even now he was wearing a pair of fancy snakeskin cowboy boots and a hat. No doubt he'd come straight from the ranch he owned somewhere farther north.

Was it near the town of Chico? Gail couldn't remember that, either.

Simon came out of the bathroom, froze as soon as he saw his father, then flipped his hair out of his eyes and ambled toward him. "What a surprise," he drawled.

Tex acknowledged him with a brief tilt of the head. "Must be, considering you disappeared without letting anyone know where you were going."

The belligerent attitude that had become synonymous with Simon over the past couple of years reasserted itself. His eyes glittered; his chin jutted forward. The transformation was so marked and immediate it caught Gail off guard. Obviously just seeing his father was enough to drag him into a dark place.

"So...how did you find me?" Simon asked.

"Ian finally got tired of me busting his balls and gave me the information I was after. But he said not to tell you it was him."

"So of course you out him first thing."

His father studied him for a second. "I'm not in the business of protecting Ian."

"No, that would require looking beyond your own concerns. But I'm afraid harassing my business manager was a waste of your time. It would've been smarter to call me."

"Why would I bother?" he said. "You won't pick up for me."

Simon shoved a hand through his hair. "Most people would take that as a sign and not show up on my doorstep."

"Ordinarily, I'd leave you in peace. You've made your wishes clear where I'm concerned." He tipped his hat to punctuate his words. "But this isn't personal. It's business. If you weren't my lead actor, I'd be banging on someone else's door."

A muscle flexed in Simon's cheek. "*Your* lead actor? What the hell are you talking about?"

With a condescending chuckle, Tex stepped forward. "You don't know? Man, you really have been in a world of hurt. I'm bankrolling your next film."

"No. Frank and Jimmy Kozlowski are bankrolling it."

"Together with a few other investors, and I happen to be one of them."

Nostrils flaring, Simon clenched his jaw. When he spoke, it sounded like he forced each word through his teeth. "*You* put up money for *Hellion?* Your name has never been mentioned in connection with the project."

Tex gave a careless shrug. "Ian knew when I came on board. I've never made a secret of it."

Gail felt her fingernails curve into her palms. Good old Ian, playing both ends against the middle. What had he been thinking? That Simon would never find out his father was involved?

That wasn't realistic. He must've been hoping the movie would be done by the time Simon learned. That was certainly possible. When there were a number of producers, a group of investors, not all of them had a say in the actual making of the film.

"Why?" Simon asked. "There are so many other projects, so many other actors. Why are you involved in *this?*"

"Frankly, it was the kind of opportunity I didn't want to pass up. A script like this doesn't come around every day. And you couldn't be more suited to the part."

Disgust etched lines in Simon's forehead. "I'm playing a serial killer, for God's sake!"

"But he's a good husband and father at the same time, very complex. That's what makes him interesting and I'm sure it's why you took the part. Anyway, not too many actors have more box office appeal than you do right now. We wait much longer, that might not be the case. So how can I convince you to get your ass back to work?"

Now Simon laughed. "You can't. I'm not going back until I gain custody of Ty."

"You won't get Ty. You've already made sure of that."

Simon folded his arms. "I wonder where I learned the behavior that brought me to this point."

"It's not your behavior I'm trying to understand. It's why you didn't bother to be more discreet."

"Maybe I'm not interested in becoming the Great Pretender, like you."

"If you had any brains you wouldn't be in this situation. You had Bella by the jugular, and you let her go. No one knows that better than me."

"That you could even suggest I go public with what happened, after the part you played, makes me want to kick your ass," Simon growled. "You were probably hoping I'd do just that. Give you a spot in the limelight again."

Tex waved his words away. "Oh, come on, your marriage to Bella would never have lasted, regardless of anything I did. It was already on the rocks." He gestured toward Gail. "This one won't last, either. One woman could never keep you happy, not when just about every female you come across is willing to lie down and spread her legs. You're too much like me."

Gail felt sick. "Out," she said. "Get out of our house. Now."

Simon grabbed her by the arm before she could get in Tex's face. "I'm nothing like you, and I'm going to prove it."

His father adjusted his hat. "Knock yourself out," he said. "But understand this—you have three days. I'll be staying at the B and B on Sutter Street until Tuesday. You don't make arrangements with me to start that damn film, I'll sue you for breach of contract and hire someone else. We'll see if the publicity from that helps you get Ty back. The judge and everyone else will think, 'Simon screwed up again, just like we figured he would.' Then hiding out here in the back of beyond will be a waste of time. Why not be realistic while you have the chance?"

"While it serves you, you mean?" Simon said. "While it gives you a film that'll make you millions more than if you hired another actor?"

"The people I talked into signing on are upset at the way this thing is going. I owe them something, too."

"But who do you owe more?" Gail asked. "Don't you care about your grandson? Don't you want a better relationship with him than you have with your son?"

Tex shifted his attention to her. "I think you shouldn't get involved," he said, and stalked out.

Rage consumed Simon. His father's nerve in showing up here and acting as if…as if he'd had nothing to do with the situation that had started everything made Simon want to put his fist through a wall.

"You okay?" Gail's voice came to him as if from far away. He knew she meant well, that she was trying to help him, but he couldn't be with her right now. Considering the rage bubbling up inside him, he couldn't be with anyone he hoped to have a relationship with afterward because there'd be no way to take back the things he was about to say.

"I need to get out of here," he muttered.

She stood in his path. "And go where? You don't even know the area."

"Who cares?"

"*I* do."

"Then you're a fool. And you'll live to regret it. Get out of my way."

"No. If you leave now you'll do something *you* regret."

On some level, he agreed with her. He thought of Ty and wanted to make him proud. But even his son wasn't enough to stem the deluge of anger whipping through him. Because trying to reclaim Ty felt like he was grasping at air. His father was right; he'd never get his son back.

He needed a liquor store, some way to dull the jagged emotions that felt like barbed wire being yanked through his heart. If he didn't do something he'd explode—or finally give his old man what he deserved. He wanted to do exactly that, but if he ever started down that road, he'd wind up in prison. He doubted he'd be able to quit slugging him.

He tried to get around Gail, but she stopped him. "No!" she said more firmly. "I won't let him take from you what you've achieved during these past two and a half weeks."

"I don't give a shit about what I've achieved. I don't give a shit about anything!" He thought his temper would frighten her. It'd certainly frightened her when he'd stormed into her office following that bogus rape accusation. But she didn't let go or back away, even when he tried to shake her off.

"I'm not giving up on you, damn it!" she cried. "Don't let him win!"

"You have no choice but to give up. Our marriage— this joke of a relationship—is over." Determined to get through the door, he picked her up and set her aside. But she came after him again, catching his arm. When he whirled, ready to shout—to say whatever he had to say to get her to accept who and what he really was—she grabbed his hand and shoved it up her shirt.

"Stay," she breathed.

The shock of suddenly having her breast in his hand shot straight to his groin. He told himself it wasn't right to take her up on the offer she was making. Not when he knew why she was making it. But the anger was like a monster inside him, a monster with a mind of its own. It demanded some kind of physical action, a release....

Still, he hesitated for a second and almost let go. He respected her too much to use her. But there was more than anger at work. He also wanted her—badly. And when her hand clenched in his hair and she turned his head to kiss him as if she wouldn't take no for an answer, he knew he wouldn't be able to refuse.

Especially when she met his lips with an open mouth and arched into him, holding nothing back.

23

Gail had never experienced anything even close to what was happening. The emotions flying between her and Simon were so charged they seemed to be sparking. Desperate to come together as fast as possible, they tore at each other's T-shirts, managed to remove them and, naked from the waist up, feasted on each other's mouths, necks and chests—gasping for breath in between.

Gail felt as if she'd just climbed aboard a runaway train. The crash was coming. But she wasn't tempted to jump off. Not yet. Everything had changed. It didn't matter that they were only temporarily married. It didn't matter that sex was against the rules *she'd* established. It didn't matter that it was full daylight and, after spending the night in Simon's sleeping bag, she didn't look her best. She was keeping him safe. That was all she cared about.

Fortunately, he was too preoccupied with touching and tasting her to notice that her hair was messy. And she was too busy enjoying the pleasure he gave her to be self-conscious.

When Simon lifted her in his arms, she warned him not to pull out his stitches, but he didn't seem concerned. He carried her to the mattress, yanked her pajama bottoms off and buried his face in her breasts while touching her in other, more sensitive areas.

"I wish I had better use of my right hand," he muttered, but he was doing just fine with his left.

Recalling all the fantasies she'd had over the years that centered on Simon O'Neal, Gail could hardly believe this was real. Especially because Simon in the flesh was so much sexier than the Simon in her dreams. He was far more aggressive than either of her former lovers—more demanding, too—but he was also careful not to take it too far. She could sense whenever he'd draw back, when he'd check her expression and responsiveness to make sure she was enjoying how he touched her.

They were both walking on the far edge of control and there wasn't a more exhilarating feeling. Gail had never let herself go to this point. She *couldn't* pull back, didn't even want to.

"I was wrong about you," he told her, his voice husky as he spread her legs.

She could barely speak. She was trembling as she clung to his arm, already close to climax. "In what... way?"

"In every way." His mouth descended on hers, mimicking what he was doing with his fingers until she stopped him.

"I want *you* inside me," she whispered. "I can't wait.

It feels like I've been waiting forever for the man I could desire this much."

His gaze locked on to hers. She wasn't sure if he was still angry, but there was a feral look in his eyes. He got up to get a condom from his wallet and put it on. But then he pinned her arms above her head and covered her with his hard, warm body.

Gail allowed her eyes to close at the solid weight of him, the delicious pressure as he pushed inside. She was lost. She hadn't protected herself against anything. She'd fallen head over heels for a man who was emotionally damaged and she'd done it in record time. Probably because, despite what she'd tried to tell herself, she'd been halfway in love with Simon from the beginning. Matt had been a schoolgirl crush by comparison, someone she'd only *thought* she wanted.

A trickle of fear ran through her as that truth crystallized. Because an even harder truth came right behind it. Simon was going to break her heart, and that wouldn't take very long, either. But as the friction increased and the tension mounted, future pain wasn't a concern. She'd never made love like this before because she'd never *felt* like this before. Despite all the reasons she shouldn't be, she was desperately in love, and her body *knew* Simon's touch, could distinguish it from anyone else's.

As she reached that first peak, with Simon's smell and body in and around her, she felt as if her bones would melt and somehow meld with his. She looked up to see him watching her. He was soaking up every nuance of her expression, reveling in every gasp, and the smile of accomplishment that curved his lips in that moment was probably the best part of all.

Simon was shaking with the effort of holding back, but he was determined to bring Gail to climax several times before allowing himself the same pleasure. He liked feeling her shudder when she reached that crest, liked hearing her moan his name. But he knew he was being unselfish partly to escape the guilt. He no longer had a heart to offer, so he had to deliver where he could.

He happened to be good at this. Today he was too worked up to have the stamina he wanted, but he was doing what he could to last.

"Again," he whispered, and closed his eyes. He needed to think of something other than the warm wetness, the clenching of her body, or it would all be over. But she didn't seem happy that he had to mentally check out in order to make that happen.

Encouraging him to roll onto his back, she got on top and that was the beginning of the end. When she took control, he could believe she was making love to him because she wanted the pleasure as badly as he did and would have no regrets—and that was all it took to render him helpless.

As soon as his hands found her breasts, wave after glorious wave ripped through him. Closing his eyes again, he succumbed to the release until he felt completely drained. Then he looked up at her, still breathing hard. He had no idea what to expect next. He was terrified she'd start to cry, feel angry that they'd broken her "rules," cling to him as if this was the beginning of forever, or—worse than anything—make him squirm by telling him she loved him.

Fortunately, she did none of those things. With a devilish smile, she bent her head for a quick peck that ended with a playful bite on his bottom lip.

"Not bad," she said. "Not bad at all."

He raised an uncertain eyebrow. "You've had better than that?" *He* certainly hadn't. Not in recent memory. Maybe it was because he hadn't been drunk, for a change, but he already knew he'd never forget this.

"A couple times." Her manner suggested she might be teasing, but he couldn't be sure. "Anyway, I think you're talented enough to make the two years we're married go a lot faster."

He still wasn't convinced she felt as cavalier as she was acting, but he was willing to play along. "You thought I might not be?"

"I thought you needed a break from your stud services, but…I'm glad I decided not to worry about that," she said. Then she got up and headed into the bathroom as if what had happened was nothing more than a casual encounter.

Thank God. Covering his face with one arm, Simon breathed a sigh of relief.

Pressing herself against the bathroom door, Gail covered her face. She was shaking and couldn't seem to calm down. But she wouldn't let Simon know how deeply their lovemaking had affected her. He wasn't capable of dealing with anything that complicated right now, even if he cared about her. And she knew he didn't. Not in the same way she cared about him.

"What have I done?" she mouthed as she stared at herself in the mirror. But it was too late for regret or remonstrance. At the very least, she was infatuated with Simon. Now that she wasn't caught up in the moment, she was reluctant to call it *love*. Even if it was, she could still salvage her pride.

"Gail?"

He was outside the door.

She hurried to flush the toilet, even though she hadn't used it. "Yes?"

"You okay?"

"Of course. Why?"

"Just wanted to be sure."

"I'm fine. Thanks. You definitely know how to show a lady a good time." She bit her lip, forcing herself to stop talking before she gave away the fact that she was completely thrown by what had just happened.

"Good. Glad to hear it. Let's take a shower."

He wanted more. And, heaven help her, so did she.

Their first encounter hadn't been bad, not by any stretch of the imagination. But, thanks to practice and a growing familiarity, sex with Simon got even more enjoyable as the weekend wore on. Gail was surprised at how quickly she became comfortable with the intimacy and how easily she lost her self-consciousness.

She'd been so worried about comparing unfavorably to his other lovers, but that was crazy. If their relationship wasn't going to last, what did it matter?

Other than a short stint here and there when they ran out to buy food and more condoms, they'd spent the weekend holed up in the house, making love, sleeping and eating. Ironically, it felt like a real honeymoon. Gail knew Josh would love to hear the dirty details of the past two days, but she planned to give Simon the same respect and privacy she was counting on from him. As if to confirm that, she ignored Josh's call when it came in.

"Who is it?" Simon asked when she set her phone back on the carpet.

Curling into him, she kissed his bare shoulder. "Josh."

"What do you think he wants?"

"To update me on how things are going."

"On Sunday?"

"He's a workaholic, like me. And he's probably dying to hear what's happening with us."

It was getting dark outside. Gail almost couldn't believe they'd spent the whole weekend indulging in hedonistic behavior. But she'd already crossed all the lines she'd intended not to cross. At this point, there was no reason not to enjoy Simon while she could.

"It's peaceful here, don't you think?" She'd been careful not to mention his father, but the knowledge that Tex was staying at A Room with a View and had been there for two days made her uneasy. She guessed

Simon felt the same, probably worse, and wondered what he planned to do about his father's ultimatum.

Maybe she'd lose Simon much sooner than she'd expected to....

"It's been perfect." He kissed her, and his tongue met hers briefly. "You don't regret what we've done, do you?"

He'd spoken casually, but she sensed that her answer mattered.

"What's to regret? It was about time I got laid, right?" She chuckled as if it meant nothing more than that, and he didn't follow up.

"Who were the other two?" he asked at length.

She ran a hand over the contours of his flat stomach. "The other two?"

"You said you've slept with two other guys."

Rising up on one elbow, she gave him a challenging look, but she was teasing and she could tell he knew that. "Do you really want to talk about past lovers?"

He surprised her by remaining serious. "Only because I'm guessing they meant something to you."

The air mattress shifted as she rearranged the blankets, which were twisted around their feet. "Hardly."

"What does that mean?"

"The first was more of a date-rape situation. He didn't like me saying no, felt I owed him more than a good-night kiss in exchange for dinner."

His eyebrows knitted as he helped her untangle the blankets. She liked him with his hair mussed and his jaw darkening with beard growth. She wasn't sure she'd ever seen him look sexier, even in the movies. "I hope you turned him in."

"I wish I had. At the time I felt that maybe I'd invited it by acting interested in him. I was so excited when he finally asked me out. Now that I'm older, I have no idea why I let him get away with what he did. But I was twenty-five and inexperienced. And I thought maybe I was weird for not *wanting* to have sex with him on the first date. He was really handsome, someone most girls would desire."

"Where is he now?"

"Who knows? I met him at a dance place some of my employees dragged me to. We didn't have any contact after that."

"And the other guy?"

"That was a much better experience. He was quite a bit older than me, very kind—a college professor complete with the tweed jackets." She smiled in memory of Skylar Henshaw's conservative wardrobe. "I liked his calm, trustworthy manner. We were together for several months."

"Why'd you break up?"

"He decided to get back with his ex-wife. She was a lovely woman, and they had children together. I never could understand why they split."

His hand slid over the curve of her waist and down around her hip in a gentle caress. "Was it because of you?"

"No, I met him at a Starbucks after his divorce. He

offered me his table because it was too crowded for me to use my laptop any other way."

"How romantic," he said dryly.

She smiled. "He was nice, like I said."

He kissed her neck, her ear. "Did he leave you brokenhearted, Gail?"

She closed her eyes. "Not really. I was ready to tell him I wanted to move on. I figured it was lucky he'd come to the same decision. Our relationship was... comfortable but not passionate. I liked that he didn't demand more from me than I was willing to give. I was building my business and didn't have a lot of time or energy for anything else. He took care of my creature comforts."

Simon raised his head. "Sounds more like a father figure."

"I guess he was. But we both understood that."

"And then there was Matt."

Gail stretched. "I didn't sleep with Matt, remember?"

"You wanted to."

She didn't correct him.

"Will you in the future?"

"Maybe." She glanced away so he couldn't tell how troubling she found that question. He'd spoken as if it wouldn't matter to him if she did.

"Why haven't you slept with anyone from Whiskey Creek?" he asked.

"I almost slept with Ted in high school."

"Your friend? The author?"

"That would be him."

"What happened?"

"His mother caught us getting naked and told her sister, who's the biggest gossip in town. The rumors going around afterward were enough to keep me on the straight and narrow. I couldn't bear the thought of news like that getting back to my father. My mother had already disappointed him. I didn't want to be next."

He ran his finger along her jawline. "What did your mother do?"

Oh, God, this, too? Gail almost said she didn't want to talk about Linda, but she supposed she might as well get it out of the way. "She left us for an old boyfriend from high school."

"Us?"

"There was no question that Joe and I might go with her. She packed up and disappeared while we were at school. We heard from her periodically that first year, but…she's the type who shies away from conflict whenever she can, and I think she hated having to speak to my father, to be reminded of what she'd done. So, once she remarried, the calls became more and more infrequent. Soon, it was just too awkward to talk at all, even at Christmas. *Especially* at Christmas."

"It must've been tough to lose your mother that way."

Probably not as tough as it'd been for him to lose his mother. At least she'd had her father. Besides, the last thing she wanted from Simon O'Neal was sympathy. "I've always had the love I need. The hard part was feeling I had to make up for what she did, to prove to my father that not all women are the same."

He rolled onto his back. "That's a lot of pressure. Must've been a relief to go to college." He paused. "You went to college, right?"

"I did. Stanford."

He whistled. "I'm impressed."

She adjusted the pillow so she could look into his face, but thanks to the setting sun and the fact that they hadn't yet turned on any lights, it was harder and harder to see. "What about you?"

"I was too busy rebelling to go to college."

That didn't surprise her. "Did you attend acting school?"

"Who needs acting school when you have a father as famous as mine?"

She heard the bitter edge to his voice. "The connection must have provided a few key contacts, but... the way I've heard it, the two of you have never gotten along." That was certainly how it had appeared when Tex showed up at the house. "I can't imagine he bent over backward to lend you a hand."

"We've always had a love-hate relationship. There were times when I was a kid that I desperately wanted to win his love. But too many other things stood in the way. He hated my mother with a passion, even though what happened was as much his fault."

"Why would he blame her? That hardly seems fair."

"He wanted her to terminate the pregnancy. When she refused, it made his marriage even more difficult than it already was. Then her family found out, and the rest of the world. He hates looking bad, wants everyone to admire him. But because of me he couldn't escape the consequences of his actions. I mean, don't get me wrong, there've been times when he's decided to be the father he never was, but…he can't sustain it."

"I remember seeing both of you from a distance at the premiere of *Now or Never*."

"That was shortly after I married Bella." It was also several years before he'd hired Gail. "He wanted to be part of Ty's life, so he was busy trying to be a good grandfather."

"What changed that?"

A muscle twitched in Simon's jaw. "He couldn't maintain that, either. If there's anything consistent about Tex O'Neal, it's inconsistency."

That didn't really answer her question. It certainly gave her no details, no specifics. But she didn't push it. He was still talking but he'd gone back to the subject of his career and his father's response to his getting into acting.

"I believe that at one point he tried to limit my options, but it was too late to do the kind of damage he could've inflicted earlier on. He hates growing old, being counted out. Feels like I've stolen everything he used to have. So he's done what he can to take what's mine."

"What does that mean?"

He grew pensive. "Never mind. He's just…not your typical father. Or grandfather."

"You've climbed higher than he ever did. That probably bothers him. And Ty's an extension of you."

"Maybe, but…his name carried enough weight to open certain doors. I owe it to his career that mine ever got a start."

"Those doors would've been slammed in your face if you didn't have the looks and talent to become who you are," she pointed out. "You should be proud of yourself."

"Proud of myself," he repeated with a self-deprecating chuckle. He didn't say so, but she got the impression he didn't hear that line very often.

"Yes, you've accomplished a great deal."

"I got lucky. It worked out."

In Gail's opinion, he was a little too quick to dismiss his success. He certainly wasn't as conceited as some people accused him of being. Even she'd accused him of that. But then…Simon had been accused of almost everything at one time or another. She'd come to believe there was a lot of misconception about him.

"I think most people in America would find that an understatement." She bent her head to rub her lips against the soft skin of his chest. "If only it could work out so well for all the starving actors in L.A."

He didn't comment. He toyed with her hair, which fell down around him. "You must've had plenty of chances to experiment with boys in college."

"We're back to my sex life? Jeez, you have a one-track mind." She touched his face, kissed him. She loved being so familiar with him.

"I'm just trying to understand what your life's been like," he said, easily rolling her beneath him.

She stared up into his eyes. "By your standards, it's

been boring, okay? You would've jiggled your knee all through it."

"Jiggled my knee?"

"That's what you do when you're bored, or anxious. Anyway, I didn't sleep around in college because I'd been trained to be cautious, and I was too busy with my schoolwork to socialize. I had to get straight A's so I could feel good about sending my report cards home to Daddy." She would've shrugged, except his weight pressing her into the mattress made that impossible. Her tone implied it instead. "Or maybe it was just that I didn't meet the right guy. I was kind of shy, and I've always been self-conscious about my red hair."

She was surprised she didn't mind mentioning that to him, although it was something she generally kept to herself. She supposed it was because she didn't have any hopes or expectations where Simon was concerned. Since she'd had to count him out from the beginning, there was no point in pretending *not* to have the insecurities that were as much a part of her as her desire for discipline and order. Considering who Simon was and the type of women he usually surrounded himself with, her shortcomings would be very obvious, anyway.

Supporting the bulk of his own weight with one hip and shoulder, he twisted a strand of her hair around his finger. "I like the color of your hair."

"Sure you do." She managed to push him the rest of the way off. "But for your information, I wasn't trying to solicit a compliment. Besides, you don't have any choice at the moment except to make do. I'm better than nothing, remember?"

He didn't seem pleased to have his words thrown back at him. "I was dying for a drink that day. And I was still angry over the rape accusation. I didn't mean what I said."

She kicked off the blankets that covered her feet. "Of course you did. But that's okay. I am what I am." With a smile to let him know she really didn't care if he found her lacking, she rolled off the mattress and onto the carpet. "Why don't we get dressed and head down to Just Like Mom's. I think it's time for a proper meal."

"Gail…"

He sounded too serious. She didn't want to hear what he had to say. She could only handle what was happening between them if she kept things light and didn't expect too much. "Come on." Resisting the urge to cover her nudity, she got to her feet. "Enough being lazy."

"I really *didn't* mean it," he said, but she was already on her way to the bathroom and pretended not to hear.

24

Just Like Mom's had purple walls, white ruffled curtains and half a dozen high chairs lined up at the entrance. The booths around the perimeter of the main dining area were done in lavender vinyl; the country-style oak tables in the middle of the floor had chairs sporting cushions with big bows that could only have been hand-sewn. Simon had never seen a restaurant that reminded him more of his grandmother's house. Not that he'd been able to spend much time there. Grandma Moffitt had been too upset about the circumstances of his birth to ever fully forgive his mother, and him by extension. She preferred her other grandkids, who were girls. But he'd always secretly liked the homey comfort of her rambler in Palm Springs.

"Smells good, doesn't it?" Gail murmured over the bell that jingled when they walked in.

The place wasn't crowded, but it was doing a brisk business for eight o'clock on a Sunday night. "Pot roast," he said.

"Mildred Davies makes the best meat loaf and beef stew imaginable. I'm sure the pot roast isn't bad, either."

Through the two-foot opening where the food came out, he saw a short, round woman with a cap of snow-white hair directing traffic in the kitchen. "That's the cook? Mildred Davies?"

"Cook and owner," Gail said. "As you can tell, she's getting on in years but she manages to keep up. After dinner you'll have to try her carrot cake. Delicious."

"Maybe I'll *start* with it." Somehow, he felt younger, more innocent and certainly more content than the man he'd been in L.A. Either the paparazzi couldn't find him or they'd been unwilling to make such a long drive on the off chance of picking up a detail or two about his private life. He hadn't heard from Bella for twenty-four hours. He had less craving for alcohol than at any previous point since giving it up. And, best of all, for the first time since the event that had caused him to unravel, he was gaining confidence that he'd be able to do what was necessary to get Ty back.

It wasn't until he thought of his father's visit yesterday morning, and the possibility of running into Tex in Whiskey Creek, that some of the old anger and uneasiness returned. His father seemed to appear every time Simon began to get on his feet.

But he wasn't going to let Tex provoke him. Tex could sue if he wanted. Simon would gladly pay restitution for any financial loss he caused the producers of *Hellion,* but he wouldn't allow his father to ruin his life yet again. He wasn't ready to jump back into the world that had nearly driven him crazy. Ty was the prize. Ty—not another movie or another fifty million dollars.

Once he was granted custody, even if it was only partial, maybe he'd bring Ty to Whiskey Creek. They could spend their summers here enjoying Gail's friendship, whenever she came home, and maybe the friendships of some of the people he'd met at the coffee shop. He and Ty could forget the opulence and excesses associated with his career, they could play baseball, eat at this tacky but homey restaurant, check out the old-fashioned soda fountain down the street, hike in the mountains....

Simon wanted to take Gail's hand, to communicate his gratitude for all she'd done. Despite his initial skepticism, her involvement in his life had made a huge difference. But ever since they'd left the house, she'd been careful not to so much as brush against him, which felt odd, considering. At first, he thought he was only imagining the change. But the more minutes that went by without physical contact, the more convinced he became that she was doing it on purpose. She was determined not to expect him to act like a boyfriend.

He appreciated that she wasn't suddenly clingy. Their current arrangement was what he'd asked for from the start. Now he had what he wanted, and yet her withdrawal bothered him. In his opinion, she was being *too* vigilant about making sure there was no emotional spillover. Why couldn't they just relax and do and say as they pleased for the time being?

He was about to broach the subject. He wasn't ready for Gail to raise her defenses again. It'd been too long since he'd felt close to anyone, and he wasn't willing to lose it so soon.

But the hostess, a middle-aged woman who wore a purple uniform with a tag that said Tilly, approached before he could bring it up. Her mouth formed an *O* the minute she recognized him, but she cleared her throat and addressed Gail. "Two for dinner?" she said in a gravelly smoker's voice.

Gail seemed amused by the hostess's reaction to his presence. He was amused by it himself. True to Whiskey Creek form, she didn't gush over him or ask for his autograph, but she was obviously flustered.

"Hi, Tilly," Gail said.

"Great to see you back," the waitress responded.

"It's great to be home. We'd like a booth, please."

Pressing a hand to her chest as if her heart was beating too fast, Tilly glanced at Simon, but looked away as soon as he met her eyes. "Right this way."

She took two menus from the holder but dropped one. When Simon caught it before it could hit the floor and gave it back, she muttered, "Oh, my God. I can't believe this."

Gail sent Simon a conspirator's smile as Tilly marched ahead of them, but someone else hailed her before they could reach their seats.

"Gail!"

Simon turned at the same time Gail did to see Callie, the friend who'd made it clear she wasn't happy to have Simon in Gail's life, sitting at a table—with Matt.

* * *

Gail wasn't sure how to react. Simon wouldn't want to be waylaid by Matt or Callie, but Callie was one of her best friends, and nothing had happened between her and Matt that prevented them from being friends, too. They'd never even been a couple.

Still, it felt awkward to stand and talk at their table, and even more awkward when Callie put her on the spot by insisting she and Simon join them.

"Are you sure?" Gail asked. "I mean…haven't you already ordered?"

"Not yet. We got here just before you." The way Callie said it led Gail to suspect this might be a test to see how she'd react now that she was married to Simon.

Gail didn't want Callie to think having Simon as her husband would make her any less receptive to her friends. "In that case…" She nearly sent Simon an apologetic glance, but knew Callie and Matt would see it, too, and recognize it for what it was. So she didn't look at him. She returned Callie's smile as she accepted, and even though Callie slid over, making a place for her, she sat on Matt's side. With Simon's right hand still bandaged, he needed to eat with his left. And Matt was so big she couldn't imagine cramming another guy into the booth next to him.

"Have you eaten here since you've been back?" Gail could feel Simon's gaze on her as she addressed Matt.

The glower that had descended on Matt's face when Simon approached the table eased, as if he'd won a small victory when she sat beside him. "Once. I plan to come as often as possible before I have to leave."

Gail took the menu Tilly handed her. "When will that be?"

"Whenever I'm capable of running without pain."

"It's terrible what happened to your knee. How's the therapy going?"

"Okay. At least I get to be home while I do it."

Tilly gave Simon his menu as Gail asked, "Who are you working with? Curtis?"

"Yeah."

Curtis Viglione was one of the best therapists in the country. He saw a lot of professional athletes. After building a reputation and a considerable clientele in the San Francisco Bay Area, he'd moved to Whiskey Creek three or four years ago—Gail couldn't remember exactly when. Now he had athletes come to his state-of-the-art center built in the hills about a mile outside town. "From what I hear, he's a miracle worker. Sounds like you're in great hands."

Matt nodded, but his eyes kept moving to Simon, who was glaring at him. Why Simon would bother with this little rivalry, Gail couldn't say. There was no point in acting possessive or jealous when he didn't really care about her. But she figured it might be part of what he felt was expected of a husband, another aspect of playing his role.

Regardless, it made her uncomfortable. She wanted her friends to like him, although she couldn't put her finger on exactly why. Maybe it was just so they wouldn't think she was foolish for marrying him.

She cleared her throat to gain Simon's attention. "What looks good?" she asked, but he didn't get a chance to answer. Tilly was still standing at the table, waiting to tell them about the daily specials. She rattled off a spiel about homemade chili and cornbread for $8.99 and beef Stroganoff with sour cream for $12.99. Then she announced that Luanne would be their server and, when she couldn't seem to think of anything else to say, finally left.

In her peripheral vision, Gail could see Tilly whispering to two waitresses at the coffee machine. They kept turning to look at Simon, no doubt excited to have a movie star in their midst. But Gail was too wrapped up in manufacturing small talk to pay much more attention than that.

"How's business at the studio, Callie?" she asked.

"Busy. I've been doing lots of family portraits. And a few weddings."

"You're a photographer?" Simon asked.

"I am." She offered him a fake smile. "I would've been happy to photograph you and Gail at your wedding—but of course you didn't really have one."

Gail jumped in before Simon could respond. "We wanted to keep it simple."

"You certainly accomplished that," Callie said. "It doesn't get any simpler than a few vows and 'I do.'"

Luanne showed up with water for Gail and Simon; Callie and Matt already had theirs. She said she'd be back to take their order in a few minutes, but Gail caught her before she could leave, insisting they were ready now. They hadn't even looked at the menu, but she wanted to get this dinner over with as soon as possible.

They all fell silent while they quickly perused the meal selections. Then Gail ordered the meat loaf, Simon the pot roast, and Callie and Matt went for the chili. After Luanne left, Matt spoke up. "So…how's married life?"

Simon gave him a smile that, to Gail's eye, looked a little too deliberately satisfied. "Second time's the charm."

"Too bad it didn't work out that way for your father. How many times has he been married, anyway?"

Gail winced at Matt's choice of subject, and the derision in his voice. She doubted he'd heard, but the fact that Tex was in town somehow made it worse.

"I haven't kept track," Simon said.

"Are you two planning to have children?" Callie asked.

Were her friends purposely trying to embarrass Simon? Gail answered, just in case. "Probably not." She'd wanted to limit the conversation on that subject by sounding resolved. But she'd seemed too reconciled to not having kids. She could instantly tell that Callie was not pleased with her response.

"Why not?" her friend demanded.

"Simon already has a son," she replied, but that didn't help.

"So?" Callie set her water down so fast it sloshed

over the sides. "What about *you?* You've always wanted children."

Gail lowered her voice. "You don't have to be so defensive of me, Callie. I'm happy the way I am. Besides… maybe we *will* have children someday. We're merely saying we don't have any immediate plans, okay?"

Callie scowled at Simon. "Just because you've had it all and done it all doesn't mean you don't have to consider *her.*"

Instead of getting angry, as Gail expected, Simon validated Callie's concern. "I understand that," he said.

His calm answer seemed to take the fire out of Callie's anger. "She's one of my best friends, you know? I care about her. I want her to be happy."

"So do I," Simon said, and he sounded so sincere Gail almost applauded.

"Great." Gail used her napkin to mop up the water Callie had spilled. "You both care about me. I couldn't be in better hands. Now…maybe you can try to get along? Because *that's* what would make me happiest."

A sulky expression turned down the corners of Callie's lips.

"We're already married, Callie." Gail leaned across the table to squeeze her hand. "I know you're mad that I didn't take your advice, but…it's over. Can we leave it for the time being?"

Her friend sighed audibly. "I'm just afraid your happiness won't last."

If she only knew… "So you're going to ruin it?"

"No."

"Hollywood marriages hardly ever succeed." Matt volunteered this, but it was unclear whether he was inviting responses or simply stating a fact.

Regardless of what he meant, Gail warned Simon with a look not to put Matt in his place. Simon could've said quite a bit about the world of a professional athlete. But what was the point? Matt was right; Hollywood marriages rarely did last, and this one would turn out to be the perfect example. "Okay, everyone's aired their complaints and expressed their worry, and it's all been duly noted by me. Can we please enjoy our dinner without making me regret that I've asked my husband to sit through this?"

Callie and Matt nodded grudgingly, but it wasn't long before they were enjoying themselves. When Simon started regaling them with stories about some of the unusual and out-of-the-way locations he'd gone to shoot movies, and the stunts he'd had to perform without a double, Matt dropped all animosity. Soon, he was so mesmerized he was talking and laughing as if he'd never viewed Simon as a competitor.

When Simon got up to go to the bathroom, Gail expected Callie to tell her again why she'd been crazy to marry him. But she didn't. "He can be charming," she admitted instead. Her tone implied she had to allow him that much.

Simon had done his best to win them over, and he'd managed it quite easily. He'd had them all laughing, gasping in astonishment, asking questions and generally hanging on every word he said. When Matt seemed more interested in becoming Simon's friend than in pouting over losing her, Gail knew his reaction to her marriage hadn't been one of true regret. If she had her guess, he'd been miffed to find that the girl he'd thought would always be waiting for him had actually moved on—and that she hadn't settled for someone less famous, less attractive or less charismatic than he was. He'd been reacting to the blow her defection had dealt his ego more than anything else, which meant that even after she and Simon divorced there'd be no Matt and Gail.

After all the years she'd believed herself in love with him, that was a little depressing. But she'd learned about her own commitment to Matt, too. She doubted she would've wanted Simon so badly today if she'd really been so enamored of Matt. He'd just made a good dream, given her someone to think about while she was working too hard to date.

"He's a lot of fun," Gail said, and stood up to go to the restroom, too. She didn't want her friends to quiz her on how she felt about Simon or ask pointed questions in his absence. She had too many conflicting emotions at the moment, didn't want to acknowledge that what she felt for Simon seemed far more powerful than what she'd felt for Matt. That made her fear she wouldn't get over him quite so readily when the time came…

Simon was just walking out of the men's room as she reached the entrance to the ladies'.

"Great job," she murmured. "They love you."

"More important, are they convinced I care about you?"

"Completely! They bought every compliment you paid me."

His smile disappeared. "But you didn't."

"I would've if I hadn't known better. You're a hell of an actor."

He took her arm. "Being an actor doesn't mean I'm always acting, Gail."

Averting her gaze, she put her hand on the door. "But it certainly comes in handy when you need to," she said.

25

It came as a surprise in the middle of the night. One minute Simon was lying next to Gail. The next they were awakened by the sound of movement, a bright light and then a series of flashes from just outside the window.

Cameras! Simon understood what was happening as soon as he opened his eyes. He'd known staying in an empty house with no window coverings would leave them vulnerable. But they'd had it so good since coming to Whiskey Creek, he'd grown complacent.

"What's going on?" Gail asked, sounding confused.

He rolled over to shield her. "Paparazzi."

Fortunately, they were both dressed. They'd come home from the restaurant, watched some television on Hulu and eventually fallen asleep. Simon had wanted to strip off Gail's clothes, to feel her skin against his while they dozed off. But things weren't the same after the restaurant. What she'd said while they were talking outside the restrooms had set him back, made him realize that she'd taken his remark—that he wasn't capable of falling in love—to mean that he'd never feel any fondness or concern for her, either.

"They've found us," he said, and shuttled her into the hall.

She hugged herself. It was chilly without blankets. "How?"

"Don't know. Someone here in Whiskey Creek must've leaked the information."

"Or Ian. He's the one who told your father where we are."

"My father's different. He may not be doing much acting anymore. There aren't too many good parts for men his age. But he's still a force to be reckoned with in Hollywood."

"I figured that out."

He pulled her up against him, to keep her warm. "I'm sure Ian didn't feel he could refuse. But..." Suddenly the obvious occurred to him. "That's it! I'll bet you anything my father did this!"

"Why would he tell the paparazzi where you're staying?"

"He doesn't want this town to be an escape. He'd rather roust me out, get me to head back home so I'll make that damn movie."

"You have quite the father."

The images he dreaded came to mind, the ones that revealed Tex as the selfish bastard he was, but Simon shoved them away. It helped that Gail softened against him, as if she wasn't opposed to letting him hold her. Somehow that made him feel better because it convinced him he hadn't lost everything he'd gained earlier. "If you had any idea…"

"What's that supposed to mean?"

"Nothing." He hadn't told a soul about what had happened. He wasn't going to break his silence.

"So what do we do?" she asked. "We could pull our mattress into a bedroom, but the bedrooms have windows, too. And we don't have a hammer and nails to put up a blanket or a sheet."

"You stay here. I'll take care of it."

She grabbed his hand. "You can't go out there! You're angry and defensive. What if you get in a fight?"

"Whoever it is deserves to have my fist planted in his face."

"No!" She tugged him back. "You'd only reinjure your hand. And we can't risk a scene. There can be no more pictures or stories of you losing your temper."

He felt he should have the right to defend himself—and his wife—which made it difficult to listen to reason. But he'd ignored Gail too often when she worked for him. "Your suggestion is…"

"We call the police and let them handle it."

Footsteps echoed on the wooden porch. The photographer was coming around the house, probably looking for another way to see in.

"My phone's charging in the kitchen," she added.

"Mine's in the living room. I'll get it."

"Wait."

"Why?"

"Maybe we can create an opportunity here."

She was always thinking. "Gail, whoever's outside is trespassing and invading our privacy. I want his ass kicked off the property. Our wedding pictures haven't come out in *People* yet, which means he'll have the first shots of us after our wedding. He'll be able to sell them for a fortune, and I'm not about to let some guy get rich out of sneaking pictures of me in bed with my wife."

"Maybe we can make a deal with whoever it is to release his snapshots after that."

She couldn't convince him on this. He'd dealt with the paparazzi for too many years. "Absolutely not. We can invite someone else to take pictures when *we're* ready. There's no need to let this asshole get away with what he's doing."

"Okay. You're right. It's just…if we give the press what they want, they'll be more likely to leave us alone."

"You're wrong," he argued. "They're insatiable."

"They're insatiable when they have some scandal to report. Our marriage is news because it's shocking and they think it's another bad move on your part. Once we prove otherwise and establish that you're happy and living a good life, they'll lose interest. Then, as long as nothing changes, they'll leave us alone."

He'd been hounded to the point that he had a hard time believing this. "No…"

"Yes," she insisted. "Their profits depend on showing the dirt in people's lives. If you give them nothing negative, they'll have to look to other actors, musicians, whatever, who might be screwing up."

He could see her logic. It wasn't until his marriage

had started to crumble that the paparazzi had become so unbearable. They wanted a front-row seat at the destruction of Simon O'Neal. Now that he was pulling his life back together there wouldn't be so much to see or report. "Fine. We'll invite someone else out here, like I said. But this guy's not the one."

"Agreed."

He dashed into the living room for his phone. But it turned out to be an exercise in futility. By the time the cops arrived, the intrusive photographer was gone.

Knowing the culprit could very easily come back, they packed up and returned to Gail's father's.

"I thought I heard you two come in last night. What happened? Air mattress pop?"

Martin DeMarco was in the kitchen brewing coffee. That meant it was Joe who'd left earlier. It must have been his turn to open the station. Simon had heard someone tramp down the stairs and head out. The noise had awakened him from a deep sleep, but he felt rested despite the early hour and the hours they'd been up in the middle of the night. No doubt it helped that he was no longer dealing with a perpetual hangover.

"We got a little surprise," he said.

Martin's caterpillar-like eyebrows drew together. "A skunk?"

Simon laughed. "In a manner of speaking." He explained about the photographer as Martin handed him a cup of coffee.

"Who do you think told the paparazzi where you were?"

Chances were they'd never know for sure. Simon had his guess, but he didn't want to say it was most likely his own father. He could hear the protective note in Martin's voice, knew he was a different kind of man. Martin would do anything to shield his children. Just being married to Gail put Simon under that same protection.

The stark contrast between Martin and Tex embarrassed Simon. But Simon had been ashamed of his father for a long time. Maybe he'd always been ashamed of him. The story of his own conception wasn't exactly something he could be proud of. The humiliation caused by his personal history had been excruciating. It was so salacious that it was brought up again and again and again in the media.

"We don't know," he said instead of admitting his suspicions.

Martin took out a frying pan and turned on the gas stove. "I can't imagine anyone around here would give you away. The only person who could provide your exact address would be the Realtor. And Kathy's good as gold. Or—" he seemed to realize she wasn't the *only* one who knew where they were "—maybe it was one of Gail's friends."

"I don't think so." Simon tried to recall the conversation they'd had with Callie and Matt at dinner last night. They'd mentioned the house, certainly. But when they parted, Matt had clapped him on the back and told him how great it was to have dinner with him.

Simon didn't think Matt would turn around and call the press. And Callie would never do anything to make Gail unhappy. She was as protective as Gail's own family. Maybe more so.

"You're right. Those kids and Gail go way back," Martin said. "You can trust every last one of 'em."

"Even Sophia?"

"Maybe not Sophia. Gail's never been too fond of her."

Smiling at Martin's blatant honesty, Simon added a splash of cream to his coffee. "She's been quite friendly. She brought us an apple pie the other night."

"Really?" He sounded more interested than Simon would've expected. "Did you bring the leftovers?"

Martin was probably joking, but with him it wasn't easy to tell. "No, but we will," Simon promised.

Gail's father dropped bread in the toaster and cracked some eggs in the pan. Then he motioned to a chair halfway around the table. "The *Gold Country Gazette*'s right there if you want to read the paper."

Now that he wasn't likely to see some terrible picture of himself doing Lord knew what, Simon thought he might. "This is local?" he asked as he retrieved it.

"It is. A weekly. They'd probably love to interview you. Maybe you'll be interested now the news is out that you're here. They always do a big spread on Matt Stinson."

"Well, I have to outdo Matt."

Gail's father actually grinned at this. "What do you have planned for today?"

Simon replied over the sizzle of eggs. "I thought I'd head over to the hardware store, see if they have the tools I'm going to need to do some remodeling. Then I've got to be at the house. Our furniture is due to arrive sometime after ten but before noon."

"What's Gail going to do?"

The comforting smells of a home-cooked breakfast rose to Simon's nostrils as he leafed through the paper. Sure enough, there was a big picture of Matt, along with an update on his knee. "When I got out of bed, she mumbled something about needing time on the computer to take care of a few details at Big Hit. It'll be easier for her to do that here, so she'll drive me and then come back."

"I can take you if you like."

Simon lowered the paper. "You don't mind stopping by the hardware store?"

"Not at all. I've got a few things I should pick up myself."

"Okay. Then I'll call her when the furniture arrives. She'll want some input on how we arrange it."

"Input?" Martin said dryly.

Simon was starting to like Gail's father. "Euphemistically speaking."

"If that means she'll need to tell you exactly where to put every single piece, then you've got the right idea."

Simon chuckled. "As far as I'm concerned, that's her prerogative. I'm not feeling any burning need to place the sofa." He trusted Gail enough to let her make much more important decisions, and he liked that.

Martin flipped the eggs. "I'm glad you two are staying here in town for a while, but I'm surprised she's willing to take so much time off work."

Simon set the small paper aside. "We were just married. Some people would call that a honeymoon."

"A three-month honeymoon? Maybe in your world, but not in Gail's. She loves the PR business. And she's done a damn fine job with that company of hers."

Setting his coffee on its saucer, Simon leaned back. Martin was so proud of his daughter. And he had every reason to be. "That's true."

When the toast popped up, Simon got to his feet. He was planning to put some in for himself, but Martin waved for him to sit down again. "I've got it."

A couple of minutes later, Gail's father sat a plate of three eggs, over easy, and two pieces of toast in front of him.

"Probably not as good as you're used to eating," he said, "but at least you won't go hungry."

Actually, the food tasted better than any Simon had eaten in a long time. But he knew the difference wasn't in the cooking. This meal told him that Martin was willing to give him a chance. All Simon had to do was prove he deserved it.

Gail paused on the landing near Simon's father's room. She knew Simon wouldn't approve of her coming to the B and B. In fact, he'd be angry if he learned. But she wasn't about to let anyone get in the way of what they were hoping to accomplish. Even his father.

Especially his father.

Taking a deep breath, she stepped up to number six, the room number Sally at the front desk had given her, and knocked.

There was no response. Had Tex left town? She doubted they'd be that lucky. More likely he'd gotten up early and gone to the coffee shop or Just Like Mom's.

She knocked again—and this time she heard movement.

"Later, for God's sake!" he yelled, and something—a pillow?—hit the door, making it rattle. "What kind of place is this?"

Tex thought she was one of the maids. Briefly, she was tempted to leave it that way and scoot. Clearly, he was in no mood to be bothered. She didn't want to tangle with him, and she didn't want him to disturb the other guests, but she had something to say and she doubted she'd get another opportunity to say it—not without Simon around.

Calling on all her nerve, she rapped at the door again. "Mr. O'Neal? Could I talk to you, please?"

Silence met her request. Then he said, "Who is it?"

His voice had lost its gruff edge. The question held curiosity instead.

"Gail DeMarco, er, O'Neal." She wasn't sure whether or not to use Simon's name. It would bring her quite a bit of clout, especially where her business was concerned. But knowing it was only borrowed for a couple of years made her feel like a cheat. And there didn't seem to be much point here in Whiskey Creek. "Your daughter-in-law."

"You don't say." A creak suggested he was getting up. She heard the bolt slide back, then the door opened and Tex peered out at her with red-rimmed eyes. "You're here alone? Where's Simon?"

"He had some things to do this morning. I came without him."

He smelled of booze. Those eyes and the sallow look of his face also told her he'd spent the previous night drinking.

"The question is why," he said.

"If you invite me in I'll explain."

The rasp of whiskers sounded as he rubbed a hand over his jaw. "I'm not exactly dressed for company, but if you want—"

"I'll wait." She had no desire to see Simon's father in his boxers.

He chuckled softly. "I heard you were a real prude."

"Ian tell you that?"

"Among other things."

He kept laughing, but the door closed and didn't open again until he was dressed. "Madame…" he said, his voice filled with sarcasm as he waved her inside.

He hadn't combed his hair. It stood up in front, gray but still thick despite his age. She could see why some women would find him appealing. He had a devil-may-care attitude that probably attracted the type of women who liked that sort of challenge. And he still had a good physique. "What can I do for you?"

"I'm here to see if you care about your son at all," she said.

Her statement took him off guard. Obviously he hadn't expected her to be so direct. He straightened for a second—and then his eyes narrowed. "What the hell has that got to do with anything?"

"It's the only thing that matters."

"Not when it comes to business."

His room now smelled like cologne. Too much of it. "When it comes to *everything*."

He finished buttoning his shirt. He wore that and a pair of jeans but not his belt or boots. "What are you hoping to achieve, Ms. DeMarco?"

She noted that he didn't do her the courtesy of using her married name. It was probably his way of letting her know he didn't think she'd be with Simon very long. He was right. But she didn't care what he was trying to intimate.

"Simon is doing better than he has in at least two years. I want that to continue. So I'm asking you to leave Whiskey Creek without further contact and find someone else to take his part in the movie."

A thunderous expression appeared on his face. "Who the hell do you think you are?"

"I'm his wife." *For now...*

"I don't give a shit. Do you realize how much—"

"That will cost?" she broke in. "I know it'll be a lot. I also know that Simon will compensate you."

"It's not just me. It's the people I convinced to invest in this. I have a responsibility to them."

"If they're like you, they have plenty of money. Fortunately, so does he. He'll repay you, and you can return what you'd like to your investors. But I'm asking you to let him out of the contract gracefully and not retaliate by dragging him into court."

"My friends won't be happy. Hardly any other actor has the same pull."

She couldn't help it; she raised her voice. She'd told herself this was a business meeting. She was here to protect the campaign she'd developed, to ensure its ultimate success. But it had become personal, too, because she cared about Simon. "Your friends don't matter as much as your *son!* Could you do what's best for him for a change? Just once?"

He threw up his hands. "Why should I? Simon's never given a shit about me!"

That was an excuse. He had to know it, at least in some part of his brain. "I'm afraid you have that reversed, Mr. O'Neal. It's *you* who should give a shit about *him.*"

Shaking his head, he laughed without mirth. "He's sure got you snowed, doesn't he? Don't you realize it's just a question of time before he acts out again regardless of what I do? Regardless of what *you* do? What's it been—two or three months since he stumbled into a bar, got drunk and started a fight? I may as well look after my friends and my money because Simon will go to hell in a handbasket no matter how hard you try to save him. He's the most stubborn son of a bitch I've ever met. And here you are, sticking up for him. He wouldn't thank you for it. You know that, right? Trust me on this—he's going to leave you with a broken heart, just like he did Bella."

"The divorce wasn't entirely his fault, and *you,* of all people, know it." In spite of Simon's past sins, Gail was clinging to the loyalty she felt to him. She was also relying on what Ian had intimated to her earlier, that Bella had done more to cause the divorce than anyone knew. She hoped to hell Ian was right, because she was determined to make some headway with Simon's father.

She expected Tex to continue arguing with her. But he didn't. He stepped back as if she'd slapped him, and a strange look came over his face. "He told you?"

Gail's heart began to pound. Simon hadn't told her anything particularly revealing. But she wasn't willing to admit it, wasn't about to let the power swing back to Tex. There was something at play here, something that affected everyone involved. What? "Of course he did," she bluffed. "He tells me everything."

"Then you should also know that *she* came on to *me*." Tex brought a hand to his chest for emphasis. "*She* was the one who wanted *me* in her bed."

Gail gaped at him. Had she heard correctly? She was sure of it, and yet she couldn't believe what had just come out of his mouth. *"You had sex with Bella?"*

He winced at the disgust in her voice but rallied. "It was a one-time thing. It didn't mean squat to either of us. She'd gotten in the habit of coming to me whenever she was upset. I helped her, gave her a shoulder to cry on. Simon's not easy to live with. If you don't know that yet, you'll—"

"When?" She was so shocked her voice had dropped to a whisper. "When did you do this?"

He cursed under his breath. "Two and a half years ago."

That was about the time Simon had started behaving badly. It was the reason he'd been unable to cope. His wife had had an affair with his own father, a sad echo of what had happened with his mother, and just as reprehensible. What was wrong with Tex? Did he have to be admired by *every* woman he met?

She swallowed hard. "How did Simon find out?"

Tex stared at her so long she thought he wasn't going to answer. Then his shoulders slumped and he sighed. "He came home unexpectedly."

"The *one* time you were together he caught you in bed? What are the chances of that?"

"Okay, we were together a few times. But it hadn't been going on for more than a few weeks." He jammed a hand through his hair. "I just blew it, didn't I? He didn't tell you a thing."

"No. If I had my bet he hasn't told a soul." He could've used it to excuse his own bad behavior. To get his son back. To make his ex-wife look a lot worse than he did. But he hadn't. He'd kept it inside. "You want to know why?"

Tex didn't answer.

"Because he cares too much about *his* son. He would never want Ty to grow up knowing such a terrible thing about Bella, the way *he* had to grow up knowing what his mother did with you."

"Our affair wasn't all that broke up their marriage," Tex said. "They were having trouble before. That's why she came to me in the first place."

"And you helped her out by seducing her."

"*She* wanted it."

"And that made you feel like a big man, didn't it? That Simon's wife could want *you?*"

He stepped back, nearly stumbled and knocked the lamp off the nightstand while he was trying to catch his balance. His hangover had put him at a disadvantage. "I don't have to tolerate your judgmental bullshit."

"And I don't care if you think I'm judgmental. What you did makes me sick. The fact that you're trying to justify it makes me even sicker."

"It's not like Simon and I have ever been close!"

"You were close when you did that, probably closer than you've ever been."

He winced. "Something would've ruined it."

"Is that what lets you sleep at night? He's your *son,* for God's sake! You know what I think?"

"Get out of here!" he snapped, but she wasn't finished yet.

"I think you're jealous of Simon," she said. "He's younger, stronger, better-looking, a superior actor and by far a better man. And you hate all that. You hate that he's replaced you in Hollywood, outdone you so easily. So you've been doing everything you can to destroy

him—at the same time you've been trying to capital-
ize on his success."

Squeezing his eyes closed, he pressed a palm to his
forehead as if he had too much of a headache to be having this conversation. "You shouldn't have tricked me."

She started to leave but turned back. "It was your
guilty conscience that set you up, *Dad.* I only helped a
little. Now get out of town before I tell Simon what you
told me. It's a miracle that he's put up with you so far."

He wasn't willing to let her have the parting shot.
"He won't stay with you. You're not even that pretty."

"Maybe not. But I wouldn't cheat on him in a million years. Especially with a morally bankrupt old fart
like you. That's got to be worth something," she said,
and slammed the door behind her.

26

Classic rock blasted from the old-fashioned boom box Simon had purchased at the hardware store as he tore out the sink, counters and cupboards in the kitchen. The furniture they'd purchased in Sacramento hadn't arrived—almost two and still no delivery—but that didn't affect him much. He'd been happily engaged in demolition since he got here more than three hours ago. It was a relief to be able to use his hand again. He knew he should get the stitches taken out because there was no more pain when he moved it.

Gail had brought him lunch a couple of hours ago, but she hadn't stayed long. She'd said she had more work to do. For starters, she was closing the deal on the sale of their pictures for $2.8 million.

Simon didn't mind working alone, but he frequently found himself thinking of Gail—the way she kissed or cuddled up to him in the night, or watched him when she didn't realize he was aware of it. The house seemed strangely empty without her, and yet he felt as if he could get lost in his current task for days. The physicality of the work eased some of the deep-seated tension that kept him so wound up.

Just as he was thinking about calling her to see when she might be back, a vehicle pulled up outside. Assuming it was the furniture he'd been expecting, or maybe his wife, he set down his hammer and headed into the living room.

He'd left the front door ajar, partly to enjoy the nice weather and partly to make sure he didn't miss the furniture delivery, but it was his father who stepped inside.

"You're making a damn racket," he said when he spotted Simon.

Simon dusted Sheetrock chalk from his hands and clothes. "So? This is my house. What are you doing here, anyway? Did you come to serve me papers?"

"Not this time." He slanted his head to look beyond Simon. "Where's Gail?"

"Gone, but she'll be back soon."

He tore the wrapper off a toothpick and shoved it in his mouth. "She's different from anyone you've been with before. You know that?"

Leery, Simon folded his arms. "Different in what way?"

"Better. Stronger. I can see that, now I've got some painkiller in me and I've had a chance to think."

Simon agreed with his assessment of Gail, but he wondered how his father had noticed so quickly. "What makes you say so?"

"Not hard to tell." He handed over an envelope. "Here."

"What's this?"

"A release."

"From the film?" Simon didn't bother hiding his surprise.

"Take a look." His father gestured for him to open it.

Simon pulled a single handwritten sheet of paper from the envelope. It said that his contract with Excite Entertainment Production Company had been terminated and all monies paid him were due back in thirty days. It was a fair arrangement, one Simon could live with. "What changed your mind?" he asked.

A faint smile curved Tex's lips. "I guess I don't want to be a morally bankrupt old fart *all* the time."

Simon had never heard his father talk this way before. "Excuse me?"

"Never mind. I owe you that much. And…" He moved the toothpick to one side and turned to spit over the railing. "I'm sorry I, uh, got involved with Bella. Sometimes even I don't know why I do what I do."

Simon wasn't sure how to react. Tex could be agreeable and easygoing at times, but he always reverted to his more difficult, narcissistic self. Still, the pleasant moments were rare and that made this an Occasion. "So you're no longer putting all the blame on her?"

"It's takes two." Tex lifted a hand in farewell. "Tell Gail to keep fighting. Looks aren't everything."

Offended, Simon followed him down the walkway. "There's nothing wrong with Gail's looks!"

"See what I mean?" Tex said, chuckling. "She might prove me wrong, after all."

Simon stopped at the gate while Tex continued on to his truck. "Prove you wrong about what? When have you ever talked to Gail?"

"Don't worry about it," his father said. "Just know that she's the best thing to happen to you in a long time. Don't take her for granted."

"Hey, I didn't expect to see you."

Gail glanced up as her father walked into the minimart section of his gas station. She'd known he'd come. A buzzer sounded in back whenever someone stepped over the threshold.

"I just wanted to stop in and say hi." She handed him his favorite flavor of milk shake, which she'd purchased at the soda fountain down the street. "Where's Joe?"

"Got a call for a tow. Old Mrs. Reed is stranded with a dead battery over at the bingo parlor."

"That's quite an emergency." She put the shake she'd bought for Joe in the minifreezer located in the tiny break room, which was more like a closet. It also contained the mop, bucket and other supplies they used for cleaning, as well as toilet paper and towels for the restrooms.

"Like what we've done to the place?" her father called after her.

He was talking about the new section of the store, where one could buy soft drinks, fruit smoothies and snow cones. She'd been admiring the new machines when she first came in. "I do. Bet it'll be a hit come summer."

"Hope so. Cost me enough."

Gail breathed deep, taking in the scents of motor oil, grease and gasoline that brought back her youth. Oddly enough, the station felt as much like home as the house in which she'd been raised. She'd spent a lot of time here as a little girl, playing with the tools or watching a small TV behind the counter while her father ran his business. When she was a teenager, she'd stocked the shelves, co-ordinated tows and written up work orders in addition to running the register. Her father had believed in keeping his kids busy. That hadn't prevented Joe from getting into trouble now and then. She'd never gotten into trouble, but she remembered closing on many Friday nights when her friends were partying after the football game and feeling left out. As an adult she didn't begrudge her father those hours. She realized he'd probably needed her help—or maybe just her company. For some of that time Joe was away at college.

"Did your furniture ever come?" her father asked.

Gail checked her phone. "I don't think so. Simon texted me an hour ago to say it hadn't arrived, and I haven't heard from him since. He said he'd call when it did."

Her father glanced at the clock hanging on the wall. "It's almost three. I'm surprised you're not over there waiting for it."

"I wanted to see you."

Stirring his shake, he tilted his head to look into her face. "Something wrong, Gabby?"

She shrugged. "Nothing serious. I guess I just wondered what you think of Simon."

"I don't know what to think yet. He seems nice enough so far. But I don't form an opinion on nice alone. It takes more to be a good man than a smile."

She nodded.

"Don't tell me you two are having trouble already...."

"No. Not at all. He treats me really well. It's just..." She nibbled on her bottom lip while searching for the right words. "I think I'm falling in love with him."

"That's good, isn't it?" he said with a laugh. "You are married to him."

"But I'd prefer not to be head over heels."

"Why not?"

She stopped trying to hide the misery she was feeling. "Because I'm scared. What if he never feels the same way toward me?"

"If he doesn't love you, what's he doing with you?"

"Isn't it obvious? I told you I married him to help him. He needs me right now. But that won't be the case forever."

Her father took a big spoonful of his milk shake and spoke after he'd swallowed. "No marriage is easy, Gabby."

"I know that. But...am I crazy to want more than I should expect?"

Her father set his cup aside and took her hands. "Look at me."

She forced herself to meet his gaze. He had every

right to say, "I told you not to get involved with Simon," but that wasn't what she wanted to hear.

"Love is always a risk," he said instead.

"I was fully aware of that coming into this. I thought I could take…whatever. But I never knew I could fall so hard."

Her father kissed her forehead. "If Simon's as smart as I think, he'll realize what he's got."

His reassurance made her feel better. She gave him a hug despite his dirty clothes and left. But as she started her car to go over to the house, a little voice inside her head repeated what Simon's father had said: *He won't stay with you. You're not even that pretty.*

When Gail arrived at the house, Simon came to the front door to meet her with his T-shirt tied around his head like a headband. His bare torso was covered in dust, dirt and sweat.

"You've been busy," she said as she got the ribs she'd bought them for dinner from the backseat of her car.

He flopped down on the top step of the porch. "I'm exhausted. I'll probably be so sore tomorrow I won't be able to move."

Captivated by his dazzling smile, she put down the sack and sat next to him. He was tired, but he was happy. She'd never seen him this relaxed, this carefree. Whiskey Creek had been the right place to bring him. She felt certain of that and proud of the self-restraint he'd exercised so far. "I got your text. Furniture's coming tomorrow, huh? What happened?"

"Truck got a flat. But I think it's for the best." His guilty expression made him look younger, almost boyish. "I've created a bigger mess than I expected."

She leaned over to peek through the open door and into the house. Whatever he'd been doing hadn't extended to the living room. She could see their mattress and bedding in front of the fireplace, apparently untouched since last night, but…the lighting was different. "Did you cover the windows?"

"I did. I wanted us to be able to stay here tonight."

She raised her eyebrows. "Any particular reason?"

His grin said it all.

Gail was done fighting what she felt. She had him for two years. Although she couldn't help hoping for more, she knew the chances of her marriage lasting longer than that were slim. She figured she might as well enjoy being with him while she could and if—when— she lost him, she'd let him go gracefully. That way, he'd maintain some respect for her afterward, maybe even remember her fondly. There was no way they could continue to work together—not after being married—but they'd have memories. She preferred that those memories be positive. "I thought you were beat."

"Not *that* beat." He slipped a hand under her blouse but only to caress the skin at her waist. "Getting you naked's been on my mind all day."

She untied the T-shirt on his head and smoothed his unruly hair. "Funny, I could say the same thing about you."

"Then what took you so long to get here? I almost called you a dozen times."

Oh, boy…she was falling deeper. There was no help for her. "Weren't you busy?"

"I will be as soon as I get you in the house. But first, a shower." He started to climb to his feet, but she pushed him back and straddled him right there on the porch.

"Actually, I like you just the way you are."

"Dirty?" he teased.

"A little dirt never hurt anybody." She leaned over to whisper in his ear. "I've always wanted to get nailed by a contractor."

He laughed. "I hope Riley doesn't know that, or I might have some competition."

She ground her hips against him. "I'm not interested in his hammer."

His teeth flashed in another smile. "I'm more than happy to show you what I can do with mine."

In one fluid movement, he sat up, then carried her inside.

"What about the food?" she asked as he kicked the door shut.

He was already nuzzling her neck, telling her she smelled good and tasted good and just the thought of her had been driving him crazy. "Later," he murmured against her skin. "Right now all I want is you."

It was well after they'd showered and eaten and rearranged their bedding so they could sleep that Simon's phone awakened him. He had a new text message. At this hour, it had to be from Bella. She was the only one who ever bothered him so late. He would've ignored it. He didn't want to leave the warmth and comfort of being tangled up with Gail. Despite her lack of experience, his new wife really knew how to make love. And this time she'd put everything she had into it. God, it was good.

But he was worried about Ty. It'd been so long since he'd talked to his son. Could something terrible have happened to him? Or maybe something not so terrible? Did he have a cold? A stubbed toe? A loose tooth?

Simon ached for the comfort of all the things he'd once taken for granted—Ty crawling into his bed early in the morning and patting his cheeks, whispering, "Daddy, wake up. I want some cereal." Ty running to him after he'd hurt himself. Ty throwing both arms around his neck and saying, "I love you, Daddy." Simon had never hurt so much over anything or anyone. The hunger to hold his son made him angry with the woman who was standing in his way, but he knew allowing that anger to overpower him would defeat everything he was doing to get Ty back. He couldn't act on it.

But thinking about Ty and Bella made it difficult to sleep.

Careful not to wake Gail, he slipped off the air mattress, pulled on his jeans and scooped up his phone, which was lying among the remains of their dinner, before going outside.

The sky was clear, the temperature cool. The stars

seemed bigger than he ever remembered seeing them in L.A. He was tempted to blame it on the smog, but knew it was probably him. He hadn't been paying attention to such details. There was a lot he'd ignored in recent years. Only now was he beginning to realize that he'd filled his life with so many possessions and so much angst and clamor, so much *shallowness,* that he'd missed the quiet, still things that brought him peace. When had he lost sight of who he really was? Of what he wanted his life to be? He was a critically acclaimed actor, but who was he on a personal level? Had he ever really known?

As he sat on the step and gazed down at his ex-wife's latest message, he frowned. Why won't you answer me? she'd written.

She had a restraining order against him, and she had to ask?

He scrolled up to read all the other messages he'd seen and hadn't responded to, but he stopped short of viewing the video she'd sent the night he cut his hand. He knew if he saw that right now he wouldn't be able to stop himself from driving to L.A. and busting into her house to get Ty.

Really? You're going to ignore me?

Maybe I should tell Ty his daddy doesn't give a shit about him anymore.

Your father's looking for you. Where the hell are you?

You said you'd never marry again. What, were you too drunk to realize you were saying "I do"? Or were you thinking with your cock again?

Who is the bitch? Your *publicist*? Were you screwing her all along?

It was hateful, spiteful garbage. He wanted to text back, to vent his anger and frustration as she felt free to do, but what would he say? That he was bitterly disappointed? That they'd created a great kid, the best, and he couldn't understand why they hadn't been able to get along?

Simon felt like such a failure—and everything he'd done to escape the self-loathing just made it worse.

Leaning back, he closed his eyes and let the autumn air calm him. He could think more clearly now than he had in months, could see that he was at a turning point. It was time to cut the past away. Sure, he and Bella had messed up their marriage. Sure, he had his regrets. But it was too late to change any of that now. So how long was he going to hang on to the wreckage?

Not anymore, he decided. He was letting go, and he wanted Bella to do the same. From here on out, they needed to handle all communication, at least any communication that didn't directly concern Ty, through their lawyers, as they'd been advised to do.

But he doubted she would. He knew why she kept jabbing him. She loved him almost as much as she hated him. As twisted as that was, he understood. He'd been struggling with the same love-hate compulsion, which was another reason he'd gotten himself into so much trouble.

Fortunately, Gail had changed everything.

His thoughts turned to his publicist and what they'd shared tonight. Something had changed, grown serious. He'd noticed it in himself as much as her. They'd approached their lovemaking with an emotional intensity that hadn't been there before, as if possessing each other mattered far more than achieving a physical release. And he'd welcomed that new emotional element, because Gail satisfied him more deeply than Bella ever could.

Somehow Gail, someone he would've considered a highly unlikely prospect, given their many differences, had managed to plug the gaping hole in his chest, to stop the bleeding caused by his divorce, his father, his mother—all of it. He wasn't sure how long being with her would feel this right. He didn't trust what he was experiencing to last. But he owed Gail enough loyalty to put an end, in *every* way, to what had come before, with Bella.

Please let me know if Ty needs anything, he typed. I will do everything I can for him. But other than that, don't contact me. He reread his words, then smiled as he added, I'm happily married.

27

"Do you see it yet?" Josh's voice was even more animated than usual.

Gail moved the phone to her other ear as she opened the link he'd just sent her. There, front and center, was a picture of her and Simon on the porch last night with the heading Hot Honeymoon. As she straddled him, his hands circled her waist and he stared up at her. They weren't photographed from the front, but there was no doubting their identities. "I'm there."

"Is that really you?"

Clearly, that was her. She looked completely caught up in the moment—and she had been. She and Simon had made love again this morning, a gentle, sweet coupling that was a stark contrast to the explosion of desire last night. She couldn't decide which she'd enjoyed more. She'd liked both. Sex was so much better when you were madly in love....

"How many sites have put this up?" she asked Josh. Their furniture had arrived. She didn't yet have a desk, but she was sitting on the new couch. Until Josh had called to report the sudden influx of Google hits, she'd been comfortable. There was only one drawback to working out of their new house—it wasn't easy to hear with Simon banging away in the kitchen.

She had to admit she was glad he wasn't in the room with her, however. She'd all but attacked him last night, and in plain view of anyone who might've been hoping for just such a pic.

"It's all over the Net and spreading as we speak," Josh said. "Isn't that great? You did a fabulous job. You both look as if you're completely *into* each other. This could be an ad for Armani or Calvin Klein. It's gorgeous! Who took the picture? I even like the old Victorian in the background. Was it Ian?"

Face burning, Gail briefly covered her eyes. "No."

"Then who? Your father?"

"My *father?*" She wrinkled her nose at the thought of Martin being anywhere in the vicinity when she'd wantonly climbed on top of Simon. "That's sick."

"Why? You have your clothes on!"

It still looked very sexual—because it had been.

"You are so conservative," he said. "Well, normally." He was obviously referring to the photograph with this clarification. He chuckled at his own joke, but Gail didn't find it funny.

"Anyway, *someone* took that picture," he said. "Was it a friend?"

"No. I'm guessing it's some member of the paparazzi. Someone was trying to get a shot through the window while we were sleeping the night before last. We assumed he, or she, left after that. No one was here when the cops arrived, and we haven't noticed anyone following us since. But apparently, whoever it was hasn't given up."

"I haven't run across any shots of you sleeping."

Big Hit would know if such photos had appeared on the internet. Google would've alerted them of that, too. "They must not have turned out—or showed our identities clearly enough. It wasn't a high-percentage shot."

Josh lowered his voice. "So…you were straddling Simon, getting him excited, and you didn't know someone was taking your picture? This *wasn't* calculated?"

She stared at the photo of her and Simon on her computer screen. Maybe Josh was happy about it, but she wasn't sure this would do Simon any favors. He needed a different slant for his new image, one that showed him as a man who'd settled down. This was far too sexy. It made him look like he was embroiled in yet another torrid affair.

"No, it wasn't calculated," she said. "As a publicist, I would've structured it very differently—maybe had him carry in the groceries or something."

"So this was spontaneous? Holy shit!" Josh cried. "Now I'm really jealous. You must be having the time of your life."

She was having the best sex of her life. No doubt about that. But she was scared to death wondering where things would go from here. And now she had to worry about how her behavior last night was going to affect the campaign and her efforts to help Simon gain custody of Ty. After they made love, he'd talked about his son for probably an hour. He missed Ty so much, he'd had to get his pictures out of his wallet and show them to her, even though she'd met Ty several times in the past and already knew what a darling little boy he was.

Could she soften the impact of this rather explicit picture? Give an interview focusing on the fact that this was, after all, their honeymoon? Passion played an important role in a marriage, but that wasn't what she'd been hoping to highlight. She doubted this picture would impress the judge who'd be ruling on Ty's fate....

"Gail?" Joshua prompted. "Did you hear me?"

She searched her memory for his question and managed to recall his last words: he'd wanted to know if she was having fun. "For now."

"So he's good in bed. As good as he seems in *Shiver?*"

Joshua wanted her to dish, but her private life with Simon was something she planned to keep to herself. "That's none of your business."

"But you *have* slept with him, even though you said you wouldn't."

"Quit digging, Josh."

"That's a yes. Oh, my God!"

She couldn't help laughing. "Stop it! We need to figure out how to spin this."

"Why? It's perfect!"

He thought so because he was one of the most sexual creatures she'd ever encountered. "We're aiming to convince a far more conservative crowd." She considered her options, then made a decision. "Call your friend at *Hollywood Secrets Revealed.* Tell her I'm willing to talk. It's time Mrs. O'Neal gave her first interview."

"Mrs. O'Neal. You're taking ownership. I like that. But what will you say?"

"I'll tell her how misunderstood Simon has been, how there's been much more going on than was reported in the media, how one side of a story is never completely accurate."

"I know the routine. But…do you really believe that?"

After what she'd learned from Tex? Wholeheartedly. Men had committed murder over less than what Simon had discovered—firsthand—about his wife and his father. It sort of made sense to her now that he'd go out looking for a good brawl, smash someone who provoked him on-set or off, pick a fight with Bella's brother. She could even understand why he might turn to alcohol to keep from thinking about what he knew, and why he couldn't tell the world that Bella had done her share of cheating. Imagine the media frenzy that would occur over something like that—Bella having sex with Simon's famous father—and how the taint of it would follow her, and Ty, for years. Gail couldn't reveal all of that information to the public, but she could certainly tell people that Bella hadn't been easy to live with and that all the blame shouldn't be assigned to one person.

"I think he deserves more credit than he's received," she said. "He's done what he can to be gallant."

"He's gone from being an ass in your opinion to being gallant? Oh, Lord."

"What?"

"You're falling for him, aren't you."

She didn't deny it. "Hard," she admitted.

Simon walked into the room as she hung up. "We've got a mess," he announced.

Of course they had a mess, but she could tell he wasn't referring to the pictures she'd just seen. He didn't know about them yet.

"What's wrong?" She closed her laptop. She'd have to tell him about the media hits, but she wanted a moment to think it through first, to be sure she was doing the right thing in offering interviews.

"The plumbing."

"The plumbing?" she repeated, somewhat relieved. After her call with Josh, she'd thought it was going to be something far more serious.

He dusted off his hands. "It's all so old. It needs to be replaced."

With Simon standing there in a T-shirt that stretched nicely across his pecs and a pair of faded jeans that fit him so well he could've stopped traffic, famous or no, it was tough to care too much about anything else. But she did her best to show the appropriate concern. "Sounds expensive."

"It probably will be. But I'm not worried about that.

I just wanted to let you know the remodel might not come together as fast as I'd hoped."

"That's fine." She was about to apologize for getting him involved in a money pit. After all, he'd bought the house to please her. But then he gazed around with a speculative eye, propped his hands on his hips and said, "Maybe we should redo the electrical while we're at it."

"Is something wrong with that, too?"

"No. It's just smart to update while everything's torn apart," he replied, and that was when she realized that he didn't mind the extra work. The opposite was true; he enjoyed what he was doing enough to add items to the list.

"I see," she said as solemnly as she could. "But you wouldn't do the electrical and plumbing yourself."

"Oh, hell, no. I'll just oversee everything and do the finish work." He hitched a thumb over his shoulder. "This place is going to look great when we're done."

"I never doubted you for a minute," she said. Then she drew a deep breath and told him about the pictures.

"An interview should handle it." A shrug indicated he wasn't too concerned as he headed back to work.

When Simon returned from getting his stitches out, Ian was there, sitting in a Porsche parked in front of the house.

His business manager opened the car door as Simon approached. "Finally!" he said with mock exasperation.

"Why didn't you go in?" Simon asked. "I told you when you called that Gail should be home." He'd left her in the midst of her interview with *Hollywood Secrets Revealed* or she would've gone to the doctor's with him.

"I have the ring you asked me to get." He held up a small brown sack.

"Great. Thanks. But I was expecting that. You still could've gone in."

"I didn't want my presence to tip her off. I assume the ring's a surprise."

"It is, but seeing you in Whiskey Creek wouldn't tip her off. You also brought some things for me to sign, didn't you?"

"I did." He scratched his head. "It wasn't just the ring, Simon. I was hoping to catch you alone."

"Because…"

"I'd like to talk to you." He motioned to the passenger seat of his Porsche. "Will you take a drive with me?"

Reluctantly, Simon agreed. He knew Ian wasn't happy with his decision to put his work commitments on hold. He'd probably get a list of all the deals that were going to hell because he wasn't there to make appearances and so forth, and he didn't want to hear it. He was fully aware of the risks he was taking and the losses he was sustaining. For once it was intentional. But he figured he owed his manager a few minutes. They'd worked together for a long time.

"Fine," he said with a sigh.

Ian pulled away from the curb almost before Simon could buckle his seat belt.

"What's up?" he asked as they gathered speed.

"This." Ian handed him a file that had been wedged between his seat and the console.

Simon glanced through it. It was a collection of articles and pictures on him and Gail. "Why'd you bring me this? You think Gail wouldn't show me the same thing, if I asked?"

"Have you read some of those articles?"

"Not word for word."

"Why not?"

Because it made him angry to read what was being said about Gail. He hated seeing how the Plain Jane garbage hurt her. So why raise his blood pressure? It wasn't as if he could do anything about what was being printed. He couldn't exactly tell the assholes who wrote this bullshit that they had no idea what she was really like. That would only make her more of a target. "Gail is keeping her eye on the press coverage. I've been busy with other things."

"Like getting in her pants? Is she that good a lay?"

Obviously he'd seen the pictures that had gone viral this morning. "Maybe. Why, would that bother you?"

Ian hung a left and drove out of town. "Of course not. I'm guessing she leaked the pictures of you and her on the porch to make your relationship seem more legitimate, but people aren't buying it."

Simon felt his eyebrows shoot up. "What are you talking about?"

"Come on, Simon. No one believes you could fall for a girl like her. There's speculation all over the place, even a few claims that it's a publicity stunt."

This was the first Simon had heard about that. Gail must not know, either, or she would've mentioned it. "What gave us away?"

"How should I know? Maybe we didn't take into consideration what a cynical world we live in. Your marriage was sudden. Your new wife is a PR pro. Maybe people are reading between the lines." He sifted through the stack and took out a snarky blog post that named the women Simon had been seen with in the weeks prior to his second marriage. The blog critiqued his usual choice of women and asserted that Gail was nothing like them. It even went so far as to say "industry insiders" believed he'd paid her to marry him to save him from the rape charge.

"Shit."

"Then there's this." Ian used his knee to steer while he found another blog post. This one had a photo of Gail and pictures of the women Simon had been with over the years. Almost all of them were famous themselves or were blonde bombshells. The heading read One of These Is Not Like the Others....

The campaign was falling apart already. Feeling a sense of loss, he shut the file and looked at Ian. "What are you getting at?"

"I think we should call it quits, don't you? If there's no benefit in pretending to care about her, why keep it up? I don't want you to ruin your career by breaking all your contracts just because of some misguided decision *I* had a hand in."

"So you've come out to rescue me."

He adjusted the heater. "To tell you you're making a mistake. I should never have gotten you involved in this."

"No."

"No, what?"

"You're wrong." Regardless of how it was being played in the media, being with Gail didn't feel like a mistake. "There will always be detractors, no matter what I do. I'm not changing course." He was finally feeling human again, sleeping most nights, gaining strength and a sense of purpose. He missed Ty but every day he felt more confident that he'd get him back. Maybe that was because he could finally trust himself to be the kind of father he needed to be.

So what if no one believed in his marriage?

He was starting to believe in it.

"Take me back. I want to give that ring to Gail."

Ian's mouth dropped open. "You're kidding."

Simon smiled. "Not at all."

"You're really going to Sophia's tonight?"

When Callie asked this, Gail was standing at the window, holding back the sheet so she could see outside. Her friend had arrived at her door carrying a copy of *People* magazine shortly after Simon and Ian drove off. One of the pictures Josh had taken at the wedding was on the cover, but Gail couldn't concentrate on that when she was so concerned about what Ian might be saying to Simon. She knew it wouldn't be anything that supported his staying in Whiskey Creek. The fact that Ian hadn't come to the door or even spoken to her would've told her that much, if she hadn't already been aware of it. Although Simon didn't want to accept it, she halfway believed that Ian had told Tex where they were because he was hoping Tex would drag Simon back. Then it would be business as usual for both of them.

"Did you hear me?" Callie prompted.

Distracted, worried, Gail murmured, "What?"

"I asked if you're really going to Sophia's."

She didn't see why that mattered right now. "I guess so."

"*What?* Now I know you're out of it. Sophia's the girl who stole your prom date in junior year, remember? She's always treated us like second-class citizens."

Gail turned. "Did you see Simon in a red Porsche on your way over here?"

Callie was thumbing through the magazine. "No, why? He cheating on you already?"

"Stop it," Gail said with a scowl.

"Sorry." Callie gave her a sheepish grin. "I have to admit I sort of like him. Not only is he…shall we say… pleasant to look at, he's very engaging."

Gail curved her lips into a superior grin. "I knew you'd like him."

"I didn't say that. The jury's still out on whether or not he's going to be good for you. It's only been a few weeks. We can't take too much for granted."

Gail dropped the smile, mostly because it was hard to act as if *she* was right when she knew it was Callie who'd end up saying, "I told you so." But she did have one argument. "Well, I, for one, am going to assume complete fidelity. Not doing so would drive us both crazy. But thanks for the advice."

Callie propped her legs up on the coffee table. "So why are you gnawing on your fingernails while you stare out the front window as if he's left for good? Why haven't you even looked at these pictures, which most women would be dying to see?"

"Because his friend and business manager cannot be trusted. Simon's trying to change, improve his life."

"And you're helping him."

"Of course."

"But what could his business manager be doing? Plying him with alcohol?"

Gail had no doubt Ian would provide drugs, too, if that was what Simon wanted. But she was more concerned that he might talk Simon into going back to L.A. and starting that movie she'd gotten him out of. Or commit him to some other project. Simon planned to return to acting, but he needed more time. And Ian certainly wouldn't take that into consideration. He'd press forward with his own agenda.

If she thought he had Simon's best interests at heart, she wouldn't mind so much, but she didn't believe he did. "Possibly."

"If you ask me, you should be more worried about Sophia than Ian," Callie said, still flipping pages. "She might be more of a test than he can handle."

"Thanks a lot!" Giving up her vigil at the window,

Gail went back to the couch and grabbed the magazine. "Let me see this."

"You know what she was like," Callie said. "No boy was off-limits."

Gail leafed through the pages. Simon looked gorgeous, as always, and she looked...determined, like she was executing a business deal. For good reason...

"That was a long time ago." She tossed the magazine on the table so she wouldn't obsess about her own imperfections, which seemed obvious when she was standing next to her movie-star husband.

Husband... She couldn't get used to thinking like that, to feeling she had such a strong claim on him. "Sophia's been through a lot in the past few years. Maybe she's changed."

"And maybe she wants to get lucky with your guy. Skip's always gone. She's probably trolling for any form of entertainment."

Gail opened her mouth to respond but didn't bother when she heard a car pull up. "They're back," she said, jumping to her feet.

Sure enough, Ian's red Porsche was parked by the picket fence. He wasn't getting out of the car, but Simon was.

"Looks like he's in one piece," Callie said, speaking over Gail's shoulder.

Gail breathed a sigh of relief. But she knew that the stronger Simon became, the more Ian's pleas would tempt him to return to his regular life. They'd planned on staying married for two years. But she doubted it would last that long.

28

Simon wanted to give Gail the ring, but he didn't want to do it while Callie was there. The edge of the hard little box dug into his thigh as he sat down to visit, but the whole time they talked he was thinking about making love to Gail later, maybe in the shower again, and then having the ring waiting on her pillow.

He hoped she'd like it. He couldn't imagine that she wouldn't, but there was a chance. He already knew she wasn't the type of woman who'd want it just because it was expensive. Giving it to her had to mean something. And it did now. He couldn't say exactly what. Everything was too new for labels. But...he wanted her to have it. That told him there had to be a reason.

When Callie asked about the renovation, he and Gail walked her through the house and talked about some of the changes they'd planned. He was getting excited about the possibilities, enjoyed challenging himself in a whole new way. He even liked how exhausted he was at the end of the day. It made curling up with his no-nonsense, tough-as-nails wife, who'd turned out to be as sweet as a woman could be, that much more enjoyable. One thing he knew—those don't-mess-with-me suits of hers hid a very tender heart.

After about thirty minutes, Gail said they had to get ready to go to Sophia's and Callie left. They were alone at that point. He could've given her the ring then and almost did. He felt like a kid with a really great Christmas gift he couldn't wait to present. But she was in too much of a hurry for him to be able to do it right. He certainly didn't want her to think he was trying to pay her for giving in on the sex issue. He'd asked Ian to buy the diamond before they'd ever made love, but she wouldn't know that and if he had to explain it, the whole thing would be ruined.

"You all set?" When she came out of the bedroom, she was wearing a pair of tight-fitting, skinny jeans and a sleeveless black sweater with a leather jacket. With her hair pulled back and pearls at her neck and ears, she looked classy, prettier than ever. But he liked the way she looked just as much when she wasn't wearing any makeup—or clothes, for that matter. He especially loved her smooth skin and how it felt beneath his hands. He loved her eyes, too, and the emotion they conveyed. She cared about him. Maybe too much. But he didn't want to think about that.

"You look great," he murmured, and pulled her into his arms long enough to breathe in her perfume and kiss her neck.

She didn't resist, but she glanced up at him as if

she was a bit hesitant to respond. "What did Ian have to say?"

"Nothing new. He wants me back in L.A. You probably guessed that."

"What for? Can't he see how great you're doing here?"

"*Great* is a relative term. In his mind I'm not working, so I can't be doing too great. I think he's mostly reacting to the fact that things have changed. He feels he's lost control of his biggest client."

"You mean he feels threatened by me."

"He doesn't like the influence you have."

She caught his face between her hands. "We'll be able to remain friends when this is all over, won't we? I mean, I know we won't be able to keep working together, but we'll still *like* each other, right?"

Why worry about later? Why not just be grateful for now? After all, he was so much better off than before. "I hope we will. The hardest part about bumping into you will probably be stopping myself from carrying you off to the bedroom."

"Why? At that point, you'll have a huge selection again."

"No one else makes love like you." There'd never been anyone with whom he could completely let down his guard, no one he could trust in quite the same way. "In case you haven't noticed, I can't get enough."

He was afraid she'd reject that compliment like she had so many others. He expected her to say he wouldn't care who he was with as long as he got what he

wanted—which was what he'd heard her say before—
but she didn't. Her hand cupped his cheek as she kissed
him, openmouthed.

"You keep this up, we won't make it to dinner," he
said.

With a laugh, she stepped away. "I can't help it. I am
so…" She seemed to catch herself.

"What?" he asked.

She hesitated, then blinked. "Glad I married you.
It's been the best mix of business and pleasure I've
ever had."

God, she'd almost told him. Right there, while her
brain frequencies were all jammed up by the sexy look
on his face and her body was growing warm in antici-
pation of his touch, she'd almost blurted, "I am *so* in
love with you!" Every time she looked at him, she grew
a little more intoxicated.

Fortunately, she'd caught herself, and a few minutes
of standing outside his immediate orbit had made it
easier to think. He'd basically told her she was a good
lay. He would not want "I love you" in response when
he'd warned her not to take their relationship too seriously in the first place.

The whole time they were at Sophia's, Gail was lec-
turing herself on how she'd handle being alone with him
once they returned home. She wouldn't say *anything,*
not one word about any kind of feeling. There was no
need to send him into a panic. She'd let her body do
the talking, since he didn't seem able to tell the differ-

ence between sex with a woman who lived for his every smile and sex with a woman who was merely in it for another celebrity conquest. Men were obtuse that way, she decided, and Simon didn't seem to be an exception.

"Would you like more mashed potatoes?"

Gail glanced up. Sophia had put on an impressive spread—medallions of beef tenderloin, garlic mashed potatoes, asparagus, carrots and a salad—and was now standing next to the table holding a bowl. Gail had expected Alexa, Sophia's daughter, to be with them, but she was spending the night with a friend because they had a school project they'd be presenting the next day. And Skip was gone again. Gail wasn't even sure Sophia had said where. They sat in her big elegant dining room in her big elegant house and it was just the three of them. She wondered how Sophia handled being alone so much of the time.

"No, thanks." Gail smiled and tried to think of something else to say but a moment later went back to her meal. Simon was doing fine carrying the conversation. She was too busy worrying. What was she going to do after their marriage ended? She'd be looking at some long, dreary days ahead. Would she ever get over him? Be able to fall in love again? If so, she doubted it would happen soon. She'd waited thirty-one years to fall in love the first time. Now that she had, she knew what she'd harbored for Matt had been nothing by comparison.

"You're quiet. You okay?" Simon murmured when

Sophia went into the kitchen to get another bottle of wine.

She swallowed the piece of asparagus in her mouth. "Fine."

His eyebrows drew together. "Maybe we should leave early. Get you into bed."

"We can't be rude. She's gone to so much work." She checked to make sure Sophia was still out of earshot but lowered her voice anyway. "And I think she's really lonely."

"I have no doubt of it."

"Callie believes she's after you."

"I can promise you she's not. She's being very polite, but she keeps looking at you as if you're the one she's hoping to impress. Take it from a fellow reprobate, she wants to win your friendship. If you weren't so preoccupied, you'd notice."

Gail *had* noticed, which was why she hadn't concerned herself with Callie's warnings. "I'm just stewing over that interview I gave *Hollywood Secrets Revealed* this morning."

"You said it went well."

"The reporter was receptive, but let's hope it was the right move. We don't want to create a backlash to our claims of peace and happiness with the media rehashing everything that happened in the past year."

"It'll be fine even if they do. We'll keep pointing to my track record since we got together. I've been perfect. That's all the judge needs to know."

For him, it really was about getting his son back.

She smiled at the pride in his voice. He was feeling a lot better about himself, and that pleased her. Regardless of what she'd face in the future, at least she would know she'd made a difference to him.

"Dessert's almost ready," Sophia called.

Simon leaned halfway across the table. "I want to mention that bruise on her cheek again and see how she responds. Do you think I should?"

Gail considered whether or not it would do any good. In her opinion, it would just make Sophia uncomfortable. "No. She's too self-conscious about it. Keeps moving her hair to make sure it's covered."

"I bet her husband did it."

Gail wondered about that, too, except she couldn't picture Skip ever striking anyone. "I don't know. Maybe not. I'd hate to accuse him and be wrong, especially here. It's such a close-knit community. Gossip like that can do so much harm."

"It's a tricky situation," he agreed.

"If she's being hurt, she needs to speak up. She can't hope someone will guess."

"But not all women can—"

His cell phone interrupted them with the buzz that signaled a text message. He took it out of his pocket and glanced at it, although he didn't seem particularly interested in what might be coming in. He obviously wanted to get back to their conversation. But then he stiffened.

"What is it?" Gail asked, but that was just as Sophia walked in.

He glanced from her to their hostess. "It's Ty," he said. "If you'll excuse me."

He got up and walked out, leaving Gail to entertain her old nemesis while he placed a call in the other room. Judging by how low his voice was, how urgently he was speaking, Gail knew he could only be talking to Bella.

Simon didn't want to look at Gail. He knew she didn't agree with what he was doing, and he hated to disappoint her. She'd just started to trust him. But he had to go back to L.A. Bella had been sobbing on the phone. He'd never heard her sound quite so desperate and brokenhearted. She'd told him how much she still loved him. That she'd always love him. That she was terribly sorry about what had happened between her and his father. That her own insecurities had gotten the best of her yet again. That there'd never been anyone in her life who could even compare to him. That she and Ty needed him.

Simon was so used to running to her rescue that it seemed natural to go now, even after everything she'd done. But he wouldn't have let that sense of obligation influence him if not for Ty. He believed Bella when she said his son needed him; he'd thought so all along, and wanted to be there for him. Although Simon wasn't interested in picking up where he'd left off with Bella, as she seemed to want, he was hoping for *some* type of relationship that would enable him to see his son on a regular basis.

Gail sat against the headboard of their new bed, hugging her knees to her chest as he randomly threw clothes into his suitcase.

"The media will find it strange that you'd abandon me to rush to her side," she said, her voice a monotone. "This could ruin everything we've established so far. You realize that."

He did. They'd talked about it on the way home. He'd take Gail with him if he could. But jealous as Bella was, he knew that would only cause more problems. It was his text about being happily married and the picture of Gail and him on the porch that'd finally caused Bella to break down. She'd told him on the phone that the minute she saw that picture, she'd feared she'd lost him for good and couldn't bear the thought of it.

"She's suddenly willing to work something out." He didn't have to specify who "she" was. "I have to take advantage of that. You have no idea how hard she's been to deal with. No one does. But she promised me that if I come right away, I can see Ty."

Gail frowned. "She's using him as a carrot. She wants you back."

"Doesn't matter. I'm no longer interested in her," he said, but he could tell that Gail didn't quite believe him. She thought it was the end of their marriage, and he couldn't promise her it wasn't. What they had was a contract to work together to help him get custody of Ty. Their relationship had turned out much better than he'd ever dreamed. But if he gained custody of his son tonight, he'd have what he wanted, and there'd be no reason to stay together.

"I'm sure she thinks you *are* interested," Gail said. "She's always been able to get you back before."

Only because she was the mother of his child and he'd so desperately wanted to maintain a regular family. "I'm not the same person I was."

"And yet you're willing to get on the same old roller coaster."

"No. She'll eventually have to face the fact that I'm over her."

In the meantime, Bella could think whatever she wanted as long as she gave him access to his son. Maybe they could build a bridge during the next few days, figure out how to put the negativity and fighting behind them. As far as he was concerned, their split didn't have to be so acrimonious. Especially now. Thanks to Gail, he was feeling healthier, more capable of dealing with the disappointment, the sense of failure and confusion caused by the divorce.

He'd gladly offer Bella more money if she'd agree to share custody. He wasn't sure what he'd be able to arrange. Bella hadn't been all that coherent on the phone; she'd just kept crying that she wanted him—but now that she'd reached out, he had to at least try.

"I don't trust her," Gail said.

"Neither do I," he responded. "But I have to do this. I'm sorry." Once he'd finished packing, he wished the limo he'd ordered while they were at Sophia's house would arrive. He had a long drive to the airport and didn't want to miss his flight out of Sacramento. It was the last one of the night. He could've arranged for his own jet to pick him up—he rarely flew commercial these days—but that wasn't easy to do on such short notice. He'd need to call his pilot, have him get the plane out of the hangar, make sure it had fuel, file a flight plan. Then Simon would have to wait for him to arrive from L.A. "Will you be coming home soon?"

"No. Not for a while."

She probably didn't want to face the media onslaught, and he didn't blame her. She'd find it embarrassing. Everyone would say that their marriage was just another fling and that he'd been in love with Bella all along. They'd say Gail should've known better than to think she could keep him. Maybe those people Ian had mentioned, who'd figured out that they'd done it for the PR, would get louder and more insistent. He dealt with the media enough—and so did she—to realize what the conjecture would be like and that it wouldn't be flattering to Gail. He already planned to offset that as much as possible by telling everyone how great she was and how much he cared about her. But he had to handle one thing at a time. "Then I'll come back here."

"No, there won't be any reason for you to do that," she said. "If you gain custody, you won't need me anymore. And if you don't, if she calls the cops because you violated the restraining order, staying married to me won't matter. After this, no one will believe you really care about me."

This was more than he could handle at the moment. He'd have to think about what to do with her later. "I just want my son. That's why I started this."

"I know. He's a great kid, so I don't blame you. What I'm trying to tell you is that I think you'll have a better chance if you stay. You should set up something consistent and reliable through the legal system, something that won't depend on her whim."

But he couldn't wait. "That could take months and months, maybe years," he said. "And even then there'll be no guarantees I'll win."

She didn't try to convince him otherwise. "True."

"That's why I have to go."

He'd dropped a shirt on the floor. She got up to fold it. Then she handed it to him to put in his bag and went about gathering up everything else he'd left—clothes, books, toiletries. "You didn't have to call a car service, you know. I would've driven you to the airport."

"I know. I didn't want you out so late. What if you got a flat tire?" He motioned at the stuff she was still picking up. "Forget that."

"You don't want it?"

"I'll get it later."

"Okay." She put the jeans she'd taken off the floor on the bed. "But before you go, there's one more thing I want to say."

He squirmed at her somber tone. This felt like a funeral. He wanted to get out of the house as soon as possible, but she deserved the chance to tell him how rotten he was for letting her down. She'd gone to a lot of work and effort to help him, and he'd done nothing except disrupt her life. True, her business was coming back from the brink of collapse. But in the aftermath of his leaving, her family would be angry with her for marrying him and her friends would have every right to say "I told you so."

He'd even messed up her love life. He knew very well that she'd once had feelings for Matt. Maybe, if not for his involvement, the two of them would've gotten together and become the perfect hometown couple.

"I'm listening." He was prepared to hear the worst. Instead, she came to stand in front of him, kissed him tenderly and said, "I've never loved a man so much. I hope you're always happy."

Completely taken off guard, he blinked in surprise. He almost pulled her into his arms so he could feel her body against his one more time, just in case she was right and everything changed after this moment. But she didn't give him the chance. With a parting smile, she crossed to the other bedroom and closed the door.

And then the limo arrived.

29

The house felt odd without Simon, probably because he'd been such a part of it. With the amount of work he'd been putting in and his excitement over the improvements, not to mention the time they'd spent here making love or simply sleeping together, it had begun to seem like a home. *Their* home. Their marriage had begun to feel real, too. But it had all ended even quicker than Gail had anticipated. He'd abstained from alcohol and behaved perfectly since they'd made their agreement, only to be drawn back to Los Angeles by Bella, the one variable Gail hadn't expected to play the part it did. She'd thought they'd have to battle tooth and nail to get Bella to let Simon see Ty. The restraining order had convinced her of it. Now she felt as if she'd been leaning hard on a door that had suddenly opened.

She should've known better than to rely on anything she'd been feeling since marrying Simon, especially the happiness and false sense of security that enveloped her while living in her hometown. She hadn't trusted it. Not really. And yet she'd embraced it—eagerly. Once she learned about Bella and Tex she should've realized that Bella had been manipulating Simon all along and would continue to do so—and that he would never be able to resist a friendly offer from her. After all, Bella had the one thing Simon cared about most. Ty trumped every other consideration.

Hugging her pillow close, Gail rolled over and squeezed her eyes shut. She'd known she'd face this day sooner or later. There was no point in feeling sorry for herself. But all the self-talk in the world couldn't ease the ache in her chest.

Maybe if she got out of 811 Autumn Lane, she'd recover faster, revert to her old in-charge, able-to-handle-anything self. If she returned to her father's place, she'd have to tell him and her brother that Simon had left her, but she'd have to do that fairly soon, anyway. Might as well get it over with.

She kicked off the covers and got up, then pulled on an old sweatshirt of Simon's. But before she could reach the hall the doorbell rang.

For a moment, she hoped it was Simon. He'd only been gone an hour. He could've come back. But she knew in her heart he wouldn't, not when he couldn't wait to see his son.

So who could be visiting at ten-thirty?

She wiped her face on her sleeve and padded out to the living room barefoot. He'd turned off the lights and locked up, but he'd replaced the burned-out porch light and left that on. Nice of him to be so considerate, she thought sarcastically, and pushed the sheet covering the front window to one side.

It was Sophia, pretty much the last person in the world she wanted to see. Wasn't dinner enough?

Gail almost didn't open the door. She wasn't sure she could put a smile on her face and pretend, as she'd done through dessert and an hour or so of small talk at Sophia's house earlier, that everything in her life was A-OK. But she also couldn't leave Sophia standing on the porch when the Lexus was parked out front, giving away the fact that someone was home. She couldn't have done that to anybody she knew, especially in Whiskey Creek.

Hoping the woman she'd once disliked immensely, and for good reason, wouldn't be able to tell she'd been crying, she opened the door.

"Hi." Contrary to what Gail had believed possible, she managed another of the fake smiles she'd been conjuring up all evening.

Sophia didn't immediately respond. She shoved her hands in the pockets of the lightweight jacket she was wearing and studied Gail carefully.

Growing uncomfortable, Gail cleared her throat. "What brings you out so late, Sophia?"

"Alexa forgot her toothbrush so I took it over to her."

"And that brought you here because..."

"I saw a limo pass by." She paused as if she expected Gail to say something, but Gail couldn't bring any words to her mouth. Initially, she'd been tempted to whisper, as though Simon was still in the house and she didn't want to wake him, but now she was glad she hadn't. Getting caught in such a pretense would've been even more embarrassing than acknowledging the sad reality.

"It was Simon, wasn't it?" she said. "He's leaving town."

Of all people to be the first to know. Would Sophia gloat? She would have when they were in high school. Gail wasn't even sure she could complain if Sophia did. She'd been slow to respond to Sophia's attempts at friendship, and she'd been less than wise to take the risks she had. "Yes."

"I thought so. I heard him call for a car after he spoke with… I'm guessing that was his ex-wife?"

"Yes." Although Gail wasn't thrilled to see Sophia put the pieces together so perfectly, she didn't see any point in trying to present the facts in any different way. As much as she and Simon had tried to pretend that nothing had changed, Sophia had watched him make his decision from a front-row seat.

"I'm sorry," she said.

"I appreciate that. So you came because…"

"I was worried that maybe you were having a hard time. I know you don't consider me a close friend, but I didn't want you to be alone if…if you needed someone." She shifted, obviously feeling awkward, but soldiered on. "I'm sure what you're going through can't be easy. I can tell that you love him very much."

Gail wished she could deny it. She wanted to say it was fine, that she'd known she was taking a chance when she married him and had been prepared for the worst—something that would salvage a bit of her pride. *It was fun while it lasted.* But Simon's defection was too new, her emotions too raw. She couldn't seem to raise her defenses.

So she didn't try. The redness of her face had probably given her away. "You're right," she said. "I do love him, more than I ever thought I could love someone. And it hurts like hell that he's gone." How was that for full disclosure? She figured she might as well give Sophia what she'd come for. The "mean girl" from high school could gloat if she wanted to.

But Sophia didn't seem to be taking any pleasure from her pain. Empathy filled her eyes, then she put her arms around Gail and gave her a long hug.

"I'm really, really sorry," she murmured and Gail could tell she meant it.

"Sometimes life just sucks, doesn't it?" Sophia added.

Gail got the impression she knew what she was talking about. "You're not happy with Skip, are you?"

Sophia hesitated as if it was difficult for her to reveal the truth. She'd been selling the "perfect family" illusion for so long. But eventually, she stepped back and admitted the truth. "No."

"Sometimes life sucks, all right," Gail said with a sad laugh. "Want to come in for coffee?"

Sophia returned her smile. "I'd love to."

They spent the next two hours discussing whether or not Gail should return immediately to L.A., what her father and brother would think of Simon's defection and how she should tell them, and whether or not Sophia should keep fighting to save her own marriage. She claimed that the bruise on her cheek wasn't from Skip, but Gail suspected the reality of that was too personal to share even within the confines of their new friendship.

Gail supposed she'd find out someday. She definitely planned on maintaining the relationship. Sophia as an adult was nothing like Sophia as an adolescent. She'd held back, too, hadn't told Sophia about the original reasons for the marriage. That was too risky to tell *anyone*.

"Look at the time," Sophia said, pulling out her cell phone. "I'd better go home."

"You could stay here," Gail said. "I have an extra bed."

"No. Skip might call." She grimaced. "He does that every once in a while just to check up. He's so afraid I'll cheat on him while he's gone."

"Do you think he's been cheating on you?"

It was another hard question, but they'd built up enough trust that this time she didn't hesitate. "I'm pretty sure he has."

"Why don't you divorce him?"

"Because he'd do everything he can to take Lex and leave me with nothing. Maybe when she gets older I'll be willing to brave that, but…not now. She means too much to me."

She'd be in Simon's situation, fighting over her child. "I see."

"I've got to go, but first I need to use the bathroom."

As she walked away, Gail was thinking how much it helped to have a friend who understood and didn't judge her for her decisions, and how easy it would've been to miss that friend in Sophia.

"Gail?" Sophia had reached the bathroom but was calling her.

"Yes?"

"Have you seen this?"

"What is it?"

"Come here."

More than a little curious, Gail headed down the hall. Sophia was standing outside the bathroom and gestured for her to peer in. There, on the vanity, was a plush velvet box sitting on a scrap of paper with Simon's handwriting.

Sending Sophia a look that said she had no idea what was going on, she read the note first. "I've been trying to figure out a good way to give you this. Now that I'm leaving, I realize there is no good way, but I still want you to have it."

She handed the note to Sophia while she opened the box. Inside was one of the giant-size diamonds Mr. Nunes had brought to show her before she and Simon were married.

"Holy cow," Sophia breathed when Gail turned to show her. "I'm tempted to believe that's a cubic zirconia but I know it's not."

So did Gail. After Mr. Nunes's visit, she also knew how much it was worth.

"Try it on!" Sophia said, and held the box while Gail

slid the ring on her finger. The setting was a simple one done in yellow gold, but it offset the diamond beautifully. The combination was stunning.

"See that?" Sophia said, admiring it. "He does care about you. I bet he comes back."

Gail smiled, but shook her head. "No."

"Why not?"

"He has too much going on in his life right now," she said. But that wasn't what she was thinking. She was remembering the moment when she'd bared her soul to him. He couldn't come back to "I love you," not to continue a fake relationship. After that, it would have to be for real.

And she'd always known he wasn't ready for *real*.

Ian climbed out of his car as soon as he saw Simon pass through the doors of the baggage claim area and into the pickup zone. "How was your flight?"

It hadn't been pleasant. As eager as Simon was to see Ty, he felt bad about leaving Gail. He kept picturing her sleeping in their new bed in their new century-old house—and wished he was there with her. She kept him sane, introduced an element of calm and rightness to his life that seemed to be missing without her. Just flying into Los Angeles brought back the past couple of years, which made him tense and irritable. The way Ian kept smiling bothered Simon, too. Ian acted as if he'd somehow outmaneuvered Gail in his quest for attention and control. But he hadn't. Only Ty could beat Gail.

"Fortunately, it was short," he said. "What's going on here at home?"

Ian had brought his Mercedes and not the Porsche, so he had somewhere to stow Simon's luggage. Simon shoved it in the trunk as Ian answered.

"Bella's been calling me, freaking out. She wants you to come over right away."

Simon checked the time—11:40—and walked to the passenger door. "Have you seen Ty?"

"No, I've just heard from Bella on the phone."

His cell rang as he slid into the seat. Hoping it was Gail checking to see if he'd gotten in safely, he pulled the phone out of his pocket, then frowned. It wasn't Gail. Of course it wouldn't be. She'd told him she loved him, but then she'd sent him off as if she never planned on seeing him again. He knew in his heart that unless he contacted her, he'd never hear from her again.

Instead, it was Bella. Already. "This is her," he said to Ian, and pressed the talk button. "Hello?"

"Oh, good!" Bella gushed. "You're in?"

"Just arrived."

"So…are you coming over?"

"On my way."

"Thank God." The sexy, breathless quality of her voice wasn't quite the turn-on it used to be. Actually, it wasn't a turn-on at all. She just sounded like she was trying too hard.

"Is Ty there?" he asked.

"Where else would he be?"

Simon wanted to be sure. At this hour, his son would

be asleep, but it'd been so long since Simon had seen him he didn't care. He couldn't wait to hug Ty's small body against his chest. "Okay, I'll be right there."

As he buckled his seat belt, Ian pulled into the steady flow of traffic. "It's good to see you, man."

Simon eyed him. "You're kidding, right?"

"No, I'm serious. Why?"

"You just saw me in Whiskey Creek."

"That was different." He tapped the steering wheel to the beat of the rap music playing on his expensive stereo system. "Whiskey Creek isn't L.A. *This* is where you belong."

"Is it?"

Ian's hands stilled and he glanced over. "What's that supposed to mean?"

Simon didn't even know. He used to love L.A., never dreamed he'd consider moving. Now, he wasn't so sure it was the best place for him. Whiskey Creek had been such a welcome change. He liked the innocence of it, the people. He had room to breathe there. "Nothing," he said. "It doesn't mean anything."

Ian put on his blinker and changed lanes in preparation for exiting the airport. "Can you believe you got out of your bogus marriage so easily?"

Simon arched an eyebrow at him. "Excuse me?"

"Now that Bella's willing to forget about that stupid restraining order, there's no need to bother with Gail."

Simon said nothing. After the initial agreement, Ian hadn't wanted his arrangement with Gail to work. That much was clear.

"Right?" Ian prodded.

"Whatever you say," Simon muttered.

Seemingly happy, Ian turned up the radio. "It's all going to work out, buddy. The way things stand now, you'll be able to start your next project in no time." He did a quick drum roll to the stereo. "We're back in business."

Considering the recent improvements in his situation, Simon supposed there was no reason *not* to return to work. He knew how fickle fame could be. If he pissed away the opportunities he had right now, they could disappear, and he could end up like his father. Someone who missed the spotlight. Someone who was yesterday's news. Besides, there were a lot of people who'd been disappointed when he backed out of his commitments. Maybe he could reschedule some of them. For the most part, he was interested in those projects, or he wouldn't have signed on for them.

But did he really want to fall back into his old lifestyle? What about the woman who'd made him happy to live in an eight-hundred-square-foot house and work as a carpenter?

Bella's house was every bit as opulent as Simon remembered. Located in Beverly Hills, not far from his, it was a fifteen-thousand-square-foot Mediterranean with plenty of palm trees and three different pools. She'd never earned much money of her own. She'd been a news anchor when he met her at an after-party, working for sixty thousand a year, but she'd quit that job as soon as they became an item.

He waited at the gate until the security guard buzzed him through, then pulled up behind her Escalade. He'd had Ian take him home to get his car, so it was after midnight, but he never knew what to expect with Bella and wanted to be able to leave at a moment's notice, if necessary.

She was waiting for him on the front stoop. Her eyes searched his face. Then she slipped into his arms. "I'm so glad you're here," she murmured, pressing her cheek to his chest.

Her perfume brought back myriad memories, both good and bad, but Simon didn't feel the poignant emotions he'd associated with that scent before. Sadness weighed on him, for what they used to have that was now lost, but he felt nothing else. Apparently a lot had changed in the past few weeks. Or maybe the changes had been taking place much longer and he just hadn't noticed because of all the drinking.

"Where's Ty?" he asked.

"In bed. Come on, we can talk in the family room." She tried to lead him into a large but cozy kitchen/family room with hardwood floors, a huge rock fireplace, granite counters and stainless-steel appliances. It was tastefully decorated, but everything about Bella was tasteful and always had been. He couldn't fault her sense of style. With her large brown eyes, olive skin and sleek black hair, she was beautiful, too.

"Would you like something to drink?" She held up

a bottle of wine—a pinot noir that was one of his favorites.

The alcohol tempted him. It felt like he hadn't had a drink in forever. But he shook his head. "No. I'm fine, thanks."

"Really?"

"I don't drink anymore." He was almost as surprised as she was to hear those words come out of his mouth, but he remained committed to them. He felt more in control of himself than he'd been in a long time; he wanted to stay that way.

"I see." Although she should be acting happy about this, which could only be an improvement in his life, he saw that her smile wilted. Obviously she'd envisioned a different kind of night than this was turning out to be. Still, she adjusted and shored up her attitude. "You look tired. What about some coffee?"

"That'd be great."

"Good. Have a seat."

He stopped her as she started to walk away. "Before we do anything else, I really want to see Ty."

She hesitated. No doubt she could tell he was much more excited about seeing their son than he was her. Simon knew that wouldn't go over too well. But he wasn't willing to deal with her until she'd given him what she'd promised.

"Of course. I'll take you up. Our boy is getting so big. Every day he looks more like his handsome daddy."

Simon followed her up a set of stairs to the second story, then down a long hall to the right wing. Had they kept going they would've come to a set of double doors—he guessed that was the master but he'd never been inside it. He and Bella had certainly made love since their separation, but not since she'd bought this house.

Ty's room wasn't far from hers. "He wanted his room decorated with race cars this time," she whispered as she opened the door.

There was a night-light burning on the far wall, providing just enough of a glow for Simon to see his son's face as he moved closer.

Smiling, he sat on the bed and pulled his little boy out from under the covers and into his arms.

"Don't wake him up," Bella whispered as if she'd thought he was only going to look.

Simon ignored her. He'd anticipated this moment for too long to hold back. "Ty, it's Daddy," he whispered. "God, I missed you."

Ty opened his eyes, smiled sleepily and tightened his arms around Simon's neck. "Daddy, where did you go? Can I go with you next time?"

Simon wished, more than anything, that he could say yes. But he wasn't sure Bella would allow him to take Ty anywhere. Not once she figured out that he didn't intend to try again with her. "I hope you can come with me someday soon."

"Maybe Daddy will stay here with us." Bella looked at him as she ruffled Ty's hair. The invitation in her eyes was clear. For whatever reason, she was ready to welcome him back into her bed, into their lives, into the family.

But Simon was no longer in love with her.

30

It'd taken two hours to get Ty back to sleep, but Simon hadn't minded at all. He'd played army men with his son and talked to him about his missing tooth and the money the tooth fairy had brought him. He'd asked about kindergarten and listened as Ty talked about his teacher and proudly recited the alphabet. Once Ty's eyelids began to droop, Simon had even crawled into bed, tucked his son up against his side and memorized the smell of his hair and the feel of his baby-soft skin as if he might never see him again. It wasn't until Ty nodded off that Simon got up to find Bella, who'd grown frustrated with the lack of attention and left more than an hour earlier.

Simon wasn't looking forward to their talk. He knew she wouldn't like what he had to say. But he couldn't avoid engaging her, not if he hoped to see Ty again.

He found her sitting in the living room, watching a reality show she'd recorded on her DVR. She put the program on pause when he came in and, bottom lip jutting in an exaggerated pout, turned to him. "Happy now?" she asked.

The bitterness in that question nearly set him off. How dared she think she had the right to keep his son from him? The lies she'd told to get the restraining order were bad enough. She seemed to feel she could stand behind those lies and that infuriated him. But he'd let his anger get the best of him before. He couldn't allow himself to make that mistake again. The goal was to establish a friendly relationship, not revert to the animosity of the past. "It was great to see him. Thank you."

She nodded, combing her fingers through her long hair as if she'd done him a huge favor instead of merely giving him what he deserved as Ty's father. "Your dad called."

Simon almost asked if they were still sleeping together but bit his tongue again. His father had plenty of women who were willing to do whatever he wanted. He didn't need Bella. As a rule, Bella wasn't attracted to men who were twice her age. Simon knew what they'd done had been all about him. Now that he and Bella weren't together, she and Tex didn't even like each other. "What did he want?"

"He heard you were back in town."

"How?"

"Who knows? That prick of a business manager probably told him."

Something was up there. Ian had told Tex where to find Simon in Whiskey Creek, too. There was a reason for that, just as there was a reason he was so excited to see Simon return to work—to make *Hellion*.

Simon suspected Ian had been offered a kickback of some kind. Everything in Hollywood seemed to come down to money. But he'd deal with that later.

"What did he want?" he asked.

"He told me to leave you alone."

Instead of crossing the floor to sit down with her, Simon pulled out a bar stool from the kitchen island and turned it to face the living room. "Did he say why?"

"You can't guess?"

"You know my father and I don't talk."

"He said you were finally happy. That you don't need trash like me messing up your life again."

When he didn't respond to the "trash" part, didn't defend her as she was no doubt hoping he would, her expression darkened. "As if what happened was *my* fault," she added.

"*I'm* not the one who slept with him," Simon pointed out.

"You slept with plenty!" she snapped, but whether she believed him or not, he hadn't touched another woman until he'd caught the two of them. Even then it was several months later, when he'd known he couldn't put his marriage back together, that he wound up in bed with a costar. After that, there didn't seem to be any reason to hold back. There were a few times Bella had realized she was losing him and attempted to straighten up, but those periods never lasted. She couldn't overcome the insecurities that caused her to provoke him.

But there was no use arguing. What had happened had happened. They'd both made mistakes. He just wanted to figure out how to go on. "I did," he admitted.

Evidently satisfied that he'd taken responsibility for his behavior, she clicked her nails as she stared at him. "So…where do we go from here?"

"I'm hoping we can make some arrangements where Ty is concerned."

"What kind of arrangements?"

"I'd like full custody." That was the only way he could put a definitive stop to her using Ty a weapon against him. "But if you cooperate with me I'll settle for shared."

"You'll never get full custody. I don't have to cooperate with you."

Simon felt his muscles tense. "Why are you still being like this?"

"Because we come as a package! You can't reject me but accept him! That's not fair!"

This made no sense. She was talking out of the hurt and anger that'd gotten them into so much trouble to begin with.

Simon tried to counteract that by remaining as calm as possible. "Bella, please. I love Ty. I'd never let anything happen to him, and you know it. That should be what matters."

"What about *me?*"

Bella acted like a child herself. "What about you?" he asked.

"What will I become? Your castoff? You think you

can toss me aside and take my son to start a new family with your publicist in some boondock town hours and hours away from here? Go live happily ever after when I'm miserable?"

Simon lifted his hands. "Even if I take him to Whiskey Creek, it wouldn't be for long. I plan on coming back to L.A. and making more movies. I'm not walking away from my career. We can work together, make sure we both have what we need."

She bit her lip. "Do you love her?"

As he'd suspected from the beginning, this wasn't about Ty. Bella was feeling left out, couldn't stand the thought that he'd managed to move on. She'd liked it far better when she knew he was suffering because of her, when she still had the power to hurt him.

"Do you really want to know?" he asked.

She didn't respond, but raised her chin as if she expected an answer.

He drew a deep breath. "I married her because I thought it would be good for my image."

She sagged in relief. "Of course. You would never be attracted to someone as…as plain as she is!"

"I'm not finished," he said. "That was how it started, but then…everything changed. She's the most wonderful person I've ever met. She makes me feel good in a deep-down, satisfied way. I love how she laughs and how she makes me laugh. I love that I know I can depend on her. I love the way her face lights up every time I walk into the room. I love that she pretends to be tough but she's really all heart. Most of all, I love the way she loves me." He smiled just thinking of her. "Does that mean I love her back?" He nodded. "Yeah, I guess it does. I was telling you the truth—I'm happily married."

Tears welled up in Bella's eyes, but he felt no empathy. She didn't need him to feel sorry for her; she was feeling sorry enough for herself. "You will never see Ty again," she said. "Now get out before I call the police."

Simon headed to the door. He wouldn't undo everything he'd accomplished by causing another scandal. But he paused before opening it. "I won't give up, Bella. I'll fight for Ty as long and as hard as it takes."

She grabbed his arm. "I think it's a mistake to forget about us, Simon," she said. "We could try again. We were happy once." She lifted his hand to her breast but he wasn't remotely tempted.

"Sorry, I'm not interested," he said, and pulled away.

Simon felt great when he woke up the next morning. He'd seen Ty. The time they'd spent hadn't been long enough to make up for the months he'd missed, but at least he'd had a couple of hours with him. And he was no longer conflicted about Bella or anything else in his life. She'd finally lost all power to hurt him. His visit to her place last night had been cathartic in so many ways, had crystallized what he really wanted out of life. He wasn't ready to go back to making movies. Not yet. He preferred to return to Whiskey Creek, where he'd been so content, and finish the house on Autumn Lane. When he did come back to L.A., Gail would be with him, but that wouldn't happen until they were both ready for what they'd face here.

He'd tried calling her last night, as soon as he got home. He'd wanted to tell her he'd made these decisions and couldn't wait to see her. His future was completely wrapped up with hers. Over the past few weeks he'd become healthier and happier. Why would he ever let that go or trade it for the emptiness of before?

He didn't plan to, but she didn't know that yet. It had been very late when he tried to reach her, and she hadn't answered.

Thinking of her the second he opened his eyes, he rolled over to search for his phone, but it began to ring before he could even touch it. Maybe she'd seen that she'd missed his call and was getting back to him.

He hoped so. He was eager to talk to her. But caller ID told him it wasn't Gail. It was his father.

Scowling, he studied his digital display. What could Tex possibly want with him? Simon couldn't even guess, but because his father had signed the release for *Hellion,* and because he felt as if he finally knew his own mind and had a clear sense of direction, he went ahead and answered.

"'Lo?"

"What the hell are you doing?" Tex demanded.

The harshness of his tone surprised Simon. He'd thought they were on better terms than usual, but it didn't sound like that right now. "I'm sleeping. What the hell are you doing?"

"I'm not talking about this minute. I'm talking about last night."

"I went to see my son. Why? And why are you so mad?"

"Because I thought you'd finally straightened up and figured out your life. I thought you understood what you had and wouldn't piss it away. And then you go and do *this*."

A sick feeling curled through Simon's stomach, chasing away the last of his fatigue. Sitting up, he rubbed a hand over his face. "Slow down and tell me what you're talking about. *What* did I do last night?"

"You're going to pretend like you don't know? It's all over the internet—on YouTube, all the celebrity blogs, AOL...."

"I really don't know what you're talking about."

"Then turn on your computer and find out. You're busted, and the media's having a field day with this one. After the 'I'm a reformed man' act you put on with Gail, they're going for your jugular. Actually, some of 'em are more interested in going after a different part of your anatomy. Castration has been mentioned as a fitting punishment."

For what? He hadn't done anything!

Tossing his phone aside, Simon climbed out of bed and hurried over to his computer. After powering it up, he did a Google search on his name. Then he sank into the desk chair, staring at the screen in silent horror. The very first hit that came up was a link to a sex tape between him and Bella. The headline read Simon's Delicious Romp with Ex Last Night Proves He's No Changed Man.

* * *

Just about everyone she'd ever known had called to tell Gail about the online footage that'd gone viral. The onslaught had started with Serge at her own PR company, because he'd been helping Josh track all the media hits relating to her and Simon, and he was first in the office. He'd awakened her. But now that word of the tape had been picked up by the major news outlets, she was beginning to hear from her friends in Whiskey Creek, too.

Although Gail had her laptop in bed and knew what the tape depicted, she couldn't bring herself to watch it. Not the whole thing. The beginning footage, with Simon approaching Bella's house and going inside, as evidenced by security cameras, was clear enough to identify him. It also revealed the date and time, which was last night, shortly after he would have arrived in L.A. That was all she needed to see. He'd left her and returned to Bella's bed within hours.

"What are we going to do?" Josh asked. He'd reached the office after Serge, so this was the first chance she'd had to talk to him. His call was the only one she'd been willing to answer. The humiliation and embarrassment was too fresh, too poignant, to cope with the sympathy of those who cared about her. She hadn't even answered the phone for her father, who must've been tipped off by some patron at the gas station. She couldn't imagine how else he would've heard.

"I don't know," she said. Her heart was aching so badly she couldn't think clearly. She dared not leave her own bedroom, dared not venture out for fear she'd be cornered. It was only a matter of time before her father showed up on her doorstep. Or maybe Joe would come. She'd pleaded with them to give Simon a chance and they had. Now she felt like she'd set them up for a strong sucker punch.

She rubbed her stomach, feeling as if Simon had hit her there. Why had she believed in him? Why had she let herself fall for his looks, his charm, his playfulness and his incredible lovemaking? Of course he was good at making love. He'd had plenty of practice both on and off the screen....

It was his happiness that had convinced her he was sincere, she decided. He'd seemed so content while he was here.

She shook her head as she remembered his boyish smile when he was demolishing the kitchen. He'd left it in rubble, just like her heart.

God, all the warnings she'd ignored... On top of everything else, what Simon had done made her feel like an idiot.

"So you've seen it?" Josh said.

"Not all of it," she replied. "But what I have seen is plenty graphic."

"It gets worse. There's no way we'll be able to spin it into anything other than what it is."

"No. And we can't claim it's not him. He left me, he went there, he slept with her. Our hands are tied. We have to let this one go, see how it affects Big Hit."

It was easier to talk about the damage this might

cause her business than her life. Although she'd admitted the truth to Josh, he hadn't been around to see just how hard and fast she'd fallen for Simon, so at least she didn't have to talk about her personal feelings quite yet.

"I doubt it'll cost us clients," he said. "Simon can't blame you for this."

"Doesn't matter. It makes me look foolish and inept for getting involved with him. And you and I both know how fickle Hollywood can be. If I'm perceived to be 'out,' we'll probably lose some of our clients, if not the majority."

"We're good at what we do. We'll survive," he insisted.

At least since the sale of the wedding pictures to *People* magazine, Gail would have deep enough pockets to carry the company for a number of months, if necessary. That was the one bright spot in her agreement with Simon. The contract stipulated that if he screwed up, she got the money, anyway.

Fortunately, she'd had the foresight to demand that stipulation.

She glanced at the diamond ring he'd left her. She'd gone to bed hoping it meant something, but now she knew better. She could sell it, too.

"So you haven't talked to him?" Josh said.

"No." He'd tried to call her once, at 3:00 a.m. After she'd talked to Serge, she'd noticed that missed call. But she'd been asleep when he made the attempt, and she definitely wasn't calling him back.

She couldn't believe he'd try to speak to her right

after making love with Bella. Maybe he wanted to tell her before everyone else did. Maybe he had enough of a conscience to want to give her some warning.

Josh sighed into the phone. "This is sad. Except for a few naysayers who didn't really matter, your marriage was well received. The campaign was working."

"Are you talking about the naysayers who were shouting that I wasn't attractive enough for Simon? Wasn't dynamic enough? Wasn't famous?" She'd known she was a regular, average person going in. But somehow, she'd let herself get caught up in the fairy tale.

"I mean those who are too stupid to know that you're amazing, that he was actually lucky to have you."

The phone beeped, telling her she had another call. Assuming it would be her father again, or Callie—Gail wasn't looking forward to the moment Callie learned what had happened—she checked.

It was Simon.

31

Gail told herself not to answer. After what Simon had done, she couldn't imagine why he could possibly want to talk to her. But her desire to hear *some* explanation won out.

Telling Josh she had to go, she called herself a fool for her weakness but switched over. "Hello?"

He didn't bother with a greeting. "I didn't do it, Gail."

Her hand tightened on the phone. She'd thought he might try to present an excuse, or ask for her help in bailing him out of this latest mess. She hadn't expected complete denial. "That's your face in the footage, isn't it?" she asked.

"It is. On the security video, anyway. I went there last night to see Ty. I spent a couple hours with him—"

"At midnight?"

"Yes. I woke him up. But I didn't have sex with Bella. I didn't even kiss her. She offered but I wasn't interested." He lowered his voice, which made him so much more convincing. "All I could think about was you."

The ache in Gail's chest grew worse because now the

betrayal she felt was complicated by the fear that her love for him was making her vulnerable to accepting what he said over what she saw with her own eyes. "If that's not you, who is it?" she asked, trying to hold out.

"I have no idea, but I didn't sleep with her." When she said nothing, he went on. "I haven't touched anyone since I've been with you. I called last night because I wanted to tell you that I think we should stay together. I don't want to lose you."

Gail pressed her palm to her forehead. She wanted to believe him so badly. But she'd just been calling herself a fool for ever trusting him. "I don't know what to say."

"Say you believe me. I've never lied to you."

He'd done some crazy things, some ill-advised things, but he was right—she'd never known him to lie. Still, caution advised her to proceed slowly. "So where did that video come from?" she asked. "How did it get made?"

"I've been trying to work that out. All I can imagine is that she set me up. She knew if she let me see Ty I'd come over. Maybe she thought it wouldn't be that hard to get me into bed. Then she'd have the proof she needed to destroy my marriage to you and wreck my chances of ever getting custody of Ty. But I didn't go for it. I wasn't even tempted."

"So...she had to do something else."

"Yes. I've watched that damn thing so many times, trying to figure it out. I bet it's the same man in the video she sent me before."

"What video?"

"It's not pretty, but I'll forward it. I think she dubbed my face over his. Notice that once the sex starts, you don't see much to identify me."

She noticed that he'd switched her to speakerphone, which meant he was probably forwarding the video he'd mentioned.

"There's just a glimpse of my face here and there," he finished.

If what Simon said was true, whoever had manipulated that footage had done a damn fine job. "Would Bella really be capable of something like that?"

"I'm sure she would," he said. "She was very upset last night. But this time she's gone too far, crossed the line."

"But it would take someone with real technical know-how. Someone who was used to editing video."

"Right. But thanks to me, she has plenty of contacts in the movie industry."

Her phone buzzed, signaling the receipt of a text message. "Hang on." She put him on speaker, too, while she watched the clip he'd sent. It was Bella with someone else, all right. A message came with that erotic footage: Ty's new daddy.

Gail was shocked by Bella's desire to inflict pain. "When did you get this?"

"The night I cut my hand."

That made sense. Maybe she was making an earlier mistake worse by wading in even deeper, but Gail had to go with her heart on this one, too. "How do we prove it?"

He blew out a sigh. "You believe me?"

She allowed herself a wry smile. "Did you think you might have trouble convincing me?"

"I was worried. I meant what I said. I don't want to lose you, Gail."

"Be careful," she teased. "You swore you'd never marry again."

"I'll settle for avoiding another divorce."

She laughed as relief flooded through her. They were in a mess, but they had each other. "So what do we do now?"

"We take the video to a specialist, see if they can prove it was doctored. We won't let her get away with this."

"Sounds good to me."

"Does that mean you'll come to L.A. and stay with me until I can get this cleared up?" he asked.

He wanted to know if she trusted him enough to stand by him publicly. Was she willing to go through what the next few weeks would require?

"I'll be on the next flight."

Gail thought she was coming to his rescue. Simon knew that was the quickest way to get her to return to L.A. But she'd done enough for him already. He was sober, he was innocent and he was angry. He'd get himself out of this latest scrape.

Ian squinted against the sunlight that poured into his house when he answered Simon's knock. Then he scowled. "Simon. What are you doing here? Why didn't you just call me?"

Simon didn't reply to the question, but asked one of his own. "Late night, huh, Ian?"

It was easy to tell from Ian's demeanor that he knew something had changed. "Not too late, no. I collected you at the airport and then I came home. Why?"

"Did you *stay* home?"

There was a slight pause. "Actually, I did."

Pushing past him, Simon headed into the living room. Fortunately, Ian lived alone so Simon didn't have to worry about barging in on anyone else. "Where's your computer?"

Ian followed him. "Why do you want to know?"

"Because you have about five minutes to prove that you didn't doctor that video, or hire someone else to do it."

"What video?" he said, but Simon could tell he knew. He knew and yet he'd been sleeping. So when did he learn if not this morning, like the rest of the world?

"The one where I'm supposedly having sex with my ex-wife."

Ian tightened the belt to his bathrobe. "Simon—"

"I know you did it, Ian," he broke in.

"No."

"Then prove it."

Hands spread wide, Ian stepped closer. *"How?"*

"Give me access to your computer."

He covered his face, then dropped his hands. "Come on, you know I'd never do anything like that. If there's a video out there, Bella must've created it herself. Or your father helped."

"It wasn't my father."

"How do you know?"

Because his frustration and disappointment this morning had been too real. Because he'd meant what he'd said when he praised Gail, and he was right about her, which lent him more credibility than he'd had in years. And because he'd apologized for the incident with Bella. Tex didn't have the strongest character in the world, but Simon believed he'd been on the level about all of that.

Besides, he'd signed the release. If he wanted to force Simon back to L.A. he'd already had a way to try and do it. He'd accepted the loss of Simon's name on his movie. *Ian* was the one who felt he stood to lose if Simon stayed in Whiskey Creek and fell any more in love with Gail. "A lot of reasons."

"But he was furious when I tried to give back your part in *Hellion*."

"He signed a release, Ian."

"That doesn't mean he was happy about it."

"He wouldn't have done it if he wasn't ready to let me go. *You* want me to make that movie even more than he did. Why?"

"Sure, I want you to make that movie. I'm your manager, and that's an Oscar-worthy part. I hate to see you screw up your life just because you're suddenly pussy-whipped. But I wouldn't do anything to hurt you."

"I wish that was true, Ian. I've been good to you. Paid

you well. Kept you on, even after what you did to Gail's business, since I felt somewhat responsible for that. But now I'm realizing a few things I should've seen before."

"No, you're jumping to the wrong conclusions," he said.

"Am I? Aren't you who told my father where to find me in Whiskey Creek?"

"Yes, but that's because he wouldn't leave me alone. I didn't want to piss him off. That wouldn't have helped you. We talked about this."

"Why didn't you tell me, from the very beginning, that he was one of the executive producers of *Hellion?*"

"I didn't know! He wasn't the person who approached us. They can sell an interest to anyone they want and often do, to raise money. We don't get to dictate that, and you know it. I found out before you did and didn't pass it along because I didn't want to upset you, but I didn't know at first."

That might be true, but there was more to what was going on than Ian wanted him to find out. "I don't think he had to push you very hard to get you to tell him where I was. You wanted him to press me to leave Whiskey Creek because there was something in it for you."

"Like what?"

"Money. What else?"

"Come on. Look at this place." He pointed to the furnishings that surrounded them. "I'm doing fine. I'd never betray you."

"Not unless it was worth it. What did Bella offer you? Or were you the one making the offer to her? When I didn't come home, when my dad signed that release, which you probably never expected, did it spook you? Did you promise her a chunk of change if she could get me back here?"

"Listen to yourself," he scoffed. "You're talking crazy."

"Am I?" Simon spotted what he'd been looking for from the beginning—Ian's cell phone. Snatching it off the counter where it was charging, he checked to see if he could get into it but it was password-protected. He held it up. "What's your password?"

Ian's eyes widened. "That's none of your business. Give me my phone!"

"Either you give me your password so I can see who you've been calling and who's been calling you, or I'm going to the police. They can get your records. You and Bella will both be busted."

The color drained from Ian's face.

"What's it going to be?" Simon demanded. "Do you tell the truth and take responsibility for what you've done? Or do I have to push it farther?"

"Shit," Ian breathed, and sank onto the couch.

Gail's stomach was a riot of butterflies as the plane landed. She knew it wouldn't be easy to look into the face of reporter after reporter and tell them all that she believed Simon was innocent. It wouldn't be easy to fend off all the paparazzi who'd be eager to get her reaction to Simon's "cheating," either. But she wasn't going to leave him in L.A. alone. Not only was she his wife, she was his publicist. She'd figure out some way to get the situation turned around.

She was staring down at her ring when everyone started to deplane. She'd have to flash it around, use it as a symbol of his commitment. Maybe that would help....

"Have a nice evening," one of her seat partners said. Fortunately, no one on the plane seemed to have any idea who she was.

With a smile and a nod, she collected her carry-on bag and made her way into the airport. Once she reached the gate, she stepped off to one side to call Simon and let him know she was in.

"Hey," she said when he answered.

"You here?"

"Yeah. You?"

"I'm at baggage claim."

"You could've picked me up curbside."

"No, I decided to park. Can't wait to see you."

"I'm nervous," she admitted. "This is going to be crazy."

"I won't let it get too bad. I promise."

Was there anything he could do? She didn't think so, but she appreciated the protective sentiment. "We'll get through it either way. See you in a sec."

Joining the flow of traffic, she headed down the escalator. There was a crowd at the bottom, most of them holding cameras of some kind. She could see the call letters of various television stations. Others were holding microphones, or lights.

Instinctively, she knew they were waiting for her. But how had they known when she was arriving?

Feeling her anxiety intensify, she hiked up her carry-on and searched the crowd for Simon. He'd said he was in baggage claim. But would he be there if all the media were, too?

Apparently so. It didn't take her long to find him. He was standing right in the middle of the crowd, wearing jeans and a leather jacket, watching her walk toward him. The way everyone was waiting, as if they'd all come to yell, "Surprise!" she almost got the impression he'd invited them here. What was going on?

When her gaze met his, she asked that question with her eyes, but he merely smiled and started toward her. The media hurried to keep up with his long strides while taking photographs and video of them both.

"What is this?" she murmured when they were close enough to speak.

"Ian and Bella doctored that footage. They've admitted it."

"They have?" She could hardly believe it.

"They didn't have much choice."

"You know what that means, don't you? You can prove that she was purposely keeping you from Ty. You can win custody."

"That's what I hope."

"So—" she glanced at all the media "—why are these people here?"

"I asked them to come and document this." Pulling her into his arms, he kissed her. Then he held her chin in his hand as he said, "I love you, Gail. I haven't cheated, and I won't. I would never do anything to hurt you."

The warmth of pure happiness poured through her as he kissed her again. The crowd grew thicker, the noise grew louder, lights flashed and cameras rolled, but she didn't care if the whole world looked on. He was letting everyone know he was completely committed to her.

They were just pulling apart when one of the reporters said, "Oh, my God! Is that your ring?"

Epilogue

"You're not having coffee?" Callie indicated Gail's orange juice as the usual suspects gathered in the large corner booth on a Friday morning in August. The weather in Whiskey Creek was every bit as beautiful as Los Angeles, maybe better, since it wasn't as hot. Simon was glad to be back.

"In all the years we've been coming here, I don't think I've ever seen you order anything else," Eve added, also eyeing the orange juice. "Of course, you've been gone a lot of that time, but still. No one loves coffee more than you do."

Simon covered Gail's hand with his. He wanted to catch her eye, to tell her he didn't mind if she spilled the big news, but Ty piped up and took care of that for both of them.

"Mama Gail can't have coffee," he said matter-of-factly. "Not for *n-i-n-e* months!"

This caused not only Callie but the rest of Gail's friends to look a little startled.

"Why not?" Callie asked him. Simon could tell she

already suspected the truth, but was seeking confirmation.

Ty had just put a big spoonful of fruit and yogurt in his mouth. This made him difficult to understand when he talked, but Simon let him answer, curious to hear what his son would say. Gail must've wanted to hear Ty explain, too, because she didn't speak up.

"'Cause that's how long it takes to make a baby, silly!" he said with a laugh.

Simon chuckled at his son's comment but no one else did. They were too preoccupied with the meaning of his words. There were ten of them today: Kyle, who was starting to rebound from his divorce; Riley and his son; Ted; Sophia and her daughter; Eve; Cheyenne; Callie; and Noah Rackham, whom Simon had just met for the first time, due to conflicting schedules. When Noah was home, Simon had been filming his latest movie, and when Simon and Gail were in Whiskey Creek for the weekend or whatever, Noah had been racing bicycles in Europe.

With news of the baby hanging out there, all of Gail's friends leaned close, pinning her beneath their curious gazes.

"You're expecting?" Sophia asked.

A blush of excitement tinged Gail's cheeks. They'd thought they were going to wait a year or two before having a baby. But by March they'd gained partial custody of Ty, who'd immediately started begging for a baby sister, and by April they'd admitted to each other that they were just as eager for a baby as he was. They'd stopped using birth control at that point, but it wasn't until a few days ago, on August 4, that they'd learned Gail was pregnant.

"Yes," she said, a grin curving her lips.

"Oh, my gosh!" Eve cried. "That's wonderful!"

"Do your father and brother know?" Riley asked.

"We told them last night," Simon said. "As soon as we arrived in town." Although they'd lived mostly in L.A. since Christmas, Simon had finished remodeling 811 Autumn Lane when they'd come for a couple of weeks in March and he'd brought out the movie props he'd promised to provide for Eve's B and B. They loved staying at their own place when they visited Whiskey Creek, had been there several times already. But they'd begun a tradition of spending their first night back in town at Martin's. Martin loved having them, and it made Simon feel good to please her old man.

"How long have you known?" Eve asked.

Gail squeezed Simon's hand. "Since Tuesday. But it's only now starting to feel real."

"That's so wonderful!" Callie said. "What about Big Hit? Will you continue to work?"

"Not for the first few months. After that, I might go back part-time, but I'm really only doing Simon's PR these days. Josh and Serge are handling the rest of our clients."

"When's the baby due?" Kyle asked.

Gail opened her orange juice and took a sip. "February 21."

Ted added sugar to his coffee. "So what do you want? Another boy or a girl?"

"A baby sister!" Ty shouted, but Gail said she just wanted a healthy child and Simon felt the same.

"Are you excited?" It took Simon a few seconds to realize that the usually reserved Cheyenne was talking only to him. The others had Gail's attention, were asking her all kinds of questions, but Cheyenne sat next to him.

"I'm thrilled about it," he said. He'd once sworn he'd never trust a woman enough to have another child, but that was before he'd met Gail. "There's nothing like that first moment, when the nurse puts your baby in your arms."

"You and Gail seem so happy together," she said wistfully.

She was looking for a level of honesty none of the others had demanded of him so far, but they hadn't lived the kind of hard life Cheyenne had. She wanted to believe in happily ever after, wanted to know it was possible, and he felt no hesitation in building her confidence.

Placing his arm around her shoulders, he gave her a reassuring squeeze while grinning at his beautiful wife. "Gail's the best thing to ever happen to me," he said, and meant it.

* * * * *

Join the people of Whiskey Creek again…

WHEN SNOW FALLS.

You'll have a chance to catch up with Gail and Simon, her family and their friends. And remember Cheyenne? You'll learn more about her as she searches for her missing past. Cheyenne's group of friends in Whiskey Creek is the one part of her life that has offered any stability. But things become complicated when she falls for Gail's brother Joe, who happens to be the man her best friend Eve's in love with…and they become even *more* complicated when another man enters the picture. Dylan's got a reputation and he's from the wrong side of the tracks—exactly the kind of man Cheyenne wants to avoid!

Find out what Christmas in Whiskey Creek is like.

WHEN SNOW FALLS
by Brenda Novak is the second book in the
WHISKEY CREEK series
and is available in November 2012.

MIRABRB313519

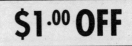
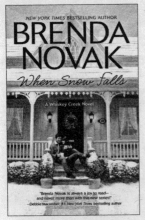

BARBARA CLAYPOLE WHITE

James Nealy is haunted by irrational fears and compulsions, but his plan is to confront his darkest fears and build something beautiful: a garden.

After her husband's death, gardening became Tilly Silverberg's salvation—and her escape. So when James demands she take him on as a client, her answer is a flat no.

When a family emergency beckons, Tilly retreats home to England with her young son, Isaac, in tow. But surprises await. Her best friend is keeping secrets. Her mother is plotting. Her first love is unexpectedly available. And then James appears on her doorstep.

Away from home, James and Tilly forge an unlikely bond. And as they work to build a garden together, something begins to blossom between them …

The
Unfinished Garden

Available wherever books are sold.

HARLEQUIN® MIRA®
www.Harlequin.com

MBCW1412

REQUEST YOUR FREE BOOKS!

2 FREE NOVELS
FROM THE ROMANCE COLLECTION
PLUS 2 FREE GIFTS!

YES! Please send me 2 FREE novels from the Romance Collection and my 2 FREE gifts (gifts are worth about $10). After receiving them, if I don't wish to receive any more books, I can return the shipping statement marked "cancel." If I don't cancel, I will receive 4 brand-new novels every month and be billed just $5.99 per book in the U.S. or $6.49 per book in Canada. That's a saving of at least 25% off the cover price. It's quite a bargain! Shipping and handling is just 50¢ per book in the U.S. and 75¢ per book in Canada.* I understand that accepting the 2 free books and gifts places me under no obligation to buy anything. I can always return a shipment and cancel at any time. Even if I never buy another book, the two free books and gifts are mine to keep forever.

194/394 MDN FELQ

Name _____ (PLEASE PRINT) _____

Address _____ Apt. # _____

City _____ State/Prov. _____ Zip/Postal Code _____

Signature (if under 18, a parent or guardian must sign)

Mail to the **Reader Service:**
IN U.S.A.: P.O. Box 1867, Buffalo, NY 14240-1867
IN CANADA: P.O. Box 609, Fort Erie, Ontario L2A 5X3

Not valid for current subscribers to the Romance Collection
or the Romance/Suspense Collection.

Want to try two free books from another line?
Call 1-800-873-8635 or visit www.ReaderService.com

* Terms and prices subject to change without notice. Prices do not include applicable taxes. Sales tax applicable in N.Y. Canadian residents will be charged applicable taxes. Offer not valid in Quebec. This offer is limited to one order per household. All orders subject to credit approval. Credit or debit balances in a customer's account(s) may be offset by any other outstanding balance owed by or to the customer. Please allow 4 to 6 weeks for delivery. Offer available while quantities last.

Your Privacy—The Reader Service is committed to protecting your privacy. Our Privacy Policy is available online at www.ReaderService.com or upon request from the Reader Service.

We make a portion of our mailing list available to reputable third parties that offer products we believe may interest you. If you prefer that we not exchange your name with third parties, or if you wish to clarify or modify your communication preferences, please visit us at www.ReaderService.com/consumerschoice or write to us at Reader Service Preference Service, P.O. Box 9062, Buffalo, NY 14269. Include your complete name and address.

BRENDA NOVAK

32993	INSIDE	___ $7.99 U.S.	___ $9.99 CAN.
32904	WATCH ME	___ $7.99 U.S.	___ $9.99 CAN.
32903	TRUST ME	___ $7.99 U.S.	___ $9.99 CAN.
32886	DEAD GIVEAWAY	___ $7.99 U.S.	___ $9.99 CAN.
32831	KILLER HEAT	___ $7.99 U.S.	___ $9.99 CAN.
32803	BODY HEAT	___ $7.99 U.S.	___ $9.99 CAN.
32724	THE PERFECT LIAR	___ $7.99 U.S.	___ $8.99 CAN.
32725	THE PERFECT MURDER	___ $7.99 U.S.	___ $8.99 CAN.
32667	THE PERFECT COUPLE	___ $7.99 U.S.	___ $8.99 CAN.
31244	IN SECONDS	___ $7.99 U.S.	___ $9.99 CAN.
28858	DEAD SILENCE	___ $7.99 U.S.	___ $9.99 CAN.

(limited quantities available)

TOTAL AMOUNT	$ _____
POSTAGE & HANDLING	$ _____
($1.00 for 1 book, 50¢ for each additional)	
APPLICABLE TAXES*	$ _____
TOTAL PAYABLE	$ _____

(check or money order—please do not send cash)

To order, complete this form and send it, along with a check or money order for the total above, payable to Harlequin MIRA, to: **In the U.S.:** 3010 Walden Avenue, P.O. Box 9077, Buffalo, NY 14269-9077; **In Canada:** P.O. Box 636, Fort Erie, Ontario, L2A 5X3.

Name: _____

Address: _____ City: _____

State/Prov.: _____ Zip/Postal Code: _____

Account Number (if applicable): _____

075 CSAS

*New York residents remit applicable sales taxes.
*Canadian residents remit applicable GST and provincial taxes.

HARLEQUIN® MIRA®
www.Harlequin.com

MBN0912BL